THE
DEAD MAN
ADVENTURES

A Series of Village Mysteries

By J. E. Rohrer

THE
DEAD MAN
ADVENTURES

A Series of Village Mysteries

© 2005 J. E. Rohrer

Ordering Information
The Books in the Dead Man series
by J.E. Rohrer are available from
Amazon.com

For discounts, contact booksreadmore on ebay.com.

Library of Congress Control Number: 2006920670
ISBN 0-9772268-2-4

DEAD MAN
BELOW DECK

This book is dedicated to the fine people
of Fort Atkinson, Wisconsin.

Chapter 1.

The Beginning

I walked past the dead man without noticing him. Well, not right past him; he was about ten feet away. This failure to notice what some people might regard as noteworthy caused the police to be suspicious. But the honest truth is I just did not see the body. After all, it was six in the morning. I was going out to pick up a newspaper and some bananas at the convenience store down the block. I was half asleep, not expecting anything unusual like a body by the door. Not exactly by the door; we have a second floor condo with a deck-type balcony. The body was directly under my deck on the neighbor's patio. My front door opened at least ten feet from that spot so, as you can see, it was not directly in front of my eyes.

Okay, maybe some people would have noticed it. But I was not your average person. The convenience store was a block away. I wandered over there in the usual way. My early morning ritual on a summer morning being unvaried if at all possible. I circled the building, staying on the sidewalk and stepping over the dirt. The building was new, so we had a lot of dirt. The dirt was sometimes a little wet and I didn't want mud on the bottom of my shoes. Then, I always followed the same route. I walked on the left side of the street until I was across from the convenience store. I crossed over and went in, being careful of cars seeking gasoline. The return trip was a mirror image of the first leg.

The convenience store was bright, clean, and airy. It was a very nice store. The people who worked there were wide awake, cheerful, neat and clean, and looked wholesome. The store had fresh bananas, donuts, and milk along with the usual conveniences. I always picked up the Milwaukee paper and this morning, a Saturday, my wife wanted me to get the Advertiser. An inveterate yard sale fanatic, she was looking forward to a full morning. Rather, she was looking to fill what would be left of the morning after she finally got up and dressed. That would be several hours from now.

Let me clarify so you don't get the wrong idea: we didn't read the Milwaukee paper because we were in Milwaukee. We didn't like Milwaukee. Nobody did. Milwaukee was not like the rest of Wisconsin. It was more like Chicago. And we really didn't like Chicago.

On the other hand, the Milwaukee newspaper was better than the one printed in Madison. The Madison paper did not even have the Dilbert comic strip. So we were driven to settle on the Milwaukee paper. Just don't think that meant we liked Milwaukee or were the slightest bit interested in what went on there.

Quite the opposite in fact. As Milwaukee grew, it pushed its boundaries out. Those of us with homes in small towns like Fort Atkinson were in danger of some day becoming part of the 'Milwaukee area.' When that happened, we would be painted with the same brush, the brush that said urban problems – crime, pollution, traffic, and racial conflict. This was unfair and not our fault. If we wanted urban problems, we would live in the city for Pete's sake. In fact, we proved our innate good sense by not living in the city. For the city to invade us was just not right. They could damn well grow in the other direction. That would be into Lake Michigan. Let them live in houseboats or in bubbles under the lake (the one they polluted whenever they got the chance).

While I was paying for the bananas and papers, a police car raced by the store, lights flashing and siren screeching. This was painful at the early hour and really not necessary. After all, there was not much traffic that had to be warned out of the way. Those guys liked to make a fuss just for the fun of it sometimes. The noise jarred our ears and caused all of us in the store to pause and gaze briefly out of the window before turning back to our respective tasks without comment.

The young woman behind the counter asked me if I had purchased gasoline (no) and would like a bag for the bananas (no). This proved to be a mistake. Since I was walking, a bag might have made it easier to carry my purchases. And, maybe, I did not look my usual debonair self with a bunch of bananas under my arm. Yes, I probably should have taken a bag, but until I had at least two cups of coffee, my brain cells did not function very well. Two large cups of coffee.

Back I went to the condo. Imagine my surprise when I saw the police car parked next to my building. Imagine my surprise when I saw the authorities clustered around the patio of the condo, right below my deck. Imagine my surprise when I saw a body on the ground not ten feet from the front door. Imagine their surprise when a middle-aged guy carrying bananas tried to push through the crime scene.

"You can't come in here, sir. This is a crime scene."

"But I need to get in my front door."

"I'm sorry, sir. But you can't come this way."

Naturally, I wilted a bit. No coffee? I had put the pot on before leaving the building. Fresh coffee awaited, unreachable. And where was I supposed to go? The car was in the garage. The keys were in the condo. The automatic garage door opener was in the car. This was a difficult problem to solve without coffee.

I could sit down somewhere and try to struggle through the paper without coffee as unlikely as that sounds. But the only place to sit was on the gurney they had brought which was next to the body, right in the middle of their precious crime scene. Impossible. So I turned away. Probably, I was going to walk slowly in aimless circles until the problem resolved itself or I fell into a coma. More likely, both would occur with my mind drifting away as my feet did their thing.

Perhaps it was just as well that one of the officers called me back. "Sir, do you live here?"

"I'm in the upstairs unit."

"Right above this body, sir?" The implication escaped me, but a feeling of unease began to disturb me.

"We would like to ask you a few questions." He said with a stone face.

"Can we do it over coffee? There is a fresh pot upstairs." Clever of me, don't you think? A chance to get at the coffee and I leapt on it.

The policeman stared at me for a moment. He seemed to think I was not displaying the proper regard for the gravity of the situation. After all, there was a dead man below my deck. Perhaps I should have been all a twitter - horrified, fearful, and excited. But heck, I saw dead bodies all the time on TV. It was no big deal. Well, if I had noticed it, I would, of course, have called it in and felt important for being so civic minded and alert. However, since I missed my chance at that moment of glory, I just wanted my coffee.

The policeman considered the situation for a moment. I thought maybe my offer of fresh coffee had dented his resolve about the sanctity of the crime scene. No such luck. "Stand over here, sir. Someone will question you later."

Stand around waiting for someone to question me? Arms full of bananas and newspapers? This could take hours. A couple of brain cells clicked together under duress and I whipped out my cell phone. I called my wife, hoping she would hear the phone ring. I did not expect her to answer it. She kept it inside a bag, inside her purse, which was usually inside a larger bag. The chances of getting through all of those barriers before the phone stopped ringing were a flat zero. But she would call me back.

And she did. "Ed! Are you all right?"

Panic.

"Yeah, fine."

"Where are you? What's wrong?"

"I'm just downstairs."

"Are you hurt? Why don't you come up?"

Trying to cut through all the fear and panic, I interrupted her and spoke as quickly as possible. Repetition was important under these circumstances so that she would hear my message even if she tried to talk. "THE POLICE ARE DOWN HERE THEY WANT TO QUESTION ME ABOUT SOMETHING PLEASE BRING A CUP OF COFFEE DOWN DON'T WORRY NOTHING WRONG BODY BELOW DECK BRING COFFEE." That should do it.

Silence. "I'm coming down."

"Thanks. Don't forget my coffee."

Chapter 2

Enter the Cops

When Betty opened the front door she was, of course, in danger of stepping into the crime scene. She peered carefully around then handed me the coffee, reaching over the tape that had been affixed to the outside wall at the door frame.

She was a sight for sore eyes, let me tell you. She had thrown on slacks and a shirt, her hair was tousled, and she had that suspicious look she gets in her eyes every once in a while. Her first reaction was always the same; I must have done something dangerous to cause this mess. This unjust view of my place in the world could be annoying, but when she handed me the coffee I knew she loved me, I loved her, and all was right in our little world.

Betty was a Wisconser through and through. Or should I say Badger? Or Cheesehead? I think she preferred Cheesehead. Anyway, she grew up on a dairy farm in the north-central part of the state. Her view of the world was forever shaped by arcane and exotic experiences that I could barely imagine. A curly-headed little scamp running madly around the barnyard, she played with her kittens and engaged in other important little-girl business. From what she told me, stepping barefoot into cowpies was a significant activity. Forgive me for not appreciating the joys of such behavior. I was the kind of kid who could not stand to have his hands sticky. Even today, I would not eat fruit unless it was cut up because of the juice. An apple I could stand if I ate it standing over the sink where I could wash up immediately. Stepping into a cowpie would be something I could handle only if I was wearing waders. I was not what Governor Arnold out in California called a "girly man." But barefoot into a cowpie? No way in hell.

A childhood of neglect on a farm full of feces must explain why my dear wife was the way she was. Not that there was anything stranger about her than there was about me. But she was more than a little odd. Take, for example, the thing about boxes and bags. She couldn't throw them away. And they accumulated. Perhaps they bred amongst themselves in the dead of night. How else could there get to be so many of them? They filled up every available bit of storage. Empty boxes and empty bags had appeared in all unused locations in every home where we had lived.

Her cousins were the same way. They were fascinated by sacks and crates, boxes and bags. They saved them for some unforeseen cataclysm, like maybe an invasion of aliens that would only spare people from slavery if they could produce one thousand cardboard boxes that appealed to alien sensibilities.

Something happened on that farm to make those girls the way they were. I shuddered to think what it might have been. Perhaps an old German lived in the woods, occasionally coming to the door of their farmhouse late at night shouting that a ransom of paper sacks must be thrown on the porch. "More sacks, more sacks! If you don't give me more sacks I will throw you into the oven like I did Hansel and Gretel!"

Okay, maybe that wasn't what happened. But it had to be something pretty strange.

The policeman stood ready to intervene if either of us stepped into the crime scene. He seemed a little disconcerted by our ability to reach over the crime scene tape to accomplish my selfish goal of obtaining coffee. This was beating the system. This was finding comfort when only discomfort should prevail. I wondered what he would have done if I had asked her to hand over a folding chair.

That proved to be unnecessary. An unmarked sedan pulled up disgorging what I imagined were two detectives. One was a beefy older man in rumpled polyester. The other was a hard looking bottle blonde with a styrofoam coffee cup in her hand. She struck me as the sensible type, no doubt because of the coffee, while he seemed like a doofus ready for retirement. This first impression proved to be completely backward.

They walked over to the little grouping Betty, the policeman, and I had formed by the door, taking in the situation at a glance. "These folks live in that unit up there," our uniform said to the detectives with a significant look in his eye.

The female detective took the hint. "We would like to ask you two a few questions. May we come in?"

Finally, I would be able to sit down and drink my coffee. "Sounds good," I said. "We can open the garage door and go in that way if you want."

The female cop looked at me. Her gaze was professional and cool. What I am trying to say is that she looked at me like I was a bug, a bug under a magnifying glass that she had caught in the back yard. She was studying me to decide where to stick the pins that would nail me to a board when she added me to her collection of trophies. Not that I would be an important addition to the collection since I was not a very interesting bug.

What she was seeing was a middle-aged guy, average in every respect. White, five feet nine inches tall (with shoes on) and weighing 170 pounds (with shoes off), you could say I was fairly average. My hair was completely white and two inches in length all over. The clipper had a two inch comb on it and I just ran it forward and backward over my head about once a week. My beard, if you can call it that, had a moth-eaten look. With glasses, jogging shoes, jeans, and a polo shirt that I got on sale at Target, she was seeing your typical guy on vacation. Not particularly fit because I don't lift weights or jog, but at least I could say I was no longer fat. I had lost 50 pounds since I topped out at 222 pounds eighteen months previously. The holiday pictures had horrified me, providing the motivation to change my eating habits. Even though I was not anywhere near movie star caliber, I was satisfied with my average appearance. It was a big step up for me.

The heavyset older one stuck out his hand. "My name is Sergeant Bill Broder and this is Sergeant Schmidt. Let's go in and have a chat." He looked like he wouldn't mind resting his feet for a few minutes.

Broder lifted the tape to let me step under and we went up the steep stairs to our second floor apartment. Betty led the way, followed by me, then Schmidt and Broder. When we got to the main floor, I pulled out a chair at our kitchen table and sat down. "Our living room furniture won't be delivered until next month, so we better sit here," I said.

"You've just moved in?" Broder was looking around at our sparsely furnished home away from home.

"Yep. This is our summer place. We just got it this year. We're still fixing it up."

Apparently, that was enough small talk for Sergeant Schmidt. She flipped open her notebook and clicked her ballpoint pen into the working position. "Names?" she asked.

"Ed Schumacher. This is Betty Betz. We're married." I always felt obligated to add that last part. Betty was afraid that people would think we were just living together.

"Occupation?"

"College professors. Texas Tech." I could be succinct, too.

Schmidt looked up in confusion, so I clarified. "We have summers off, so we bought this place. It's cooler here in the summer."

She nodded, not really interested. "What can you tell us about the body downstairs?"

"Nothing. I didn't know it was there until I got back with the paper this morning." My answer sounded weak even to me.

Schmidt narrowed her eyes suspiciously. "You walked out that door at what time?"

"About six." I felt compelled to elaborate. "The body might have been there, but since I was pretty sleepy, I wouldn't have noticed it."

Schmidt and Broder exchanged disbelieving glances. Since Schmidt seemed at a loss for words, Broder broke in.

"So you're a college professor," he said with an indulgent smile.

"Yep. Absent-minded professor." I appreciated the excuse he was giving me.

"What were you doing last night?"

"We got here from Texas about five p.m. We were pretty tired, but Betty called her cousin and we made plans to go out for a fish fry. No food in the house, of course. Betty, what time did we get back from that?"

Betty looked startled. "Around seven probably," she said. "We watched some TV then went to bed early. We were tired."

No doubt about that. Driving up from Amarillo would have been tiring enough. But the night we spent in a motel outside Fort Leonard Wood, Missouri provided no rest at all. Our decrepit and neurotic cat was traveling with us. Betty had given him something to relax him for the drive since he goes nuts in the car. The tranquilizer did not make him sleep, but we found out that it relaxed him in ways we did not anticipate. In the middle of the night, I got out of bed to turn down the air conditioner. The cat was in my spot when I got back to the bed. Naturally, I picked him up and dropped him on top of Betty. Then I lay back down, only to discover something hot, wet, and smelly was all over me. Perhaps it was my fault. Maybe I squeezed him when I moved him and that forced a nasty squirt out the back end. Whatever the cause, we spent the next hour wide awake. The bed was a mess, I was in shock (imagine that stuff on your naked body), and Betty was trying to clean up. The cat seemed to be happy enough, though.

Broder wrote this down. Not the part about the cat squirt since I didn't tell him that story, but about our going to bed early. Maybe I should have told him the cat story. It would have proven I was not capable of murder. With all the provocation the cat gave me, the possibility of killing it never crossed my mind. Drop kicking it off the balcony would not have been out of the question, though. Maybe it was just as well I did not tell that story to Broder since we had sneaked the cat into the hotel room without asking permission. What if the hotel had called in a report on us for making a strange and noxious smell in their hotel room.

"Did you folks hear or see anything unusual last night?"

Betty and I both shook our heads.

Broder apparently had finished his assessment of us and concluded we were not dangerous. We might have killed the guy below the deck, but we weren't likely to kill someone else right away.

"Thank you for your time. Sorry to have disturbed you." Then he smiled at me. "We might have a few more questions." His smile broadened. "Don't leave town."

11

Chapter 3.

A Clue Points at Me

When the detectives left, we tried to get back into our Saturday routine. Actually, it was our every day routine when we were in Wisconsin. We read the paper and drank coffee. The big news item was the presidential campaign. Wisconsin was seen as a battleground state. Both major party candidates were stumping in Madison, Milwaukee, and the smaller cities. A few weeks before, the Green Party had rejected Nader and picked someone else as its nominee. All this was pretty exciting politics for those who were interested.

Betty eventually showered and went to an estate sale.

"If you see a bike that's in good shape, I wouldn't mind having it," I said.

She gave me an odd look. "For you to ride?"

"Sure. Why not? You said you've seen several bikes at sales that were really cheap."

She still had that mystified look.

"I don't want one with skinny tires or lots of gears. Just a plain bike. And I want a banana seat."

"Banana seat. I remember those. They were from the sixties, right? I don't think they make them anymore."

"A banana seat would be a lot more comfortable than a regular seat."

She just stood there for a moment, shaking her head. Then she put her arms around me. "I'm very lucky to have you," she said.

"And I am very lucky to have you," I answered.

"You better believe it, buddy," she said. Then she went out in pursuit of junk and, hopefully, a cheap but functional bicycle.

I went into the spare bedroom we have set up as an office and got on the internet. After checking my email accounts, I did a little computing for a few projects. I didn't get paid for summer work, but when a project was hanging out there ready to progress to the next step, I couldn't resist. My job was to test hypotheses using data collected from surveys. It made me feel good to find the answers to life's little questions, even if no one else was really interested.

Frankly, I forgot all about the dead guy under my deck. It was really none of my business and, besides, the police were handling the problem. I didn't even look for the story in the Milwaukee paper because I figured it was too soon. Not that Milwaukee papers would care much about a single body found out in the boondocks. They had bodies all over the place in that town.

By noon I was ready for a break. After a few pushups to get the blood circulating and to tone up the flab, it was time for my walk. The village of Fort Atkinson, "Fort" for short, was a real jewel. Our place was on the edge of town, but we could walk downtown in just thirty minutes. Traffic was fairly light if you stayed on the residential streets. The Rock River ran through the center of town. I peered over the wall and watched the water for a few minutes, then strolled over to the hardware store. The ad for True Value that was in the morning paper said they sold small engines.

There was a kid working in the power tools section who looked like he was about 15. I figured he had to know more about small engines than I did, so I hit him with my question.

"Do you have a gasoline motor that can be mounted on a bicycle?"

He looked at me like I was nuts.

"You know, on the axle. So I won't have to pedal." You have to draw a picture for some people.

"Why don't you buy a skooter?"

See, this was the problem with teenagers. They didn't understand service. I asked the guy a simple question and he gave me guff.

"A chain saw turns a chain. A bike has a chain. Would a chain saw drive a bike?" I was giving him hints, hoping his brain might start to work.

"I don't think that would work. The chain saw would cut your leg off."

What an idiot. Not getting any help, I left, planning to go back later when an adult might be working there.

Have you ever noticed that everything cost a lot of money and was a lot more complicated than it needed to be? Back before all homes had utility lines, some washing machines were made that had gasoline motors. Creative teenagers put those motors on their bicycles - instant motorcycle. Now, you had to spend thousands to get a motorcycle. Then you had to register the monster, get plates and insurance, and worry about theft. Or, if you didn't want to go 100 miles per hour, you could buy a scooter. The state of Wisconsin still wanted you to register it, and, of course, it would have to be in compliance with a bunch of safety regulations.

Why did a vehicle have to cost thousands of dollars? I bet you could mass produce Model T's with little modern engines for about $500 bucks each. Heck, you could put a lawnmower engine on a golf cart and drive it around Fort. More to the point, why were we paying a lot of fees for safety inspections and vehicle registration? To pay our share of road maintenance costs, you say? On the other hand, if you rode a bicycle, you didn't have to register it and it did not have to pass inspection. You were still using the road, so what was the difference?

The answer had to be the bicycle lobby. Those guys and gals in the spandex pants who were spending hundreds on whiz bang racing bikes had the money that swung votes and made favorable laws. You think I am kidding? The Yuppie lobby got what it wanted. Heck, the Democratic nominee was one of those spandex guys. The Yuppies even had their own presidential candidate. Now that was political power.

Where was I? Oh, after striking out at True Value, I walked back to the condo. We were the first and, so far, the only people living in the place. We had purchased it sight-unseen, based on location and price. It was either a very smart move, or we were just lucky because we were quite satisfied with it. Of course, a number of small issues had to be resolved as with any new construction. Trim, tile work, and some painting were still needed. The window in the garage had not been finished.

With all this going on, I was not surprised to find the garage door open when I got back home. On the other hand, I did not expect to find our friendly neighborhood detectives standing by my garbage which they had apparently seen fit to dump on the floor of the garage.

They seemed surprised to see me when in I wandered like a lamb to the slaughter. Detective Schmidt turned to me, then held out a baggie with a wallet in it. "Have you ever seen this before, Mr. Schumacher?"

After a brief perusal I answered, "No. Where did you find it?" Perhaps the exercise had moved all of my blood into my feet. Otherwise, I would have guessed where they found it right away.

Broder pulled out some handcuffs and grabbed me by the arm. "You have the right to remain silent..." I didn't hear the rest. Apparently, if your jaw falls open wide enough, it makes you go deaf.

Chapter 4.
They Take Me Downtown for the Third Degree

It was my first ever ride in a police car. I guess I should have paid more attention to such a memorable event. Wasn't that always the way? When the really important things were happening to us, we were too caught up in the moment to appreciate just how momentous it was.

They led me into an interrogation room and told me to sit down. There was a mirror on one wall, so I knew we were being watched by a steely-eyed police Lieutenant. This person would decide whether or not to call the District Attorney. If the DA said they could make a case against me, I was toast, innocent or not.

That was when I remembered Betty. When she got back from shopping, she would wonder where I was.

"Don't I get to make a phone call?" I sounded a bit grouchy and scared, even to myself.

Schmidt glowered at me, then said, "Yes. Use that phone in the hallway if you have the right change."

What century was she living in? I whipped out the cell phone and called Betty, who answered right away.

"Where are you?"

This was going to be tricky. "I'm with the police detectives. They had a few more questions."

"Are you all right?" She sounded panicked. I could not be sure she had understood what I was saying.

"I am at the police station."

"I can't hear you. You're breaking up." She was wailing.

"I AM AT THE POLICE STATION COME GET ME POLICE STATION CAN YOU HEAR ME NOW?"

"What?"

"POLICE STATION POLICE STATION POLICE STATION!" I was shouting to make myself heard.

Schmidt took the phone away from me. "You abusive bastard," she said. Broder just shook his head at me. What were you supposed to do besides yell if the person couldn't hear you?

Personally, I liked to read books that were over thirty years old. Forty or fifty years old was even better. If this book is being read by someone fifty years from now, you may not understand the importance of the cell phone in transforming human society. Almost no one had a cell phone a decade before the dead guy was found under my deck. By 9-11, when the terrorists knocked down the Twin Towers in New York City, the cell phone had become more than ubiquitous, it was a necessity. When family members were interviewed after 9-11, they invariably spoke about how frightening it was not to be able to reach their loved ones immediately. Immediately? Before cell phones there was no immediacy to telephone communications. You called the person. They were certain not to be at home. You left a message on the answering machine. If you did not hear back in a couple of days, you figured the person had heard the message but forgot to return the call. So you called again. But in the early 21st century, we were thrown into a panic if we could not communicate instantly.

It should be fairly obvious that lack of instant communications was not inherently more dangerous today than it was ten years ago. Yet in 2004 people panicked if they couldn't speak to each other. People used cell phones to talk to each other on airplanes, in public restrooms, while shopping, and even while driving. Half the people in the country seemed to have their cell phones permanently jammed into their ears. The mystery to me was what they found to talk about all the time. The state of panic people experienced when disconnected was an artificial result of a technological change.

Do you get it? The technology made us crazy. And we did not know it was happening to us.

Where was I? Oh, the interrogation room. Schmidt sat across from me. Broder stood to one side. The lights were bright and I was stinking in my own sweat. The questions were coming rapid-fire. The chair was hard. I had to urinate, but I was not going to ask to go yet. I would try to tough it out. After all, we had only been in the room five minutes.

"How do you know Jack Wilson?"

"Never met him." Cool under pressure, that's me.

"Why did you kill him?"

"Didn't kill nobody." Started to crack at this point.

"Then how do you explain his ID being in your trash?"

"Can I go to the bathroom now?"

"NO!" Schmidt leaned across the table with a sickening smile. "Now, Mr. Schumacher, why don't you make it easy on yourself? Just tell us what happened. Maybe this guy was a burglar. You surprised him in the house, there was a fight, you threw him off the deck, then left him there hoping no one would notice." After she heard what she just said, she frowned. Obviously, it did not sound quite right even to Detective Schmidt.

The door opened and a guy in a nice suit stepped in. "Officer Broder" he said. "May I have a word with you?" Broder got up.

"Wait!" I was getting upset now. "You aren't going to leave me in here alone with her, are you?"

Broder gave me a funny look.

I didn't want him to think I was a wimp. "That's okay. I can take it. Go ahead. Take your time."

He left and Schmidt glowered at me. She, obviously, was uncertain about what was happening out in the hallway. Fortunately, we did not have long to wait because the suspense was killing us both.

Broder was back in five minutes and he said the magic words. "You can go now. But we may have more questions later, so don't leave town."

"That's great. Where's the men's room?"

After taking care of the necessaries, I wandered out of the building wondering where the nearest bar might be. A car screeched to a stop right in front of me. It was Betty.

"What's going on around here?" She was really cranked.

"Heck if I know," was all I could think of to say.

She took me home. Fortunately, there was beer in the fridge.

Chapter 5.

Cocktails at the Country Club

That evening I was sitting on the deck, smoking my pipe. A Miller High Life was resting comfortably in my stomach and a pad of notepaper was in my hand. My best thinking happened with a pipe in my hand and some paper for taking notes. I used a mechanical pencil to jot down stray thoughts. A pen would work but not as well.

The time had come to review events. Betty had asked what was going on. It was a good question. Here is what I had written down.

Friday p.m. – returned from Texas.

Saturday a.m. – dead man below deck.

Saturday p.m. – police station (wallet in trash).

It was a short list. The emotional impact of those events did not come through. I had the feeling that events were building up to some kind of cataclysm. What, really, was going on?

I started to write down more specific questions.

1. Who was the dead guy?

2. Who killed him and why?

3. Why was he under my deck?

4. Why was his wallet in my trash?

5. Why did the police let me go?

That last question was a good one. Why did they let me go? The evidence, though circumstantial, seemed to point right at me, provided I was an idiot. After all, it would not have been very smart to kill the guy then leave him right under my own deck. On the other hand, for all the cops knew, I could be crazy or stupid or even both. Some folks had certainly thought so in the past. But since I was writing the list and I knew I was not guilty, my alleged craziness or stupidity was irrelevant.

"Hello up there!"

Bob Johnson was down on the sidewalk, looking up at me. Bob was a nice young fellow. He sold us the condo. As far as I could tell, he was one of the owners of the development company. The building we were in was an eight-plex. Three more eight-plexes were planned to fill out a square that would contain 32 units. Bob and his partners would clear a tidy sum when the rest were sold.

And that was not the whole story, either. Our complex was at the edge of town. Most of the housing out there was relatively new at the time. Acre after acre of new homes, duplexes, and apartment buildings was spreading to the south of us. Demand for housing, Betty and I theorized, was coming from people who were commuting into Madison. If a couple had jobs in Madison and Milwaukee, Fort Atkinson was a central location. Property was cheaper in Fort than it would be in either city. One spouse could jump on the interstate headed west and the other could head east.

"I hear you had some excitement around here," Bob said.

"Yup. Just a little."

"Yah, if a dead body is 'just a little'." I didn't answer, so he went on. "That's really too bad. You guys are new in town and something like this has to happen."

He had a point. "Not exactly like the Welcome Wagon, is it?" he asked.

"Meat wagon is more like it."

"Is everything cleared up ok? Are the police going to leave you alone now?"

"Guess so. They took me down to the station today, but then decided to throw me back. Too little to eat, I guess."

Bob chuckled. "You guys must be pretty shook. Tell you what, the company has reservations out at the Fort Atkinson Country Club for tonight at seven. Why don't you let us bring you as our guests? Have a couple of steaks and relax."

That sounded pretty good. "Let me ask Betty. Steak would just about hit the spot."

Bob was ready to move on to his next task. He was an energetic guy. "Tell you what, we will just plan on seeing you there. Hope you can make it." He turned to go then turned back. "Oh, our senior partner, Moody Jorgenson, especially was hoping you guys could make it. He would like to make up for the poor hospitality you have gotten so far." Then with a wave, he was off and running to the next money making opportunity. Those business guys are something else.

My pipe was out, so it was a good time to go ask Betty about dinner. She was sitting on the bed, reading. When I walked into the bedroom, she looked up with a frown.

"I had a strange dream last night."

Uh oh.

"I dreamed about a first aid box. There was a big billboard in my dream with a picture of a first aid kit."

"Really?"

"What do you think it means?"

"Maybe it means you're feeling anxious."

"Why would I be feeling anxious?"

"Because you are a Nervous Nellie."

"No, I am not!"

"Yes, you are."

"Am not!"

"Are too."

"I think it means there is going to be an accident. I think it means I should go out and buy a first aid kit."

"Okay, buy a first aid kit. By the way, Bob Johnson invited us out to the Country Club for dinner. His company has a table and they wanted to be nice since I nearly got the electric chair today."

She considered this. "We don't have any food in the house." She thought some more. "I could wear my new shoes."

"What new shoes?"

"Well, you asked me to buy you a bicycle at the estate sale, but I found some shoes instead. They are really nice. You will enjoy seeing me in them. They're red and they have heels." She jumped off the bed and whipped open a shoe box to reveal a bright red pair of suede shoes with one-inch heels.

"Those will kill your feet," I observed.

"Sometimes a woman has to suffer to make her man happy," she said sadly.

Off we went to the Country Club after looking up the address in the telephone book and consulting the city map. As you might expect, it was an impressive building sitting on the edge of what looked like a pretty nice course. Too nice for me to play. I was a duffer, myself. Duffers should not waste money on good courses.

Jorgenson and Johnson were already there when we arrived. Bob introduced us to Jorgenson, who was a beefy guy with a big smile and a loud laugh. He welcomed us like long lost cousins, called the waitress for a round of drinks, cracked a few jokes, and generally started the evening off on a warm and friendly footing.

The steak was good and the beer was welcome, also. I had already consumed one back at the condo, so the one I had at the Club kind of went to my head. Alcohol was disinhibiting which in me resulted in a tendency to be mouthy. My opinions, never far from the surface, would start rising to the top like soap bubbles. When those bubbles burst into a conversation, sometimes they caused a bit of a disturbance. I was not sure why; people should be able to enjoy a bit of controversy without getting mad. Unfortunately, once I got going on politics or religion, a lot of folks got downright hostile.

In this case, I started talking about regulations that prevented your average citizen from driving any kind of inexpensive homemade vehicle that he could dream up. That led me to several related topics, culminating in a call for the elimination of the federal income tax. I was warmed up at this point and started on my lecture about how much money the government wasted on unnecessary tomfoolery, such as high school teachers. Just give the kids a box of computer programs and send them home for Pete's sake. Once a kid could read and write, he could teach himself anyway. "I don't remember any teacher ever teaching me anything," I asserted loudly. "I just learned it by reading the textbook."

At this point people all around the room were looking at me. Woops. One thing I had learned was that you can attack a lot of sacred cows, but if you go after the school system, you are going to make a lot of people really mad. Teachers worked their tails off, they didn't get paid much, and they had to put up with parents who thought their kids were smarter than they really were. It was a tough job. So they got mad if you said they were inefficient.

But what really made them mad was if you said teens didn't need the social interaction they learned at school. Why this upset them so much was a mystery to me. But the fact was, and it was a fact I had just pointed out at length, most of the bad habits teens picked up they learned from other kids. Spiked hair, tattoos, pierced body parts, drugs, and pregnancy all resulted from interaction with other kids. The obvious solution was to keep them away from each other.

Then what would we need the teachers for? They could organize and manage internet courses. Of course, this would require smarter teachers. Ouch. This was usually where somebody threw something at me.

Finally I shut up. All eyes stared at me for a moment, then returned to their meals. I figured my name was mud and our hosts were feeling humiliated. We would never be allowed into the Country Club again.

But Jorgenson's smile was a mile wide. "Ed," he said, "You have some fascinating ideas. We are going to have to get together and have some serious conversations. Sometime soon." Then he called for the check.

Chapter 6.

My Country Wants Me

The next morning was a Sunday, so we went to church. We were Presbyterians in Texas, but since Betty grew up Lutheran, we decided to be Lutherans in Wisconsin. We preferred a traditional service backed by liberal theology, so the Irish Lutheran church was just right for us.

Betty wore her denim skirt and one of my old shirts with the sleeves turned up at the ends. I wore a black blazer with khaki work pants and a bolo. This made me the most dressed up fellow in the sanctuary. The other guys were coatless and wore open-necked shirts. It was a pretty casual group. Most of the parishioners were even more casual; they did not show up at all. We had visited this place three times now and it was never even half full. Even so, they had three pastors running the service. One was a comedian, one might have been senile, and the third wanted to hug all the women.

"How can they afford to have three pastors?" Betty wondered aloud.

"Hopefully, they aren't paying the old guy. He doesn't seem to be all there. And the masher probably would be willing to work just for the feels."

Lutherans were different from Presbyterians. Both groups were mainline protestant, of course, but the Lutherans were close cousins to the Catholics. Betty didn't like it when I said that, but it seemed true to me. It was amazing to me that during the Reformation Lutherans and Catholics went around killing each other. After all, they were theologically pretty close together. They agreed on about everything except the old guy in the big hat in Italy. And, frankly, it seemed to me that even the Catholics ignored him most of the time.

I could afford to be objective about it since my ancestors were Anabaptists. The Anabaptists were pacifists, so both the Catholics and Lutherans could kill them without too much trouble. They deserved killing apparently because they thought you should only be baptized once as an adult. That way you might understand what you were signing up for which, as any marketing expert could tell you, was bad for business.

It seemed to me that Anabaptists had to learn to be good at running away. If they could not fight back and everyone wanted to kill them, then they must have slipped out of a lot of back doors. Otherwise, they would have all died and I would not be writing this book.

Anabaptists must have been naturally cantankerous. Otherwise, they would not have chosen to be on the side that was guaranteed to lose every time. The natural selection process would have favored those who were smart enough to leave town before they were drowned by the authorities. All this could explain why my natural opinionated stubbornness was counter-balanced by a healthy survival instinct. It was bred into me.

The Lutheran church service had nice music that sounded as if it was written for a harpsichord. They also had a standardized service that repetitively used the same prayers and other liturgy from one Sunday to the next. This was a good plan since human failings and spiritual problems tended to repeat themselves as well. Lutheran pastors were weak on sermons, but all were good singers. Pastors who could not sing must have joined another denomination. Maybe this was why pastors in the fundamentalist churches always seemed so angry; they wanted to be Lutherans but weren't allowed because they couldn't sing.

Of course, you could find a Lutheran church that was fundamentalist if that was what you wanted. The Missouri Synod was pretty hard core as were the Norwegian Lutheran and the Wisconsin Synod. Farther south, a small town may have ten denominations of churches within its boundaries. In Wisconsin, a town of the same size would have ten varieties of Lutherans. And one Catholic church which, as I wrote earlier, was pretty much the same thing except for paying lip service to that guy in the Vatican.

You might be wondering why I am spending so much time on churches in this chapter. Don't worry. It will prove to be quite relevant later on.

The service was relaxing and brought us all a sense of peace as it was designed to do. In fact, it was so relaxing that one of the parishioners fainted during his kid's baptism. That happens when you stand up too fast after falling asleep in church. They just propped him up in a pew and went on with it. The rest of us appreciated the drama since we were getting a little dozy as well.

After the service, we chatted with Betty's cousin Andrew for a few moments on the sidewalk outside of the church. It was a nice cool morning with a gentle breeze. Andrew was a nice guy who did some kind of investigative work for state government. We made plans to look for each other at the concert in the park that was scheduled for Monday evening.

Betty and I drove back to the condo, then I went into the den for a little work. After checking for email messages, it was time to do a little computing. Some colleagues had asked for a report on a survey we had done, so it was time to run the basic descriptive statistics which then were imported into a word processing file. The output did not look quite right for a nice report, so I started editing. Move this, delete that. Type 'p=.0000'. Copy, paste, delete, type. Copy, paste, delete, type, faster and faster. I was going to make a mistake if I did not slow down. Copy, paste, delete, type. My eyes were tired and I was filled with a nervous tension. Copy, paste, delete, type. I had to quit. Just a little more. Had to stop. Almost done. Copypastedelete typecopypaste deletetype.

I had to physically tear myself away from the computer. Staggering, I ran out of the den. In the living room, I dropped for twenty-five pushups. When I got up, my face was hot and I was still jittery.

So I set out for my daily walk. The compulsion to keep at the repetitive motion on the computer had never before been this bad. Other times, I just kept going until I was too tired to stop which was no later than six in the evening. That was not a big problem. I have known guys who didn't stop computing all night long, eventually collapsing in their offices onto the floor. Then they would go out and get a big cup of coffee and start again. Compared to that, my little bout of compulsiveness was peanuts.

A walk around a small town in the Midwest was a good cure for almost anything. Fort Atkinson was like most such towns, but it was also unique in several ways. Take, for example, the Milk Shrine. You might think that having a Milk Shrine meant that the locals worshipped dairy cows like some sort of strange Hindu cult. However, reality was even stranger.

Way back when, one of the early governors of the state of Wisconsin was a fellow by the name of Hoard. Governor Hoard thought that the schools should teach in English rather than German. This argument was reminiscent of contemporary concerns about Spanish in the public schools. Anyway, the voters kicked him out of office for being anti-German. (Lesson for politicians who insist on language purity in the public schools—the growing Hispanic population might get even with you in the end.)

Ex-Governor Hoard started a newspaper in Fort Atkinson. He was a big believer in the dairy farm and promoted dairy farming constantly in his newspaper. Not surprisingly, the Milk Shrine, which was really a museum, contained a lot of stuff about Mr. Hoard.

Anyway, you walked into the Shrine expecting to find an altar, then you noticed it was a museum. You also noticed a lot of propaganda about how great the family farm was. I was okay with that point of view, being a bit of a populist myself. For the Shrine to promote farmers was kind of nice in a state like Wisconsin.

But wait, the story is not over yet. After you made it through most of the display, you started to realize that a lot of what you were seeing had to do with the mechanization of modern agriculture; machinery that no small independent farmer could hope to buy. If he did, he would not be a small farmer any more.

By the time you got to the end of the show, the sponsorship of the Shrine had become evident. It was Big Agriculture all the way. What appeared to be idealistic promotion of the small dairy farmer was actually heavy-handed lobbying by large corporations.

What did this tell us about Fort Atkinson in particular and the state of Wisconsin in general? It told me that the core values of the general public lie in populism, but the insidious forces of financial consolidation were quietly transforming the economy in ways the average person did not like. At his core, the average guy knew what had happened and it made him cynical and embittered. But he did not know what to do about it, except perhaps to attend county fairs and try to enjoy the best of small town life for as long as it lasted. After all, we could not control or predict in what ways the big corporations would choose to change it.

Twenty-five minutes after I started my walk, I was in McDonald's, resting and drinking a well-earned Diet Coke. When Betty came with me, it took quite a bit longer to get to McDonald's. She was a slow walker. Besides, this day I was cranked up by my computer work.

A smiling fellow in a nice suit slid into the seat opposite me. "Mind if I sit down?" Very polite, but he was already sitting which spoiled the effect.

"Sure. I was just leaving anyway."

"My name is Will Johnson," he said sticking his hand out. (The reader will note that our developer who was introduced earlier also was named Johnson. That coincidence has absolutely no significance to this story, so you can ignore it. Johnsons are all over the place in Wisconsin.)

For Will Johnson to try to shake hands was a little unusual. If I had been back in Texas, I would not have taken notice because people were very friendly there. They shook hands on any occasion and always said hello when they saw each other or even when they saw strangers. I think it was a Baptist thing. Of course, they also got quite angry very easily and would not hesitate to pull out a concealed handgun and shoot you if you got out of line. They seemed to believe this was necessary because of the high crime rate by which they meant Mexicans. Mexicans carried knives and stabbed each other all the time over women the Anglo Texan thought. The Anglos carried guns so they could defend themselves against the Mexicans. It was ridiculous, of course. Mexican-Americans were very nice, polite, kind, and considerate people, except maybe outside of a Gentlemen's Club at one in the morning. People could get hurt under those circumstances. But there was no good reason to be there anyway, so who cared?

People in Wisconsin were less likely to shake hands, say hello, or even look you in the eye. This was how they showed courtesy; they didn't want to intrude. So when Johnson introduced himself, I knew he was selling something.

"Ed Schumacher. Nice ta meetcha". There was a certain way to exchange the ceremonial greeting, including correct pronunciation of words. I was working on blending in.

"How's it goin'," he asked with a smile.

"Just fine. Nice weather for a walk, don'cha know."

"Yah. That's for sure."

It was my turn, but I couldn't remember what came next, so I just let an awkward silence develop. After a moment, I chugged down my soda and stood up.

"Well, I guess I better get back to it," I said.

"Mind if I walk along?" This guy definitely wanted something. But I didn't really want a new friend.

"Well, I'm getting my exercise. Can't mess around."

Johnson's demeanor became a little more serious, a little less friendly. "This will only take a minute. Maybe we can have a chat while you walk."

This guy was official. Police, no doubt. Always one to support law and order, I didn't argue with him. So out we went.

I headed in the direction of the hardware store where I had unfinished business. The way to get there from McDonald's was down an alley behind the store. This was out of the way of prying eyes and gave Johnson a chance to make his pitch.

"What can I do for you?" I asked.

"Maybe I can do something for you. I bet you have a few unanswered questions about the police matter over at your place."

"Yup."

He waited for me to reel out my unanswered questions, but I just looked at him, so he went on with his line.

"Mr. Schumacher, the police made a mistake with you, but it really wasn't their fault. You were set up."

"Set up? How so?"

"Saturday morning at about six somebody called the police and reported the body. The tipster implied you had a fight with the dead man the night before."

"No kidding?" I was shocked. And angry. How are you supposed to defend yourself against false accusations delivered anonymously?

"Calm down," Johnson said. "We know you didn't do it."

Taking a deep breath, I relaxed a little. "Okay, that's good. How do you know?"

"Because you have just about the best alibi I have ever run across in twenty years of law enforcement."

"I do?" I was feeling pretty smug about being special until it occurred to me that being in bed with my wife was not all that strong as alibis went.

"Yes sir. You see, the medical examiner placed the time of death as being Thursday night. You were not even in town. We traced your credit card expenditures to a motel outside of Fort Leonard Wood, Missouri. We called the place and they were able to give an accurate description of you with no trouble at all."

He suppressed a grin. "The manager seemed to be a little upset with you. Something about a very bad smell being left in the room you rented. I wouldn't recommend going back there if you can help it."

Oh, the incident with the squirting cat. "That's a big relief," I said. "Wait a minute. Are you saying that the dead guy was under my deck from Thursday night until Saturday morning?"

"That's correct."

"You mean, I not only didn't notice him Saturday morning, I also didn't notice him when we got back in town Friday evening?"

"That's correct." He gave me a break. "Well, I guess there was no reason to look under the deck."

Maybe not, but I had walked right past the spot when I went out to check the mail Friday evening. Since the authorities had a lot on their minds and shouldn't be burdened with unnecessary information, I did not bother to mention the business about the mailbox. I was sure the body had been there in its usual spot. I just was not paying attention, as usual.

"Thanks for sharing this information. Your buddies, the detectives, didn't tell me anything except not to leave town. Which raises an interesting question: why are you telling me about this now? Not that I don't appreciate it."

"Mr. Schumacher, this is a little awkward, but please hear me out. First of all, I am not with the local police. I am a Secret Service agent." He let that sink in for a moment.

"We have a problem. Word has reached us that an assassination attempt will be directed at the Democratic presidential nominee, John Kerry, within the next week. We traced the information to Fort Atkinson." I was completely lost. "What does that have to do with me?"

"Mr. Schumacher, have you ever heard of a militia group called the Fist of God?"

"No. Who the heck are they?"

"They are the same kind of people who blew up the federal building in Oklahoma City." Johnson could not repress a look of anger. With an effort, he smoothed his features and got back to business. "The only terrorist group in this area is the Fist of God, so they are probably the ones who are planning the assassination attempt."

"What good does it do them to kill John Kerry?"

"This group is very right wing. They think the federal government was taken over by communists a long time ago and that state governments are almost as bad. They consider themselves to be true patriots because they want to restore the government to the principles that it started with. Or at least, they want to change the government to the way they would like to believe it originally operated. That means a lot fewer laws, less government involvement in education, no income taxes, no environmental protection laws, and that sort of thing. And, of course, they are radical fundamentalists when it comes to religion."

"Militant Libertarian fundamentalists?"

"Sort of, except that a lot of Libertarians are in the ACLU. These Fist of God guys don't like lawyers."

"That's pretty weird. But what does it have to do with me?"

"The Fist of God is the action arm of a movement. Basically, they provide the foot soldiers who are willing to get killed for the cause. But they don't have a lot of education, they don't have high paying jobs, and most of them are just not too bright. Organizing terrorist campaigns takes money. You have to arrange travel, purchase guns and explosives, buy vehicles. These guys don't have any money, so somebody is financing them."

At this point, Johnson took a breath, looking at me appraisingly. "We need to find out who is financing the Fist of God, so we can shut them down." He put his hand on my shoulder. "You can help us with that. Mr. Schumacher, your country needs your help."

Well, of course. It was about time they recognized it. "How can I help? I don't know any of these people."

"But you do, Mr. Schumacher, you do. And they are very impressed with you. If you play your cards right, you might be asked to join them."

"This is nuts. I don't support any militias. Hell, I'm practically a socialist! Why would they think I would join them?"

"Because you had a nice conversation at the Country Club last night. You sounded off about government regulations and generally came off as a right-wing nut case."

This hit a little too close to home. "Well, maybe I did get carried away a little."

Johnson smiled indulgently. "We all do once in a while. In this case, it works to our advantage. Jorgenson is involved somehow with the flow of money into the Fist of God. We need you to make nice with them, gain their confidence. You're a smart guy; you can do it. Just tell them you supported Pat Buchanan."

"I did not support Buchanan!"

"You support the Reform Party."

"That's Ross Perot's party! Buchanan's people hijacked the party during the last election. I would never support Buchanan!"

"Calm down, Ed. I know that you know that, but Jorgenson doesn't know that. You can let him think you like Buchanan, can't you?"

This was going to be harder than it had first appeared. Pretend to like Pat Buchanan? Ouch!

"We need you to meet with Jorgenson when he asks you out for that little chat he wants to have with you. Go along with him. Find out what you can. But be cautious. The Fist of God is a dangerous group."

We agreed that Johnson would meet me at McDonald's at one p.m. every day for the next week to check on progress. How was I to know what a mess this would get me into? After all, when your country needed you, you really had a duty to respond. And respond I did in my own special way. Maybe that was the problem. Johnson really didn't know who he was dealing with. My wife says I am a little nutty. Of course, she really shouldn't talk. People in glass houses shouldn't throw stones, right?

Chapter 7.

Enter the Militia

When I got back to the condo, I checked the mail. A slip of paper was in the box telling me that I had a package to retrieve from the post office. By this time, Betty was back from lunch with her cousin, so we jumped in the car and set off for the post office.

The package was a cardboard box about the size of a suitcase. It was addressed to me. We jumped back in the car and headed home.

"Aren't you going to tell me what that is?" Betty asked.

"What what is?"

"The package."

"Oh that. No big deal."

"You're not going to tell me?"

She was looking pitiful, so I relented. "Look, we will be home in a minute and I'll open it. Then you'll see."

Five minutes later I was running my pocket knife down the seam that closed the box. Out came my pride and joy: a bicycle motor. It was beautiful.

"What is it?" Betty asked.

"It's a motor for a bicycle. I ordered it off the internet."

"You don't have a bicycle."

"Yes I do. I went across the road to Goodwill and got one this afternoon on the way back from my walk. It's down in the garage."

Installing the motor was easy, even for a guy like me who had no mechanical aptitude. The motor was electric and would take me up to 20 miles per hour for 25 miles. Pretty cool. It assisted the pedals rather than replaced them, so I could get my exercise while riding without being in danger of having to pedal up a hill that was too steep for me. Any hill would be too steep for me.

Betty didn't like it. "You'll kill yourself."

"Any kid can ride something like this!"

"You're not a kid."

"Don't worry about it."

"But I am worried about it. That proves it's dangerous." Yeah, right.

"No, it doesn't."

"Then why am I worried about it?"

"Because you are a Worry Wart."

"Am not!"

"Are too."

"Am not!"

"I'm going for spin. See you later."

Later that evening as I was resting on the deck, smoking my pipe, and considering my new assignment, a voice called up from below.

"Hello up there!" It was Jorgenson.

"Hey," I replied.

"Mind if I come up?"

"Nope. Door's unlocked. Come on in."

We met at the top of the stairs. "Care for a beer?"

"Don't mind if I do," he said with a grateful grin.

We cracked open a couple of Millers and made ourselves comfortable in the wicker chairs on the deck.

"How's it goin'?" I asked him.

Jorgenson stretched his legs out in front of him and settled into the chair. He took a long swallow from his bottle before answering me.

"Good. Busy." He sighed. "You would not believe how much hassle the government puts you through to run a business these days."

"Bureaucracy, eh?"

"Bureaucracy, taxes, inspections, fees, accountants, lawyers, delays. If it's not one thing, it's another. It's amazing that anybody can make any money any more."

He sighed again. "Well, that's my problem." He switched gears. "Bob tells me you and Betty are college professors. Texas Tech, isn't it?"

"Yup. We have summers off and Betty has family in Wisconsin, so we decided this should be where we locate our summer home. It's too hot in Texas in the summer."

"Makes sense to me. You're liking it okay, I hope?"

"We like it a lot. Nice town. And we really like our condo. You guys did a nice job."

"Thanks. We put a lot of thought into it. By the way, a fella moved into the unit behind yours. Older guy. Met him yet?"

"Nope. I should go around and say hi."

"Do that. We want everybody to get along." Jorgenson hesitated.

"What do you teach at Texas Tech?" he asked.

"Not much teaching. Mostly I do research. Statistical analysis of surveys."

"That's pretty impressive. Never did understand statistics myself. More of a deal maker, I guess. But we occasionally need some help understanding our data. Do you know anything about market research?"

"Marketing and epidemiology are a lot alike. In epidemiology we study whether certain groups in the community have worse health or different behaviors. Marketers study market segments. It's pretty much the same idea, using similar statistical methods."

Jorgenson leaned forward. "Maybe we could help each other," he said seriously. "Our business is expanding faster than we can keep up with it. In addition to this complex, we have projects going on all over the area. We operate with a lot of credit. If we make a wrong move, we could get overextended. For example, look at this development. Just two units sold. Six empty in this building. The second building is going up soon. If we get ahead of ourselves, we could be in trouble. Some forecasting could help."

"I couldn't promise accuracy. No crystal balls in my closet."

"No, no, of course not. But I would sleep better if I had some numbers that said we were headed in the right direction. If you could take an objective look at our data, you might save us from making a mistake."

"Be happy to give it a shot. What kind of arrangement were you thinking of?"

"Oh, a retainer would be best for us. Can't predict how much work we would throw your way, so I would like to just keep you on the payroll in case we need you."

He hesitated. "I will have to think about how much I can offer you." He leaned back again. "Well, that's enough business. Let's talk politics. Did you really mean those things you were saying at the Club?"

Now we were getting down to the real business he was concerned about. I tried not to look nervous. "Sure I did. We waste a lot of money in this country. Tax dollars. The average person would be better off if we cut out a lot of the baloney."

"Darn right," he said enthusiastically. "Did you see some of the dumb ideas the Democrats plan to talk about at their convention this week? Those guys promise everything to everybody. And who is going to pay for it? I can tell you who. Me and you." He was steamed.

"Can't argue with that. Of course, the Republicans aren't much better. Bush has run up the deficit in nothing flat."

Jorgenson groaned. "Ain't that the truth. Sometimes I wonder what the hell he thinks he's doing." He hesitated then said, "Some of us would like to turn the system in a different direction. A direction that lets the business man do what he does best without a lot of hassles. Business is what makes America great. But we are going to kill the business climate if we keep going this way."

Now was my chance to be helpful. "It isn't just opportunities to make a profit that are at stake from my point of view. It's quality of life. Wouldn't it be great if everybody with energy and a brain could be his own boss, live his life the way he wants, and have enough left to save up for a rainy day? Wouldn't it be great if we didn't have to pay $25,000 for a car, if every kid didn't need a college education just to do office work, and if retired people didn't have to pay taxes on the money they earn off their pensions?"

Jorgenson loved it. "Damn right," he said. "Damn right."

He stood up a happier man. "Well, I guess we can't solve all the world's problems right now. Have to get on with making a living, putting bread on the table." He turned to go. "You know, a group of us likes to meet in the bar at the Club every now and then to grouse about all this stuff. Would you like to join us some time?"

"Be happy to. That would be fun. Just tell me when."

"I'll be in touch."

Bingo.

After Jorgenson left, Betty and I settled in for the evening. As she flipped through the television schedule, she mentioned a few shows that looked interesting. "BBC has something called 'The Village.' Have you ever heard of that?"

"Sure. Old reruns. Patrick McGoohan. He's a spy that has been captured by some unidentified bad guys."

"Never heard of it. What else was McGoohan in?"

"Remember 'Secret Agent Man'? He was in that. It was a good show. He was a spy in that, too."

"'Secret Agent Man'? I remember the song, but I didn't know there was a television series." She looked up quizzically. "Hey, you were singing that song this afternoon."

"Me?"

"Sure, you were dancing around the living room singing Secret AAAgent Man."

"Not me. Must have been somebody else."

Chapter 8.

Money Grows on Trees

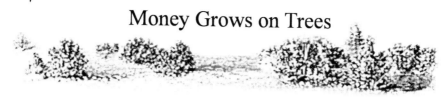

The weather on Monday morning was nice as usual. After showering and putting the coffee on, I traipsed down to the convenience store to pick up the paper and bananas. When I got back to the condo, I took a quick peek under the deck to make sure no surprises had been deposited there by unknown benefactors. It was mercifully clear of corpses.

Betty and I read the newspaper, she still in bed and I in my chair. The Democratic Convention was scheduled to begin that evening in Boston. The Republicans were saying that the whole show was just a show. Which, of course, it was, as would be the Republican Convention in September.

The story about an unidentified dead fellow in Fort Atkinson still had not appeared in the paper. It was old news by now, so my guess was that it would not be reported in the Milwaukee paper at all. The slim chance that a reporter would call me for an interview had evaporated. Fifteen minutes of fame was allocated to us all. This must not have been the event that would give me my quarter hour.

The paper finished, I retired to the den for some much needed computing time. This time the ghost in the machine did not attempt demonic possession of my spirit, so it was every bit as relaxing as it should have been. My latest survey was giving up its secrets without too much difficulty. After learning that people who have a mentally ill family member are at greater risk of suffering from frequent mental distress themselves, I declared victory and quit.

It was about noon and I was eager to check in with my personal secret service agent. Hopping on my newly motorized bicycle, I zipped over to McDonald's for a little discreet lurking. Agent Johnson did not appear. After fifteen minutes (patience had never been my strong suit), I motored home. Of course, there was some pedaling involved but not much.

Munching on a granola bar and slurping a Diet Coke, my brain began turning over the situation as it stood at the moment. The questions seemed to be these:

1. Was Jorgenson really the financier for the Fist of God?
2. How could I worm my way into his confidence enough to find out?
3. How could I accomplish number two without being detected as a spy?
4. What would happen to me if I was caught? This one did not bear thinking about.

At this point another question occurred to me.

5. Why was Johnson listening in on my conversation at the Country Club with Jorgenson before I had agreed to spy for him? The answer to that question seemed obvious: Jorgenson was under surveillance and my presence was just fortuitous for him. But, frankly, I did not much

like the idea that someone was listening to what I had to say without getting my permission first.

6.   Was there any connection between the dead guy being under my deck and the Fist of God investigation? The answer to this one appeared to be 'no,' but the chances of two very odd circumstances happening to me in the same week were slim. After all, my life up to this point had been very quiet and uneventful. No connection between the two events was evident, but I had a nagging feeling that something had to tie them together.

At this point, I ran out of questions. And I definitely was short on answers. With a sigh, I returned to the computer for a chore that was no fun at all: online banking. It was something that you just had to do once in a while, like cleaning the toilet. Since our bills were going to our address in Texas, it was prudent of me to check my bank balance online periodically and to occasionally fire off payments for utilities and the like.

Doing the little chores life assigned us on schedule instead of putting them off was a sign of virtue and responsibility I had always felt. Of course, the people I would deride as procrastinators might just say that I was overly compulsive. In this case (as in so many others), my point of view on this issue was proven to be correct because a little surprise was waiting for me in the computer: an unexpected and unexplained deposit had appeared in my checking account. It could have been a deposit that I had forgotten to record, one that I had completely lost from my memory in regard to where the money came from and what it was for. After all, forgetfulness had always been part of my nature. On the other hand, even I would have trouble forgetting $100,000. Someone had deposited 100K in my bank account. For some reason, this struck me as odd. I thought about mentioning it to Betty, but she would just have said there was something dangerous about receiving 100K for no reason. She would probably want me to report it to somebody. And she would expect me to figure out to whom I should report the windfall. This was too difficult to deal with and no reason for urgency presented itself, so I just logged off and went on about my business. I could tell her about it later when I had more information. No need to worry the poor woman. Thinking of my dear wife, I knew just what would make her happy.

"Betty!"

'Yes?"

"Let's go over to Culver's and get some ice cream?"

Silence. A moment later she was standing in the doorway. "Did you just say you want to walk to Culver's for some ice cream?"

"Yup. Sound good to you?"

"Always. But what about your diet? You never want to break your diet."

"Oh, we've been pretty good lately. We deserve a treat."

"What's the occasion?"

"Oh, nothing. Just feeling rich at the moment."

So off we went for ice cream.

Chapter 9.

Concert in the Park

That night a couple of hundred people were gathered around the bandstand. The tubas, the horns, and the various other instruments along with their players were already in place when we arrived. We saw Betty's cousin Andrew leaning against a tree, so Betty and I dragged our folding chairs in his direction.

"Hey, Andrew. How's it goin'?"

"Just holding up this tree to make sure it doesn't fall down."

"You're doin' a fine job. It's not even lookin' wobbly."

As we settled in for the show, Betty and Andrew exchanged small talk about relatives, some of whom were throwing guilt trips her way about not visiting them yet. We were living in Wisconsin now, why hadn't we come to see them? The relatives sent these guilt trip messages through Andrew. He was the nearest family member and so it fell on him to pass the guilt on to Betty. It sounded a bit convoluted to me, but I was not one who could judge these things. Usually, when someone threw a guilt trip at me, I didn't even notice.

The concert was pleasant. The quality of the music was a little uneven, but when they got to the Army and Marine anthems the band did an excellent job. John Phillip Sousa's work was delivered with verve. You could tell the band had practiced marching music quite a bit.

By the time we were allowed an intermission, it had become apparent to me that the audience could be broken into several distinct groups. First, we had retired people. This was the largest group. They must have arrived first because their folding chairs were clustered closest to the bandstand.

The next largest group was the kids, who were busy playing on the swings and jungle gym. They yelled and had a good time until a stern-looking woman from group A came over to shush them.

The third largest group, oddly enough, was the bicyclists. At least twenty people clad in spandex were scattered around, their bikes on the ground next to them. These people did not have folding chairs, instead they just sat on the grassy turf. Personally, I would have been reluctant to do that. Chiggers leave a nasty bite when they get their teeth into me. While I have never been the recipient of a chigger bite in the butt, I would be reluctant to take the risk.

The cyclists were scattered between our tree and the old folks. They chatted among themselves in a desultory way during the intermission. Betty, Andrew, and I did, also. Andrew had a bone to pick with us. "Hey, you guys didn't tell me about the excitement you had over at your place."

"Excitement? Oh, you mean the dead guy."

"Yes, I mean the dead guy. That's big news. Why didn't you call me? All the relatives will want to hear about it."

"Nothing to tell. Dead man below deck. End of story."

"That can't be all of it," Andrew protested.

"Yep. Except they took me downtown for the third degree. Then they let me go."

"That must have been pretty scary. Did they tell you what it was all about?"

"Nope."

"Well, why did they let you go? You look pretty guilty to me." What a jokester.

"They let me go because I didn't do it. In fact, I couldn't have done it because the guy was killed on Thursday when we were still driving up here from Texas."

Betty looked over. "How did you find that out?" Damn. She never misses a trick.

"Andrew, tell me this," I blustered on. "What possible reason could there be for a murder in Fort Atkinson? I mean, why would somebody leave a body lying around in plain site?"

"I don't know. We don't have many murders around here. A suicide now and then is all we get and that is usually a cop doing himself in."

"Maybe it was politics?" I asked.

Andrew looked at me like I was from Mars. "Politics? We don't get that excited about politics." He thought for moment. "Most likely, it was some drug deal out of Milwaukee. Or Chicago. You know how those city people are. If they didn't have money, we wouldn't even let 'em get off the highway at Fort Atkinson."

"What's their money have to do with it? Are you saying it's okay to do business with drug dealers?"

"Well, it's okay to sell them ice cream."

The band started up again, so we turned eyes front. I am afraid I dozed off soon after that.

Chapter 10.

The Old Guy at the Burger Joint

It was raining on Tuesday morning, so I drove to the convenience store. The Democratic convention was still the big news item. The nomination was locked up by John Kerry, so the whole thing was theater. Even so, the press seemed to think it was important for reasons that escaped me.

My computing that morning focused on cancer. Dr. Lee, an oncologist, was interested in why some people with terminal cancer chose not to be resuscitated while others preferred that everything possible be done for them. My opinion was that when you were a goner, you might as well check out. Interestingly, our survey data showed that the closer to death the patients were, the more likely they were to want heroic efforts to keep them around. Maybe my own attitude would change if I was at death's door. I hoped I would be more consistent than that, but you never could tell, could you? And that was Dr. Lee's point: people changed their minds and doctors should listen to what patients preferred in extremis, not what they originally thought they would prefer.

With these morose thoughts in my head, turning off the computer at noon was not difficult. Betty was about to go out for lunch with her cousin Wendy. Wendy worked at the Fort Atkinson hospital. She was a dietitian.

"Hey, Jorgenson called this morning," I told her. "He invited me over to the Club for drinks this afternoon."

"That's nice. It's a boy's thing, I assume."

"Yep. No girls allowed."

"I didn't want to go anyway."

"Well, you can't even if you want to."

"You couldn't make me."

We grinned at each other. "Oh," she said. "Wendy invited us to a church supper tomorrow evening. I told her I would check with you."

Wendy and her family were members of some kind of bible church. I hesitated.

"You don't want to go, do you?"

"No, I don't mind."

"Really?"

"Really." This would be an opportunity to probe the secrets of the bible thumpers. It might help me understand the Fist of God crowd.

Cranking up the chariot, I headed over to McDonald's to meet my supervising secret service agent. While I was nursing a cup of coffee in my usual spot, a smiling fellow whom I had never met sat down across from me.

"Thought I better introduce myself," he said, "since we are neighbors. I'm Skip Cavanaugh."

"Neighbors? Oh, you must have the unit right next to ours. Nice ta meetcha."

We shook hands. Cavanaugh appeared to be in his sixties. He was a dapper fellow, wearing Dockers, a nice pair of shoes, a sport shirt, and a fishing hat.

"We don't make too much noise for you, I hope?"

He smiled at that. "No problem there."

"Oh, by the way, I have a router for my internet connection. You might be able to get a free connection since you are right next door." I was trying to be neighborly in my own geeky way.

This amused him. "I'll keep that in mind," he said with a broad smile.

"You're a fisherman, I guess. We saw your boat parked by your garage."

"Yes indeed," he said. "I get out whenever I can."

"Lived around here long?"

"No. I just retired. Used to be in banking. Moved here from Madison."

He seemed to be a nice fellow, easy to talk with and interested in everything. Before long I was telling him about the mystery of the corpse. I even spilled the beans about the mysterious deposit into my account, something I still had not confessed to Betty. I figured since he was a banker he might have some useful ideas about what to do with that situation.

Cavanaugh thought about it for a few minutes, stirring his cream into his coffee thoughtfully. "Well," he said. "The first question is, of course, how did they get your account number? Your bank has your account number, so, most likely, they made an error. If so, then they will figure it out eventually. When that happens, they will take it back. So you better not spend it."

That seemed like good advice. He was more interested in the dead body. I could not give him any theories about why the murder was committed or why the body was placed under my deck.

"What do think might be going on with that?" I asked him.

Skip grinned. "Bankers always think everything can be traced back to money," he said. "Somebody is protecting money or trying to get more."

"How does killing somebody help you get or keep money?"

"Look at it this way," he explained. "What might you expect would be the consequences of this death?"

We mulled that over for a minute when an idea struck me. "A dead body could slow down sales of the condos, don't you think?"

"Sure it could. Buyers might be put off by that. And there have been no new sales since it happened."

"Why would somebody want to derail the development?"

Cavanaugh had an explanation for that one. "These small towns often have a strong resistance to economic development. Local folks are concerned that the quality of life they have always enjoyed will go downhill. Traffic increases, crime waves hit, prices go up. Some places have passed strict ordinances to make it hard for developers because they don't want village life to change."

This made him chuckle. "When I was in banking, I hated that attitude. Now that I'm retired, I am a lot more sympathetic to the local yocals. After all, I am one."

It was a pleasant chat, but both of us were ready to move on with our day's activities. We split up and I mounted my trusty steed to head for home.

Before I could go, however, a sedan pulled up next to me. My old friends, detectives Broder and Schmidt, leaped out and stood on either side of me. This looked ominous.

"Still in town I see," said Broder.

"Yes sir."

"That's good because we have some concerns that we need to discuss with you."

"Oh? What's up?"

"There's been another murder."

"No kidding. Who?"

Schmidt leaned over toward me. "Don't play dumb with us," she snarled.

Now I was getting nervous. "Why would you think it had anything to do with me?"

"Because the stiff is a friend of yours, fella by the name of Johnson. You were seen talking to him right here a few days ago."

This shook me up pretty badly and the cops noticed my reaction.

"What can you tell us about it?" Broder asked me.

"Well, it's kind of a long story." They waited with blank stares. "It's like this. Johnson was a secret service agent. Somebody from this area was threatening a politician and he wanted me to keep my ears open."

Their faces showed frank disbelief. "You don't expect us to swallow that cockamamie story, do you?" Schmidt's irritability was straining her ability to control it.

"It's true."

"Yeah and maybe the real truth is that you killed him."

"That's crazy! Why in hell would I want to do that? I had no reason to want to kill him!"

"Really? We figured you had lots of reasons." Broder was giving me the once-over like I was already convicted and sentenced. "Like maybe a hundred thousand reasons."

"What?" Then it hit me. One hundred thousand reasons. Uh oh.

"We will be talking about this with you soon. Don't leave town." Broder was about as menacing as anybody could be without actually attacking you.

My ride back to the condo was a blur. How did they find out about the money? I had to admit, now that they knew about it, they had to think it looked suspicious. How was I going to explain why I suddenly had that big wad of cash? Damn. What a mess.

Chapter 11.

Enter the Lion's Den

Back at the condo, I figured I should clean up a bit for drinks at the Country Club. After all, my Levi's, jogging shoes, and gray T-shirt were a bit on the casual side. After carefully considering my options, I changed into my Justin black boots and threw on the black blazer. Blazers looked good with T-shirts, don'cha know.

The question running through my mind was this: why was I even going? The secret service agent who had enlisted me in the undercover assignment was dead. This provided two reasons to bail out. First, I no longer had a boss. Second, his death proved this was dangerous business.

On the other hand, a chance to drink beer with some guys, no matter the circumstances, was still a chance to drink beer with some guys. Ultimately, I decided that the undercover role was over, but that didn't preclude me from having some fun.

The group clustered around Jorgenson at the Club was about what you would expect: middle aged white guys in polyester suits. Introductions revealed that they included an insurance agent, a commercial real estate appraiser, a banker, a building contractor, and a fellow from the zoning office of the local government. The conversation revolved around how hard it was to make money since the government was always throwing up obstacles to prevent entrepreneurs from doing their patriotic duty (i.e., driving the economy).

Since I was no longer under cover, I felt free to tell them what I really thought. When Jorgenson teased me about seeing me whizzing around town on my motorized bike, it gave me my opening.

"Yep, ten dollars for the bike and a couple of hundred for the motor. It gets me where I'm going. And how much did you pay for that caddy you're driving, Moody?"

Jorgenson laughed. "You've got a point there, Ed."

"You wouldn't believe how hard it is to do something economical. The other night we went to a movie that showed a scene from India. Lots of motorized rickshaws or whatever running around. Miles per gallons for those little vehicles must be pretty good. That's all we need for running around Fort Atkinson most of the time. And if more people drove them, we would reduce our dependence on foreign oil. This would mean that we would be less involved in military action in the Middle East, which means the average Joe in the Middle East would have less reason to hate us, which would mean that we would not have to worry about terrorism. And to top it off, we could manufacture that stuff locally instead of having to build it in Korea and pay to ship it half way around the world."

I was warming to my subject. "So little fuel-efficient vehicles are in the public interest, besides being cheaper. Almost anybody can afford to buy and drive something like that. But for some reason, the economy does not make it easy to get them. You should be able to yank a bike motor off the shelf at Walmart. Heck, they're afraid to sell a scooter because of state regulations against them, much less a bike motor. Briggs and Stratton has stopped making motors that might be used to power a homemade vehicle because they are worried that some dope will kill himself and the family will sue them under product liability laws."

Now I was making myself angry. "I bought my bike motor off the internet. Before I ordered it, I went into a bike shop down in Whitewater to ask about bike motors. The guy running the place said he could fix me up with one that cost over five hundred dollars. Any other product was just imported junk, he said. Then he gave me a flyer for the company upstate where he buys his bike motors. Turns out the upstate guy gets his bike motors from, where else? Overseas via the internet."

By now, I was standing up. "The bike store fellah is doing alright. He has a lot of high end stuff in there, including a Lee Iacocca motorized bike on sale for nine hundred dollars. So I said to him, 'Look, I know you want to market to yuppies so you can meet your income goals. But if I paid those prices, I would just be supporting the yuppie materialist culture. What happened to Henry Ford's philosophy of an affordable car for everyone? The Wright brothers were bicycle shop guys. They built an airplane out of spare bike parts. What happened to the spirit of frugal creativity, making things everyone can enjoy?' He had no idea what I was talking about. So I walked out."

At that I sat down. After a pregnant pause, the group broke into cheers and applause. They didn't particularly care what my opinions were, they just enjoyed the show. That's the great thing about beer with the guys, unless it leads to a fight.

Jorgenson clapped me on the back. "You're right about one thing. We sure don't have anything that equates to a Model A these days."

He grinned at me. "You know, business is tough right now. My construction projects are way ahead of sales. Cash flow is a bitch. Getting together with the guys like this once in a while takes some of the pressure off. You added a heck of lot of entertainment value today. Just wanted you to know I appreciate it. Hope you can make it some other time." He seemed to be completely sincere.

I had to take advantage of this brief moment of guy-type intimacy to ask him a question. "Hey, have you ever heard of a group called the Fist of God?"

He was completely mystified. "Never heard of it. But I don't listen to rock music, so I'm the wrong guy to ask."

Back at the condo, I settled into my usual spot on the deck with pipe in mouth, notepaper in hand. Jorgenson was convincing and I believed him. He had no knowledge of the Fist of God militia. It was starting to look like Johnson had been completely wrong about this investigation. On the other hand, something had gotten him killed. I just could not believe that Jorgenson had anything to do with it.

Betty stuck her head out past the sliding glass door. "How was your little party with the boys?" she asked.

"Just fine. And the girls who popped out of the cake were really sweet."

"I'll just bet they were."

"Yep. I would have to say they were downright wholesome."

A voice called from below. "Hello up there." It was Cavanaugh, our neighbor.

"Hey Skip. Betty, this is Skip Cavanaugh. He lives next door. Skip, this is Betty. She runs things around here."

"Nice to meet you, Betty."

"Skip, if you have a minute, come on up. I have something I want to ask you about."

Betty looked at me quizzically.

"Financial matters, dear, you wouldn't be interested."

She hit me then went downstairs to let Skip in.

I told Skip the whole story, leaving out nothing. I told him about the undercover assignment, the dead secret service agent, and how the cops thought the 100K in my account was payment for a hit on said agent. I told him about Jorgenson and the Fist of God and how I believed him to be completely innocent of any involvement with a militia group. "He's just a business guy trying to do the right business thing. He would not go in for any violent insurrection. Hell, he's a capitalist. Violence disrupts business. He would regard bomb-throwing as a giant pain in the ass."

Skip carefully considered all that I told him. He seemed to accept my conclusions without question. He did not appear to harbor any doubts that maybe I really was a hit man.

"Well, you certainly have gotten yourself into a tangled mess, haven't you," he said sympathetically.

"Just minding my own business and trying to be helpful." It seemed like a weak answer. Was it possible that I was somehow responsible for the mess I was in?

"Ed," he said forcefully. "Try not to worry about all this. It will resolve itself sooner or later. Just relax."

"But what about the cops thinking I killed Johnson?"

"You didn't do it, so it should turn out okay. If they decide to press charges against you, then just get a lawyer. After all," he paused with a grin, "you have a hundred thousand bucks you can use to hire a good one. For a fifty-fifty split, a good lawyer should be able to get you off the hook."

It seemed like a good point. I had nothing to worry about.

Chapter 12.
Homeschoolers are Hardnosed

Wednesday started badly. The cat decided it would wake me up a bit earlier than usual. It walked on me for a while, it stuck its paw in my face, and when I tried to burrow under the covers, it kept poking me with its paw. They say cats stroke their owners because that was how they got milk to let down from their mothers' breasts when they were kittens. I doubt it. If a kitten poked it's mother in the breast the way that cat poked me, it would go hungry for awhile.

After I had slid even deeper under the covers, the cat started knocking around the items on the bedside table. Glasses went on the floor along with the cell phone and a paperback book.

Enough. I got up, started the coffee, and showered. For some reason, I was tired. Most likely, the stresses of the past week were getting to me. Dead bodies, police inquiries, undercover work, more dead bodies, more police inquiries…it wasn't fun anymore. Then, when I weighed myself, I was up two pounds. Didn't that just add icing to the cake?

After trucking down to the convenience store for the paper, I took Betty her half along with her coffee. She took hers with cream whereas mine was black unless we were driving somewhere. Under those circumstances, you couldn't trust what you were buying, so I asked for sweetener. Better safe than sorry, right? The stuff may have been sitting on the burner for hours.

The paper contained some interesting commentary on the Democratic convention. The Democrats were coming on strong for national security. This stance appeared to make them indistinguishable from the Republicans on that issue. The Democrats wanted to spend a lot of money on new social programs, of course. They could get away with saying that because in the Clinton administration the federal budget was balanced whereas the Bush administration had run up the deficit. The Republicans had lost their ability to present themselves as the gurus of fiscal responsibility.

For most of us, these were not the real issues at stake in the election. The two major parties were asking us to choose between two rich guys who never had to worry about paying the light bill, who never bought bologna in order the stretch the meat budget. One party wanted to give our tax money to corporations, the other wanted to give it away to other groups, some of whom deserved it and some who did not. What a choice.

Shrugging off politics, I went in to work on the computer. Dr. Lee's cancer project, a bioterrorism drill project, and revising a manuscript for a journal all danced around the screen. I was multitasking to beat the band and it was stressing me out. Why did I do it? I was on vacation for Pete's sake. I guess I did it because not doing it stressed me out more. By noon, I was exhausted and needed a break.

Dragging my tired brain out to the deck, I stretched my legs out and tried to calm down. Jorgenson was rushing by, his fat legs moving at a rapid clip on the sidewalk below. "Hey, Moody! How's it goin'?" I called down to him.

He slowed down then turned to walk back toward me. "The usual thing," he said. He looked pretty harried.

"Come on up and have a cup of coffee. You look like you need a break."

He hesitated then replied, "I think you're right. Be up in a second."

After making a brief call on his cell phone, he climbed the stairs. Coffee mugs in hand, we settled on the porch.

"Read the paper this morning, Moody?" I asked him.

"Sure, I flipped through it. Politics, politics, politics."

"Yep, both parties are big spenders, aren't they? But neither one seems to understand what the little guy needs."

Moody looked at me. "You know, Ed, I can't figure you out. Sometimes you sound like a Libertarian, other times you're a Green. What gives?"

I tried to put it succinctly. "It's like this, Moody. Like it our not, lots of people are working for low wages with minimal benefits. We can't keep increasing taxes so we can give them financial help. That would require perpetual economic growth, raping the environment, and constant pressure on the people who are actually paying the taxes. Keeping the cost of living low would be a better idea. We don't need to constantly come up with new consumer goods that are just overpriced toys. Slow economic growth is better than a mad frenzy. Otherwise, we will all end up going crazy."

He wasn't buying it. "Yeah, yeah, I understand your words. But why do you care so much about the little guy? You're smart, you seem to have made good money. You don't have to worry."

"I couldn't disagree with you more on that one. None of us are safe. You and I are only about six months away from being greeters at Walmart. A lawsuit, a big health problem, or a bankruptcy could destroy our revenue stream and wipe out our retirement assets. Heck, after retirement it is almost guaranteed that, if we live long enough, we will end up broke. When we get to that spot, we will want the cost of living to be damn low."

I leaned forward. "Fact is, the reason I worry about the little guy is simple: 'there but for the grace of God go I'. And I can't think of any reason why God should continue giving me all the lucky breaks."

His faced turned gray and his shoulders slumped. "You may be right," he said. "Maybe we are all just one step from the poor house."

He stood up slowly. "Well, enough philosophy for one day. Time to get to work. Sometimes there is no getting around doing the tough things and making the hard decisions. Business is a gamble and sometimes you just have to take the risks and deal with the stresses."

I was not sure what he was talking about, but since I had upset him enough for one day, I let him go away without further comment.

Back I went to the computer, getting more and more stressed as I tried to deal with my anxieties by getting more accomplished. The faster I worked, the more I worried about making mistakes and misjudgments. But my value in the world depended on providing what people expected of me: intelligent work, delivered faster than anyone else. Maybe I was just like Moody Jorgenson, hustling to stay alive.

By five o'clock my back was killing me and my head hurt. Betty found me on the deck and reminded me that we had agreed to attend a church social with her cousin. I groaned.

"You said you would go," she pointed out.

"I know. I'll go. Just let me smoke my pipe for fifteen minutes."

"Okay. I'll be getting ready."

The church social was actually a good thing. I found it relaxing. The group was small and appeared to be composed of regular people, mostly working class folks. If they were like most Americans, they tended to want bigger houses and better cars. No doubt, they lived mostly on credit from paycheck to paycheck.

We took our paper plates through the food line, eating several kinds of 'hot dish'. I parked myself and my plate at a table with Betty and her cousin. It was a large round folding table, so a few other adults joined us. Betty's cousin Wendy had a husband and a couple of kids who were seated at another table with several teenagers. The man and wife who sat with us were sober in appearance. The man wore a white shirt and tie and black slacks. He had a bushy black beard. The woman was dressed in a rather plain print dress.

We chatted about home schooling for awhile. All of the people in the church seemed to be into that form of education. Apparently, they helped each other in order to share the load. We talked about the differences between virtual education and home schooling. From their point of view, virtual education was a bad idea because it involved supervision from the school. The parent was provided computer programs and other curricular materials which she passed on to the child. About every two weeks, more often if needed, the teacher from the school would touch base by email to see how the student was doing.

It sounded perfect to me. Kids would only advance if they mastered the material, teachers could handle a lot more students than they could in face-to-face instruction, and the kids would be exposed less to the bad habits they might pick up from other kids. Why wasn't virtual schooling the way we could get local school budgets under control? The only thing wrong with the idea that I could see was that virtual schooling seemed to have started with the primary grades. I could envision it being more useful for high school kids. High school was largely a waste of time when I went through it. You could have learned everything you needed to learn in about half the time if virtual schooling had been available.

The people at my table disagreed strongly. They were home schoolers through and through. They wanted no involvement from the school system. And, they either wanted their property taxes cut since they didn't use the schools or they wanted the school district to pay them back for the value of the education they provided. They were pretty hard core.

"But why are you so set against getting help from the school system? They can buy materials like computer software in bulk and get better prices. They can come up with a standard curriculum, so you don't have to do that."

This really got us to the heart of the matter. "Because of government propaganda," the man with the bushy beard asserted loudly. "The government pushes crap like evolution and accepting homosexuality. The government wants us to become Godless and accept a secret dictatorship."

His wife hushed him. There was a moment of silence. "This is interesting. I sure would like to hear more about your point of view," I said.

The man and his wife exchanged looks. "Sorry," he said. "We are better off keeping our opinions to ourselves. Government agents have been known to persecute people like us when they realize we are onto their agenda."

This made me chuckle. "That seems a little paranoid. It's not like you're the Fist of God militia or something."

The man and his wife looked startled. "What about the Fist of God?" he demanded.

"Nothing," I backpeddled. "I thought it was an urban myth. Does it really exist?"

"No," he said belligerently. "It does not exist and never has." With that he and his wife got up and left the table. No one else would speak to us, so Betty and I went home. Add that church to the list of places I can't revisit because of my big mouth.

Chapter 13.

A Near Miss

Wednesday had been a bad day, but Thursday proved to be much worse. I woke up exhausted, having tossed and turned all night. The room had been stuffy and my senses were acutely tuned to everything that was going on around me. The cars that drove by on the highway a quarter of a mile away seemed to lack mufflers. The water heater was noisy. The air conditioner sounded like it was powered by a jet engine. I got up twice during the night to use the bathroom. Betty was snoring, something she didn't usually do. When I finally got to sleep, the damn cat stuck his paw in my mouth.

Staggering out to make coffee at five a.m., I felt like it would take a gallon of the stuff to get me going. After showering, I went out for the newspaper in a daze. The woman at the counter looked at me oddly; I probably looked like I was hung over. The paper contained nothing remotely interesting, so I went back to work on the computer.

The task that morning was to develop a bioterrorism drill for a municipal health department in Texas. The scenario I had dreamed up was for a militant group to start dousing the public swimming pool with nasty bacteria that would cause dysentery. I was going to send data about the hypothetical cases of sick kids to the health department to see if they could analyze it accurately and rapidly. By ten o'clock it was shaping up, but I was ready to quit.

Betty wanted to check out some shops in a little town just past Whitewater called East Troy. This sounded fine to me, so off we went. East Troy had a nice little square at the center of town with a few shops encircling it. The weather was nice, so I sat on a bench smoking my pipe while Betty picked through a gift shop. By eleven o'clock, we were ready for an early lunch. We decided to try a mom and pop restaurant facing the square.

Usually I liked these little independent restaurants. Ordinary people trying to make a living providing a useful service to the community was an activity worthy of support from my point of view. The waitress was friendly, revealing a couple of missing teeth while she chatted with us. The water glasses did not look very clean, though, and the potato chips were stale. I ordered a hamburger but could not finish it. It tasted bad. Sniffing it, I could not say for sure that the meat was spoiled, so I tried to eat the thing. But I just could not get it down. Being a burger kind of guy that was an unusual experience for me. In fact, I don't think it had ever happened before. We left that place a little disappointed.

During the twenty minute drive back to Fort Atkinson, my stomach started to give me trouble. Belches started to demand release. Betty was worried that I had food poisoning and was tempted to make me drive to the hospital in Fort Atkinson rather than home. Aside from the gas and some tingling in my arm, my symptoms were not that bad, so I just drove home.

The gassiness cleared up after I drank a Diet Coke, but I didn't feel like going back to work in the den. A brilliant idea struck me; maybe I needed to take the afternoon off. I would go fishing. While by no stretch of the imagination could anyone describe me as a fisherman, I did have a license and a pole. Catching anything has never been important to me; the fresh air and quiet rush of the river were the sources of satisfaction that came with dropping a line in the water.

Fastening my pole to my bike with a bungi cord, I set off for the river. My route led down Madison Avenue through the center of town. Traffic was light, even at the main intersection in the village which was right by McDonald's. I caught the green light and continued on through town toward the hospital. Turning left, I was on the river road in another five minutes.

As I peddled along, I was reminded of why we had wanted our summer home to be in a small town. It was very peaceful. Life was good. In a few minutes, all the businesses and houses were gone and I was alone on the heavily wooded road. The river glimmered off to the right, visible only occasionally through the trees. A gentle breeze was blowing in my face.

At this point a couple of people on ten speed racing bikes pulled up level with me. The bikes looked like they were top of the line and must have cost them quite a bit to buy and maintain. The bikers were wearing, of course, spandex biking shorts that looked pretty silly, but if they had padding in the seat, they might have been worth wearing. My tail end was already pretty sore. Maybe not; a guy has to have some standards. The bikers also had helmets on with visors pulled down over their faces. That looked a bit over the top in regard to the level of protection a person really needed, but there was a reason for everything.

I nodded a greeting to them, not speaking to conserve my wind. I was peddling to assist the bike motor which made me huff and puff a little.

The biker on my left did something that surprised me quite a bit. He reached into his shirt pocket and pulled out a switchblade knife which he clicked open then swung at me viciously. I gasped and pulled my bike to the right, wobbling and slowing down. The biker on my right was not accommodating. He also had a knife and was driving it straight toward my side. Opening up my throttle to its maximum, I jammed the pedals as hard as I could and accelerated just out of reach.

Now I was cranking the pedals as fast as I could. Unfortunately, the bikers could easily match my pace. They were on racing bikes and they knew how to operate them. The only reason I was not already lying on the road with knife wounds was simple; racing bikes required the rider to have his butt up in the air as he hunched over the handle bars. This made swinging a knife rather awkward.

But not awkward enough. They caught up with me and renewed their attack. I dodged their swings as best I could. Even so, they managed to inflict some cuts on my arms that burned like fire.

By now we were starting down a steep hill. This enabled me to pick up some speed. Since the road was rough, the bikers had to devote their attention to controlling their bikes. They held off their attack for a moment, no doubt waiting until our speed was again reduced.

As we raced down the hill at a fast pace, I saw with horror that the road made a sharp turn to the left at a bend in the river. How was I going to get out of this? I would have to slow down to make the turn. These maniacs would get me for sure. I could sense a feeling of murderous satisfaction coming from my attackers. This spot was where they had wanted me to go all along. They had been herding me like a lamb to the slaughter.

I couldn't slow down or they would get me. As I bounced down the road toward the turn, I could see a glimmer of river water through the trees. There was no choice; I had to go for it.

So I did not slow down at all. The bikers dropped back a bit, no doubt wondering what I was doing. The bank dropped off steeply from the road to the river. Shortly after leaving the road, I was fifteen feet in the air, aiming for a gap in the trees. Branches slapped my face and my back wheel banged off of a branch. Then I was out in the sunlight. The bike and I cartwheeled in the air. Afraid of landing on it and breaking a leg, I kicked it away from me in mid air. Then there was a splash and water was all around me. Not sure which direction I should go to find the surface, I just swam until I bobbed to the top.

Miraculously, my glasses were still on my face. However, they were spotted with water droplets, so that I could not see much at all. I could tell where the trees were - that was the bank. That was not the direction I wanted to go since my evil friends would no doubt be waiting for me. I starting swimming out into the center of the river, figuring that was the only safe way to go.

I have never been a strong swimmer and my clothes and shoes were weighing me down. But I had no choice. I just kept up my awkward stroke until I was too tired to continue. Then I treaded water while I caught my breath. Fortunately, I've always had a knack for dog paddling.

No movement from the bank seemed to be coming toward me. Perhaps they were watching me, but at least they had not jumped in after me. After five minutes or so, I struck out for the bank on the opposite side of the river.

When I reached it, I was exhausted, so I just held onto a friendly branch for awhile to rest. Then I dragged myself out of the water and struggled my way up the bank. Muddy and tired and dripping wet, I shook off my glasses and looked around. I could see no sign of my attackers and could hear nothing that sounded threatening. So I started the long walk home.

It took nearly three hours to find the nearest bridge then walk home. This gave my clothes time to dry, though my jogging shoes were still squelching a bit when I got to the condo. Taking them off inside the door, I trudged tiredly up the stairs.

Betty was standing at the landing looking down at me sternly. "What happened to you?"

"Nothing much."

"Your face is scratched. Your clothes are ripped. Your shoes are wet."

"Okay, okay. I went fishing."

Her face cleared up a little. "Oh. You fell in?"

"Yep."

Then she got angry. "You shouldn't go fishing without me. You might have drowned," she stormed.

"A guy can go fishing without taking his wife!" Now I was mad. She was always trying to baby me.

"Never again," she insisted. "Promise me you will never go fishing again without me!"

"That's ridiculous. Next, you'll have me wearing diapers."

We didn't speak to each other for a couple of hours. Finally, I figured enough was enough. "Look, I know you were upset. I'm sorry. How about if I take you out somewhere?"

Betty gave me her scared and angry look for a minute, then softened. "Where are you going to take me?"

"You like that Club 26 place down the bypass south of town. How about that?"

This was acceptable, so off we went. Instead of going into the restaurant, we sat at the bar which was a very impressive circular affair made of heavy wood. Betty had a fancy martini and I had a couple of ales. Then, we went over to Culver's for ice cream. Forgiveness seemed to have been achieved.

When we pulled into our garage back at the condo, Betty looked around quizzically and asked, "Where's your bike?" Damn. She never misses a trick.

Chapter 14.

Time to Get Serious

Thursday night I slept like a log because I was exhausted. I woke up in a terrible mood. I was stiff all over. And I was seriously angry.

The only good news was that somehow two pounds had disappeared off my weight. Apparently, being chased by homicidal maniacs on bikes, swimming a river, and walking several miles to get home was a good routine for losing weight. Maybe I could start a new weight loss program. How much, I wondered, would people pay to go through that routine?

The previous evening Betty had extracted a full confession from me about the events of the day. "I told you that you would kill yourself on that motorized bicycle," she scolded me.

"I didn't kill myself. I'm still alive."

"Pure luck!"

"The bike didn't almost kill me. Those damn yuppies with the switchblades did."

She grabbed me by the shoulders. "Look at me," she said. "I want you to report all of this to the police tomorrow. Promise me."

"Okay. No problem."

She was dead right. Enough was enough. These guys should be tracked down and arrested. Then they should be thrown into the slammer for a very long time.

I woke wrathful and ready to take action. Broder probably would not be in his office until after eight, so I went about my usual business until then.

When I called the police station and asked for Broder, he wasn't immediately available. Leaving a message for him that basically said I wanted to report an attempt on my life, I hoped for a quick response. And quick it was. He called me back in about five minutes. We agreed that I would come down to the station to make a statement that morning.

Since I was once again a pedestrian, it took me about 25 minutes to get there. He led me into the same interview room where he had given me the third degree. Schmidt was already there with a tape recorder. I did not know who might be watching from behind the one-way window.

After I had recounted the whole story about the attack of the bicyclists, there was a moment of silence. Then Broder asked, "And why do you think these guys would want to kill you?"

"The best theory I can come with is drugs," stealing the idea from Betty's cousin Andrew. "What else is worth killing people for?"

"Why would drug dealers want to kill you?" Broder was deadpan. I suspected he already knew the answer.

"On Monday, we went to the concert in the park. We were talking about the dead body you found at my place. The drug theory came up. And here is the interesting part -several people with racing bikes were sitting around us. They could have heard the whole discussion and thought I was getting too close. Maybe they wanted to shut me up before I drew attention to them."

Broder and Schmidt exchanged glances. "Actually," Broder said, "you might have something there. For your information, we are now operating on the theory that the hundred thousand was deposited in your account to frame you for the murder. That's a lot of money. Nobody is going to throw away a hundred K unless a lot of money is at stake. That points to drug dealers, probably a big distribution network."

This was great news, but I had to ask, "Why did you decide I was being framed?"

Schmidt and Broder avoided my eyes for a few seconds. Finally, Schmidt could not contain herself. "Because you have friends in high places. We were told to operate on the theory that you were a chump instead of a perp. Personally, I'm keeping an open mind on the subject. We might still tag you for that killing."

Broder put a restraining hand on her arm. "No, no. We don't think you had anything to do with it. You can forget about it."

Then he got back to the attack. "Do you think you can identify the guys who attacked you?"

"I didn't see their faces, but I saw their bikes. I might be able to recognize them. And the helmets were pretty distinctive: they had blue visors that completely covered their faces. And, of course, they had those stupid shorts on."

Broder looked doubtful.

"Hey, I bet if you interviewed some people who were at the concert in the park you would be able to get at least one name for one of the bikers who was there. I know I would recognize some of those guys. If you had some names, you could search their homes for bicycles, shorts, helmets, switchblades, and drug paraphernalia. You might be able to build up quite a bit of evidence."

Broder twirled his pen around for a minute. "Would you be willing to look at people in a lineup? Would you be willing to testify?"

"Damn right. I want to get these guys."

He stared at me, dead earnest. "I have to warn you that this crowd has proven they can be dangerous. That means you have to watch yourself. I would suggest that you avoid dark alleys for a while."

That sounded like good advice.

Trudging back home, I had a lot to think about. I was feeling very virtuous about my commitment to nail the drug ring. I was also scared from the top of my head right down to the bottoms of my feet.

When I got home, I happened to run into Skip Cavanaugh. He could see that I had a lot on my mind, so he invited me up to his place for a chat. I updated him on all the events of the last 24 hours. He didn't look greatly surprised. "You sure are getting in deeper and deeper, aren't you?" he said gravely. "You'll be lucky if you don't end up getting yourself killed."

"You're right about that. I just don't know what else I can do at this stage."

"Well, hang in there. Things can't get much worse"

He was wrong about that as it turns out.

Chapter 15.

Loose Ends

This next part is difficult to write about, so I will try to keep it short. The good part or what at first seemed like the good part was that my new bike motor arrived that day. I had never intended to stop with a little electric bike motor. A 40cc gasoline motor was being offered on the web for $250 on sale, so I jumped at it. It was illegal, of course, but if you rode it on the sidewalk you didn't break the laws about having licensed motorized vehicles on the street. Go figure.

The motor arrived, and I spent the day trying to put it on a new Schwinn I had picked up at Kmart. After several hours, it looked about right, but I could not get it to start. In frustration, I ran it over to a motorcycle shop where the manager treated me like an idiot. He agreed to work on it for a few hours, after which it still did not run. The purchase price for the motor and new bike plus the charge for the labor made my new motorbike a thousand-dollar waste of money. So much for doing things the cheap way.

While I was wasting time and energy on the motor bike, Elric the cat was dwindling away. He had begun to lose bowel and bladder control a bit at a time a few days before. The vet gave him some medicine and told Betty that she could not allow the cat to turn the condo into a toilet. By midday, it was clear what had to be done.

Betty could not do it, so I took Elric over to the vet's office to be put to sleep. I stroked him while the vet injected him, then held his paw while he went to sleep. They gave me his collar to take home. That evening, Betty and I sat out on the deck and had a good cry. It was not a good day. Elric had been with Betty a long time.

Chapter 16

Another Body

The man was wearing a black ski mask pulled down over his face. He was carrying two heavy five-gallon gasoline cans. It was very dark around the building. He appreciated his luck; the night sky was overcast, so there was no light from the moon or the stars. Building lights had been turned off.

Moving quietly, he walked to the nearest door. Bending over it, he did something with the knob and it swung open. He slipped inside the building, bringing the gas cans with him. The door closed without a sound.

Inside the room, he quickly opened one of the cans and laid it on its side. The gasoline gurgled out onto the carpet in large gulps. Leaving it to empty itself, the man carried the other can into the next room where he opened it and began pouring it directly onto the rug. The gasoline splashed out and quickly formed a large pool around the man's feet. The entire downstairs area was rapidly filling with fumes. The man began to get a headache. Empty, he tossed the can aside. Then he returned to the first room, emptied what was left out of the first can, and tossed it into a corner. He was in a hurry now. He had to finish this task and disappear before he was noticed.

He walked to the door and opened it. Propping it with his foot, he took out a book of paper matches and struck one. The brisk breeze blew it out. He tried again with the same result. Stepping back into the room and allowing the door to close almost entirely, he lit the third match and threw it on the floor.

Betty and I were sleeping like the dead when the door bell began ringing incessantly. I jumped out of bed and ran out on the deck wearing only my pajama pants. Skip Cavanaugh was down below. "Fire!" he shouted. "Get out! Now!"

He was right. The next wing of the building was on fire. The unit on the ground floor was spewing smoke and flames out of its front door. I ran back into the bedroom and thrust an armload of clothes at Betty. "Fire. Get downstairs. Now. Go out into the garage."

I grabbed some clothes for myself and followed her down. "Get in the car," I shouted, hitting the automatic door opener with my elbow.

"Wait," she screamed. "Elric is still up there!"

"No, Elric is not up there," I said. Then she remembered, a crushed look on her face. Damn cat. I missed him, too.

I tossed her the keys. "Move the car out to the street. I'll be right back." His collar was on the counter. I swept it up and ran back down, out through the garage, and over to the street where Betty was pulling up to the curb.

We could hear sirens and then a fire truck screeched around the corner on two wheels. A heavy rain was falling and we were soon drenched. We dressed hurriedly under the downpour while the firemen grabbed their equipment and went to work. It would have been more modest to dress in the car, but we simply were not that limber any more. Just getting into and out of the car was a challenge; putting on clothes would have been impossible. Modesty would just have to take a back seat to expediency.

By dawn it was apparent that the alarm had been called in time. The rain had probably helped a good deal as well. The building was blackened on one wing, but the fire had not spread to the upstairs unit or to any of the other wings. We did not have a strong odor of smoke in our condo, though outside the building the stench was overpowering. The air conditioner, cable television, internet service, water service to the units, and the lawn sprinkler system were all out of commission. Bob Johnson, who showed up about five a.m., assured us that everything would be in working order by the end of the day. He would have to wait until a complete damage assessment had been made before he could say how much new construction would be required to repair the burned wing. However, he fervently hoped the building was not totaled. So did we.

Betty and I went to one of our favorite restaurants for breakfast, feeling like something the cat dragged in. Or like something he would have dragged in if Betty ever let him out of the house. We probably smelled like we had just come from Hell.

Eggs over easy, wheat toast, and lots of coffee were what I needed. Betty needed some pancakes as well. She was pretty shaken up. The waitress did not ask us what was going on, though she had to wonder. This was Wisconsin and it would have been nosey to pry into other people's business.

We went back to the unit. We still had no water, so we could not get cleaned up. There was nothing else I could do, so I went out to my favorite spot and lit my pipe. The situation had gotten so bad I was smoking at seven in the morning. This had to be a very bad step for me.

The firemen were gone, but a couple of guys were poking around in the burned part of the building. Then, a car pulled up and my buddies, the police detectives, disembarked. They walked over to my deck and looked up.

Broder said, "Trouble follows you around, doesn't it?"

"No kidding. I hadn't noticed."

Even Schmidt had to chuckle at that one.

"Mr. Schumacher, we're going to put a man on duty out here for you." He looked at me carefully to see if I understood his implication.

It took me a minute. "Hey. You're not telling me that this was aimed at me, are you?"

Broder just shrugged his shoulders. "We don't know the cause of this fire. But it is quite a coincidence, don't you think? Anyway, better safe than sorry. We will provide twenty-four-hour coverage for a couple of days. A car will be parked out front."

I thanked him, still stunned. The likelihood of a connection between the fire and the attack of the rabid bikers had escaped me.

As Broder and Schmidt started to get back into their car, a man from the burned apartment ran over to them. "You guys are cops, right?" he asked.

They must have said yes because then the fellow burst out with the news. "You better look at this. There's a body in here. Burnt to a crisp, I'm afraid. Not a pretty sight."

"Ah shit," Broder said. "Not another stiff." But it was indeed another stiff. I was happy that this time it was not right below my deck. It was at least thirty feet away.

Another crew was summoned. The crime scene was carefully studied and catalogued. The body was bagged and taken away. I sat on the deck most of the day watching people work. The internet was down and I was completely lacking in energy, so I just sat there.

About four in the afternoon, Broder came back. Once again, he did not bother to walk up the stairs but just stood down below and spoke up in my direction. "Mr. Schumacher, you happen to know a guy named Jorgenson?"

"Sure. He's the developer for this complex. Nice guy." I chuckled sympathetically. "He's gonna be pissed when he hears about this mess."

Broder shook his head. "Not much danger of that. That stiff we found in the ashes was your buddy Jorgenson. Do you have any theories about how that ties in with your nasty network of drug dealers?"

For once, words failed me. Jorgenson? What the heck was he doing in that building in the middle of the night? And why was he dead?

Chapter 17.

The Pieces Fit Together

Betty had gone over to her cousin's place for sympathy while I loafed on the deck all day. She correctly figured that she would get more emotional support from her cousin than she would get from me.

When Betty got home, she told me, "I called my cousin Andrew and told him about the fire. He invited you out for a beer tonight. He said Salamone's at six. I figured you would want to go, so I told him you would meet him there. If you don't feel like it, I can call him back and tell him."

"Sounds like a great idea," I said. "I want to run some ideas past him. Maybe we can figure out what's going on around here."

By this time the water was back on, so I showered and changed clothes. Then I headed out on foot. The patrolman out front stopped me. "Where are you going, sir?" he asked.

"Just over to Salamone's for a beer with a friend."

This clearly created a dilemma for him.

"Why don't you stay here?" I suggested. "Betty is upstairs."

"I don't think you should go out, sir." He was not liking my plans.

"Don't worry. It's only a ten minute walk. If you give me a phone number, I can call you when I get there."

He agreed to that plan, though reluctantly.

The best way to walk to Sal's was to go straight over on Commonwealth, turn left on a side street, then cut through the back parking lot of the Citgo station. That brought you out only a block from the restaurant. I called the patrolman when I was in front of Sal's to tell him the coast was clear.

When I walked in the door, Andrew was already sitting in the bar. "Hey, Andrew. How's it goin'?" I asked.

"Better for me than for you, I bet."

"That's a sucker bet. But I'm sure glad you suggested this. I want to go over the whole story with you and see if you can figure out what's going on."

We ordered Millers because this clearly was going to be thirsty work.

"Okay," I said, "first we find a dead body under the deck. That's Saturday morning. A secret service agent tells me the body had been there since Thursday, so I'm in the clear. But the agent also tells me a militia group called the Fist of God wants to assassinate the Democratic presidential candidate, John Kerry. Supposedly, this group is in Fort Atkinson. He tells me that a real estate developer is tied in with the Fist of God crowd. He might even be their financier. The theory is that business types don't want Kerry elected because he would be bad for business. So they manipulate this militia group into knocking him off. The militia does not like Kerry because they think he is a Godless communist or something. Are you with me so far?"

Andrew nodded. "Sure. I get it. It's pretty farfetched, but I can follow the argument.

"Okay, let's see. I guess the next thing that happened was that somebody snuck a hundred thousand bucks into my checking account."

"Wait a minute. I haven't heard about this part. A hundred grand? Who did you have to kill for that?"

"Terrible choice of words, Andrew. My secret service agent turned up dead and the cops originally thought that I killed him for the hundred K. But later they decided it was a set up. I was being framed for the murder. But since 100K is a lot of money, the cops figured that the murder had nothing to do with politics. Instead, it must be connected to drug dealers somehow."

"Ah hah!" Andrew said. "I knew it."

"Yes, you did know it. You said drugs were probably tied in with the first murder. And you must have said it a little too loudly at the concert in the park last Monday. The drug dealers probably overhead you say it. That's the only reason the cops and I can come up with for why some guys would first try to frame me then try to kill me. The dealers thought I was getting too close. Now I'm a witness who might be able to help identify them and they really don't like that."

"Wait a minute," Andrew said. "Why would they think you were a threat to them before you could identify them? This doesn't hang together right."

"That part is a little murky. And here are some more murky parts. Who was the first dead guy and why was he killed? Why was he left under my deck? Why was the secret service agent telling me some malarkey about militia if he was really after drug dealers? And if he really was after drug dealers, why did he want me to check out the real estate developer? And here is the latest bit of murk. Who set fire to our building and why did the real estate guy turn up in the ashes burnt to a crisp?"

Andrew just shook his head. "We've got too many players in this game," he said. "There are too many theories about what is going on. Militia, real estate, and drug dealers can't all be involved. It's too much."

"Oh, I forgot to tell you another theory. This one is from my neighbor Skip Cavanaugh. Skip said that maybe the local anti-development crowd is against real estate projects and they stashed a body next to my building to throw off sales. This would cause the real estate guys to go bankrupt and development would stop."

Andrew frowned. "That won't hold up," he said. "Nobody is radical enough around here to commit murder to stop economic development. We might not like development, but we wouldn't kill to stop it."

"Okay, then you tell me how it all ties together."

Andrew gave it his best shot. "Try this. We can work backwards from today and see if we can determine what might have caused each event. First, we have the real estate guy fried in his own building. If I knew nothing else about the situation, I would guess that he was setting the fire and got caught in it. He screwed up big time."

This made sense to me. "You mean he was in danger of going bankrupt because the units weren't selling, so he needed to clear out the inventory. And the insurance money would help to settle his debts."

Andrew nodded. "Sure. It happens all the time."

He considered how to explain the rest of it. "That brings us to the biker attack. It does appear to be an escalation of a campaign against you. The frame-up didn't work, so they had to take drastic action. The question is why were you dangerous to them? You didn't really know anything about them before they attacked you. What were you doing that they would regard as a threat?"

"All I was doing was hanging around with the real estate guy to find out if he was connected to the militia."

"That must be it," Andrew said. "They didn't know why you were hanging around with the developer, but they could see you were doing it. If that was threatening to them, then they were connected to the developer somehow. You might learn what that connection was if you kept on."

"Keep going. You're doing fine. What could the connection have been between the drug dealers and the business guy?"

Andrew was on a roll. "Money, of course. The problem with drug dealing on a large scale is that you end up with a lot of cash that you can't explain. So you need to launder it by running it through legitimate businesses. The developer needed cash and the drug dealers needed a place to unload their cash. It was perfect for both of them."

Now it all made sense. I started running with Andrew's theory. "They killed the secret service agent because they could see he was investigating something and, having guilty consciences, they figured he had to be after them. So they took him out."

Andrew jumped in again. "The first dead guy was probably another cop who got too close. Same story. Kill him before he can figure out what's going on. Leaving the body under your deck and the wallet in your trash was just a matter of convenience. You were a convenient patsy."

I finished it. "And my developer friend was still losing money. Only now he didn't just owe it to the banks. He owed it to a very nasty crowd of drug dealers. He was desperate to raise enough cash to settle up with them, so he tried the arson thing. He was no good at it and died in the attempt."

Poor Jorgenson. He just wanted out from under debt. I bet if he had pulled it off he would have retired and become a greeter at Walmart. And been grateful he got off easy. He just got in too deep, chasing the businessman's dream of a big profit.

Andrew had figured it out. We ordered another round on me. I toasted him for his brilliance. Then we called it a night.

As I walked out the door, I wondered: What did the Fist of God have to do with all this?

Chapter 18.

Confrontation

It was amazing how a couple or three beers could lead to brilliant thinking. The beer and the brainstorming had explained everything. I was feeling pretty smug as I walked back home. That lasted until I got behind the Citgo station to cut over to my street. It was dark back there. That was when I remembered the drug ring still wanted to kill me. Didn't Broder tell me to avoid dark alleys? Maybe beer didn't make me as smart as I had first thought.

When I looked over my shoulder, I could see someone on a bicycle quietly rolling toward me around the corner of the gas station. And when I looked forward, I saw another biker coming around the other corner of the station. This was not good. I couldn't outrun them when I had wheels. What chance did I have on foot?

All I could do was try, so I sprinted directly away from the station and down the side street. The bikers had to negotiate past a cement barrier that had been placed behind the station to prevent cars from using it as a through street. That gave me a few seconds to gain some distance on them. My only chance was to run between houses, cutting through yards, and trying to dodge around obstacles that would slow down the bikers. I had to avoid open spaces. If I ran into a field or a parking lot, they would have no trouble running me down.

I ran as fast as I could. Dodging around houses kept the speed down a little which was good for me. I was not a runner and had never been one. Now I was a 49-year-old college professor who smoked a pipe. The hundred yard dash would have taken me a week to complete.

As I ran through one back yard after another, dogs were starting to bark and I could see lights going on in the backrooms of the houses on the street. If I could just keep away from the bikers until somebody called the cops, I might survive this experience after all.

Then I stopped. I was facing a board fence and could see no way past it. The bikes skidded to a stop on either side of me. My breath was coming in harsh pants and I felt a stabbing pain in my chest. I kicked out at one of the bikers and heard a sharp grunt of pain. Grasping the opportunity, I jumped directly onto him and he went down. Rolling over him, I staggered to my feet and started running again. Skidding around the corner of the nearest house, I nearly fell over a recycling bin filled to the brim with empty cans and bottles. I dumped it over as I went past. It made a welcome racket, a racket that was repeated when my attackers followed me around the house.

My left arm went numb and I was running with an awkward gait. I staggered across the street and stopped, leaning on a lamp pole. I was in bright light. Surely they wouldn't do anything here.

The bikers had no intention of leaving until their task was finished. They pulled up on either side of me. I couldn't breathe. The pain in my chest was unbearable. Gasping, I fell to my knees, then over onto my back. One of the bikers stood over me, then he knelt on my chest. Darkness was clouding the corners of my vision as I fought for air. He hesitated a minute, thinking perhaps that mother nature would do his job for him. Then he decided to make sure. He brought his arm back for a vicious swipe at my neck with his switch blade. I could see his face clearly since he was not wearing the visored helmet. I guess he was committed to leaving no witnesses this time.

Then, just as he started to swing his arm down toward my throat, I heard a sharp sound like a firecracker. The biker's face dissolved into blood and he fell directly onto me. As everything went black, I heard more shooting.

Chapter 19.

Conclusion

When I woke up in the hospital, the nurse gave me some ice water and let me rest. My first visitor was Skip Cavanaugh. "It looks like you're going to make it," he said.

"Yep, 'fraid so."

"Do you remember what happened?"

"Most of it. But I don't know who shot the biker. Whoever it was, I owe him a big favor."

Skip smiled. "That would be me if it ever happened. But there is something you need to know before you start talking to people about it. We had to clean up the scene a little bit."

"Clean it up? How much?"

"Well, we got rid of the two dead drug dealers. No one actually saw them except you. Officially, they were never there."

"I don't get it. Why was that necessary?"

Skip cleared his throat. "Speaking hypothetically, if a government agency was investigating a situation that involved national security, our new laws would permit a high level of discretion to be exercised by the relevant authorities." He could see I was mystified. "It's like this. Suppose a bunch of drug dealers killed a drug enforcement agent who was investigating them. The agency would be very eager to catch these guys. If the case involved a terrorist group, then the agency could skip all that stuff about warrants, keeping complete records, and reading people their rights. If we grab the terrorists, we can hold them until they get old and gray, especially if no one knows we have them."

"Okay, I get that part. But what do drug dealers have to do with national security?"

"The case has to do with national security. The drug dealers are involved with the case, so we can do what we want."

"You mean like moving in next to me, tapping into my computer, and listening through my walls?"

"Yes, just like that." He grinned without any embarrassment whatsoever. "Look, Ed, at first we did not know your role in all this. We thought maybe you were with the bad guys. As soon as I figured out you were clean, I did what I could to keep the cops off of you."

"And I appreciate it." I hesitated, "Skip, were both the guy under my deck and Johnson DEA agents?"

"No, just the guy under the deck. Johnson was a genuine secret service agent following up on a potential threat from a suspected terrorist organization."

"The Fist of God."

"Right, the Fist of God."

"Okay, this is the loose end that's killing me. What is the story on the Fist of God?"

This made Skip chuckle. "One of the local bible churches is tied in with home schooling. Some of their teenagers must have had too much time on their hands, so they invented an on-line role playing game in which they were fighting the US government. They were religious revolutionaries. One of their scenarios was to assassinate John Kerry."

"You mean it was all a game?"

"Yes. The National Security Agency picked up on their email discussions from monitoring the internet for key words and phrases. At first reading, they seemed to be quite real. So, NSA alerted the secret service which sent in Johnson. The drug dealers killed him on the false premise that he was investigating them. Since it was labeled a national security case, we were able to exercise extraordinary powers to get it cleaned up."

"What happened to the kids?"

"We told their parents to make them quit. We also told them that the government is watching them very closely to see if they might be teaching their kids anti-American attitudes."

"That will do a lot for their paranoia."

He laughed. "Well, I don't think they could get much more paranoid."

He got serious. "Ed, you won't be seeing me again. In fact, you never saw me. I never lived behind your place." He gave me a pat on the shoulder. "It was nice working with you. You did pretty well, considering how much we kept you in the dark."

"Thanks. I wish I could say I enjoyed it."

Skip turned to go, but I stopped him. "Skip. Good luck. And take care of yourself."

"Thanks. I always do," he said and quietly slipped away.

After he left, a couple of women in white coats came into my room. "Hi. I'm Dr. Baker, your surgeon. This is Sarah Spivey. She was helping in the operating room."

"Hi. I behaved okay, I hope. I don't remember anything about the surgery."

The two women exchanged smiles. "You were one of our most memorable patients, Mr. Schumacher. We enjoyed working on you."

At this point, Betty burst in. She was giving me hugs and kisses and asking if I was alright. Dr. Baker said I appeared to be mending well, so she moved on to the next patient. She said she would check on me later. So did Nurse Spivey.

"The staffs' bedside manners are great," I told Betty. "Who says the quality of health care in America is poor?"

Betty gave me a funny look. "Well, you are something of a celebrity."

"How so? Because of all the criminal activity that's been going on around us?"

"No, not that. My cousin Wendy tells me that you caused quite a stir in the OR. The whole hospital is talking about it."

"What did I do?"

She sighed. "Anesthesia does funny things to people sometimes. For some reason, a certain part of your anatomy was rock hard all through the triple bypass. The nurses enjoyed that."

"Oh. Sorry about that."

"Not your fault. But it reminds me that there is something we have been forgetting to do lately."

"You're darn right. And we should start doing it more often."

She took my hand. "That's what I wanted to tell you before all these nurses start thinking you aren't being taken care of at home. We are going to do that thing a lot more in the future."

"Why put off till tomorrow what you can do today?" I asked.

"You aren't suggesting..."

"Yes, I most certainly am. Come over here."

"You dirty old man. You're BAD."

Chapter 20.

Epilogue

They let me out of rehab in time to go back to work at our jobs in Texas. A few things had changed in our lives. For one thing, Skip did such a good job 'cleaning up' after the case that there was no proof left concerning much of what happened to me. Since there were no drug dealers, there was no attack on me either at the river or before my heart attack. The police told Betty I had hallucinated the whole thing and that she should put me into some kind of treatment program. Betty now claimed she never met Skip Cavanaugh. Bob Johnson said the unit behind our condo was never occupied. It appeared that the only people who believed my story were the bible thumping home schoolers. Maybe they should be in treatment, too.

Betty thought maybe I had been working too hard and lost my grip on reality. She figured if I kept acting like my usual self the university would want to push me into early retirement which might be the best thing for me. We would settle down in Fort Atkinson year round. I would still have to work because I'd get anxious if I didn't. So I figured I'd start a little retail outlet for affordable transportation. Maybe I would buy used bicycles, import motors for them, and sell them on the cheap.

After all, what else was I going to do with that extra hundred thousand dollars?

DEAD MAN
TO
STARBOARD

This book is dedicated to all those Baby
Boomers who have struggled with a
period of unemployment, particularly
those who were managers.

Chapter 1.

Face Out of Context

The wet road cast off reflections from the street lights, but there was enough light to see the man in the street in front of me. Being observant was not my strong suit, but even I could not miss seeing the guy.

At first, he looked like a crumpled heap of old clothes tossed into the middle of Main Street. He was about a block from the signal at the corner by the Sentry grocery store. You know the one I mean: if you turned one way you headed toward the hospital, if you turned the other way you headed toward the Holiday Inn Express.

The body was wet, of course, because everything was wet. The poor guy's wet clothes glistened in my headlights as I slowed my Ford Focus. For a minute or so, I just sat there, the car idling. After all, this was not something you saw every day and I was having trouble taking it in. Was that what it appeared to be, a body in the middle of the street? Finally, I got out and walked toward it hesitantly.

He clearly had been a business type. He was wearing a blazer, white shirt, tie, dress slacks, and wingtips. He was face down and his head was turned at an angle. A puddle of what had to be blood surrounded him.

The sound of another car stopping gradually registered. A car door opened and the sound of footsteps approaching caused me to turn and look. An elderly man stood there. He wore a stunned look on his face, one that probably mirrored mine. The driver's side door of his pickup stood open and the overhead light illuminated an elderly woman who was busy talking into a cell phone.

I started to call 911 then realized the woman in the other car was already talking to them. I was in shock and everything seemed to be in slow motion, especially my rational thought processes. Perhaps I should have checked the body for a pulse, attempted first aid, or thought of some useful action to take instead of just standing there. But all I seemed to be able to do was stare blankly at the body.

"Well, this is a mess," I said.

The man next to me hesitated, then replied laconically: "Yup." He looked me over with a frown, then said again, "Yup. Sure is." He looked like a farmer with his overalls and seed hat.

We stood there saying nothing more while we waited for the police to arrive. The woman got out of the car and came over, standing on the other side of the man and peering around him to direct a frown at me.

Why was she frowning at me? I could be a little slow on the uptake sometimes. Then it dawned on me. She thought I had hit the guy with my car. Just because my car was there first and I was standing by the body, she assumed I was the guilty party. Pretty darnn unjust, don't you think? Some people were just plain judgmental, always ready to believe the worst of their fellow man.

A siren could be heard approaching quickly. Then another. The city police car pulled up and we could see an ambulance coming. It was starting to look like I would not make it home any time soon. Since I couldn't seem to stay awake past ten in the evening, this was going to be a real hardship.

The level of activity picked up right away. The police officer moved us away from the body. The EMS team rushed over with a stretcher and started to examine the body. The crackle of radios punctuated the night air. Traffic was starting to become blocked, so the cop began directing it around the scene. The elderly couple and I just stood around, waiting for someone to ask us what we knew. Which was, of course, exactly nothing, but going home would probably not have been seen as acceptable behavior. So there we stood, shifting our weight from one foot to the other every few minutes.

Another car pulled up and two people I had met before emerged. They were police detectives. The senior officer was named Broder and the number two was a tough woman named Schmidt. Frankly, I was a little relieved. Those two would know that I was not at fault.

Both of them recognized me right away. Without needing to discuss the division of labor, Broder took the old farmer and his wife off to one side and began taking their statements. Schmidt walked up to me. I gave her a smile and said, "Hey. How's it going, Detective?"

She ignored my sally and glowered at me for a minute, then said, "Looks like you've really done it this time, Schumacher."

Shoot. This was not fair. This woman should know I was an honest citizen who would never run over a pedestrian. Come to think of it, I had never liked Schmidt, not from the first time I met her.

On the other hand, wasn't this what the police always do? They accuse witnesses of being the perpetrators. Maybe real perps fold under pressure when the cops accuse them, making for a speedy resolution of a crime. On the other hand, given the number of unsolved crimes in this country, maybe the police should rewrite their rule book.

Being a curious sort, I had to ask her about it. "Is there some kind of rule book for cops that tells them they are supposed to make every witness feel like he is a suspect? Something like "Interrogation for Dummies?"

Usually, I was not this impolitic. Okay, often I was. But when it was important, I could usually keep my mouth shut. If I sound a little defensive on this point, it is only because my wife keeps telling me that I embarrass her at cocktail parties by offering outrageous opinions. People should be able to exchange ideas openly without everyone getting upset, don't you think?

Schmidt's face turned red and the muscles in her jaw bunched. "Actually, Mister Schumacher, we only accuse people of running over pedestrians when we actually find their cars in the middle of the street right next to the victim."

My survival instincts began to awaken, belatedly. "I see your point," I told her. This was not the time to be a smart aleck. Even I could figure that out.

Schmidt flipped open her notebook and said flatly, "Now, tell me what happened." So I did. "I was driving up the street and saw this body, so I stopped."

She waited a moment, ballpoint pen poised. "That's all?"

"Yup. That's all."

She snorted with disgust and flipped the notebook closed. "Listen, you turkey, I don't want any of your guff." She was getting wound up, no doubt about it.

"You hit the guy, didn't you? Ran right into him. You been drinking? Come from a party? Driving a little too fast? Half asleep? You didn't even call anybody, you bastard!" Her eyes were slitted and she was breathing fast. She was starting to scare me.

"Enough of this, you damn jerk. I'm reading you your rights. You have the right to remain silent. You have the right..."

At this point, Detective Broder came over and put a hand on her arm. "What's up?" He asked her. She was sputtering with anger. He held up his hand. "May I ask a question or two?" He asked gently. She took a breath and waited. "Did you see any damage to his car?" She froze. "Do you smell alcohol on his breath?" Her face got even redder. "Is he behaving in an erratic or unusual way?" He glanced at me then amended the question, "I mean, unusual for him?"

She took a breath, then let it out slowly. "Okay, you handle it," she said curtly and walked away.

"Thank you, Detective," I told him. "She was really going after me."

Broder looked me over carefully. "You're not out of the woods yet, Mr. Schumacher. Mr. and Mrs. Swearingen did not see you hit the victim, but they can't say you didn't hit him, either. We need to know where you have been, where you are going, and what you are doing here at this time."

"I was at church. The Irish Lutheran Church. We had a meeting in the basement. I was just going home, minding my own business, when I saw the body. That really is the whole story."

Broder nodded. "Okay. We need to look over your car. It will only take a few minutes."

Sighing, I stepped to one side. I pulled out my cell phone and called my wife. Betty had a system with her cell phone. She kept it in a little bag inside her purse. That meant when it rang she had to first locate her purse, then get the bag out, then get the cell phone out, then punch the correct button. All of these steps took time to accomplish, so generally the phone stopped ringing before she answered it. Not to worry; she would call me back.

She did. "Hello!" Was my cheery answer when she rang me.

"Where are you?"

"I..."

"Are you hurt?"

"No..."

"Why aren't you home yet?"

"But..."

"Should I come get you?"

"No..."

"I'm coming right now!" Then she hung up. Fortunately, Fort Atkinson, Wisconsin, was a small town, so the fact that Betty did not have a clue where I might be located was irrelevant. She would be there shortly.

The examination of my car did not take very long. Even so, Broder kept me there another forty-five minutes while he went through the victim's wallet and made a few calls. Betty showed up and stood with me while we waited. It was the middle of June, so the evening air was comfortable. I told her the whole story while we waited. She was appropriately sympathetic. "Are you okay? Do you want to sit down? They shouldn't make you stand all this time." That's my Betty, always in my corner. Well, to be honest, she was usually in my corner. But every now and then, she mistakenly thought I was in the wrong. Then, I caught hell.

Finally, Broder came over. He was looking pretty grim. "Is there anything else you want to tell me," he asked?

"Like what?" I was mystified.

"Why didn't you tell me you knew the victim?"

That threw me for a loop. "Who is it?"

He paused for effect. "His name is Tom MacFarlane. He was at the church meeting with you. In fact, he has been attending that meeting with you and three other guys for the last six months. It appears that you knew each other very well. What I would like to know is why you didn't mention that to me?"

Tom MacFarlane? He was a good friend of mine. This was terrible.

I gulped air and gave it my best shot. "You know how sometimes you run into people in places where you don't usually see them and you don't immediately recognize them? It's like they are out of context, so your brain does not make the connection."

Broder looked at me, then said. "No, I have never heard of that." Then he shook his head slowly. "But somehow I can believe it about you, Professor Schumacher."

Chapter 2.

Interrogation

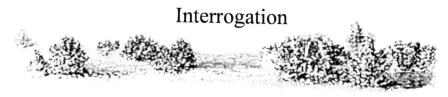

At this point, I should tell you a little about myself and Betty and how we came to be in Fort Atkinson, Wisconsin. Physically, I was an average guy: 5 feet 9 inches tall, 170 pounds, not big on exercise, constantly working to control my weight. You might say I was a little eccentric; Betty certainly did. I liked a beer now and then, and I smoked a pipe.

Betty grew up in Wisconsin and had relatives scattered around the state. We had been living in the Panhandle of Texas until recently. Over a year ago, we bought a condo in Fort Atkinson, so we could spend our summers here. Last summer was the first time we lived in "Fort". It was a great summer, but it had its stresses, culminating in a heart attack for me. My doctors and Betty felt that a period of group therapy was indicated for reasons that escaped me. What they called erratic behavior and a tendency to imagine things was greatly exaggerated, of course. But I was alone in that opinion.

When we were back in Texas, we tried to settle into the old routine, but Betty finally concluded that I was too prone to stress and needed to retire. I never agreed to complete retirement. I was only 50 years old at that point, but scaling back seemed wise. So, we sold the house in Texas and moved all of our stuff into the condo in Wisconsin. This was a major exercise in downsizing and not without stresses of its own. Not for me because I didn't cart around as much childhood memorabilia as Betty did. She seemed to have kept every childhood toy she ever owned.

Betty is a very sharp cookie. She is a physician who went through the Washington University Medical School in St. Louis on a scholarship. She had her quirks, but who didn't? And she puts up with me which I sincerely appreciate.

Betty and I live with a little cat we call Fritter. Fritter was our second cat. The first one died the previous summer while we were in Wisconsin. When we were driving back to Texas, we stopped at a restaurant in Solon, Iowa, that claimed to have the best pork fritters around. They were right about that. Anyway, when we came out of the restaurant into a light rain, we saw a little kitten dashing around the parking lot. The kitty ran from car to car, hiding under them and whining pitifully. This behavior was going to get the kitty killed, so we felt obligated to rescue it. Betty banged on several nearby doors to try to find the owners, but everyone said it had probably been dumped. It was a cute little thing, so we kidnapped it. Or should I say catnapped? Kitnapped?

During a good portion of the next two days, which was how long it took us to drive home, the cat continued to cry. Betty was ready to throw it out the window of the car, but I persuaded her that the little thing would calm down eventually. I suspected Betty was mourning the cat we had recently lost and felt that liking the new one would somehow be disloyal. Betty is a very loyal person.

Sensing who its protector was, the kitten spent most of its time nestled between my legs while I drove. It must have bonded to me during that period because it has exhibited a strong attachment to me ever since.

Fort Atkinson is a nice little city. I like to call it a village, but it is really a bit large for that. Like many similar towns in Wisconsin, Fort was trying to attract the tourist trade. Madison was thirty miles in one direction and Milwaukee was just over an hour in the other direction. And, of course, you could always aim for attracting tourists from Chicago.

Small places like Fort had an ambivalent attitude toward tourists. On the one hand, tourists brought a lot of spending money with them, which could be used to fuel the local economy, thus increasing tax revenues to support the school system and other essentials. On the other hand, some tourists were a pain in the neck, especially those from Chicago. And, of course, Chicagoans believed Wisconsin was their playground. Wisconsin was a great place to visit, cut loose, drive too fast, act pushy, and generally make a mess. The locals were very polite and would never tell the folks from Chicago what they really thought. Maybe it would do them good, but delivering that kind of criticism would be out of character. Well, I could tell the folks from Chicago what people in Wisconsin really thought. Should I? Would that be disloyal to Fort? Being the kind of guy I am, I have to believe that the truth, although painful, is constructive.

So, here goes. Listen up people from Chicago and learn. If you pay attention on your next trip to Wisconsin, you will hear the locals use the term 'FIBs' among themselves while they are preparing your ice cream. Do you know what a FIB is? Everybody in rural Wisconsin knows what it means and they all agree on the accuracy of the term. The second two words are Illinois and Bastard. You can guess what the first word is pretty easily.

Were you shocked that the nice people in Wisconsin would have this attitude? If so, then maybe you should think about how your crowd earned the name. Next time you visit, try to behave yourself.

Fort was making a serious effort to attract tourists. A river ran through downtown, so they built a river walk that was nice, if small, and made for a pleasant ten minute stroll. Unfortunately, the year after they finished it, high water covered it most of the summer. This year, the water was gone and the river walk was in great shape. However, some of the storefronts downtown were vacant and others were clearly on their last legs. As it had for the last one hundred years, the economy continued to suck resources away from the small towns into the cities. Local businesses could not seem to compete with malls in the larger cities. Even locally, the chain stores were healthier than those that were locally owned and operated.

The mom and pop store, which exemplified the entrepreneurial spirit in my mind, was dying out. There were two good reasons for this: quality and cost. Frankly, I liked the Pizza Hut Bistro better than some locally owned restaurants. And if McDonald's ever turned itself into a coffee shop and cafe similar to Starbucks (but with lower prices), I would be a regular patron. And yes, I shopped at Wal-Mart. The big chains could buy supplies in volume and they have developed standardized systems to maintain efficiency and quality. How could a locally owned store hope to compete?

Where was all this headed and what did the future hold for towns like Fort? Was tourism the only option? Let's hope not. Tourism was a zero-sum game. If Fort succeeded in attracting tourists, then some other small town in Wisconsin would get fewer of them. If all the small towns had to compete against each other for a limited supply of the tourist business, then some would lose and die out. This process of fighting over the crumbs from tourists seemed demeaning to me. And competing against each other seemed almost like cannibalism; the survivors eating the weaker of their fellows.

I hoped there would be another way. If the internet reached it's potential, then anyone would be able to live in rural Wisconsin and still compete in the global market place. Maybe I was dreaming, but I sure hoped it worked out that way. Then, maybe, we would see a reversal of the flow of resources into the cities. Our main problem would be keeping out the FIBs. After all, we didn't want them to actually move to places like Fort. Short visits were bad enough.

Anyway, there we were in Fort in our condo, the day after finding a friend's corpse in the middle of Main Street. It must have been a Thursday morning because I had run across the body (correction: discovered the body) when driving back from my support group, which always met on Wednesday evenings. We were doing the usual thing that morning - reading the paper and drinking coffee. I always made the coffee since I was up first. Usually, I brought it to Betty in the bedroom, who was sure to be both prone and groggy, along with a donut from the local convenience store and part of the newspaper. I claimed the front page for myself since I was doing all of the work.

That morning, about nine, the doorbell rang. Opening the door to our deck (our condo was on the second floor), I walked out and looked over the rail to see who was there. It was Schmidt and Broder. Great. I trotted down the stairs and opened the door.

"We need to talk to you down at the station," Broder said. Schmidt looked unusually happy this morning. That was a bad sign.

I sighed. "Let me tell Betty where I'm going. I'll be right with you."

They put me in the back seat of their unmarked Ford Taurus. None of us said anything during the five minute ride to the station. I just watched the town unfold outside my window. Quiet, middle-class neighborhoods, the homes were tidy without being obsessive about it. We lived in Lubbock for a couple of years in an upscale neighborhood. Folks were nuts about their yards. Green grass was unnatural to the area, but they poured gallons of water on their yards every day. I suspected they had Midwest envy, though they would never admit it. And green grass was not enough; they wanted their yards to look like putting greens. Frankly, I never liked that place, not after receiving the anonymous note about how the condition of my yard was bringing down property values.

Fort Atkinson was different. People had green yards because it rained a lot and the sun did not scorch the grass. But if they lived in an arid climate, they would not have spent time and money trying to make it green. They had too much common sense for that. And they just weren't pretentious enough to bother with trying to reach superior standards of appearance. Maybe the real difference was the natural egalitarianism of the Midwesterner; we didn't aspire to be better than our fellow man. In fact, those who had money were careful not to flaunt it. In Texas, it was a different story. The extremes between rich and poor were right out in front of everybody. There was no shame about wealth and precious little resentment from those who didn't have it because the poor were hoping for the day when they could be filthy rich, also.

The detectives led me into an interrogation room after we arrived at the station and climbed out of the car. Broder directed me where to sit with a gesture. I was on one side of a small table, they were on the other. Broder's face was blank. "Mr. Schumacher, we have to go over a few more things with you."

"I thought we had all this taken care of last night."

"Some new evidence has turned up."

"Really? Like what?" I was trying to be chipper.

Schmidt leaned over the table and, with a malicious grin, said "one of the swabs we took from your tire tread had the victim's blood on it." Then she actually chuckled. "Based on the posture of the body and its condition, forensics tells us that your car could have killed the victim without damage to the front bumper, grill, or fenders."

"How the hell could I have done that?" This was pretty farfetched. But it got worse.

"By driving over his head while he lay in the street, Mr. Schumacher, by driving over his head." She leaned back and crossed her arms with a satisfied smile. "You see, the victim was drunk and probably had just passed out in the street." She was enjoying this immensely. "It's perfectly understandable. It had been raining. It was dark. Your vision is not as good as it used to be." She was right about that. "You just did not see him down there on the road, so you drove over him. When you heard the crunch, you backed up. Since you had not been drinking, we can probably get you off with manslaughter if there is not something else going on."

"What are you talking about?" I was really mystified.

"We look for three things when we investigate a case." She held up two fingers and a thumb. "Motive, means, opportunity. We have taken care of means and opportunity. We just need to find out your motive."

Broder stepped in at this point. "Let's take this one step at a time. Tell us a little more about your relationship with Mr. MacFarlane."

"Well, we have this support group that meets in the church basement. We have been meeting for about a month. Tom was a member along with me and three other guys."

Now it was my turn to lean across the table. "Look, you guys, Tom was a good guy. Everybody liked him. He had been through a heart attack and a divorce and his life was a mess, but he was never a jerk. He was always considerate of other people. Nobody would want to murder him, unless it was his ex." The last comment just slipped out. I really did not mean it seriously. But, it lay on the table in front of us, taking on a life of its own.

While they were off-balance, I tried to take the initiative. "Hey, there was a puddle of blood leaking out of the body. Water was all over the road. You had me waiting so long the puddle probably spread to my tire." Surprisingly, that actually made some sense. "See, you guys, there is a simple explanation."

Broder did not seem surprised at my stroke of brilliance. "We thought of that. That theory also fits the facts. But you can see why we needed to talk to you about it." He offered no apology for Schmidt's belligerent approach.

Broder stood up and motioned me toward the door. "Thanks for coming in. We appreciate your help."

I bolted for the door, but he stopped me with a glance. "Mr. Schumacher, we may have more questions for you about the ex-wife's relationship with her husband. A men's support group might have discussed some pretty intimate issues that would have a bearing on the case. Mr. MacFarlane's fears and feelings may have been revealed to a large degree."

Well, no kidding, especially after a couple of beers.

Chapter 3.
The Downsized Boomer's Support Group

Back at the condo, Betty was outraged at the way the detectives treated me.

"They knew all along that there was a simple explanation for the blood on your tire," she insisted. "They were just giving you a hard time to see what they could learn."

"You're right. And that Schmidt enjoys giving people a hard time. She's a very angry person."

Betty hesitated. "Well, you do tend to bring that out in some people."

It was time to change the subject. "I am calling the group together for a wake."

"When will it be?"

"Sometime in the next couple of days. I hope all the guys can come."

"You can't do that at the church, you know."

"Oh. I guess you're right. We can meet at Sal's. It does not have to a big thing. I don't want to reserve a room somewhere, just hoist a few in memory of Tom."

"Can I come?"

"Of course. You can be the designated driver."

"The other guys can get their own designated drivers. I'm going to take care of my man." She put her arms around me. Sometimes, she acted like I needed protecting. That was ridiculous, of course. After all, I was the man, wasn't I? I was supposed to protect her, not the other way around.

She was like this even before my heart attack. Betty is just an anxious person. She worries about nothing, or everything, depending on how you want to put it. If there ever was anything really serious to worry about, she would be great to have in your corner because she is a champion worrier. Unfortunately, when there is nothing to worry about, she keeps doing it. I guess when you are a world-class worrier you have to keep practicing to stay in training, so to speak.

After my heart attack, Betty and my doctors insisted that I be in group therapy. They seemed to think I was a little loopy. Then, after we moved up here, I asked my new cardiologist if there was a support group for his patients. He said 'no,' but it sounded like a good idea. Before you knew it, five middle-aged guys who had survived heart attacks were meeting in the basement of the Irish Lutheran Church. This was a support group, not group therapy. We were all too cheap to want to pay for therapy. And this was better than therapy, anyway.

By the end of our second meeting, we knew we were going to keep doing it. We kicked around different names and finally settled on the Downsized Boomer's Support Group, DBSG for short. All of us were in the Baby Boomer demographic, all of us had experienced stressful career transitions, and all of us were living on less money than we had earned earlier in our lives. Technically, not all of us had been 'downsized', meaning laid off. But the net result was pretty much the same no matter how you got into the predicament. The truth is a middle-aged guy did not have much market value in the first decade of the twenty-first century, especially if there was a heart attack in his medical history.

You have heard about the founding member of the DBSG. A heart attack and a bit of eccentricity resulted in a voluntary surrender of a six-figure income. Now, I was planning to sell battery powered bicycle motors out of my garage which was okay with me. After all, I was a humble guy. I thought I could adjust to not being a big shot. I had enough invested in my retirement plan that I would be okay as long as I didn't start drawing from it too soon.

Tom MacFarlane was the second guy to sign up for the group. Tom was a mess. He was an insurance salesman and a very likeable guy, but somehow he managed to mess up his life pretty badly. His heart attack was worse than mine; he nearly died on the table. His recovery was slow. Whereas I lost my excess weight before the heart attack, Tom was still fifty pounds too heavy during the recovery period. He may have been a bit too fond of beer, not that I would ever criticize an appreciation for such a fine and wholesome beverage. Tom's divorce had become final two years before the heart attack. He was struggling with child support payments. His son, a senior in high school at the time of Tom's death, was reputedly a juvenile delinquent. And to top it all off, Tom was convinced his employer was going to downsize him. His income had been dropping for years due to low sales. It was only a matter of time before they cut him loose altogether. Let's face it, Tom was over the hill and he knew it. He was renting a mobile home and still owed money on a seven-year-old Chevy Cavalier. No wonder the guy needed a support group. The only bright spot in his life was his girlfriend whose heart was apparently much bigger than her brain.

Robert Navis was another member of the DBSG. A former VP for strategic planning for one of the largest accounting firms, Robert had a very high opinion of himself. I didn't know what his salary had been before his company was brought down by the backwash from the Enron scandal, but it had to be a lot. He was pretty smug about being a Six Sigma black belt. That did not mean he knew karate. In big business, it meant you had been trained to analyze and control operations to a high level of efficiency and quality. Personally, I thought it was just another fad, but what did I know.

At the time of Tom's death, Robert was an independent consultant. Cynics liked to say that whenever a manager said he was becoming an independent consultant, it meant he got fired. Whatever the real story was, Robert still had some resources left. While I had to wonder how much consulting business was coming his way, he drove a Volvo and obviously did not buy his clothes at Wal-Mart.

Maybe this description did not do justice to Robert. Sure, his preference for 'Robert' over 'Bob', his expensive clothes, and his smug confidence that prosperity was just around the corner could be irritating. But, underneath it all, he was just as scared as the rest of us. He was okay.

George Schilling was an interesting character. When he wanted to, he talked like an announcer for National Public Radio. When he was being natural, he sounded like he was back in the streets of Milwaukee where he grew up. George was trained as a technical writer and apparently had enjoyed some good jobs writing documentation for manufacturing firms. Now he sold snowmobiles. He said he enjoyed it. He also said once he showed the world he could sell products, he would move back up the income ladder. He might even have believed it.

Louis Smurfit was the last person to join the support group. Louis was a nursing home administrator who had been unemployed for two years. A secretive little guy, Louis was older than the rest of us by a few years. He said he was being passed over for jobs because during his career he had been bold enough to take on 'turn-around' situations, nursing homes that were in trouble. He had brought them back from the brink. But on paper, it looked like he was associated with poorly performing facilities. Some of the blame was rubbing off on him. The fact that he was 60 years old had nothing to do with his inability to get a job, he said. And he would not accept anything that paid less than six figures.

Louis was a quiet, closed-in kind of guy, but you could sense the rigidity inside him, an intense anger toward an unjust world. Maybe we all felt that way. After all, we all carried around a lot of hard-earned experience that should have had value in the business world. But, for some reason, wet-behind-the-ears MBAs were being chosen for the good jobs. Sure, the Boomers were slower, had health problems, and got a little forgetful now and then. But maybe the real problem was that older guys were more likely to call a spade a spade. If a business move made no sense to them, they were likely to say so. Younger guys were more ambitious and more compliant. Okay, it was just a theory, but there might be some truth in it.

The ironic side of all this was that the senior managers who hired the brash young MBAs were pretty much the same as the guys in the DBSG. They just had not been downsized yet. Like all successful businessmen, they attributed their success to their own superior abilities. They didn't seriously consider the possibility that someday it could happen to them. In a dog-eat-dog world, the dog doing the eating was shortsighted; he did not realize that sooner or later he would be the main course for someone else, someone who might be sniffing around his rear right this minute.

In a nutshell, this was why downsized boomers needed a support group. When it finally happened to them, the hotshot business guy was truly in shock. Being unemployed and short of money was simply unbelievable. His self-esteem was shaken to the core. How could this be? It took a long time to readjust your self image from hot shot to ordinary guy. You came out a better person in the end, but it was a painful process.

Our group liked to call this dynamic the Boomer Lament. "I'm really a big shot, it's just that nobody recognizes it right now." Yeah, right. Get over it. Get over yourself.

Chapter 4.

The Wake

The wake was on Friday evening. We were seated around the table in one of the large booths at Sal's. Betty was on my left. Louis, Robert, George, and I were sharing a pitcher of beer while Betty sipped a glass of white wine. Betty did not hold her liquor very well and she knew it. It was one of her more endearing qualities. I didn't mean that knowing she shouldn't drink much was endearing. I meant that when she had a couple, she got loose, which could be a lot of fun. Strike while the iron is hot, I always say.

We toasted our fallen comrade and told little stories about him. We had a few laughs at his foibles. All in all, it was a nice event for the first hour. Then a serious-looking man in a suit came up to us.

"My name is Steven Winters. I was Tom's boss. The people at the office heard about the wake you were holding for Tom, so I thought I should come over and pay my respects."

The rest of us shifted in our seats uneasily. We all remembered that Tom thought his boss was planning to oust him at the first opportunity. It was probably true.

On the other hand, the guy was trying to be nice. "Let's put a couple of tables together so we have more room," Betty suggested. She was right. We had to give Winters a break.

We slid out from behind the booth and rearranged the furniture in the bar. One of the waitresses came over and helped us push the tables together. After a short period of confusion, we were resettled and pouring another round. Winters ordered another pitcher. His stock went up a bit at that point. He probably knew, or suspected, that we had our doubts about him and was trying to pour oil on the waters.

We were all quiet for a few moments, then Winters raised his glass. "To Tom MacFarlane," he said simply. We all drank soberly.

"I only knew Tom for a couple of years," Winters said, "but folks tell me he was a great salesman at one time. Ten years ago, he was bringing in more business than all the other guys combined."

Nobody responded to that. The use of the past tense was obvious.

Betty changed the subject by asking the guys what they had been up to lately. The conversation drifted along lazily for another half hour, then suddenly stopped. A woman was standing beside the table, waiting to be noticed. When we were all looking at her she said, "I'm Wanda, Tom's ex-wife. May I join you?" Betty leaped up and grabbed a chair for her while the guys sat frozen in fear.

After she was seated and had ordered a mixed drink she said, "I heard about the wake through the grapevine, so I thought I would drop by." Gossip got around quickly in a small town, since it had a shorter distance to travel.

Nobody knew whether we should toast Tom again with Wanda present, so the men were quiet while the women complimented each other on their purses and chatted about the woeful shopping situation in Fort. We slowly started to relax which was a mistake.

The door to the bar swung open with a bang and a buxom blonde rushed in. She looked around wildly, saw our table, and strode over to us. She was a sexy woman, with heavy makeup, tight jeans, and plenty of cleavage showing. A cloud of perfume surrounded her.

"Everybody's talking about the wake," she said, "so I just had to come over." She dabbed a tissue to her eye. "I will miss Tom so much. He was such a dear man."

She turned to me and said, "My name is Brenda Stone. Tom was my steady boyfriend."

Now I knew who she was. Tom mentioned having a girlfriend who was a real bombshell. He was not exaggerating. But with Wanda there, things might get tense.

My guess was that we now knew the real reason Wanda had joined the wake. She was hoping to run into Tom's girlfriend. This could get ugly.

But introductions were in order and I knew of no way to stave off disaster. "Ed Schumacher," I said. "This is my wife Betty." I did not mention Wanda. Louis, Robert, and George introduced themselves as well. Then Wanda said, "My name is Wanda. Wanda MacFarlane."

Brenda hesitated, then said brightly, "I didn't know Tom had a sister."

Wanda was gritting her teeth. "I'm Tom's ex-wife."

Brenda seemed to shrink a little. "Oh. Nice to meet you."

Wanda stared at Brenda coldly for a second. Then she asked in a low voice, "Just how long did you know Tom?"

Brenda paled. "Oh, just a year or so."

Wanda spat out the next words, "Like hell!" She was out of her chair, grabbing Brenda by the hair.

The next few minutes went by in a blur. The two women were rolling around on the floor, kicking and screaming. The waitresses were screaming. The glasses and the pitcher fell to the floor. Wanda kneed Brenda in the groin. Brenda bit Wanda's ear. Wanda gouged her nails into Brenda's cleavage. Wanda ended up on top of Brenda and drew back her fist for what looked like it could be a knock-out punch. At this point, Louis and George managed to pull Wanda off of Brenda, no doubt saving the poor girl's life.

Wanda was a mess, with her hair in disarray, stockings torn, and lipstick smeared across her face. Brenda looked a lot better, though she had one breast hanging out of her low-cut top. The guys all had their faces directed toward the ceiling with involuntary eye twitches toward Brenda's heaving chest. All in all, it was a wake to remember.

Chapter 5

Betty Analyzes the Wake

The next morning, Saturday, was fairly typical for Betty and I, at least at first. I made the coffee, then picked up a newspaper and some donuts at the convenience store. After spending some time glancing over the news, Betty cranked up the laptop and began browsing for medical jobs in the area. She was in no hurry to go back to work, but also hated the idea of digging into her savings. On the other hand, she liked to go to the outlet mall and was realistic enough to know that sooner or later she would want to have an income. She was hoping for a part-time position with no call schedule.

At about nine o'clock, Betty emerged from the bedroom and stood in the doorway waiting for me to look up from my reading. "That was some party you guys had last night," she said.

"Sure was," I replied with a grin.

"The waitresses didn't think it was very funny."

"But the cops did."

Betty pointed her finger at me. "By the way, I saw you looking."

"Looking at what?"

"Don't play innocent with me!"

"Oh, that. A guy would have to be blind not to see that."

"You are not allowed to look at stuff like that."

All this raised an issue that had always bothered me. "Hey, explain something to me. If a woman wears a low-cut top, why do men get in trouble for looking at her breasts? That seems like entrapment to me."

"Entrapment only catches people who are doing something wrong."

"But why do women expose their breasts if men are not supposed to look?"

"Men are supposed to notice, but not look." She could tell this made no sense to me. "Men are slime," she announced. "Looking is when your eyes bug out and your tongue flaps down to your chin, which is what you guys were doing last night. Admit it, that floozy got you hot."

"So, she was attractive. That does not mean I got hot."

"She was not attractive. She was a bimbo."

"At least she was not a homicidal maniac like that Wanda."

"Wanda had a good reason to go ballistic. Any woman would have done the same."

This was amazing. "Wait a minute. You're on Wanda's side? She assaulted Brenda. She should be in jail."

Betty just sniffed. "Brenda is trouble. That's obvious. You men can't see the noses in front of your faces."

"But she seemed very nice."

"Nice? How many times do I have to tell you? Women can't be trusted, especially when they're being nice."

Sometimes, I thought Betty was a little hard on her own gender. This time, though, she went on to make an interesting point. "Let me ask you this, smart guy. How did Brenda know our table was the one doing the wake? The bar had four tables full of people. She walked right up to us. Then she pretended she didn't know any of us."

"She tricked us?"

"Of course, she tricked you! Men are easy to trick."

"But you would never do that to me, would you?"

"Of course not. Tricking you is no fun because it's too easy." With that she went back to her computer.

Betty could have been wrong about Brenda. The facts on which she was basing her conclusion seemed to be pretty thin. On the other hand, Betty was almost never wrong. I have never figured out how she does that. Her accuracy was uncanny.

When faced with a puzzle, I always started by making a list. The first question on the list was "Who killed Tom." Now why was I assuming a murder had taken place? Most likely, it was a hit and run. But the police were interviewing people as if a motive was involved. Your garden variety hit and run had no motive. Maybe they knew something about the case that I didn't know.

I decided to run with the theory that Tom was murdered. Somebody had deliberately crushed Tom MacFarlane's head.

This led to the next question on my list. "Who would want Tom dead?" Naturally, the first person I thought of was Wanda, who was obviously prone to violence. A distant second choice was Winters, who might want to replace Tom with a more productive salesman. That seemed unlikely. Winters did not seem like a bad sort. And why crush somebody's head when you could just fire him?

My theory was shaping up. Wanda had run Tom down in the street. But how did she know he would be in the street? Was it blind luck? Did he just happen to be crossing when she was driving by? Did she recognize him and grasp the opportunity in a fit of rage? A lot of coincidences were involved, but then I guessed everything that happened in life resulted from a lot of coincidences.

Still, something did not fit properly. The police would have developed this theory long before I got around to it. They would have checked her car as they did mine. If they had found any evidence that she had run into anything, she would be in the slammer.

How, then, did she do it?

Betty came out of the bedroom. "Where's Fritter?" she asked. Betty did that a lot. I mean, she looked for the cat to make sure it was okay. She did this about ten times a day. A little odd, I know, but who was I to talk about oddness?

Glancing around, I saw the cat on top of the kitchen cabinets. "She's up there," I said.

"Oh, you are a bad little cat. Get down from there before you hurt yourself." The cat ignored her.

Have you noticed how when people are looking for something they generally look down? Seldom do they look up to find what is missing.

Up? Was it possible that Tom had died from a fall instead of being run down by a car? It was time to revisit the scene of the crime.

"Betty," I called. "I'm taking my walk now."

Thirty minutes later, I was standing on the sidewalk near the spot where I found Tom's body, my neck bent back and my eyes scanning the rooftops. First, I should clarify something: Fort Atkinson had no skyscrapers. Anybody who died from a fall off a short building would have to land on his head. That could explain Tom's head injury.

Tom's body had landed in the street next to a rather innocuous building that looked like a vacant warehouse. On the night I found the body, I noticed the McDonald's which was next door. The McDonald's had its lights on whereas the warehouse had been dark.

Some kind of repairs or construction work was taking place on top of the warehouse. Workmen were banging around up there, yelling at each other. At the very top, they had placed a derrick for lifting supplies from the ground. Yes, it was the kind that swivels. Was that derrick swiveled out over the street the night Tom died? Who could say? It was dark and nobody ever looked up.

Chapter 6.

The Ex-Wife

My theory was speedily revised. Wanda had killed Tom with a blow to the head, swung his body out over the street with the derrick, then dropped him so that the next person to drive by would get the blame. She must have lured him up there before killing him since Tom was a hefty guy. Fiendish, of course, but she seemed capable of that sort of thing to me.

In our society, we tended to assume that the perpetrators of violent crimes were men. And most often this was the case. However, well-known exceptions exist. In Texas, a woman ran over her estranged husband several times, then claimed it was an accident. In Iowa, a woman killed her estranged husband by stabbing him in the heart, then claimed she did not mean to kill him. And everybody knows about the famous case in which an unhappy wife took a kitchen knife to her husband's manhood while he was sleeping. In each of the cases just mentioned, similar ingredients could be found. These ingredients were A - a man, B - a woman, C - anger, D - a convenient weapon, and E - the guy was bested by the woman. Damn, it was a good thing women didn't get violent very often; all the men would be exterminated. Then who would women blame for everything that went wrong?

At this point, there was little doubt in my mind that Wanda, the ex-wife, was the killer. But I did not have any proof whatsoever, so there was no point in taking my theory to the police. My experience with that crowd made it clear that my theories would not interest them. Still, I could not let it rest. Were women allowed to kill off men just because they were angry with them? Was this what our society had descended to? On behalf of my gender, I could not let the matter rest.

Walking back to get my car took half an hour. Ten minutes later, I pulled up in front of Wanda MacFarlane's house. Her name had been in the telephone book and a quick telephone call secured an appointment. Ordinarily, I avoided angry women for obvious reasons: they scared the crap out of me. When I was an enlisted man in the army, an angry general did not scare me. Later in life, angry deans and university presidents did not scare me. But angry women? You would have to be stupid not to be scared of them.

Steeling my nerve, I climbed out of the Focus and strode to her front door, lifting my hand toward the doorbell. The ranch-style house was in a nice, well-kept neighborhood. A late-model minivan stood in the driveway. The door swung open before I could ring the bell. She invited me in. Taking a deep breath, I followed her through the door into the living room. The carpeting was plush and the furniture looked both new and expensive.

"Nice place," I offered.

"Thank you," she said. "Please sit down."

We sat, then she asked, "Exactly what do you want to talk about, Mr. Schumacher?"

I cleared my throat. How was I going to approach this? What exactly did I hope to accomplish? She wasn't going to confess for Pete's sake. Suddenly, I wished I had not embarked on this little investigation.

"Please, call me 'Ed.' I'm just trying to understand what happened to Tom. He was a friend of mine, after all. That little scene at the wake suggests there might be more going on here than meets the eye." I smiled weakly at that point to soften the words.

She stared at me for a moment, then said, "Yes, I see what you mean. Obviously, there is more than meets the eye regarding Tom MacFarlane. His friends probably never heard the real story since he was so good at slanting the facts to make himself look good."

Getting this woman to speak her mind was not going to be difficult. "Can you elaborate a little?"

"Tom MacFarlane was a loser. He sold a lot of insurance when he first started out, but he has been going downhill for years. He drank too much, flirted with everything in skirts, and goofed off at work. He was a lousy father and a lousy husband. He ripped off little old ladies. He was a deadbeat dad, and he was bad in bed."

By my count, that was ten bad things about Tom in one brief speech. She must have been practicing its delivery because venom dripped from every word.

"Deadbeat dad? You mean he defaulted on his child support payments?" This did not sound like the guy I knew and liked.

Wanda hesitated. "No, he never actually defaulted. He would 'forget' and then the payment would be late. Tell me this, Ed, why do ex-husbands hate making child support payments? It's their duty. Don't the selfish bastards care about their own kids?"

"Wait a minute. Maybe I can see it from the point of view of the guy a little better than you can. Should I try to explain?"

She sat back. "Yes. Please do. I would really like to understand this."

"First, it's obvious that you live in a nicer house and drive a more expensive car than Tom did. So, he was not living high on the hog while his kid went without essentials."

"He was drinking up his money. That's why he didn't have a better house or car. Besides, he didn't care about nice things."

"You may be right. But you can see how he might dislike making payments that don't directly benefit his kid."

"All the payments benefited Tom Junior. What are you talking about?"

"Well, you got half of the family assets in the divorce. You got a few years of alimony. That's fair. But what portion of the child support payment is being invested in this house? This house is an investment that benefits you, not Tom Junior. From Tom senior's point of view, the money that should have gone to meet Junior's needs was actually funding your investments, not to mention paying for a new car."

"You men all stick together!" She was pretty angry at this point. "Well, let me just tell you something about your great, self-sacrificing, noble buddy Tom. He ripped off little old ladies. Yes, he did. He talked them into spending all their money on nursing home insurance, insurance that they never got to use because they died too soon. He tricked them out of their life savings."

"I don't believe it."

"I can prove it. There's a man I know whose grandmother was ripped off by Tom. You can ask him if I'm right or not. His name is Willy Bundt. He lives here in Fort Atkinson. Maybe you should talk to him, Mr. Schumacher. Now, you can get out of my house."

At this point, a young man with bad posture entered the room. He was wearing a snazzy bicycling outfit, spandex pants included. Even so, with his greasy hair, nose ring, and sneering expression, he looked like a punk to me. "Mom, what's going on?" he asked.

She turned to him and said firmly, "Everything is under control. This man is just leaving." She stood up to emphasize the point.

As I walked out the door, Tom Junior was right behind me. He followed me to the front step. Turning halfway toward him, I asked if we could talk later. Naturally, I did it in a low voice. He hesitated, then said okay. We made a date for McDonald's that afternoon.

Chapter 7.

The JD

The lunch crowd was leaving when I walked into McDonald's. I deliberately got there early so I could think about what I had learned over a leisurely cup of coffee. Wanda was still the number one suspect, but she had mentioned someone named Willy Bundt who was worth thinking about. He was displeased about the long-term care insurance that Tom had sold his grandmother. If she really had blown the family nest egg, then Bundt had a serious reason for hating Tom. Maybe Bundt hated Tom enough to kill him.

Reflecting on my conversation with Wanda, it occurred to me that perhaps I had not carried it off with sufficient finesse. After all, she had blown her stack. True, her angry outburst had resulted in my receiving some interesting information. Even so, when the person you were interviewing threw you out of her house, you probably failed some kind of important test on how to interview a suspect.

Having people blow their stacks at me was not that unusual. In fact, it seemed to happen with some regularity. Apparently, I just naturally seemed to hit a nerve with some people. Betty said I should just learn to keep my mouth shut, but I really didn't know when I was crossing the line.

For example, when we went to the Fort Atkinson town meeting a couple of weeks ago, I innocently set off a few folks. The meeting was to discuss the Wal-Mart proposal to open a supercenter in Fort. Public opinion was strongly against it. The city fathers held the meeting to ratify what everybody knew was going to happen to the proposal – it was going down for the third time.

Betty and I went to the meeting with her cousin Andrew. Andrew was some kind of investigator for the state of Wisconsin. We sat together on folding chairs and listened while person after person stood up and argued against the proposal. Maybe the fact that the meeting was taking too long partly explained what I did. Maybe the hardness of the chairs was another part of it. After all, my tail-end had gone to sleep and I simply had to stand up or I might have ended up completely paralyzed. So, when the moderator asked if anyone else wanted to express an opinion, I just had to stand up.

Betty looked at me with alarm. Andrew was a little surprised, but he didn't seem concerned. Of course, Andrew did not know me as well as Betty did.

"Madam Moderator," I began, "all of these good people are obviously very sincere. And we can all see why they are worried about the proposal. Local businesses will be hurt if Wal-Mart opens a supercenter. And the nice, attractive appearance you are trying to create for the tourist trade will not be helped at all." Appreciative murmurs could be heard around the room.

"On the other hand," I went on, "is this tourist trade strategy a sure thing? After all, any tourists you attract will have to be diverted from some other cutesy small town in Wisconsin. It is impossible for every town in Wisconsin to be a tourist attraction." The murmurs had turned to grumbles by this time.

"Besides, is it neighborly to steal business from your neighbors in the next town?" The moderator was frowning and making gestures like she wanted me to stop. But I wasn't finished.

"The most important concern, though, is our dignity: how dignified is it to suck up to tourists to make a buck? Most of them are FIBs, aren't they?" Betty was tugging on my sleeve, trying to interrupt the flow. The moderator was banging her gavel.

"So, if tourism is not the answer, then what is the alternative to Wal-Mart? I think we need to arrive at a third alternative." The grumbles had turned to heckling, the gaveling was manic, and the sergeant-at-arms had his hand on my shoulder. I didn't think anybody heard my final point. That was unfortunate because it was brilliant.

Later, back at the condo, Andrew told me he thought I was out of line. Letting Wal-Mart in was a bad idea.

"I didn't recommend letting Wal-Mart in," I protested.

"It sounded that way to me. It sounded that way to everybody."

That was one of the crosses I had to bear - being frequently misunderstood.

Betty had a different take on it. "You embarrassed me. If you ever say you are going to a town meeting again, I will hide your car keys."

I couldn't help chuckling at that. You could walk anywhere you wanted to go in Fort Atkinson. Who needed car keys?

As the reader may or may not remember, I was about to tell you about my meeting with Tom Junior at McDonald's. Junior arrived just a few minutes after two, bought a milk shake at the counter, then sat across from me in the booth I had chosen near the back of the restaurant.

"Hey," he said. He was obviously uncomfortable.

"Hey," I replied. "Thanks for taking the time to talk to me. I'm just trying to get a handle on what happened to your dad."

"Who cares? He was a shit." This kid was carrying around some 'baggage' as the psychologists liked to say.

"Besides, it's pretty obvious. He was standing in the middle of the street like a dork and somebody ran over him. He was probably drunk." He concentrated on sucking his milkshake through the straw.

"Well, sure, that's the way it looks." Suggesting foul play seemed cruel, so I changed directions. "Hey, that's a pretty snazzy biking outfit you've got on."

This change of subject seemed to appeal to him. "Thanks. Gotta nice racer, too. It's chained up outside."

"Wow. Those things are expensive."

"No shit. I got a couple thou wrapped up in gear."

"Now that's impressive. You must have a pretty good part-time job."

"I do okay." His eyes became hooded and his face took on a furtive look. "Why did you ask that?"

"I only meant that the support your Dad paid your mother probably wasn't enough to cover all your biking gear."

"He didn't pay shit. Worse than that, he tried to mess up my job."

"That's a shame. Why would he do that?"

Junior looked me full in the eye with a defiant smirk. "It don't matter why he did it. He poked his nose where it wasn't wanted. People I work with didn't appreciate it." He tossed his empty cup toward the trash can, missing it by a mile. "And they wouldn't appreciate you sticking your nose into our business, either. Get it?"

With that parting remark, he left.

Naturally, I was too stunned to move for a while. Had he just threatened me? In a couple of minutes, I refilled my coffee cup and sat down to think the situation through a little more fully.

Was I wrong or did we now have another party with a motive for killing Tom? Junior obviously was dealing drugs. Tom didn't like it, interfered, and may have been killed for his efforts. I couldn't see Junior killing his own father, but the crowd he was working with would not have hesitated.

Darn. Now there were three suspects: the ex-wife, Willy Bundt, and a drug kingpin. This situation was getting messier and scarier.

Chapter 8.

The Warning

Andrew and I met at Sal's that evening. Andrew was a sensible guy and bouncing some ideas off of him seemed like a good idea. I filled him in on how my investigation was progressing.

"What do you think you are doing? The police are there to handle this sort of thing." He looked genuinely alarmed.

"Now wait a minute. I don't have any proof about anything, just hearsay and speculation. They wouldn't appreciate my opinions. They would tell me to butt out."

"That is exactly what they should do. And it's what you should do." The sentence structure was confusing, but I knew what he meant.

"You know how police detectives are. They might figure it out and they might not. They might have to work on more urgent cases. It can't hurt for me to nose around a little."

"It could hurt you. Terminally."

He didn't get a response to that one. I just sipped my Miller High Life.

Andrew sighed. "This kid sounds like bad news. He's a drug dealer. That makes him dangerous."

"Maybe not." My response startled him. "Did you know that the federal Bureau of Labor Statistics did a study on people who had been drug dealers when they were kids to see how they turned out?"

"You're kidding me."

"Nope. It's true. You can find it on the web. Anyway, former drug dealers are significantly more likely to be self-employed, independent business people when they are adults. Legitimate business people. Entrepreneurs. The backbone of the economy. The American way."

Andrew pushed his chair back in disgust. "You have the most backward way of looking at things of anybody I ever met. You can't be saying that kids should deal drugs!"

"Nope. That's not what I said. I just pointed out that not all teenage drug dealers spend their lives in jail. The facts show otherwise." I paused. "On the other hand, a lot of teenage drug dealers are incarcerated before they become legitimate, independent businessmen. And it is possible that they become self-employed because no one wants to hire them." The truth is I did not really know how to interpret the report from the Bureau of Labor Statistics. But it had to be relevant, somehow. "Anyway, just because Junior is dealing drugs now doesn't mean he is beyond redemption."

Andrew's response was direct and to the point. "Yeah, but you could still get killed." At that point, he said he had to go and left.

I sat there for another couple of minutes to finish my beer. Andrew was right that I always looked at things from a different perspective than most people, leading me to different conclusions. Take, for example, the food poisoning outbreak back in the panhandle. I can't tell which state this happened in since it might get me into trouble. Let me just point out that the panhandle of Oklahoma was near where I lived and worked, as was eastern New Mexico, Colorado, and Kansas. Let the actual location remain nameless.

At the time, I was working with the health department of the city in question on some other projects. Since I knew something about statistical analysis, they invited me in on the food poisoning situation.

The basic facts were these: some people became ill after eating at a certain Mexican restaurant. They complained to the health department. The inspector found some procedures that were not optimal. You have heard of that sort of thing – temperature not right in the beans or something like that. Lab results came back on the sick folks and it was definitely food poisoning. The Mexican restaurant got its wrists slapped.

All cut and dried, right? No, not from a researcher's point of view. A researcher needed to rule out alternative explanations before he accepted a hypothesis. You couldn't prove a particular restaurant was guilty of spreading food poisoning germs unless you considered other possible sources of the infection.

A lot of people had food poisoning germs in their bodies on any given week. They were carrying them around from somewhere they ate or maybe they picked them up in their own kitchens. The only way to be sure this particular restaurant was at fault was to survey some people who did not eat at the restaurant and compare their rates of food poisoning to the rates for people who did eat at the restaurant.

Believe it or not, health departments never did it this way. They inspected the kitchen of the accused restaurant, found something that was not perfectly clean, and concluded that the accused party was guilty. They usually were guilty, but nobody actually proved it.

In this particular case, my arguments raised questions that the health department tried to answer. Investigators from the state health department and the Centers for Disease Control came to help. The comparison of the restaurant's patrons to people who ate elsewhere showed that eating at the Mexican restaurant increased the risk of food poisoning, but not as much as a few other things did, like being poor.

We also found that most of the victims were employees of an upscale health food restaurant who were having a party at the Mexican restaurant. Did we check out the health food restaurant? The answer was 'no'. Turned out some places have to consent to an inspection and others do not.

We discovered that the first person to become ill was the owner of the health food restaurant. This person called a friend at city hall who called the health department and told them to nail the Mexican restaurant.

Naturally, I said that the entire process had to be changed to eliminate political influence and racism. After that, people in the state capital stopped communicating with me. That's what came from thinking about things backwards.

Sighing, I put down my beer glass and called for the check. If people thought being an oddball was easy, they were wrong. It was lonely being an oddball, not that I didn't enjoy it at times.

Out in the parking lot as I was fishing the keys out of my jacket pocket, two men in biking outfits sauntered over to me. "Hey," I said.

"Hey, yourself," said the one on my left, then he shoved me hard against my car. My keys dropped to the pavement with a jingle. The one on my right gave me another shove from his side when I tried to turn toward my first assailant. They took turns after that, bouncing me back and forth between them. Finally, I completely lost my balance and fell onto the parking lot. One of them pushed my face into the gravel that was scattered over the pavement and said, "Smart guys mind their own business. You're smart, aren't you?" He laughed. "Take this as a warning. We can get rougher if we have to."

I stayed down until I heard them walk away. After a few minutes, I got up and looked around. They were nowhere in sight. It was time to go home, so I picked up my keys and left.

Chapter 9.

Ditto

The cat and I were having our usual love-fest the next morning when Betty came in to observe us. In the mornings, Fritter usually jumped in my lap and demanded to be petted. She never did that with Betty. She tried to get away when Betty picked her up. I tried to explain to Betty that being held has to be the cat's idea, or they won't go along with it. Betty was still hurt. She knew a lot more about cats than I did. She grew up on a dairy farm where the barn was always full of cats.

On this particular morning, which was a Sunday, the cat had turned onto her back to let me scratch her tummy. Her head was lolling to one side and she was completely relaxed. Betty said, with heavy irony, "Perhaps I should leave you two alone."

I just grinned. Was it my fault the cat liked me better? On the other hand, Betty deserved some sympathy. She had always liked cats. Playing second fiddle to me with this one was hard for her.

"Maybe we should get another cat," I suggested. "I could leave town for a couple of days to make sure it bonds with you."

"Do you really think we should get another cat?"

"Sure. Besides, Fritter needs someone to play with."

"I don't know. She might not like having another cat around the house."

Then Betty changed the subject. "Speaking of being around the house, are you thinking about getting a job?"

"I have a job. I sell electric bicycle motors."

"I'm talking about a real job. Working for somebody else."

"I'm self-employed. That is a real job."

"No it isn't. Nobody sees it that way. Remember when we went to dinner with the pastor and his wife before we left Texas?"

Yes, I certainly did remember. After we explained that Betty would eventually be finding a medical position after our move to Wisconsin and I would be self-employed, the pastor's wife turned to me and asked with a sweet smile, "Does that mean you will have dinner on the table when Betty gets home?"

Please don't get the wrong impression. The pastor's wife was a very nice person and I liked her a lot. However, in this case, she was completely out of line. I blew my stack. "Of course not. I will be working, too." The pastor and his wife were stunned to silence by the vehemence of my outburst. I tried again. "Self-employed people work just as hard as anyone else." No response.

"I have always worked hard and don't intend to stop working." Silence.

On our last Sunday in church, the Pastor announced from the pulpit that we were leaving. He said Betty would be practicing medicine in Wisconsin. He said nothing about me.

"Yes, I remember that the pastor and his wife thought I was going to loaf around doing nothing."

"Well, that is what self-employed sounds like when people hear it. It sounds like it means unemployed."

"Is this what our country has come to? Self-employment, small business, independence, entrepreneurship, all these things were virtues at one time. Now being self-employed means you're a bum." I was steamed.

Betty put her hand on my arm. "It's not just me and everyone else. It's you, too. Otherwise, you wouldn't be so defensive about it."

"I'm not defensive!" I yelled. "You always say I should express myself when I don't like something you do instead of suppressing it and building up resentment. You say resentment makes me passive-aggressive. So, I'm not being passive-aggressive. I'm just being aggressive! Stop saying I'm unemployed!" Then I stomped down the stairs and went out the door.

Betty was out on the deck. "Where are you going?" she called down to me.

"I'm taking my walk now."

"What about going to church?"

"Don't feel like going."

"Do you have your cell phone with you?" Betty liked me to have my cell phone with me. I guess she figured that I would call her if I died. That seemed improbable to me, but maybe there was a logical process there that escaped me.

"Yes. Got it. Bye." And off I went.

There is nothing like a good walk to burn off negative emotions. Within thirty minutes, I was feeling better. As I emerged from the residential streets and approached Fort's downtown area, the traffic picked up. In search of less noise, I crossed the main street bridge then turned right so I could cut over to the other bridge. There was less traffic that way.

There was an open spot by the river where no businesses had been built yet. I wandered over to listen to the sound the water made as it rushed along the bank. I stood there for a few minutes, gradually shifting into a state of tranquility. We all seek tranquility, don't we? It was a lifelong quest and a daily challenge.

The sound of a car pulling up behind me brought me out of my trance. Turning, I saw a hefty guy get out of his black Ford Bronco. The man's belly hung over his belt and his pants were bagging very low in back. He wore a denim vest and had chains dangling in various places. He reached back into the truck and pulled out a baseball bat.

"You Schumacher?" he asked.

"Maybe." I didn't like to lie, but on the other hand confirming my identity appeared to be unwise at this juncture.

"Yeah. You're Schumacher." He started smacking the palm of his hand with his bat.

"You been asking questions about Tom MacFarlane. How he got killed." The fat guy was speaking in a low tone, continuing to smack the bat into his palm to punctuate each sentence.

I did not respond. Silence seemed like the best policy.

"You cut it out. Now. Or you will be the next dirt bag to end up dead. Get it?"

"I understand you."

Then Fatso got back in his Bronco and drove slowly away. He took my tranquility with him.

Betty was messing around in the kitchen when I got back to the condo. She said 'hi' guardedly when I came in, then asked how my walk went.

"Fine. Walking is good for me."

The cat jumped on my leg and climbed up, wanting to be picked up. Sometimes, she liked me to walk around holding her. She liked the view, I guess.

"We spoil that cat, you know," Betty said.

"I know," I responded with a grin.

"I'm sorry I'm jealous of the cat."

"It's okay. I understand. When you're ready, we can get another one that will like you better."

"Okay. But I'm not ready yet."

"Hey, would you like to go over to Culver's and get an ice cream?"

Betty's face brightened. She loved ice cream. And Culver's had great ice cream.

"Right now?"

"Why not?"

So, off we went. The flavor of the day was Apple Pie, so I tried it. Betty had a malt. As we were walking out, she asked me how I liked the Apple Pie flavor.

"It was good. Sweet."

"Sweet as apple pie?"

"Yup. Sweeter than apple pie."

"Sweeter than me?"

"Nothing is sweeter than you."

She smiled and we went back home.

That evening Fritter the cat entertained us by doing hops and flips. She was a very talented cat. When the mood struck her, she would spring straight up in the air to about chest height. Other times, she would do back flips in the air, one after another. Then she threw her favorite toy, a green mouse, up in the air and did a back flip as it fell to the ground. Fritter, the acrobatic cat. Truth is we both loved that cat. A couple of middle-aged folks, dotty over a cat. Well at least it was cheap entertainment. And it didn't require that I stay up past ten o'clock.

Chapter 10.

The Girlfriend

Monday morning came around on schedule and that meant I should get to work. It was time to work on my list. The sun had been up for an hour. The paper was read, half a pot of coffee was in my stomach, and I was bursting with energy. I cranked up the computer. The cat climbed up my back and sat on my shoulder, eager to help. She leaped onto the desk and sat in her favorite spot for computer work: the modem. The modem was warm, so she liked to sit there in comfort and watch me while I worked.

Writing things down always helped me to make sense out of them. I decided to start with what I knew for sure and then move on to hypotheses about things I was less certain about. Where to start? Cause of death. After some thought, I realized this had to be considered unknown. Was it a hit and run or a blow to the head or a fall from a building?

That was all I knew. Apparently, I knew almost nothing. Time to move on to speculation about who killed Tom and why.

Point number one: who did it? My suspects were Wanda MacFarlane, Winters, Willy Bundt, and the local association of drug dealers. Wanda because she was angry with Tom. Winters because Tom was holding back the insurance business. Willy because he inherited less money than he had hoped. And the drug dealers because Tom was a threat to their business.

Point number two: how was it done? Any of the suspects could have run Tom down in the street, but that would have required that they knew when he would be in that particular location. Wanda's car must have been cleared by the police, so it seemed unlikely that she had done the dirty deed. Knocking Tom on the noggin and throwing him off a building would have been easier for Winters, Bundt, or the drug dealers than for Wanda, which was another argument against Wanda being the killer.

But why would any of them want to choose such a dramatic way of committing murder? Bundt would have wanted to keep the murder as discrete as possible, unless he was so angry that he wanted the world to see the punishment Tom had received. On the other hand, perhaps the drug dealers wanted a public display to discourage anyone else from bothering them. Taken all together, it was starting to appear that Wanda was the least likely suspect after all. And, to be honest, the Winters' motive seemed far too weak to take seriously. That narrowed down the list of primary suspects to Bundt and the drug dealers.

It was time for a break from all that thinking. When I went into the kitchen to refill my coffee mug, the cat rushed over to the couch and raised a paw toward it. This signaled a clear intention to claw the fabric. I pointed my forefinger at her and said "EH!" This sound was not easy to spell; Betty said I sounded like a seal when I admonished the cat in this way.

Fritter and I had arrived at this pattern over a period of months. Being a cat, she liked clawing the furniture. Being a person, I did not approve. By accident, Fritter discovered that she could train me to react in a way she enjoyed by threatening to claw the furniture. Initially, I would shout "stop that!" or "no!" at her, but that did not stop her. After awhile, I started throwing things at her to distract her - cat toys, balls made from wadded up paper, and little pieces of wood. Of course, she never brought any of these items back. Instead, she would jump at them while they were airborne, then return to the couch and raise her paw again. Eventually, I was keeping a box full of ammunition ready to throw at her. Picking up all that junk was a pain in the neck. So, we compromised; she would start to claw and I would bark like a seal. This was how my cat trained me to bark like a seal on command. Sometimes I wondered if I really was the king of my castle.

After we tired of the game, I returned to my list, but I could not expand it any further. More information was needed. Then a burst of inspiration rattled my brain: why not talk to Tom's girlfriend Brenda and see if she had any information that would help me solve the problem?

Brenda and I agreed to meet at McDonald's, which seemed to have become my second office. She arrived almost as soon as I did, so I offered to buy her a cup of coffee, which she accepted. When I brought the two cups, hers and mine, back to our table, she had made herself comfortable. Her legs were crossed, and she was leaning languidly to one side with her arm draped over the adjacent chair. Her low cut tank top fit nicely and her skirt was slit up the middle, exposing plenty of thigh. Bright red lip stick and matching sandals completed her outfit.

When I handed over her coffee, I unfocused my eyes in a vain attempt to avoid seeing down her front. After seating myself I looked at her more directly. She was clearly amused. Brenda knew what kind of effect she had on me, despite my efforts to conceal any reaction.

"How's your day going?" I asked.

"Just fine," she answered. "I have the rest of the day off and now I can enjoy myself. I'm sooo happy that you called me. I would love to talk about poor Tom. I just can't get used to him being gone." Her eyes filled with tears.

"I don't want to upset you."

"No, that's all right. It's good to talk about it, don't you think?" She opened her eyes wide with this query. She had very expressive eyes.

"I hope so. When I talked to Wanda, it didn't turn out so well."

Brenda scowled. "I believe that, for sure. What did she do? Go after you with a cleaver?" Brenda did not like Wanda very much.

"She threw me out of her house."

"Oh, my! What did you say to her?"

"Just asked her some innocent questions."

"Like you're going to ask me? I promise not to throw you out." She smiled sweetly.

"What I am trying to do is understand Tom's situation a little better. He was a friend of mine and now I find out that there was a lot about him that we never talked about. Maybe we should have. Maybe things would have turned out differently."

"There, there," she said, patting my hand and giving it a squeeze. "None of us should feel guilty. It was just one of those things."

"Heck," she said. "If anyone should feel guilty, it should be me."

"Why should you feel guilty?"

"Well, he was such a wonderful guy. I just didn't appreciate him enough."

"I'm sure you did a lot to make him feel better."

She chuckled. "Yes, you betcha. And it was worth it. That man was great in bed, let me tell you." She laughed outright at the expression on my face.

"So why should you feel guilty?"

"Well, it's like this. I kind of hate to mention it, but you look like an understanding man. Tom and I did not have an exclusive relationship if you know what I mean."

This called for a moment of silence. "You mean....?"

"Yes. I was seeing another man. An older man. Oh, he's not as nice as Tom, but he is so needy if you know what I mean."

"That kind of thing can be awkward. Did this other guy know about Tom?"

"Oh, yes. And he was jealous."

"Wow. It's a good thing they never met each other."

"Oh, but they did. They knew each other very well. After all, they were both in that cute support group you guys have."

The hinge of my jaw failed at this point, causing my chin to strike somewhere near the center of my chest. "No kidding!"

"Oh, yes. Of course, I can't tell you who it is."

"No, of course not." Darn!

We chatted a bit longer, then I said I had to get on with my day. Brenda walked out of the restaurant with me.

"I'm so glad you suggested this. You're a nice person." She put her hand behind my head and pulled me down for a kiss on the mouth. It was not what I would call a sisterly kiss. Having put me into shock, she went on her way with a cheery goodbye.

Stunned, I tried to get my legs moving to take me the rest of the way home. They carried me about ten steps. At that point, I saw Betty's car. She had the window rolled down and was glaring at me.

"And just what was that all about?" she demanded.

Naturally, I was incapable of speech.

"Get in," she said. "We're going home."

You can imagine that the next hour was not very pleasant. It went like this:

Betty: "Why were you kissing that woman?"

Ed: "I didn't kiss her!"

Betty: "I saw you kissing her!"

Ed: "That was her kissing me."

Betty: "Same thing."

Ed: "Not the same thing at all. I didn't want her to kiss me!"

Betty: "Then why did you let her do it?"

Ed: "She caught me by surprise."

At this point Betty relented. She admitted to having seen the whole thing. "In fact," she said, "that bimbo did not decide to kiss you until she saw me waiting in the car. Then she turned back and let you have it."

"Why did she do that?"

"She's trouble. I told you that. Women can't be trusted."

This gave me another thought. "Hey, if you knew I was innocent, why did you give me such a hard time?"

"Consider it an inoculation. Against temptation." She gave me a steely glare, just in case I was feeling the pull of temptation.

"You need to get a job to keep you out of trouble," she said.

"I have a job."

"Electric bike motors. I haven't seen any bike motors. Where are these bike motors?"

"They will be here soon. I can't start selling them till I have them."

"You better get busy. We can't have you running around town talking to floozies."

As you can imagine, this entire episode was exhausting. Afterwards, I needed a break and some beer, not necessarily in that order, so I walked over to the grocery store. A burly guy in uniform was wheeling a rack full of fresh bread in the front door when I arrived. I mumbled a greeting and wandered toward the beer section. After a moment, I realized that the bread man was startled to see me. Did I know him from somewhere? I hate it when I meet people I am supposed to know, but because they are in the wrong place I don't recognize them. Who did I know that was big and fat and mean looking?

Then it hit me: the guy who threatened me with a baseball bat was the bread delivery man.

Chapter 11.

The DBSG Meeting Gets Carried Away

The next morning, a Tuesday, was fairly typical. After collecting the newspaper and a small bunch of bananas from the convenience store, we quietly sipped our coffee as time slowly drifted by.

Betty was remorseful about how hard she had been on me the previous day. She said she was sorry. I assured her that she was forgiven. I said I was sorry for not dodging Brenda's lips. Next time I would be more alert. Betty reminded me that since I was to avoid women like Brenda, there would be no 'next time.' Naturally, I agreed wholeheartedly. I had learned my lesson: floozies are bad. Stay away from floozies.

While we were having this conversation, sharp claws were digging into my leg, then my back and shoulder. At first I thought Fritter was reinforcing Betty's points. But then I realized the cat, though very intelligent, was not that brilliant. Besides, if Fritter was a person she would have been a floozy. It turned out that she was just trying to reach a point high enough for her to transfer to the top of a door. When she did so, the door moved back and forth slightly under her. She balanced precariously on the swaying portal. Did she have a reason for going up there, besides the thrill of possibly falling? Who could tell what went on in the mind of a cat? That was one of the reasons I liked them; they were inscrutable.

The time to update my list was overdue. Taking paper, coffee mug, and a mechanical pencil into the fresh morning air out on the deck, I went to work. The list of suspects now looked like this:

Wanda.

Willy.

Winters.

Brenda's boyfriend.

Drug dealers on bikes.

Drug dealer driving a Ford Bronco.

At this point, a pause was in order. Why had I scribbled drug dealers twice on my list of suspects? While logically I had to believe that only one drug dealership was involved, my two threatening experiences with drug dealers had been dramatically different from each other. The first experience had involved two men, clearly serious bicyclists, and actual physical assault against my person. The second had involved a ruffian who looked more like a drug dealer should look. He was dressed like a gangster and looked like a biker. But he looked like a Hell's Angel biker, not a bicyclist. He had threatened me with a bat, instead of whacking me with it. The other two would have tapped me at least once or twice for practice. All things taken into account, I had to leave open the possibility that these two threats were not from the same set of drug dealers. Unfortunately, my list of suspects was getting longer.

The door bell rang. A fellow with a clip board was standing by our front door. I trotted down the stairs and swung open the door with a cheery, "May I help you?" My friend with the clip board spoke the words I had been yearning to hear for three weeks: "Gotta a load a boxes for yah. Wherdya wantum?" My bike motors had arrived.

It was truly an exciting moment. I raised the garage door and moved my car to the street. The driver backed his truck up to the garage and offloaded three pallets stacked with boxes. I signed the clip board and our business was done. All I could do at that point was gaze with rapture at my inventory. My new life was about to begin. In order to better savor the moment, I returned to my spot on the deck to smoke my pipe and appreciate my place in the universe. As I went through the living room, Betty asked: "Was someone at the door?"

"It's nothing. Don't worry about it," I called back to her. I should have known that response would pique her curiosity. Still, it was a couple of hours before she wandered down to the garage. For some unfathomable reason, she was not delighted about having the garage serve as a warehouse for my electric bike motors.

"Where are you going to park your car?"

"Outside."

"In the winter?"

"These will be sold before the snow flies."

Betty looked at me like there was something wrong with my mental processes. "You are not going to be able to sell all of these things by Thanksgiving. That's if you can ever sell any of them at all."

That seemed a bit cruel to me. She was entitled to her opinion and I wanted her to be honest with me about her opinions, but her lack of faith in me was demoralizing. It was a good thing that our support group was meeting that evening because this was exactly the kind of situation we needed to talk about. By that I mean wives who did not have faith in their men's abilities to bring home the proverbial bacon.

We convened at a coffee shop in Cambridge, which was only a few miles down Highway 12 from Fort Atkinson. After we had assembled and each of us had purchased a large coffee, we called the meeting to order. All of us bought the robust coffee of the day; none lowered himself to buying a foofy drink with froth and a load of calories. As usual we went around the table to review what had been going on in each of our lives that week. As moderator, I saved my story until last.

George went first. George was a technical writer and probably the most verbal guy in the group. He announced proudly that his wife was close to finishing her doctorate in mathematics, which he believed would make her highly marketable for a university position, since women were still in short supply in the math field.

"Does that bother you any?" asked Robert. Robert considered himself a big-time corporate executive. He was intelligent, smooth, and aggressive.

"Why should it bother me? It's great."

Robert just smiled and shook his head.

"What's your point?" George demanded.

Robert did not answer this sally. We all shifted in our chairs uneasily. Finally, I said, "Well, some guys might find it demoralizing for their wives to be highly marketable when they are not doing as well."

"I'm doing fine. It's true that I haven't found a writing job, but selling snowmobiles is good training for re-inventing myself as a salesman. I will move right up the ladder after I prove I'm a good salesman." Now it was Louis's turn to shake his head. Louis had been unemployed for two years. He was holding firmly to his plan to wait for a job that was at an appropriate level for his talents. No low-level sales jobs for Louis, no sirree.

"How are the snowmobile sales going?" I asked. "Are they hard to sell in the summer?"

"I'm turning out to be darn good at it," George said.

Robert stepped back into the conversation. "Does your store sell all-terrain vehicles?"

"Yes, we do. Why do you ask?"

"According to a story I saw in the paper this week, sales of all-terrain vehicles have surpassed sales of snowmobiles for the first time."

"Geez," I said. "That means the hooligans can tear up the landscape in the summer even more than they do with snowmobiles in the winter."

George could not let that pass. "That sounds like more Green Party propaganda, Ed. Sometimes I think you're a tree-hugger."

'I'm not a tree-hugger. Maybe I don't like snowmobiles and ATVs just because they are so blasted noisy." This wasn't sounding very supportive, so I changed my tune. "But don't get me wrong, George. I think it's great that you are breaking into sales. If people want to buy snowmobiles, then they should be able to buy snowmobiles. It's a free country."

Louis smirked when I said that. He was a died-in-the-wool cynic and figured I was lying through my teeth about my true feelings. Maybe he was right.

"Selling is a legitimate way to make a living. Tom MacFarlane was in sales." After I said that, I wondered if it was a good argument. Surprisingly, Louis broke in at this point. "Sure. There is nothing wrong with selling nursing home insurance." Then he spoiled it by speaking ill of the dead. "Not that Tom was very good at it."

The conversation veered into reminiscence about the wake. We all agreed that it had been one for the record books.

"That Wanda was a real shrew," George said. "No wonder Tom couldn't live with her."

Robert laughed. "No kidding. But look at who he ended up with."

"What do you mean?" Louis asked.

"Well, that Brenda was quite a character. She fits a stereotype, don't you think?"

Louis frowned, "She seemed okay to me." George agreed with Louis and I kept my opinions about Brenda to myself.

Changing the subject slightly, I took the opportunity to tell the group about how my own sales efforts were progressing. I also recounted Betty's lack of confidence in my ability to market the electric bike motors and how it made me feel.

"She wants me to be the breadwinner. She wants me to have a big paycheck rolling in so she won't have to worry about money. Being self-employed makes her nervous, which I can understand. But it's her lack of confidence in me that I find demoralizing."

The other guys all stared moodily into their mugs. At various times, most of us had admitted that our wives had lost faith in us and it was hard for all of us to take. We were the heads of our households. Sure, our wives considered themselves liberated and deserving of perfect social and economic equality. But when it came to protecting home and hearth, each of them expected their men to be out in front, especially when the going got rough. It was hardly fair, but at the same time it made us feel good that our women wanted to rely on us so much. At the same time, it made us feel bad that they were starting to doubt our abilities to successfully play that role. What would happen if they completely lost faith in us? Would they decide we were not the men they thought we were when they married us? Would they decide we were losers and ditch us?

Robert was the first to speak. He cleared his throat hesitantly, then said, "You know, Ed, she may have a point."

"What do you mean?"

"Maybe those motors won't sell. What makes you think there's a market for electric bike motors?"

"They're Green. Lots of people have sympathies for environmental issues, living simply, keeping the cost of living down. My motors don't use gasoline, which is in scarce supply. Heck, if we had more electric-powered vehicles, maybe we would not be caught up in a war in the Middle East."

"The Greens are a bunch of goofballs," Louis said. "And there aren't that many people who will alter their lifestyles on the basis of Green principles. Lots of people talk like they're Greens, but they drive SUVs." Trust Louis to have a cynical point of view.

"Come on, Louis. Look around you. The city of Cambridge proves my point. They are a giant advertisement for a 'small is beautiful' philosophy. They have given the town a facelift so that it looks quaint, choosing to support small locally-owned businesses. They won't let the farms be subdivided, so the county won't become one big suburb. You could use an electric powered bike to go anywhere in Cambridge. You sure don't need an SUV."

But Robert agreed with Louis. "You can't really think Cambridge restricts land use the way they do because the local politicians are idealistic. Business is business."

I did not understand his point and told him so.

"Who do you think benefits from restricting land use they way they do? I'll tell you who: the local businesses. The restrictions on development keep other businesses from coming into town. That means more profit for the businesses that were here first."

Robert pounded on the table to emphasize his point. "And I'll tell you something else: somebody in this town has a lot of clout and they are using it to promote local profiteering."

"Do you have any proof of that or are you just sounding off?" George asked.

"The proof is right in front of this coffee shop: Highway 12. They just finished a major road construction project that routed the highway right down the main drag, right past the local retail establishments. All over the rest of the state, the improvements being made to Highway 12 are in the form of bypasses that take traffic around the downtown areas of small towns so the people on the highway can get where they are going faster. In Cambridge, they did just the opposite. Can you offer another theory as to why they would do that, except that some people plan to make a lot of money by slowing down highway traffic right in front of a bunch of quaint retail establishments. The decision they made about the highway has paved this street with gold."

Our voices had risen during this argument. The proprietor of the coffee shop came over to our table to calm us down. "You gentlemen are disturbing our other patrons," she said.

We all apologized. Then curiosity got the better of me. "Ma'am, you're a local business person. Maybe you can settle this argument for us. Is it true that the decision to route Highway 12 through downtown Cambridge instead of onto a bypass was politically influenced by local business people who saw a way to enhance their profits?"

In retrospect, what kind of answer could I have expected from a question like that? The local business person gave me what I deserved: she threw me out. She threw the entire group out and said we were not welcome to have our meetings in her shop in the future. She suggested that we take our business to other towns in the future. We were not likely to be welcome anywhere in Cambridge.

Driving home, down Highway 12, it occurred to me that one of the disadvantages of living in rural Wisconsin was the flip side of what I liked about it: it was not urbanized, so not many people lived there, which meant that fewer coffee shops were available. I was in real danger of running out of coffee shops that would serve me if I did not learn to be careful about what I said in public.

It was about eight p.m. and the light was starting to fade. Turning on my headlights helped a lot, since I was out of Cambridge and virtually alone on the road. My night vision left me about 1985, so I avoided driving on unlighted roads when possible. Interstates were okay at night because they were wide and you could usually avoid running into things with, of course, one major exception: deer. It was just a matter of time before my car tangled with a deer. It seemed to happen to everyone eventually. The car would be totaled when that happened. Since I liked my little Ford Focus, it was going to be a sad day. But did I really think I could dodge a deer with the car? No. So, like death and taxes, hitting a deer was something you knew you would have to suffer through when your turn came along.

While I was mulling over the unavoidable tragedies of life, like being thrown out of coffee shops and hitting a deer, somebody ran into the back of my car. It was just a gentle nudge, but the shock nearly caused me to lose control of the vehicle. After a little swerving, it came back under control and I looked into the rear view mirror. The vehicle behind me had no lights on, so I could not see it clearly. As it inched closer to nudge me again, I got the distinct impression that it might be a black SUV. Stomping on the gas pedal caused my trusty little car to shoot forward. I kept the pedal all the way to the floor, trying to get away.

Our speed climbed quickly to 75, then 85, with my follower only inches from my rear bumper. The road was fairly straight between Cambridge and Fort Atkinson, but there was at least one curve. I knew because my car didn't make it. The engine was roaring when the road started to curve to the left. Directly in front of me was a long driveway that ran up a hill. I chose the driveway, which turned out to be gravel. Having learned to drive on country roads, I knew better than to hit my brakes on gravel. Instead, I let off the gas and fought the steering wheel. The steep slope of the driveway slowed the car just as I pulled up in front of the farmhouse at the top. The house was well lit. I could see the flicker of the television through the panes of the living room window. No one came to the door. I supposed the location of that driveway had led a few other crazy drivers up to the front door in the past. As I reversed the car, I looked around carefully, but the black SUV was gone. I didn't see it anywhere on the remainder of the drive home.

Chapter 12.

Bullets Fly

When I arrived, Betty gave me a hug. "You're shaking! And dripping with sweat. You must have the flu. Are you feeling sick?"

"I'm fine. Just tired." I opened the fridge and fished out a Miller. Then I parked myself in my Morris chair and put my feet up. I loved that chair. It was very comfortable.

"You are not fine. You better go to bed early."

"That might be a good idea."

"Can I bring you anything? You look awful. Like death warmed over."

"I'm fine. Just let me rest for a minute."

She sat down in her recliner. She had been reading when I arrived and her book was by her side.

"Let's just read for a while, okay?"

"Okay," she said. I knew she wanted to get back to her book.

We sat there a few minutes and I started to doze off. Then the window cracked. It was loud and both of us jumped. We sat there in surprise for a moment, then we walked over to look at the damage. The crack was a bad one. "Darn it," I said. "Just what we need." Getting this fixed was going to be a hassle.

"What could have done that?" she asked.

"A bird probably flew into it."

"What do think caused that hole? It's beak?"

There was a round hole about the size of a quarter at one end of the crack.

"That must have hurt."

"What kind of bird would do that?"

"It shouldn't be too hard to find out. We just look for a pug-beaked woodpecker. It's probably laying dead down there on the ground."

"Look at that," Betty said, pointing at the ceiling in the middle of the living room. A long stream of plaster dust was falling from a small hole in the ceiling. "What a mess. I better get the vacuum out."

"Get down," I said.

She looked at me blankly.

I sank to me knees, pulling her down with me.

"What are you doing?" she demanded.

"Somebody's shooting at us."

Betty started screaming. I wrapped my arms around her as I pulled my cell phone out of my pocket and called 911.

A couple of hours later we were back in our respective chairs. The police had been very efficient. They measured angles and brought in a tall ladder so they could dig the bullet out of our cathedral ceiling. They had done a lot to reassure Betty. They promised that the patrols would drive by frequently throughout the night. She was calm now and starting to get angry.

"Drive-by shootings? This sort of thing isn't supposed to happen in Fort Atkinson. Milwaukee is where they do that sort of thing. Not here. And why should they pick us out to shoot at?"

At that moment, the door bell rang. It was my favorite pair of detectives, Broder and Schmidt. They accepted our invitation to sit on the couch, then pulled their notebooks out.

"It seems there was a little excitement here tonight," Broder said. "You two must be pretty shaken up."

"Are you going to catch whoever did this?" Betty demanded.

"We'll do what we can. It was probably random, which makes it more difficult. But maybe somebody saw something. We will canvas the neighborhood."

That mollified Betty somewhat.

"First, though, we need to ask you some routine questions. Can you folks give me a rundown on your activities lately? Do you have any idea who might have wanted to do this?"

"We are just normal people with normal lives," Betty said. "No one hates us enough to want to shoot at us."

Schmidt looked at me thoughtfully. I suspected that she didn't quite agree with Betty's assessment.

"Even so, let's run through where you have been and who you have talked to," Broder said. "Maybe something will turn up." He turned toward me. "What have you been doing the last few days, Mr. Schumacher?"

I stared at my shoes for a moment. Without looking at Betty I said, "Somebody ran me off the road on the way back from Cambridge tonight."

Betty's face went blank with surprise. Broder asked, "How do you know they were trying to run you off the road?"

"Whoever it was banged my rear bumper while I was driving at highway speed. He chased me for a few miles with his lights off. It sure seemed like he was trying to run me off the road. I ended up on a gravel driveway about halfway between Cambridge and Fort."

"What were you doing in Cambridge?"

"My support group was having a meeting at a coffee shop there."

"Was there some kind of incident that made someone angry?"

I considered that question carefully, then answered, "Not enough to try to kill me."

Betty, Broder, and Schmidt exchanged glances. "We know the place," Broder said. "We will pay them a visit and see what they have to say about it."

Broder sighed. "What else have you been doing this week, Mr. Schumacher?"

"Not too much. A guy delivered some boxes today. I talked to him."

Betty broke in. "You talked to that Brenda woman." She turned to Broder. "You know the woman that was in the fight at Sal's the other night? Ed talked to her at McDonald's."

"What was that conversation about?" Broder asked.

"Trying to find out more about Tom MacFarlane." It wasn't necessary to remind them who Tom was.

Broder sighed again. "Did you talk to anyone else?"

"Hmmm. There was Wanda MacFarlane."

Betty was startled. "I didn't know about that."

"And her son, Tom Junior. And a few drug dealers."

The room fell silent. "Drug dealers?" Schmidt asked with an evil grin. "Maybe you could elaborate on that for us. Just a little bit." Have I mentioned that she didn't like me?

"Well, it seems that Tom Junior is running errands for drug dealers. His dad found out and tried to interfere. They warned him to stay out of it. When I asked Tom Junior questions, they did the same thing to me."

"Oh my God," Betty gasped.

"They just told you to lay off?"

"They pushed me around a little. They were both dressed like serious bicyclists. I know there is a gang of drug dealers in this town that distribute drugs via bicycle. Anyway, they shoved me around some."

"I imagine they did, Mr. Schumacher. They tend to get physical." Broder sighed. I heard him mumble something about bicyclists under his breath. Then he asked, "What else?"

"Well, there was another drug dealer. He caught up with me while I was taking my walk. He was driving a black Bronco. Big guy with a baseball bat. He threatened me. But he didn't hit me with the bat," I said brightly, shooting Betty a reassuring smile. She did not smile back at me.

"By the way, detectives, I know how you can find that guy. He is a big, heavyset fellow who delivers bread to the grocery store over by Culver's ice cream shop. He must be distributing drugs along with the bread. It's a perfect set up, don't you think?"

Schmidt and Broder just stared at me for a moment. "When he threatened you, was he wearing his bread delivery uniform or his spandex biking suit?" Schmidt asked, dead pan.

"Neither. He was wearing a lot of chains."

Betty was holding her head in her hands, her face covered.

"Okay, so you don't believe me." I stood up in anger. "But why would I make all that up? It's the truth. And somebody did take a shot at us tonight, didn't they? Who would want to do that?"

"Most anybody," Schmidt said.

Chapter 13.

Another Death

Wednesday morning was a little tense. Betty started in on me before I finished my second cup of coffee.

"Why didn't you tell me about all this?" she demanded. "You were keeping everything to yourself. And we could have gotten killed because of it."

"Tell you about it? Last summer when wild things were happening you thought I was imagining it all. Since you thought I was delusional then, why would you believe me now? And besides, I didn't want to scare you. You either would have been scared or you would have thought I was nuts. There was no upside in telling you."

"But I want to know about these things," she said.

"You know, since somebody shot at us that means you have to believe me," I pointed out.

Betty hesitated. "Not necessarily. You could be misinterpreting what you see and hear while at the same time irritating people enough to make them want to kill you."

"So you agree with Schmidt!"

She was saved from answering when my cell phone rang. It was Schmidt. "Speak of the devil," I told Betty. "She wants to talk to me downtown. They have some new information." Then I left.

The interrogation room was so familiar to me by this time that I was almost comfortable there. Broder and Schmidt were not accusing me of anything (at the moment), so I just relaxed and sipped the coffee I had picked up at McDonald's, which was only a block away. Come to think of it, Tom's body was lying in the street not far from the police offices in the city building. He was within sight of our protectors when he died, most likely. Granted, it was after hours. But even so, it was pretty bold to murder somebody in clear view of the police station.

Broder got right to the point. Picking up one piece of paper from the small pile in front of him, he said, "First, someone saw a black SUV in your neighborhood about the time of the shooting. We don't know for sure if it was a Bronco. And it is a very common color for an SUV, so it might be unrelated. Still, it's progress." He laid down that document and picked up another. "Second, we checked around and Tom Junior is under suspicion concerning drug dealing in the area." That piece of paper went down and a third was lifted up. "Third, about three this morning a gun was heard being fired over on the east side of town. The squad car that answered the call found a body dead of a shotgun blast." Broder paused for effect, then went on. "The victim apparently had been riding an expensive racing bike. He was dressed like a serious bicyclist."

I was delighted. This information appeared to vindicate me in some way, though right at that moment, I was not sure how. "You mean the guy was blown off his bike by a shotgun? What have we got here, a drug war?"

The pencil Schmidt had been playing with broke in half. Broder went pale. "Don't even think that. This is not Milwaukee. We will investigate this matter. We are asking, no insisting, that you refrain from any amateur investigations into drug crimes. We need no wild talk about drug wars. You will only muddy the waters and you might get hurt. Your wife might get hurt."

He had me convinced. "Okay, okay. No amateur sleuthing into drug dealerships. Got it. No problem. I'm outta that business. You can count on me."

I was feeling pretty darn good. Drug dealers did exist in this town. Tom Junior was tied in with them. And the cops believed me about the dealers being bicyclists. Since I was on a roll, I decided to try for the goal line. "Hey, what you guys need is a bike patrol." Broder, who had been rising from his seat, froze in mid-air. "Some cities have them, you know. Of course, I know some of your guys have been hitting the donuts pretty hard and chasing drug dealers on bikes might be tough on them. But if the cops had electric battery power assisted motors on their bikes, they would have the edge, right?" Broder and Schmidt were staring at me, mesmerized. I had them right where I wanted them. "And I know just where you can get some of those motors. Get back to me. We can help each other on this." I leaned across the table. "Think about it. Fort Atkinson could be the first police department in the country with a bike patrol that uses electric motors. You would be on the national news." Having nailed them with a sure-fire sales pitch, I exited.

Trotting down the steps in front of the city building, I was on cloud nine. I was vindicated by the police, somewhat, and I was about to make a big sale. Life was good.

A few loose ends were still floating around, of course. Come to think of it, we actually did not know the truth about anything, including Tom's death. But at the moment, I was willing to assume the drug dealers did it. After all, they were willing to kill each other, so killing a snoop would have been no problem for them. The point was I didn't need to worry about that stuff anymore. The cops were on it now. And I might have helped bring this promising juncture to pass.

The loose ends I was allowed to consider had to do with the minor mysteries, like which of the guys in the support group was chasing after Tom's girlfriend? And was Winters really planning on firing Tom? This was minor stuff. There was really no reason why I couldn't look into it.

The insurance office was just down the street about ten blocks, on the other side of the bridge, so I wandered over there. On the way, I stopped at a print shop and had a hundred business cards made up. They had my name, my email address, and the words "electric bicycle motors."

You will never guess who the receptionist was at the insurance office: Brenda. Tom had been dating someone from his own office. And after meeting Brenda, I was sure that everybody in the building probably knew about their relationship.

"Hey, how's it going?" was my opening sally.

"Good enough," she answered. "How're things with you?" She giggled. "Betty is doing okay, I hope?"

This caused me to gulp and remember why I was there. 'Hey, Mr. Winters isn't around, is he? I would like to talk to him for a minute."

"Still asking people questions?" She smiled at me. "Well. That's fine. And he's here. Just go over to that office with the open door. He's in there. He'll see you."

He was and he did. Winters welcomed me with a hearty handshake and offered me a seat. After commenting on the weather (it looked like rain) and the heat (we wished it would rain sooner rather than later), I said, "I don't know how to ask this, exactly. Tom was my friend and I'm trying to find out a little more about his life, things I should have asked him about before he died."

Winters nodded. "I understand. We all need to find closure after a person dies. We are left with things we should have said or done. What can I tell you that will help?"

"Let me just ask it straight out. Tom thought you were going to lay him off. His sales were down. He was worried about it. He was worried about his future. Did he have any reason to be worried?"

Winters stood up and closed the door, then returned to his seat. "Tom was not a productive salesman, hadn't been for years. But under our system, if you sell less, you make less money. It doesn't cost the company to keep you around. And I admit I pressured him to produce more, especially shortly after I was transferred to this office. But after I settled in, I realized that Tom was serving as a mentor to the younger sales reps. Besides he was always cheerful and was good for morale in the office. No, I was not going to fire Tom. I guess I should have reassured him about that."

I was really getting to like this guy.

Winters snapped his fingers. "You know, you just explained something I have been wondering about. You know Louis Smurfit? He has been coming around here for weeks trying to get me to hire him. He was convinced that I would have a vacant position soon. Louis must have gotten the idea from Tom."

"Geez. Going after your friend's job before he has even been fired is a little opportunistic, don't you think?"

"You're right. It's the kind of aggressive behavior that might actually make for a good salesman, though. What bothered me was the way he was dating Tom's girlfriend. Now that is a bit low." He chuckled. "That woman keeps no secrets, let me tell you."

Louis was dating Brenda? And he wanted Tom's job? Did this mean that Louis had two motives for wanting Tom out of the picture?

Shaking my head to clear it, I stood up and headed for the door. "Thanks for talking so openly with me. I really appreciate it."

"Before you go, can you tell me how Tom's boy is holding up?"

"Tom Junior is having problems. He was in trouble before. Now he acts as if he doesn't care that his dad is dead. He believes Tom was worthless, a loser. Wanda put a lot of those ideas in his head, I'm sure. She is carrying around a lot of anger."

"That's too bad." He seemed sincere about the sentiment.

Winters walked me to the front door of the office suite. Hanging on the wall by the door was a large sign that had the word STARBOARD at the top. The white space under the title was empty. To the left of the starboard was a row of eight by ten photographs of each member of the sales team, hanging on hooks. It was clear that the picture of the best sales rep could be moved from its regular hook to the hook on the starboard, so that the star of the month could bask in fame and appreciation.

"What's this?" I asked, purely out of curiosity.

"This is our starboard. We put up the name of our best salesman. We change it every month. This month we left it blank. With Tom being dead, nobody wanted to focus attention on sales. It seemed a bit crass. So we left the name off this month."

"You said it's for the name of the best salesman. But you meant the guy with the most sales."

Winters looked at me. "Right."

"But it's possible to be good in other ways than just total sales, right?"

"That's right," he said, looking at me thoughtfully.

After a moment of silence for Tom, I went on my way.

That evening Betty and I had a good time. We went to the restaurant she liked out on Highway 26. That place had a large handsome bar in the front room and a nice dining area in the back. We sat at the bar for a drink before dinner. Betty had one of those fancy martinis she liked and I told her about the events of the day. The news from the police interview was interesting to her. I even told her about my visit to the insurance office, about Brenda being the receptionist, and recounted all that Winters had told me. Betty asked questions as I went through the story.

"You know," she commented, "I kind of enjoy hearing about your little investigations."

"I know you do. But it's nice to hear you say it."

"We can call you the Silly Sleuth."

"How about the Delusional Detective?"

Betty laughed a little too hard at that one. She had to wipe tears from her eyes.

"It wasn't that funny."

"I'm sorry, dear. I know you enjoy sleuthing. I like to see you happy. You are happy, aren't you"?

"Yes. I'm happy. I'm glad we moved to Wisconsin. I feel a lot better. I used to get pretty compulsive about my work. It wasn't healthy. Now I can work a little, then take a break. I couldn't do that before."

Betty had one more point to make on sleuthing. "On the other hand, that doesn't mean I want you to get involved in anything dangerous. Dangerous is out. No drug stuff." She was giving me her stern look.

"Okay. I don't like having the bejeezus scared out of me, either. No more investigations into drug dealerships."

"Shake on it," she demanded.

So we shook hands across the table, then sealed the deal with a kiss.

When we got back home, Fritter and I played tag for a bit before we went to bed. The way we did it, it was Fritter's task to chase me. I had tried chasing her, but she wouldn't run. She would just stare at me when I ran up to her. But she was willing to chase me. In a couple of leaps, she could be ahead of me. To make the game interesting, I changed my route at random, running into different rooms. This game tired me out in about five minutes, so it was not long before I was flopping down on the bed next to Betty.

"I'm glad we have a unit on the second floor," she observed.

"Why is that?"

"If we were on the ground floor, somebody driving by might see you chasing the cat around in your underwear."

"I don't chase the cat. She chases me."

"Do you ever win the game?"

"Hah. That shows what you know. The victory is not always to the swift, nor to the strong. Sometimes it's to the guy in his underwear who makes unexpected turns."

Betty chuckled. One of the things I loved about that woman was the way she laughed at my jokes, even when she had no idea what I was talking about.

Chapter 14.

Andrew Connects The Dots

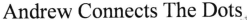

The next day, Betty and I took her two teenage nephews to a matinee. It was a remake of the old Willy Wonka movie about a chocolate factory. As we were walking out of the theater, the young men were chatting happily about the movie.

"Do you guys remember the part where all those dudes on motorbikes were delivering candy?" I asked them.

"Yeah. That was cool!"

"Those bikes were pretty quiet. And I didn't see any exhaust coming out of their engines. I think they were electric."

"Awesome. Electric bikes!"

"Do you think kids would like to ride electric bikes?"

"Sure! Anybody would want one!"

"Let's go back to our place. I've got something for you guys." I gave each of them a box with a bike motor with the understanding that they would pass out my business cards to any of their friends who might want to buy one. The boys went away happy. It gave me a good feeling to spread a little joy in the world.

That evening, Andrew and I met at Sal's for a beer and to catch him up on events. I began by assuring him that I had learned my lesson and would never again get involved in any dangerous sleuthing. A little harmless sleuthing was still a possibility, though.

Andrew listened carefully to the whole story. "Let me see if I have this straight. Your list of suspects now includes the ex-wife, Louis Smurfit, Winters, drug dealers on bikes, a drug dealer who delivers bread, and this guy Willy Bundt. Is that right?"

"Nah. Winters is out. I like him."

"Don't you think murderers can be likable?"

"It seems un-like-ly. Get it?" That made me laugh. I loved it when I made a pun.

Andrew was not amused. Maybe he didn't get it.

Andrew pulled a sheet of paper out of his jacket pocket. "Betty called me earlier and told me about the black Ford Bronco. Just out of curiosity I ran a list of all the black Broncos owned by residents of Fort Atkinson. "I can't show you this list because it's confidential. But I distinctly remember one name on the list because it was a little unusual." He folded the paper so that only one name was visible, then showed it to me. It was "Willy Bundt."

Taking a swig of my beer, I considered this revelation and what it might mean. "Willy Bundt is the drug dealer slash bread delivery man?"

Andrew nodded. "I followed up by calling the store and asking for the names of the bread delivery guys. One of them was Bundt. That clinches it."

"Well, I'll be darned. So that means Bundt had two reasons to kill Tom: his anger over the long term care insurance and Tom's interference in the drug business."

Andrew held up his hand. "Now wait a minute. All this proves is that the guy who threatened you was Willy Bundt. It does not prove Bundt is tied in with the bikers. From what you said, I would guess that he would look pretty silly on a bike."

We discussed the case for quite a while, but could not settle on a provable case against any particular suspect. Louis had two motives, but outright violence did not seem to be his style. Wanda was angry enough, but too small in stature to have easily done the dirty deed. Bundt was big enough, but he was a bread delivery man. Could a bread man actually be violent? Maybe the business with the bat was all an act. We had to agree that the biker drug dealers were the most likely suspects.

"Why was the druggie-biker killed, Andrew?" I asked. "How does that fit in?"

"That is the part that is easiest to understand. The regional office for the distribution network probably heard about Tom's murder and concluded that the local boys were out of control. They needed to deliver an object lesson to all their people: 'don't draw attention to yourselves, especially from the police.' I think we can ignore that death. And I suspect that the person who killed Tom has been caught and punished - by his own partners in crime. End of story."

But, for once, Andrew was wrong.

Chapter 15.

Reenactment

Thursday started with the usual routines. After reading the newspaper, I parked on the porch to enjoy the fresh morning air. One of the neighbors emerged from his condo, glanced up at me, and called out, "Good morning!"

"Perfect weather," I called back. "Whadeyahknow?"

Let me briefly digress. The word 'whadeyahknow' in my experience had always been misspelled. The uninitiated may have believed that 'what-do-you-know' was slurred together as 'what'dya know' in common parlance. Even National Public Radio operated under this misconception. However, a true Midwesterner pronounced the phrase as 'whadeyaknow.' Try saying it slowly.

Wha. De. Yah. Know.

Now say it fast ten times. It definitely came out as 'whadeyaknow.' Perhaps someone at NPR would read this book and correct its spelling. And maybe they wouldn't.

"Whadeyahknow?" I asked.

"Not much. You?" This, by the way, was the correct response. Even NPR knew that.

My neighbor wandered around the corner of the building, returning shortly with some mail in his hand. This reminded me that I had not checked the mailbox in several days. Some bills might be resting in there. Since receiving a nasty note from a creditor was one of my least favorite experiences, I trotted down the stairs to check the box.

Two post-it notes were stuck to the inside of the front door. In block letters, the first one read, "DON'T LET THE CAT OUT." The second one elaborated on this point. "THE CAT WILL TRY TO ESCAPE. WATCH OUT!" I shook my head. Betty's anxieties were showing again.

The mail box was empty except for some advertising flyers, so I returned to my place on the deck. The means by which Tom MacFarlane was killed continued to elude me, and it was bothering me. I just could not get the problem out of my head. The only hope I had of forgetting about the problem was to dream up a scenario that explained all the known facts.

My favorite scenario went like this. Tom was drinking in one of several bars a few blocks from where he died. At some point, a couple of thugs stuck a gun in his back and forced him to walk down the street to the building that had its top floor under construction. They directed him to walk up the stairs to the top floor, then directed him to walk out on the arm of the crane. Then they moved the arm over the street.

Then what? They didn't shoot him, so how did they make him fall from his perch into the street? And was it really possible to gain entry into a construction site after hours? I couldn't figure it out. But I had an idea about how I might be able to shed some light on the matter.

That evening when it was cool I took my walk, using the opportunity to swing by the construction site. It was dusk and well after quitting time for the workmen. The sidewalk in front of the building was separated from the street by a chain link fence. A sawhorse blocked the sidewalk between the fence and the building. A sign hung from it that said, "Sidewalk Closed.' Glancing furtively in all directions to make sure no one was in sight, I moved the sawhorse to one side far enough to enter the blocked-off area. Fifteen feet down the sidewalk was a door into the building. Actually, it was a doorway, since the door had been removed. So I walked into the building.

No furniture was in evidence. Heavy dust coated the floor except where the workmen had been walking to and from the other rooms and the stairway. The fire door that led to the stairs was not locked. I climbed up the cement stairs as quietly as possible, even though it seemed unlikely that anyone would hear any noises made inside the building.

By the time I emerged on the top floor, I was breathing heavily. Tools were scattered around in untidy piles. Scaffolds reached up into the darkening sky as if they were the skeletons of those who had died in defiance of the forces of nature, perhaps paralyzed at the moment of death by bolts of lightening.

The crane was sitting at the edge of the roof with the boom slanting out over the street. The arm of the crane was narrower than I had expected. Only an acrobat could have walked out on that boom without losing his balance and falling. A person could have crawled out to the end of it by straddling the thing and pulling himself forward with his arms, but how could you be sure that you would be able to force someone to do that, even at gunpoint?

The cool breeze fanned my face as I looked out over the street. Gradually, the spookiness of the place faded and I realized how peaceful it was up there. Peace, how elusive and precious it was. The cares of the world were remote, held at bay by some kind of magic. But I knew that once I went back down those stairs, the responsibilities, fears, and pressures of life would return in full force. Why not just stroll out on the arm of the crane? A person who was relaxed could make it all the way. And he could be very relaxed if he did not care about falling.

Chapter 16.

Denouement

It was nearly ten when I pulled up in front of the house occupied by Wanda MacFarlane and Tom Junior. Darkness had set in completely and it was far too late to be calling on people in their homes, especially when those people neither expected you nor liked you. But I was in no mood to wait.

Wanda answered the door. Her face showed several emotions in rapid succession. First surprise. Next anger. Then fear.

"What do you want?" she asked.

"I need to talk to you."

"About what?"

"You know about what," I said roughly.

She turned with a sign of resignation and led me into the living room. I should have been surprised that she let me in, but somehow I wasn't.

She sat on the couch without a word. I sat down in a chair without waiting for an invitation. We sat and stared at each in silence for a moment.

Finally, I asked it the only way I knew how, straight out. "Did Tom send a letter to Tom Junior before he died?"

Wanda gasped, then swallowed hard. She hesitated, then said, "How did you know?"

"I didn't. I guessed. I just got to thinking that maybe he committed suicide. And I was sure he would not have done that without trying to explain himself to his son. A letter is the usual way a suicide handles that kind of communication."

I leaned forward. "Once I got that far in the scenario, I realized that you would have seen the letter first. And being the kind of person you are, you would not have given it to Tom Junior without reading it first. Tom Junior would not have liked having his mother open his mail, so it would be easier just to hide the letter or throw it away. Once you did that, you couldn't tell the police about it because then Tom Junior would find out what you did."

Wanda had gone pale and was holding her hand over her mouth.

"Have I got it right?" I demanded.

"Yes, you have it right," she said in a low voice.

"That's what I thought. And it makes me wonder how many other times you prevented Tom from communicating with his son."

Wanda's eyes shone brightly as her anger flared. "That was my duty as a mother. I had to protect Tom from his father's wild ideas. The man might have said anything."

"You mean he might have said something critical about you."

"Yes!" she shouted. "That is exactly what I mean!"

In the brief silence after her outburst, we both realized we were not alone. Tom Junior stood in the doorway. His face was blank. There was no way to discern how much he had overheard.

I stood up. "You two have some things to talk about, so I'm taking off now. But Wanda, if you don't call the police and tell them about the letter first thing in the morning, you can be sure that I will do it for you." Then I went home, figuring that I had caused enough anguish for one day.

Chapter 17

The Truth Unveiled

Friday morning was bright and sunny. After reading the paper, I sat on the deck and watched the birds dive-bomb the neighbors. This show had been playing for a couple of weeks. When the neighbors came out of their house to play with their dog, the starlings would attack them. The kids loved it and would run around screaming. The woman of the house also ran around screaming, but she didn't seem to enjoy it as much. The previous week she told me the starlings had built a nest in the rain gutter over her garage. She and the kids did not want to disturb the baby birds by moving the nest. So, they were putting up with the daily air raids.

They weren't the only ones. Pedestrians walking by frequently received similar treatment from the starlings. For some reason, the birds left me alone even though I walked to the convenience store every morning. Several of us stood on the sidewalk one morning discussing the mystery. What motivated the starlings to attack some people and not others? My theory was that the starlings thought the dog, a Chihuahua, was a cat. They were actually attacking the dog. The retired sheriff who lived across the way said that would not explain why pedestrians were attacked. After all, not all of them were walking their pets. And the ones that were had dogs that actually looked like dogs from the air. His theory was baseball hats. He thought starlings hated baseball hats. I could not refute this because I could not remember whether all the victims had been wearing baseball hats. This made me wonder if the birds only attacked certain colors of hats, or certain sizes, or hats representing ball teams they didn't like.

This particular morning I was mulling over the mystery of the bird attacks while watching one such attack occur. Perhaps it was the shape of the hat. Maybe from the air, the bill of the hat made the person look like a giant bird, perhaps an ostrich. Are larger birds prone to eating smaller birds? Was this why the starlings attacked baseball hats? To drive away larger birds?

Yes, if you looked at it from the birds' point of view, everything changed. It all made sense. Most things do if you try looking at them from a different perspective.

The headline on the front page of the paper was about a group of seven state governors who were calling on the president to offer more incentives for the development of renewable energy sources. National security required that we reduce our dependence on foreign oil supplies, they argued.

They were right on target from my point of view. That was my politics showing, but also my desire to sell electric bike motors. Robert was probably right. Businesses trying to make a buck were behind every policy decision, even when those decisions appeared to be motivated by the public interest. But what difference did it make what the motives were if the public benefited?

Inside the paper there was a short story about Tom MacFarlane. Suddenly, the mystery of his death was solved. A suicide letter had been discovered. The deceased wrote that he was despondent about how his career, initially so promising, had somehow faded. He was slipping backward, with lower earnings each year. His health was bad, having suffered a heart attack. 'Family tensions' were also mentioned in the letter, according to the reporter. The police had declared the case closed. An obituary for Mr. MacFarlane was printed on page such and such.

An unrelated story briefly described the killing of a bicyclist in Fort Atkinson. The biker was discovered to be dealing drugs, according to police sources. The police statement indicated that the killing was most likely an internal issue for organized crime. They did not expect new developments in the case any time soon. This file also appeared to be closed. Broder and Schmidt were having a productive week.

And, at that moment, the door bell rang: it was Broder and Schmidt. I let them in and we all trudged upstairs. After we had arranged ourselves on the living room furniture, I opened the conversation by saying, "It looks like you guys have wrapped up two cases at once. You must be satisfied with yourselves."

"Just doing our jobs," Schmidt growled.

Broder ignored her. "Thank you, Mr. Schumacher. We try to serve the public as best we can. Which, by the way, is why we are here. We wanted to update you about the shots that were fired through your window."

"I'm all ears."

"This is for your information only," he said, then added, "and of course for your wife's information." He continued, "Our undercover agents have learned that our original theory was correct: the dealers who were working with Tom MacFarlane, Jr., were seeking to discourage your interest in the case. They fired the shots. However, since this drew too much attention to their operation, the kingpins decided a lesson in discretion was required, as well as a change in local leadership. They eliminated the person who made the decision to fire a weapon at your home." Broder leaned forward. "This, however, does not constitute a 'drug war,' in any way, shape, or form. This was just a business decision to replace a local manager. It is imperative that there be no loose talk about 'drug wars.' We take this very seriously and hope you will as well." He gave me a steely look.

"So, the shooting was poor performance on the part of a local manager who has since been downsized, permanently. Now, it is back to business as usual."

Broder looked surprised. "That seems to sum up the situation accurately," he agreed. He hastened to add a footnote, however. "Please be confident that we do not take drug trafficking lightly and will pursue these miscreants continuously within the limits of our resources."

He must have realized that his statement sounded pompous and generated no confidence in my mind. Shaking his head, he decided to stop while he was ahead. Gesturing to Schmidt, he got up and they headed for the stairs down to the front door.

"One more thing, Detective Broder," I said. "Can I assume that it was the drug dealers who also ran me off the road?"

Broder hesitated, so Schmidt spoke up. "We have no evidence that the incident you reported ever occurred. There were no witnesses other than yourself. You might have imagined the whole thing."

My mouth fell open and Broder could tell I was about to protest. "However," he broke in quickly, "in answer to your question: yes, you may assume that if the incident involving the car chase occurred as you described it, then it was probably another attempt by the drug dealers to scare you off." Then they left, leaving me frustrated and unsatisfied.

I went out on my deck to smoke my pipe and try to gain some perspective. After a few minutes, I adjusted to the official doubts about my sanity. After all, it was not the first time people had questioned whether I was imagining things. That was life or at least my life. My mind drifted over the entire episode, not just how I had been affected personally. I became somewhat philosophical.

There I sat, mulling over the life and times of Tom MacFarlane and all the men like him. Men who began their lives as the brash and self-confident crowd dubbed the 'Baby Boomers.' They were self-indulgent and irreverent. They tried pot and created a sexual revolution. They even flirted with political revolution. They brought a war to a crashing halt with mass protests. They helped bring down a president who exceeded his authority. Then they grew up, became blatant materialists, and hustled hard to earn the big houses and expensive cars that they were sure they deserved. And now, they were over the hill, replaced by young MBAs who were clueless about how the initial promise of life could turn to dust and failure. They couldn't make their mortgage payments and their families sure as heck did not want to move into duplexes.

How did you adjust to a role of diminished importance, diminished power, diminished status, diminished income, and diminished respect from families who were led to believe that the gravy train would never end? Over the next decade, how many of these men would blow their brains out, jump off of buildings, crash their cars into viaducts on empty highways, or mysteriously drown while fishing? Somebody had to tell them, convince them, that the money, the cars, and the houses weren't that important. The idealism they had flaunted so bravely as young people was right and true and better after all. But then the downsized boomers would ask, "Why did I spend my whole life chasing worthless stuff?" How did you answer that question without telling these men that their values had been all wrong? On the other hand, couldn't you say the same about most generations? Has there ever been a generation that did not eventually drop the idealism of youth in favor of materialism?

Chapter 18.

Epilogue

That afternoon, after a light lunch that consisted of toast and unsweetened tea, I was back on the deck smoking my pipe when Willy Bundt walked up to my front door. He rang the bell, not seeing me on the deck. "Hey," I called down to him, pretending that I didn't recognize him. "Can I help you with something?"

Bundt peered up at me hesitantly. He clearly was nervous. He spread his hands. "Can I talk to you? It's okay. See? No baseball bat." He was wearing his bread uniform and looked harmless enough, so I went down and let him in. He followed me back onto the deck and we sat in the wicker chairs we use for deck furniture.

I said nothing, letting him start the conversation. He cleared his throat, then said, "I came by to apologize."

"Really?"

"Yes. I was out of line. Threatening you that way was ridiculous. I'm sorry."

"Why did you do it?"

Willy shifted in his chair, clearly uncomfortable. "You were asking questions about Tom MacFarlane. Wanda is a close friend of mine. In fact, I care a lot about her. I was trying to protect her."

"You thought she killed Tom."

He smiled sheepishly. "It seemed like a possibility. She couldn't get over being angry with him. I tried to make her see that was all in the past, but she just couldn't let it go. When Tom died, I couldn't help thinking that she had finally done it. I know she wanted to, sometimes."

"Is that why you ran me off the road and fired a bullet through my window?"

Bundt was genuinely startled. "I don't know anything about that. It wasn't me. I promise you, it wasn't me."

I believed him. It must have been those darn drug dealers, still trying to scare me off.

"Why did you decide to come tell me about it?"

"The police dragged me in for questioning. They traced all the people who owned cars like mine. They have me dead to rights on threatening you. I would really appreciate it if you wouldn't press charges against me. I have never done anything like it before and never will again."

We didn't exactly part friends, but we shook hands and I thanked him for coming to see me. I also wished him the best of luck with Wanda. He was probably going to need it.

A few minutes after Bundt left, the phone rang. It was Winters.

"Ed," he asked, "is there any chance you could come over to the office about five this afternoon? We are having a little ceremony for Tom MacFarlane."

"Sure thing. That's very nice of you."

"Can you bring Tom's son? And the guys in your support group are welcome, also."

"I'll do my best to round them all up."

It took about an hour to reach everyone, but all agreed to attend the event. Even Tom Junior said he would come, though he didn't sound enthusiastic. I offered to pick him up, but he said he had his own transportation. Betty insisted on being present as well.

We all gathered in the reception area of the insurance office at five. Robert, Louis, and George had each asked me what was happening, but I didn't know what Winters had planned. Somehow, I had confidence that it would be appropriate and appreciated by all of us.

Winters stood by the starboard, which was draped with a cloth, and encouraged us to gather around him. All of his office staff and sales reps were present along with my group, so it was a big crowd. Brenda was there as well. Betty ignored her.

"First," he announced, "after consultation with staff, we all agreed that the least we could do was to honor Tom by shifting him to the starboard." He pulled away the drape and Tom's photo could be seen hanging on the hook on the board. The words "Sales Rep of the Month" were affixed above his photo. Tom Junior was obviously startled.

Winters continued his presentation. "As I said, this was the least we could do. Why stop with making Tom the sales representative of the month? So, we had an award made for him." Winters opened a box to remove a plaque made of dark wood. An engraved piece of bronze was in its center. "Tom," he said, looking at Tom Junior, "will you please step forward to receive the award for your father?"

Tom Junior screwed up a scowl but did as he was asked.

Winters positioned himself next to Tom Junior, holding up the plaque so that it faced the group. "The award reads," he said, "Awarded to Tom MacFarlane by the Fort Atkinson Office of the American Insurance Corporation for Being the Best Overall Sales Representative for the period 1985-2005. Mr. MacFarlane will be remembered by his friends and colleagues for his unfailing good humor, honesty, and concern for others. He was a mentor and friend to all who knew him." Then Winters handed the plaque to Tom Junior and shook his hand. Everyone in the room clapped. Tom Junior broke down, tears streaming down his face. Come to think of it, there was not a dry eye in the place.

Later that evening, Betty and I sat in our chairs, reading. She looked up and said, "That was a nice ceremony today."

"You bet. Winters gets my vote for manager of the year. Of the decade."

"What do you think will happen to Tom Junior now? Will he turn out okay?"

"Winters mentioned to me that Tom Senior left all his life insurance to the kid. It's in trust, so Tom Junior can't blow it all at once. But it's enough to get him through college if he wants to go."

"That's nice. At least a little good will come of all this." She changed the subject. "Will you get another member to replace Tom in your support group?"

"The Downsized Boomer's Support Group is officially defunct."

"No! When did that happen?"

"When we were leaving the insurance office after the ceremony, Robert told me that he had accepted a job as a VP for strategic planning for an accounting firm down in Georgia. Apparently, they lost a lot of executives due to some scandal and they needed new leadership fast. He is headed out there immediately."

"That still leaves three of you."

"Would you want to talk to Louis every week? I don't. I'll call George for a beer every now and then. Truth is we weren't helping each other that much."

Betty reached over and patted my arm. "I think you were. And I think you could help other people. You are just burned out right now. I hope you will start the group up again some day. There is a real need for it."

"Maybe I will, someday." I said. "In the meantime, I'm selling bike motors. So far, twenty-three kids have sent me an email message wanting to buy one. These things are going to sell like hotcakes." And they did. For a while.

DEAD MAN
IN GALLEY

This book is dedicated to the true academics in
the world, who value publications over money
from grants and contracts despite pressure from
their universities to do the opposite.

Chapter 1.

Woops Defined

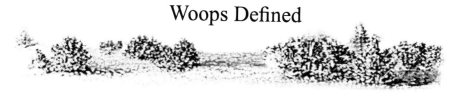

It started out simply enough. In fact, it was a great opportunity. A publishing company had asked me to arbitrate a dispute they were having with some of their authors. I had published a fair amount, so the job seemed like it would be fairly straightforward. All I had to do was interview the parties involved, smoke my pipe while mulling over the issues, then deliver a Solomon-like decision that would be fair and reasonable. Piece of cake, right? And the money they were offering was good, also. What more could a semi-retired college professor ask? Good money, easy work; it was a no-brainer that I would jump at the opportunity. But, of course, as anybody with half a brain could tell you: if it sounded too good to be true, it probably was.

In all fairness, the publishing company was not misleading me. There was no possibility that they could have foreseen how messy the assignment would become. By messy, I mean there was a seamy underside to the story that involved lust, big money, and death. No one could have known the depth of evil that had impeded the completion of paperwork necessary to publish a medical research report. But it was there, bubbling away like a witch's cauldron. This particular witch's cauldron was cooking up a spell that lured me out of my safe and tedious existence into a situation that went beyond challenging and descended into life-threatening. This kind of thing could be mildly diverting unless it was your life that was being threatened. Then, it was downright fascinating. After all, nothing was more interesting than an ax flying toward your head, a bullet being fired in your direction, or the possibility of poison in your stew. The threat did not take any of these forms, but it was real enough.

These were my thoughts as I drove back from the latest round of interviews in Madison. My home was in Fort Atkinson, which was only 30 miles from Madison. The usual route was to take Highway 12 through Cambridge. The highway ran through a 20 mile stretch of nothing after you left Cambridge. This was good news and bad news. It was good news because it meant that no children were going to ride their bikes out in front of me, and no stop lights or stop signs were going to impede my progress. The bad news was that if my car left the road, several days might pass before I was found.

These were the thoughts rattling around in my head as I drove down that tree-lined highway in the early evening dusk. While I was accelerating on the outskirts of the sleepy village of Cambridge, a loud clunk came from the engine compartment. Not being mechanically inclined, my general policy was to ignore all unexplained noises that came from my car. This noise, however, may have had some significance, though what I could have done about it was not clear to me.

At highway speed, I let off the gas, but the pedal stayed down. The car continued to accelerate. That was odd. Assuming the cruise control was malfunctioning, I tapped the brake pedal. Nothing happened. I stepped more firmly on the brake. Nothing happened. I pumped the brake madly, eyes wide open, and sweat pouring out of every pore. None of that helped; the car continued to accelerate.

Having traveled that road many times, I knew what lay ahead. In fact, one time in the not too recent past I had driven down that highway at a high rate of speed and lived to tell the tale. That time, however, both my brakes and my accelerator were working properly. This time, slowing down even slightly was not an option. Since my car was a little Ford hatchback, there was not much danger that my speed would go over 90. But hitting a stand of trees at 90 miles per hour was plenty fast enough to ruin your day, your car, and your life if you had one left to ruin by the time you came to a complete stop.

Rational thought was difficult when your engine was roaring and you were fighting the steering wheel. I did manage to wonder if the simultaneous malfunction of the two systems, brakes and accelerator, could have been random bad luck. Considering the feathers I had ruffled in the last few hours, I had to reject that idea. Of course, I had never suspected that the forces I was challenging would stoop to murder. If I had thought it even a remote possibility, I would have been more circumspect. After all, you didn't spit in the eye of a killer.

Millions of dollars were at stake. Hundreds of millions, more likely. Of course, that amount of money provided sufficient motive for murder. Why did that not occur to me while I was tweaking the tails of the rich and powerful, especially when there had already been one death? The previous death was classified as an accident, but if I lived to get out of my car, I was going to have to question whether or not the poor fellow had been deliberately sent to his great reward. If I was alive fifteen minutes from now, I would call the first death a murder, but would I have the courage to tell anyone of my suspicions?

On the other hand, if I was dead fifteen minutes from now, perhaps the police would make the necessary connections to link my death with the first one. That would provide some consolation. But would they bother to check the condition of the brakes and accelerator in my smashed car? I didn't know what normal procedure might be, but at least some of the police officers I knew would just say 'good riddance to bad rubbish' and close the file on poor old Ed Schumacher.

Some of the people I knew in law enforcement were nice to me, one I even considered a friend. But there was another one who thought I was some kind of dangerous nut who caused nothing but trouble. That shouldn't affect the professionalism of the officers sworn to protect, but it did.

At that precise moment, as if on cue, the wail of a police siren became loud enough to be heard over the roar of the engine. A quick glance in the rear view mirror revealed flashing lights, nearly on my bumper. A bullhorn was shouting for me to bring the car to a stop and pull over.

Stop and pull over? That was exactly my problem, wasn't it? How nice of them to point it out to me. The police were supposed to help in emergency situations, weren't they, not blame the victim?

Emergency situations? The jumble of thoughts flying through my head suddenly ended. I finally remembered that little-used device between the bucket seats: the emergency brake. My hand leaped down of its own accord, grasped the handle, and pulled up with all its strength. Right away I learned two things. First, I learned that emergency brakes worked very well. Second, I learned that slamming on the brakes when you were traveling at a high rate of speed with a police car on your tail could make a big mess. It could also make you very unpopular.

Right away, my Ford slowed and the police cruiser rammed into my rear end, jolting me forward. My car started to fishtail, with the front sliding toward the left-hand side of the road. I ended up skidding sideways down the highway. My driver's side window was facing toward Cambridge, the direction from which I had just come. With a detached interest, I noted that the police car was also skidding sideways. It was a county vehicle. Its nose was pointed toward the right side of the road, so the driver's side window was toward me. The two cars were skidding in tandem, like figure skaters. The driver of the county cruiser was only a couple of feet away from me, since our windows were facing each other and the cars were close together. He was scowling as he fought to control the skid. His heavier vehicle slid closer to me until the two cars were touching. Then, he over-corrected and his car started to turn toward the left, pushing mine with it. Together, we turned completely around. Now the county car was on the left-hand side of the road, traveling east but facing west. His tires smoked and screeched as he slid backwards. My car was snuggled up against him, facing the other direction. About this time we left the road on the left-hand side, sliding into a stand of trees. After much crunching and banging, we came to a halt.

For a moment we sat there quietly. I, for one, was enjoying the peace of being at rest. It was very quiet, except for the occasional creak of wood from the damaged trees and a gentle hiss that was probably steam escaping from a radiator. Leaves and branches were scattered over both cars, and there was the sweet smell of forest in the air. I could not see any damage to my car from where I sat, but the county car had several broken windows.

Where I came from, when something like this happened, there was only one word that captured the entire essence of the situation. So, I said it: "woops." It expressed how I felt exactly, though in retrospect I think I should have said "double-woops."

The driver's side door of the county car was only inches from my own. The deputy's head was leaning against the side window. A whirring sound came from my car as I lowered my electric window. I reached out and knocked on the glass of the car next to mine. "Are you alright?" I asked. Okay, it was a dumb question, but what else was I supposed to say? It was the best I could do under the circumstances.

The deputy slowly straightened in his seat, then lowered his window.

"Are you crazy?" he asked.

"You said to slow down, so I did." It seemed like the wrong time to admit a mistake. Now, I realize that a mature person always admits his mistakes. But we live in a world where our lawyers advise us to behave differently. By this time, I was starting to think about how much trouble I might be in, so I tried to shift the blame. Not mature, not noble, and I'm not proud of it. But that was what I said and I am perfectly willing to admit that I am not perfect, especially under stress.

The deputy gritted his teeth, then asked, "Can you start your car?"

In response, I put the gear shift into 'park' and turned the key. The ignition whined for a few seconds, then the engine started. It rapidly raced up to a high r.p.m.

The deputy nodded in satisfaction. He had to raise his voice to be heard over the racing engine. "Can you move your car?" he asked.

"My accelerator is stuck and the brakes don't work," I answered.

He looked at me with a blank expression for a minute. A cut over his left eye was producing a trickle of blood that was running down the side of his face.

"Reach down and pull up on the gas pedal."

That had never occurred to me. I tried it, and, sure enough, the engine's roar turned into a gentle rumble.

"Now, put it into gear and give it a little gas. If it moves, drive up onto the road and just turn it off. Then come back and help me out of this car."

I nodded. First releasing the emergency brake, I pushed the gear shift into 'drive.' The car went into gear with a small jerk, then climbed off the grass and onto the road. Turning off the key caused it to drift to a stop. I jumped out and ran back to the county car.

The deputy had his door open and had fallen out onto the road. He insisted that I drag him all the way to where my Ford was stopped. The guy was only average in size, but he felt like he weighed over 200 pounds. Of course, I was just five-nine and had never done much physical work, so 25 pounds seemed heavy to me. His bulk felt like a ton.

It seemed like it took me an hour to drag him to my car, though it was probably only a few minutes. I helped him sit on the road, leaning against my back bumper. We were both gasping for air at this point. Slumping beside him, I leaned back against the bumper and tried to catch my breath.

After a minute or so, I asked the deputy, "Should I call 9-1-1?"

"Naw," he said, "I called dispatch while you were moving your car."

The situation looked like it was under control for the moment with a few minutes available for rest and recuperation. As any pipe smoker knew, when you have fifteen minutes to kill and you would like to calm your nerves, you broke out the fixin's and had a puff.

So, I got the works out of the back seat of the Ford and sat back down next to the deputy. Part of the enjoyment of pipe smoking was the ritual you went through. Open the pouch, put a little tobacco in the pipe, push it down gently, put the pipe in your mouth, close the pouch, light it up. At that time, I was using kitchen matches to light my pipe because the smell of burning matchwood was so nice.

The deputy was leaning back against the bumper with his eyes closed. He looked like he was in pain. But that might have just been due to the fact that he felt compelled to say something nice to me.

"I want to thank you for helping me out of the car," he said.

"No problem," I answered modestly. "It was no big deal."

"Might 'a' been," he answered. "It smelled like the gas tank ruptured. Don't want to stay in a wreck with gas all over the place."

Now I swear I had already thrown away my match by the time he said that. That's my story and I'm stickin' to it, as the country song said. But even if my fingers had let the match fly into the air after he mentioned gas instead of before, so what? Sometimes it took a moment to connect the sense of what you were hearing to the actions you should or should not take. You can be sure that if I had realized gasoline was flooding out of the car I would never have thrown a hot match onto the ground.

The spreading pool of fuel had not reached us, but it was only a couple of feet away. Looking at the bright side; if the gas had flowed two more feet in our direction we both would have been crispy critters. Instead, a sheet of flame shot straight up into the air, then raced toward the county car. A loud 'whump' signaled that the car had become engulfed in flames. Then it exploded. Bits of metal and burning branches fell all around us. The deputy and I covered our heads with our arms and cowered. Until my face touched my arm, I did not realize that the pipe was still in my mouth. Discretion being the better part of valor, I reached back and pushed the pipe, pouch, and matches under my car and behind the tire. The deputy's eyes had been closed when I lit up, so maybe he did not know from whence the spark had come.

Woops again. Triple woops. This just wasn't my day.

More police cars, an ambulance, and a fire truck arrived in due course. The deputy was placed on a stretcher and moved into the back of the ambulance. Through the open door, I could see him talking briefly to another deputy, gesturing toward me. I stood up and walked around my car assessing the damage. It was less than it might have been. The left side was scratched and there were dents in the driver's side door and the front and rear fenders, but the fenders were not pushed against the tires. None of the windows were broken. I figured that a couple thousand dollars would fix the exterior and repair the brakes and accelerator.

The ambulance left to take the injured deputy to the hospital. His comrade-in-arms came toward me. I leaned against my car to wait for him, knowing that he would doubt my story. "License and registration, please," he said.

Pulling out my wallet, I quickly found the license and handed it over. Then I opened the car door and climbed in to look for my registration. The deputy watched me closely until I found it. "Step out of the car, sir," he said.

I did and he directed me to walk back to his car with him. We sat in the front seat while he checked his computer, which told him my car was not stolen and my license was valid.

Then he asked me to tell him what had transpired. "When I was leaving Cambridge," I said, "the gas pedal went all the way down and the brakes stopped working. The other deputy was pretty close to me when he told me to slow down and pull over. The only way I could slow down was to put on the emergency brake. That worked, but he rammed into me and we both lost control."

The deputy nodded. "He says you pulled him away from his car before it exploded. You saved his life."

"It seemed like the thing to do at the time," I answered modestly.

He gave me a flat stare. "At this point, Mr. Schumacher, I don't know whether we should throw the book at you or give you a medal. But I want you to know that I will do what I can for you. We don't take it lightly when a citizen steps up to the plate the way you did."

He started his car. "I'll give you a ride home," he said. "Your car will be towed in and examined. We will call you and tell you how to get it back in a few days. In the meantime, I suggest you get a rental."

Ten minutes later he was dropping me off in front of my condo in Fort Atkinson. As I got out of his car, he said, "We have your address. Someone will be in touch." He handed me a card. "If you need any help, give me a call," he added.

"Thanks," I said. I stood there watching as he drove away. What a nice guy. He could have been pretty tough on me. Then I remembered that I had left my pipe fixin's under my car. Woops again.

Sighing at my own stupidity, I let myself into the building and climbed wearily up the stairs to our second floor unit. My wife Betty was sitting in her recliner, reading. "You're back," she said with a smile.

"Yup. I'm back."

"How did your day go?"

"I managed to reach most of the people I was scheduled to interview. It was interesting. There is a lot going on beneath the surface."

Betty smiled. "I'm glad you're doing this. It's nice to see you taking on a challenge." Little did she know how big a challenge it was. "How was your drive home?" she asked.

"Could've been worse," I replied. As long as we have been married, I should have known that not telling her everything right at that moment was a mistake. But I was basking in the glow of her approval, so I let it drop. Besides, I didn't want to scare her. We were a happy couple until the next morning when she noticed that my car was missing from the garage. Oh well, it was nice while it lasted.

Chapter 2.

The Contract

"Do you think I should take my walk now?" I asked.

She did not reply. Instead she just gazed steadily at me with her pretty yellow eyes.

"It looks like rain. Maybe I should wait."

She squinted her eyes slightly, still watching me quietly. Did she understand that my words were an attempt to communicate? It really didn't matter. She was beautiful and she adored me.

"But it might rain this afternoon. So I better go now."

Fritter the cat didn't argue. She just followed me to the door as I started out on my walk.

I always thought that people who talked to their pets were nuts. Betty had started her new job a month ago, and after a month of working at home alone, I was either changing my mind or going nuts. Betty said I had to get a job or I would get strange. Or 'stranger' as she liked to add. Of course, I did have a job – I was selling bicycle motors out of my garage. But business had fallen off after a brief burst of sales. I had about 50 boxes of electric bike motors stacked in the garage. If they didn't sell by January, I would have to dump them at a loss. I was pretty sure I could do that on ebay, but, of course, I would have preferred to at least break even on the venture.

By nature, I was not a 'people person', meaning that mostly I kept to myself. Betty and I did not go out for social events very often. A cocktail party was very unpleasant for me and I avoided them like the plague. But working at home had shown me the limits of my hermit-like tendencies. What really struck the point home was when I realized that I was drawing out phone calls with telemarketers just for the enjoyment of having someone with which to converse. Telemarketers were under-appreciated, I had decided. They were always respectful, cheerful, and they laughed at your jokes. After about ten minutes, they suddenly lost interest, but that was okay. They had to make a living, after all. And you could be sure that I wasn't going to buy anything from them, since I was frugal to a fault. Betty would say that my frugality was just plain cheapness, and it was one of my worst faults, of which I had many.

Cheapness is a good thing, though. Betty's bank account had swelled since she married me because I didn't like to go out and spend money. Besides, she couldn't enjoy recreational shopping when I was holding back, so she spent less than she did when she was single.

Cheapness is also an essential part of my weight control plan. Since I didn't like to buy groceries or spend much money in a restaurant, I ended up eating less. Naturally, I let people think I was eating less because I had so much dietary discipline, but really I was just saving money. Did you know you can eat fast food and not get fat if you only buy one item off the dollar menu? It's true. And if you only eat a piece of toast for breakfast, your grocery bill will be a lot lower than if you buy bacon, eggs, milk, juice, and the like.

As a result of my frugality, my size 34 pants were loose on me (most days of the week, anyway). My weight was usually below 170 pounds (which was about right for a guy like me who only reached 5-9 when he had his shoes on). And I felt a lot better than I did when I weighed 222 pounds. So, don't under-rate the value of being cheap.

Walking was my only form of exercise. For me, the most effective walking had always required a destination. That fall, I usually walked to McDonalds and rewarded myself with a newspaper and a cup of coffee. My favorite type of newspaper story had to do with drug company shenanigans. On this particular day, another installment in the Pacex trial story was making the news. Pacex, which was a pain medication manufactured by a company called DrugCo, had been accused of causing heart attacks in some of the people who took it.

According to the Associated Press, Pacex was rushed onto the market a year before patents ran out on DrugCo's other lucrative drugs. A former DrugCo CEO confirmed on the stand that Pacex was important to the company's financial future. He denied, however, that DrugCo put profits over safety by rushing the medication to the marketplace in 1999. The increased heart attack risk was a complete surprise, he said.

Plaintiffs in over 4000 lawsuits claimed otherwise. The drug had to be pulled from the market under pressure from the Food and Drug Administration when studies showed it increased the risk of heart attack or stroke if taken for 18 months or longer. An investigative reporter for a west-coast newspaper analyzed the composition of the FDA board that approved Pacex and found two interesting tidbits of information. First, many of the board members had lucrative consulting contracts with pharmaceutical companies. And second, if those board members who had financial conflicts of interest had abstained from voting on Pacex, it would not have been approved for release onto the market as early as it was.

The good news for DrugCo was that Pacex earned $2.5 billion for the company in 2003. This was despite the release three years earlier of a study showing that Pacex users had five times as many heart attacks as people using an older painkiller. DrugCo responded to the study by saying that Pacex was not bad for your heart; instead, the other medication was unfairly 'heart-friendly'. When compared against sugar pills, Pacex won hands down.

That last part made me chuckle. We would hope that a brand new medicine would be better than a sugar pill, wouldn't we? The sugar pill comparison seemed like an unfairly easy test to me.

The Food and Drug Administration was driven to rebuke DrugCo on the 'heart-friendly' claims because they lacked scientific proof. Finally, in 2002 DrugCo added a warning about cardiovascular risk to the Pacex label. Ultimately, DrugCo decided that retreat was better than defeat and pulled the drug from the market.

The head of clinical trials for DrugCo continued to deny that the company had skewed its research findings to make Pacex look safer than it was. Prosecutors, however, produced an email message written by that same executive suggesting that patients with heart disease should be excluded from research projects to decrease the number of heart attacks among those people who were taking Pacex. Plaintiffs claimed that if the studies had included the same kind of people who were intended to buy the drug, it would have been shown to be far more dangerous than sugar pills.

Woops. Maybe the sugar pill comparison was not so dumb after all.

When I got back from my walk, the first thing I did was check for new email messages. The usual spam had arrived: advertisements for low-cost mortgages and male 'enhancements', which claimed to make soft things hard and short things long. In addition, a message was waiting for me that looked promising: Afzal Arif, editor of an online medical journal on whose editorial board I was serving, wanted to arrange a transatlantic telephone call with me to discuss a business matter. Naturally, my reply was enthusiastic, and we set the time for 11 a.m. Arif was in London, so it was late in the day for him.

When the phone rang, I snatched it off the hook eagerly.

"Hello?"

"Is this Professor Schumacher?" Arif's accent was pure Oxford English.

"Speaking. How are you, Dr. Arif?"

"Just fine. The weather is perfect here this week. Everyone is enjoying the summer."

"Same here. It is hard not to be in a good mood when the sun is shining."

"I agree." Arif changed the subject at this point, getting right down to business.

"My reason for calling has to do with a problem we are having with one of our manuscripts. Given your extensive experience in writing for publication and serving as a reviewer, I was hoping you could help us out. Also, you are in the right location, I believe. Is Madison, Wisconsin, near where you live?"

"Yes, it sure is. Madison is only thirty miles away." This was a stroke of luck, I thought. "What exactly is the nature of the problem?"

"The manuscript in question was written by a team of researchers who are located at the Medical University of Madison. As you know, the lead author is normally the person with whom we correspond. The lead author is responsible for making the necessary changes to the document. This is done online. For example, if the order in which authors names appear should be changed, the lead author makes the necessary changes in the appropriate screen on our website. We then review the changes before finalizing the manuscript for publication."

Arif cleared his throat, then continued. "The manuscript was accepted for publication with no changes. In fact, the reviewers were very enthusiastic and urged rapid publication because of the importance of the findings. We converted the manuscript into its final form, called the galley proofs."

The system Arif was describing was fairly typical for online medical journals. However, Arif worked for Acmemedpub, which was one of the pioneers in the field of online publishing and also one of the largest players. They had refined their manuscript processing system so that it was highly efficient.

"Yes, I am familiar with the process."

"Normally this all works very well. Of course, small difficulties, glitches, if you will, occur regularly, but we are able to overcome them without much problem. In this case, however, an unusual circumstance has arisen."

"What is that?"

"The lead author, who also was the corresponding author, has died, unfortunately."

I pondered the implications of that for a moment. "This means he can't make the final changes in the manuscript. Can't you just make one of the other authors the correspondent?"

"We have done that. But the new corresponding author wants to dramatically revise the thrust of the manuscript, completely reversing the findings and conclusions. The deceased lead author obviously would not have agreed with the new conclusions." Arif hesitated a moment. He may have been consulting his notes.

"These are the issues we at Acmemedpub must resolve. First, is the new corresponding author allowed to make such dramatic revisions, or should he be required to submit a new manuscript? We have already made a decision on this question and the answer is 'no.' The corresponding author will have to write a new paper and submit it for peer review.

Our second question is more difficult: does the dramatic nature of the revisions suggest that something is fundamentally wrong with the original paper? If so, then perhaps we should withdraw our agreement to publish it.

Our third question is even more difficult: since our reviewers were enthusiastic, should we go ahead with publication, even though the new corresponding author no longer supports the conclusions? We could give him the option of removing his name from the manuscript. This step would be unprecedented and we may not want to establish such a precedent."

"How can I help?" I asked.

"Our editorial board has decided that it needs more information. Two kinds of information are needed. The first is technical: if the paper was technically correct, then some board members desire to proceed with publication, post haste. The second information requirement has to do with ethics: is it ethical for us to proceed with publication when one of the original authors disagrees with the conclusions of the paper? As you know, if he wrote part of the paper, he should be included as an author. But if he does not agree with the paper as written, then some board members believe that the paper cannot be published."

"This is a fascinating dilemma."

"Isn't it, just. But we need a fairly rapid resolution of the matter. Would you be willing to interview the corresponding author at the Medical University of Madison, review the data to verify its accuracy, and submit a brief report of your findings and recommendations to the editorial board? We need the report as quickly as possible, preferably within a week."

"I can rearrange my schedule to accommodate that. Of course, this level of commitment goes well beyond the level of activity normally expected of a reviewer."

"We agree. We are prepared to compensate you in the form a flat fee of $1000 per day for five days. Given the location, travel expenses would not be provided. We would call you our 'consulting research ethicist.' Would this be acceptable?"

It was a lot more than I had made on my bike motors. Come to think of it, the bike motor business was a net loss. I had not actually earned any income for several months. I took a deep breath so that I could sound as if the amount of money was trivial, but I would nobly make the sacrifice for the public good.

"No problem. This should be an enjoyable experience."

Arif was very pleased. "Wonderful! We will be sending you a contract today. Please sign it and return by fax immediately." He sounded very relieved.

"Good enough. I will call to set up the appointments as soon as we have taken care of the contract."

Arif hesitated. "Professor Schumacher..."

"Call me Ed."

"Umm, Ed, it goes without saying, of course, that we are trusting you to behave with the utmost discretion in this matter. Acmemedpub's reputation as a responsible publisher of medical research is very important to us. No matter how critical your conclusions might be, please do not reveal them to anyone except the board. And it is most important that nothing about this matter reach the news media. Very hush-hush, you know."

"No problem. Low profile is my specialty." Perhaps that was a bit of an exaggeration, but I was sincere when I said it.

After I hung up the phone, the cat and I skipped around the house shouting for joy. Well, I shouted and she skipped. She may not have known what we were celebrating, but she seemed to enjoy the event anyway.

By this time, Arif had sent me the contract, along with a link to the manuscript so that I could study the galleys. I printed the contract, signed it after skimming it quickly, then faxed it back to him. I also printed out the galleys so that I could read them carefully over a leisurely cup of coffee.

I made my list of the necessary preparations for completion of my assignment. First, study the galleys. Second, get a hair cut. Third, buy a nice suit. Fourth, set up the interviews in Madison. Fifth, go out for a beer to celebrate.

This list showed how seriously I was taking the assignment. Ordinarily, I cut my own hair with a buzzer, even though Betty did not approve of the result. But I wanted to make a good impression. I was hoping for follow-up work. Being a consulting ethicist sounded like a pretty darn good job to me.

My first stop was a return to McDonald's where I purchased a cup of coffee and settled in to study the research paper that was causing all the fuss. The study was entitled Randomized Clinical Trial of a Performance Enhancement Drug. The authors were three men from the Department of Urology at the Medical University of Madison. The lead author was Pritpal Gupta, MD, who I assumed was the dead man in the galley. The second author was William Cosgrove, MD, and the third author was Kim Lee, PhD. Cosgrove was almost certainly the new corresponding author who was attempting to redirect the paper. Dr. Lee had to be the biostatistician who crunched the numbers for the project. The study was sponsored by Pharmamax, the drug company that had developed the medication being studied.

Like most medical research articles, this one was succinct, running only six pages in length. Over three hundred subjects were recruited to participate in the study. Only men who were over 50 years of age, complaining of some degree of sexual dysfunction but who were otherwise healthy, were eligible to participate in the study. The men were randomized into either a treatment group, which received an experimental medication named Erecta, or a placebo group. Sexual performance was measured at baseline, meaning before the treatment was started, and at three month intervals for a period of nine months.

The results were striking. The first finding of the study was that the medication achieved its purpose: men in the experimental group reported higher levels of satisfaction with their sexual performance and more frequent sexual intercourse than men not receiving Erecta.

The other significant finding from the study was completely unexpected to the investigators. Nothing about the chemical composition of the medication had created a concern about its impact on the cardiovascular system, but the men in the experimental group experienced heart attacks at three times the rate of that found in the comparison group. Interestingly, both groups had higher heart attack rates than is normally found in men over 50. Ten men died during the study. The manuscript concluded that Erecta should not be used in the treatment of sexual performance problems until further research had established its safety.

The negative conclusions were unusual, not because it appeared to be harmful, but because it had almost appeared in print despite its sponsorship by the company that had created the drug. Drug manufacturers were famous for requiring researchers to sign agreements that precluded publication unless the company approved of the findings. And they were unlikely to approve a study that said their drug should not go on the market. Negative studies were buried and forgotten. More experiments were done until one or more showed that the drug was good for what ailed you. Then it appeared in print.

Of course, I am not saying that all drug companies played dirty pool with their research projects. But it had happened often enough to be considered very common.

By this time, developing a scenario that explained the problem with the dead man in the galley was pretty simple. Most likely, the lead author, Dr. Gupta, had felt a moral obligation to publish the findings because of their importance. It was equally likely that Pharmamax was not told he was doing so. The second author, Dr. Cosgrove, was probably a junior researcher who had just been following Gupta's lead. When Gupta died, Cosgrove decided to be cautious and informed the company about the manuscript. He, no doubt, received a firm attitude adjustment that was the legal and financial equivalent of a smack in the head. His new goal was to change the findings to show that Erecta was the best thing for your sex life since the discovery of sea food, or failing that, to prevent the study from being published.

Betty frequently told me that I was negative, cynical, and paranoid. She was right, so I knew I had to verify my scenario very carefully before jumping to the conclusion that Cosgrove had been manipulated to change his tune. The purpose of my interviews would be to probe into the goals and motivations underlying Cosgrove's behavior.

This was the responsible way to proceed. Even so, I really did not have much doubt about my theory. A drug company that could come up with a 'superstud' pill that was better than the next best product on the market stood to make many millions of dollars. They had a lot at stake. And the willingness of drug companies to slant the evidence so that doctors and patients didn't learn about the negative complications of a popular medicine had been demonstrated more than once.

One thing was certain: if Acmemedpub published the original article, their goal of keeping the whole episode low-key would not be achieved. The news media would be all over the study the very same day. Pharmamax would scream 'foul' at the publisher, reformers would scream 'foul' at Pharmamax, and the Food and Drug Administration would be compelled to try to protect its political rear end while not alienating the drug industry. Still, I vowed that the matter would remain 'hush-hush' until my report left my computer and arrived at Arif's office. When the publisher had suspected they might be dealing with an ethical problem, they had been dead right. Their ethical problem would be whether they should tell the truth about a life and death matter or duck and run. I fervently hoped they would choose to tell the truth.

My next stop was the hair cutting place, which was in a strip mall only a block from our condo. No one was there ahead of me, so a pert young lady moved me straight into a chair. She chatted amiably as she worked. Her name was Jill and she gave me a scissor cut that was excellent. She did not strike me as being very intelligent, in the academic sense, but I had generally found that common sense, even wisdom, could be independent of IQ. Kindness, honesty, and other virtues might be more common among people of average intelligence. The working person was not called 'the salt of the earth' by accident, but because he (or she) possessed virtues that kept society on an even keel, despite the self-centered and irresponsible behavior of the people who ended up in "leadership" positions. Jill seemed like a solid and sensible person. And, as I said, she gave me an excellent haircut. When I asked her what she thought of all the scandal surrounding Pacex, she replied, "Oh, you mean that pain medicine that causes heart attacks? Well, those old people with arthritis who took it were in a lot of pain. It was worth it to them to risk a heart attack. After all, when you're old, you could have a heart attack any day anyway."

"But they didn't know that Pacex increased their risk of a heart attack. Shouldn't they have been told?"

"Well, sure, I guess. But who reads those little inserts they hand out with the medicine at the pharmacy? Nobody, that's who. Everybody knows that something weird could happen when you take a pill. If you aren't willing to take a risk, then you shouldn't take any pills." Maybe she had a point.

My next stop was a men's clothing store. A man was coming out when I reached the front door. He was holding a suit hanger covered in plastic. I didn't recognize him at first, but he spoke to me.

"Good morning, Professor Schumacher."

I did a double-take, then realized the man was Sergeant Bill Broder of the Fort Atkinson police department.

"Sergeant Broder! It's good to see you. How yah been?" Broder was a solid guy; I really was pleased to see him. Unfortunately, his car was parked at the curb with his partner at the wheel. The partner, Sergeant Schmidt, was not my favorite person, nor was I hers. The truth was she hated me for some reason I was not able to discern and tried to throw the book at me every chance she got. I was careful not to look toward the car for fear that I would either have to pretend I didn't see her or wave and have her pretend not to see me.

"Can't complain. Could be worse," he responded. "And yourself?"

"Good enough. Could be worse."

Broder hesitated a moment, then asked reluctantly, "You, mmm, aren't getting involved in any more sticky situations, are you, Professor?" Twice in the previous couple of years, circumstances had led me into contact with the authorities. That was how I met Broder and Schmidt.

"No, no," I assured him. "Those other times were freak situations. Not likely to happen again."

"Yes, of course." He did not look entirely convinced, but he shook off his doubts. "Glad to hear it. Well, must be moving on. Have a nice day, Professor."

"Not a problem. Same to you."

The men's store was typical of its ilk. Any small town was likely to have one just like it. It was located on Main Street. The styles were conservative. I suspected that their main customers were retirees who needed something to wear to church, to weddings, and to funerals. You can be sure I had not darkened the door of such a place for several years.

An attractive saleswoman swooped in on me as I entered the door. She was being hopeful, since I am sure that I did not look like their usual buyer; I was wearing Levis and a t-shirt.

"I need a suit," I said. "And I don't want to spend any more than I have to."

"We can take care of you. We are used to that kind of request. What size do you wear?"

"Forty regular."

With an economy of motion, she directed me toward a rack where she found suits in my size that had two pair of pants. She pointed out that having two pair of pants that were of different colors, one in the same fabric as the jacket and one different but compatible, would allow me to vary my ensemble more cheaply than I could accomplish by buying two suits.

I agreed immediately. "Ah, ha," I thought craftily, "she doesn't know that I have no intention of buying two suits. What a deal!"

"Would you prefer navy or gray?"

"Gray."

She looked doubtful. "Why?"

"Matches my hair." She decided not to argue, but instead did an end-run.

"What style of trousers? Pleated or flat-front?"

"Flat-front."

"Oh, on you pleated is better. Flat-front is better when the gentleman is portly."

I was definitely not portly. "Okay, pleated."

She gazed at my lower half critically. "We have to size the trousers properly. Do you always wear your trousers that low?"

Low? They must have been dragging again. "No, but they tend to slip down," I said apologetically.

"Do you wear a belt to hold your trousers in position or just as a decoration?"

Was that a serious question? "To hold them up. But they slip anyway."

"That's the cut. We can take care of that problem." She pulled some trousers off the rack.

I was very relieved that she could take care of my sagging pants problem. Perhaps this was the point where I lost control over the experience of buying my new clothes.

"Let me recommend an additional navy blazer. The blazer will go with both of your suit pants, which means you actually will be getting four combinations out of two jackets and two pairs of pants. That's like getting four suits for the price of one suit and a blazer."

Wow. That sounded like a real bargain. "Okay. Let's do it."

Before I got out of there she had sold me two pair of shoes (one brown and one black because black shoes definitely should not be worn with a navy blazer), two belts (one black and one brown), four shirts (to match the jackets), and four ties (to match the shirts). I was feeling a warm glow until they rang up the bill. My face must have gone pale when they presented it to me. My gasp was the same sort of gasp I expected to let loose when I finally saw the Grand Canyon. Only this time the hole was not going to be in the ground, but in my bank balance. Apparently, the key to making a big sale was to hit the buyer with such a large sticker shock that he was unable to think straight. I paid the total with a credit card then staggered out to my car.

When I arrived back at the condo, I called Cosgrove at the Medical University of Madison. He was obviously expecting me to contact him and was eager to meet at the earliest opportunity. We set up the appointment for nine the next morning. This would give him time to make his rounds before sitting down with me. He gave me directions, which I dutifully scribbled on a piece of scrap paper.

Then, I parked myself in front of the television to wait for Betty to come home. As always, I turned on the science fiction channel, hoping that some new and interesting alien creature would be devouring a small team of heroes. I liked to guess which heroes would be eaten, and in what sequence. Ironically, given my new assignment, the commercials were touting a new medication that was available for the treatment of female sexual performance. Its scientific name was Ambrosia, and it was being sold by, you guessed it, Pharmamax. The commercial showed a sad looking woman sitting in bed next to a disappointed looking man. Next, she visited her doctor, who smiled expansively and held up a pink pill. The scene cut to the bedroom, where the man was lying passed out in bed. The woman was sitting up reading a magazine and sporting a smug look on her face.

Betty arrived home around seven. Betty was a physician, and something always seemed to come up that delayed her departure from the office. As a woman who valued her leisure time, she found this irritating. But that was the price she paid for making her living doing clinical work. The pay was good and so was the prestige, both of which she also valued.

She collapsed into her easy chair as soon as she got home. Mustering up her energy, she asked, "So, did you do anything today?" Since she had gone back to work, she had taken the attitude that I was not working, just because I was not making money. Truth was, I worked on the computer all day long. So far, though, none of my efforts to sell my bike motors had generated much in the way of results.

I told her about my new job with quite a bit of pride, sort of like a cat who brought home a dead mouse and laid it on the door step expecting praise. And I was not disappointed.

"That is great news! " Betty said, clearly delighted. "I'm so happy for you."

She basked in a warm fantasy of early retirement for a moment, then said, "Tell me again. What, exactly, are you supposed to do?"

"I'm to be the consulting research ethicist who figures out whether a particular article should be published. The lead author died and the second author wants to change the conclusions."

"Tell me again what this research is about."

"The medication is supposed to improve sexual performance in men over fifty. The experiment showed that it worked, but it also increases the risk of heart attacks."

"Why does the second author want to change the findings?"

"That's what I will try to find out tomorrow."

"Well," Betty said firmly, "I hope they publish it the way it is."

"Why?"

"Because men are too preoccupied with sex. When they get older, they should be willing to give it up."

"You can't be serious."

"Yes, I am serious. Men will turn this into a recreational drug. Medicines are supposed to cure disease, not be used for recreation." Now she was on a roll. "I'm sick of all that spam I get on 'male enhancement.' A bunch of dirty old men want to have sex all the time. They should leave their wives alone. And did you read about that sex offender in Sweden who convinced his doctor to prescribe Viagra for him, then got arrested for committing another rape?"

"Wait a minute. Just today I saw a commercial for a female enhancement medication. Is that for dirty old women who should leave their men alone?"

"That's different. Women should be allowed to enjoy sex just as often as men. It's only fair."

"Besides," she continued to argue. "Viagra can cause blindness." Betty seemed to think that clinched the argument in her favor, but I had an answer for that one.

"Blindness is a rare complication. Besides, it usually only causes blindness in one eye. Guys have a spare, so it's worth it. And, anyway, anybody can figure out that it's not the Viagra that causes the blindness, but what you do with your dingus once you get it working again."

Betty laughed. Then she changed the subject abruptly. "What's for dinner?"

"I didn't make anything. We have pizza in the freezer."

"There is too much salt in frozen pizza. And it's too fattening."

"I could whip up some pancakes."

That mollified her. Calories apparently were not an issue with pancakes. Betty loved breakfast food.

After dinner, which we enjoyed as usual in front of the television, I headed over to Sal's to have a beer with Andrew, Betty's cousin. Andrew and I had scheduled this event a week previously, but that was no reason I could not use it as a convenient excuse for celebrating my new opportunity to work as a consulting ethicist.

Andrew was already holding down a table at Sal's when I arrived. "How's it goin'?" I asked.

"Can't complain," Andrew said. "Could be worse." Andrew was a Lutheran, so he was careful not to be too upbeat. After all, if you were happy, you must have been doing something you shouldn't. That was how Lutheran theology seemed to influence Lutherans or so it appeared to outsiders like me.

I told Andrew about my good fortune and he was happy for me. "So," he said, "you're a consulting ethicist now. That's sounds pretty important. I didn't know you were so ethical. This is a new side of you for me. I'll have to think about that."

"I never claimed to be more ethical than the next person. Let's just say I have an academic background that allows me to tell other people when their research ethics are slipping."

Andrew still seemed to think that was a stretch for me, but he let it pass. "Does this mean you are going out of the electric bicycle business?" he asked. I had been trying to sell electric bicycle motors out of my garage for several months without too much success.

"Naw, this consulting gig might be just a one-time thing. I will keep trying with the bike motors for awhile."

Andrew laughed. "Do you really think you can sell those to anybody?"

"Maybe not. Maybe no one will buy them. But that just goes to show what's wrong with our economy."

"This I have to hear. Go ahead, tell me what's wrong with our economy."

"Well, we waste a lot of money on luxuries then have too little left to provide the basic things people need to have a decent quality of life. That applies to energy just as much as it does to medicine. People are complaining about the price of gasoline, but instead of conserving, they buy big gas-guzzling SUVs. They live in the suburbs and drive miles and miles to get to work or go to the store. It's nuts."

"What else can they do? They don't have any choice. And high gas prices are killing their budgets."

"There is too a choice. And until the price of a barrel of oil gets a lot higher, people won't be ready to stop wasting energy."

"Wait a minute! You can't be saying that prices should go higher! Everybody else wants them to be lower."

"Imagine this scenario for a minute. Imagine paying eight bucks a gallon for gas and quadrupling the price of oil. Think of the improvements that would lead to in our economy."

"Improvements? Like what?"

"For one thing, companies that own large office buildings would tell their employees to work at home, so they can cut their air conditioning and heating bills. Many meetings would be held at coffee shops and fast-food establishments. Many other meetings would occur online, with each participant actually being in his or her home office instead of being at a central business location."

"That sounds good. What else would happen in this fantasy of yours?"

"Wind turbines would be put up over large buildings if the price of making your own was less than the cost of buying it. Or, buildings could be built underground. That would use renewable energy and it would clean up the air."

"Okay, that sounds good."

"People would trade their SUVs for compact cars. Others would start using electric vehicles."

"Oh, ho! This whole idea is just so you can sell your bike motors."

"No! I invested in the bike motors because the world would be a better place if people used battery powered vehicles!"

"Where are they going to drive them? They would be a hazard on the roads."

I had an answer for that one. "We let them use the network of low-speed lanes being built in most cities around the country."

Andrew was mystified. "What are the 'low-speed lanes' you're talking about?"

I smiled in triumph. "Bike trails, of course. Right now, the main users of bike trails are better educated, healthier, and wealthier than the average person. They are of no benefit to disadvantaged people, decrepit old people, or even to the average person in the community. Taxpayers have spent a lot of money to produce a network of roads that isn't being put to good use. Electric vehicles should be allowed to drive on them."

He was irritated. "What kind of electric vehicles?"

"Well, golf carts, for example."

"I don't want golf carts on my bike trail!"

I had forgotten that Andrew frequently rode on the bike trails that encircled Fort Atkinson. So far, I was not having much success selling my vision of the future to Andrew. But it was too soon to give up.

"And other changes would happen," I said, "if the price of oil quadrupled. These would be good changes. Some recreational activities would start to take place in neighborhoods where people live, instead of across town. Zoning practices would change so that grocery stores, coffee shops, and restaurants would be opened within easy walking distance of residential neighborhoods. Smaller homes would be built because smaller homes cost less to heat and cool. The average price of a new home would drop for the first time ever. Maybe school teachers and policemen would actually be able to buy a house for themselves again." Andrew was nodding about lowering the price of a home. Prices had gotten way out of line.

"Developers would put up mid-sized wind turbines to provide power to new neighborhoods. Playgrounds would fit nicely under these neighborhood energy sources. Schools would encourage students to study at home online, which would allow the bright ones to move at their own pace instead of the brain-numbing rate that goes with the traditional lecture format. Classroom efforts would be focused on those children who need personal attention or tutoring. Some school activities would be decentralized back to the neighborhood level."

Andrew sat quietly for a minutes, absorbing what I had said. Then he announced: "If the kids aren't in school they will be out getting into trouble. That will never work."

I had to just shake my head in defeat. If I couldn't convince him, then I would never be able to convince anyone.

We switched our focus and began a discussion of modern pharmaceuticals and how they were affecting society.

"Look at all those TV commercials," I said. "The drug companies are pushing all kinds of pills on people."

"So, what's wrong with that? If the medicine helps people, why shouldn't they be told about it?"

"They didn't know they needed it, but then they see a commercial and suddenly they need it after all? That sounds pretty dubious to me."

"Maybe they knew they had a health problem but didn't know there was a new medicine for it. So when they saw the commercial, it was a good thing."

"Yeah, lucky for them. The problem is that every pill has side effects. Sometimes the medicine is worse for you than the health problem it's intended to treat."

"You aren't saying our government would let drug companies sell pills that aren't good for people, are you?" Andrew was just teasing me; we both were cynical about the kind of nonsense corporations could get away with. Besides, he knew that remark would get me cranked up.

"You're darn right they would. Americans take more medicine than people in any other country, but we are a long way from being the healthiest people in the world. Our health statistics put us about 30th or 35th in the world, not in first place. But the total amount spent on medical care per citizen is much higher than it is anywhere else. A heck of a lot of money is being wasted."

"So, it's the American Way. It's a market, so business people are going to make money in it. Nothing wrong with that."

"Maybe that would be true if everybody had all the essentials. But we can't justify wasting billions on unnecessary services when a lot of people are suffering because they can't get basic medical care. It's immoral."

"Now you sound like a socialist. Next you are going to say we should have socialized medicine like those European countries."

"Why not? It's not like we would need to raise taxes to do it. There is enough money floating around in the medical care system to take care of the basics for the whole population. Of course we need a national program."

"It will never happen in the United States."

"Maybe not. But it's pretty clear that employers are getting tired of paying for health benefits. They have figured out that their products will sell better around the world when they can lower the price, which they could do by eliminating health benefits. You just wait; someday soon the corporate lobbyists will start pushing the federal government to allow everybody into state Medicaid programs. And Medicaid programs won't let people have all the latest medications the drug companies have dreamed up. It would be too expensive."

"You know who wouldn't like that: the old folks would get very upset."

"Yep. And that is who a lot of the commercials are targeting. But those new medications are not going to cure old age. Nobody gets to live forever. What I want to know is why, after a full life, are people so afraid to die? They want every new pill, hoping it will help them live longer, and they get downright angry if somebody says it's a waste of money because they are still going to die, whether they get the new pill or not."

"You mean they get mad at people like you?"

"Yep."

"Well, it's no wonder, if you're saying stuff like that."

Andrew could be really obtuse at times.

Chapter 3.

The Big City

My trek into Madison began at 6:30 in the morning. The place was only thirty miles away, but I know myself well enough to anticipate getting lost. Fort Atkinson and the surrounding towns were nice places to live, but Madison was a big city, by my standards, with big city traffic. I usually avoided the place. The Madisonians sometimes acted as if they still lived in a small Midwestern college town. They should have looked around; those days were gone. They had sacrificed small-town quality of life for economic growth many years ago.

A parking place on a side street did not appear to be available, so I splurged and went into a parking garage. With an hour to kill, I wandered down State Street, the main drag near campus, in search of a place to get some breakfast. It was October so the air was brisk. Since it was early in the day, few students were out and about.

State Street had a lot of funky places that catered to students, but somehow I found an old-fashioned diner. After first buying a newspaper from the machine out in front, I seated myself on a vacant stool at the counter. A waitress who looked like she had been working there for thirty years gave me a menu and offered me coffee, which I accepted. When she returned to take my order, I chose a cinnamon roll. "Butter with that, Hon?" she asked. Since I knew it would be slathered with icing, I declined the butter. It was indeed covered in white icing, and it was darned good. After I gobbled it down, I settled in to enjoy the coffee and read the paper.

On the front page, below the fold, the big news was a federal audit of the research programs at the Medical University of Madison. Well, well, well, I thought. Is this serendipity or what?

According to the story, the feds were very irritated with the University. Their audit, which began as a routine affair, had been delayed by concerted foot-dragging on the part of the University. After eighteen months of wrangling, the feds announced that the University was being fined three million dollars for transferring funds around willy-nilly, without asking permission first. Money that was given to the University for one project would be moved to another. The spokesman for the feds pretty much admitted that the extent of impropriety was impossible to assess. "We gave them a list of 150 transactions to justify. They could not find any of them, much less explain them. It is clear that the University's grant accounting system does not meet the basic requirements of an accounting system: it cannot account for expenses."

Reading between the lines, the federal spokesman seemed to wish he could have been announcing more serious penalties. The University spokesman, on the other hand, was blasé about the entire matter. "Our acceptance of this penalty in no way constitutes an admission of error on our part. What we have here is a difference of opinion about how our funds should be managed." This kind of arrogant defiance really irritated the feds. Retribution would come to the University, some day, somehow; of that I was sure. On the other hand, I doubted that the university in Madison was doing anything unusual. Every university, in my experience, had a constitutional inability to keep its right hand out of its left pocket.

My thoughts turned to Betty, as they often did. I was worried about her. Since she had started her new job, she was working long hours and coming home very tired. Her usual anxieties were exaggerated, and that is saying a lot. For example, she was worried that the cat would escape from the house.

"Tell me not to worry," she would say.

"Don't worry about it. She won't run away."

"You're just saying that. You don't know."

"Well, of course, I don't know."

"Then you do think she's going to run away!"

And so it went.

So I worried about her. She was always tired and she was always worried. Hopefully, this would all get better. But what if it didn't?

Chapter 4.

Interview with William Cosgrove

Dr. Cosgrove was waiting for me at the reception desk in the urology clinic when I arrived. He shook my hand enthusiastically, then led me into his cramped little office. The name plate on his desk labeled him as an assistant professor. Ah ha, I thought, this guy is a novice. And he doesn't have tenure, so he has to worry about job security.

Cosgrove skipped the small talk and went straight to the issue at hand. "Mr. Schumacher," he said, apparently not realizing that even if I was only a Ph.D., I still should be addressed as 'doctor' or at least 'professor.' What a beginning: one sentence into the interview and already I didn't like him.

"I hope we can resolve this little problem quickly," Cosgrove said. "As you probably know, universities operate on a 'publish or perish system,' so we need to get this paper corrected and into print as quickly as possible." He said 'we,' but I was pretty sure he was just talking about his own needs.

"'Publish or perish' was the dominant principle in the academic world twenty years ago, Bill," I said, "but today universities will take funding over publications any day." Notice that I called him 'Bill' rather than "Dr. Cosgrove." I outranked the neophyte in academic terms and didn't intend to let him think he was top dog.

My remark set him back a bit. "Well, maybe you're right about that, but publishing is still important. On the other hand, of course, we can't publish a paper with errors in it. Dr. Gupta was a great researcher in his prime, but he was out in left field with what he wrote in this paper."

"Didn't you get to see the manuscript before he submitted it?"

Cosgrove had the decency to look embarrassed. "Yes, well, he gave me a draft, but I didn't really have time to study it. I just trusted him to get it right."

"Are you saying you didn't know that he had concluded that Erecta was not ready for marketing, that it needed more study?"

He squirmed in his chair. "Yes, I knew that, but I hadn't thought about other ways to analyze the data. If you've read the paper, you know he included men who were known to have heart disease and obese men who probably also had heart disease. That obviously increases their risk of heart attacks. The analysis should have been limited to men who were healthy. Pharmamax helped us re-analyze the data by excluding those men and the results came out much different—completely the opposite, in fact. Erecta does not increase the risk of heart attacks in healthy men."

He looked at me carefully. "Do you see what I mean about how those unhealthy men skewed the data?"

"Dr. Gupta adjusted for that in the statistical analysis. The reviewers felt that he did the analysis correctly."

Cosgrove's blank expression revealed a lot to me. This guy had no idea how statistical analysis should be performed. He was just following the Pharmamax party line.

"I don't understand how they can say that," he said. "You can't compare apples to oranges."

"How many projects have you worked on that were large and involved complex statistical analysis, Bill?"

He sputtered. "This is my first one. But it doesn't matter. The correct way to do the analysis is obvious." Yes, it appeared to be obvious if you were clueless about the right way to do it. "Listen," he went on, "Pritpal obviously had developed some kind of bias against the pharmaceutical industry. That's ridiculous; we practice medicine here and we know the value of new medications. The nation, the world, needs the drug industry to continue with its R&D efforts full steam. They are producing amazing breakthroughs every year."

"Some of those 'breakthroughs' are not quite as amazing as they first appear."

"For instance?" he demanded.

"What about HRT?" HRT was short for 'hormone replacement therapy', which was used to treat the symptoms of menopause.

"The complications from HRT are greatly exaggerated," he asserted with impressive confidence.

"In the sixties when the drug companies started promoting HRT to treat menopausal symptoms, the risk of cancer had already been known for over thirty years. The recent findings about the increased risk of cancer and other problems should not have surprised anyone who had done their homework. Some critics have gone so far as to say that the industry redefined menopause as a disease so that they could sell a treatment for it."

Cosgrove was glaring at me. "Look," I said, "I'm not trying to say HRT is bad because obviously some women benefit from it. What I am saying is that sometimes drug companies exaggerate benefits and minimize risks in their enthusiasm to get a drug to market. Acmemedpub has to take an objective stance on this, a stance that puts scientific validity and the public interest on the front burner."

Cosgrove gritted his teeth. "That sounds okay as long as you guys are not as biased as Pritpal was. You have to get your facts straight."

"That's what I'm here for. Do you suppose you can help with a few of those facts?"

"Sure. What do you need?"

"First, I would like to review your correspondence with Pharmamax regarding the Erecta project."

"I guess that would be okay." It probably violated a few regulations, but he didn't know that.

"Next, I would like to review the University policy on conflict of interest."

"Oh, that's easy. We will pull that out for you."

"And I would also like to see your University policy on institutional conflict of interest."

"Isn't that the same thing?"

"No, not really. Do you have an institutional conflict of interest committee?"

"Heck if I know. I will have someone look for it." He picked up the phone and asked someone to locate the files I had requested.

"Just a few more questions. Is Erecta primarily a therapeutic drug or a recreational drug?"

"That is a ridiculous question. It's therapeutic, of course."

"Is it likely that some abuse of the drug will occur after it's on the market?"

"That is always a possibility. We can't prevent that from happening. Why is it relevant?"

"In any ethical analysis, we have to weigh the benefits against the risks. We have an ethical duty to do what is in the best interests of patients, while also respecting the patients' own preferences about how to live their lives. These requirements are not easy to reconcile. I was just trying to get the facts straight so I could think about it."

"Oh, sure." He obviously had no interest in this line of reasoning. "By the way," he said, "before I forget, there are three more things I have to mention. First, our statistician will talk to you in a few minutes. He can explain the technical issues. Second, Dr. Jones, the vice president for research, would like to meet with you this morning. My secretary will escort you to the administration building after you have reviewed those files. The third matter is a bit unexpected." Cosgrove picked up a pink telephone message note from his desk. "Dr. Gupta's widow heard somehow that you were going to be in town. She would like you to come over to her house and talk to her."

"That's awkward. I don't want to intrude on her grief."

"I understand. But it's her request. The address and phone number are on this note." He handed it to me.

"How did he die, anyway?"

"Apparently, he just keeled over at home. These things happen to guys his age. He was over sixty."

A knock on the door signaled that the files I had requested were ready for me. Cosgrove stood up, eager to be rid of me.

"One more question, Bill."

He waited, poised impatiently behind his desk. "Sure, but I have patients to see. Fire away."

"Do you have any financial relationship with Pharmamax?"

His face became guarded, his eyes hooded. "We have a research grant from them, obviously."

"Do you have a personal consulting arrangement with them? Have they provided you money or resources other than the research grant? Have they paid for any travel on your behalf?"

"We're done here," Cosgrove said and marched out of the office.

Chapter 5.

Review of Project Records

The secretary led me into an unoccupied examination room and handed me a folder, then left me alone to study the documents.

The conflict of interest policy clearly stated that employees could not accept gratuities, fees, or other items of value from any company or individual if, in so doing, it affected the performance of their duties. However, no committee or other mechanism had been created to monitor the staff to see if conflicts were occurring. The only way any action would be taken was if someone's colleague ratted them out. An accusation would lead to an investigation by the vice president for research and development, the man I was scheduled to meet with next. It was interesting that he was vice president for both research and development. Development, in universities and in many other organizations, means fund-raising. Combining research administration with fund-raising suggested that the University viewed the activities as being similar. I had to sigh about that. At one time, research was about generating new knowledge; now it was measured in dollars.

The next set of documents was interesting. These chronicled the correspondence between Pritpal Gupta and the office in Pharmamax that was charged with monitoring the conduct of research projects. Federal regulations were strict about monitoring, so Pharmamax periodically sent out site visitors to verify that all the files were in order. Unfortunately, in the case of the Erecta study, the records were not quite complete. The site visitor had noted that several dozen doses of the experimental medicine were unaccounted for. They were not in the storage area and they had not been given to patients. They were just lost. Dr. Gupta had been warned that if he didn't find them the matter would have to be reported to the VP for research. That was interesting. I wondered what was going on with the missing meds.

As I was closing the file, someone knocked on the door. When I opened it, an extremely attractive woman in her early thirties was revealed. She had a bright smile on her face. "Hi," she said, "you must be Dr. Schumacher."

"Yep, that's me."

She thrust out her hand for a shake. "I'm Allison Smart, the Pharmamax representative in this area."

"Pleased to meet you."

She pointed at the folder in my hand. "You've been reviewing the project correspondence, I hear."

"Yes, that's right."

"Those are supposed to be kept confidential. Dr. Cosgrove should not have given them to you."

"You got me there." I gave her my most winning smile. "Maybe I was testing him."

She laughed. "Nice try, but it won't wash. You're busted. But I'll let you off the hook if you let me brief you on the project. You should get the company's point of view. I'll buy you dinner. The company will pay for it."

"Tell you what: we can have dinner and you can brief me, but I'll buy my own."

My response introduced a note of worry into her expression. "Okay, if you insist. There is a four-star restaurant that I like to take people to. We can go there."

"Not on my budget. I saw a Mexican restaurant on the edge of town as I drove in this morning. Near the intersection of Highway 12 and the interstate. Let's go there."

She scowled with distaste. "If you insist. How about six o'clock? That way you can get on the road before it gets dark."

"Good enough. See you there."

Ms. Smart took the folder from me and left the room.

Chapter 6.
Interview with Kim Lee

A soft rapping sound got my attention. Obviously, my mind had wandered as I considered how to deal with the drug rep. The rapping was the sound made by a tall Chinese man who stood by the door. I jumped up to greet him.

"You must be Dr. Lee. Thank you very much for talking to me about this project. I'm sure it will help a great deal."

"I am pleased to be of assistance," he said. He had a slight accent.

"You know why I am here?"

Lee hesitated. "Dr. Cosgrove said you are sent by the Journal."

"That's right. We just want to verify a few of the facts. But first, can you give me a little background on yourself, so I know who I'm dealing with?"

Lee blinked, then answered, "I have been here, in this job, for twelve years. Before that I was in graduate school at the University of Michigan, where I was given a Ph.D. in biostatistics. I came to the United States from China."

"You are too modest. I looked you up on the internet, and, unless I got the wrong Kim Lee at the Medical University of Madison, you have an impressive list of publications."

"Thank you. Yes, I am listed on twenty-six articles. My role is to compute the statistics and write down the explanation."

"You must be an associate professor with tenure by now."

Lee's face froze. "I am a research assistant professor, so I am not eligible for tenure."

"But you should at least be an associate professor."

"Promotion is based on grant money. I have not been the principal investigator for a funded research project, so I am not eligible for promotion."

"Well, that's unfortunate. Not too surprising, but still unfortunate." I changed directions. "At least they acknowledged your contribution to the Gupta article. You are listed as a co-author. The statistical analysis was complex, so I am sure the paper could not have been written without your help."

"Thank you."

"The reviewers were impressed with how you did it. Some wanted to rush to early publication because it was so good."

"Thank you. I am pleased to learn that they liked my work." He was starting to relax a little.

"What we don't understand is why Dr. Cosgrove thinks the results of the project should be completely reversed."

Lee said nothing.

"Did you perform the statistical analysis for Cosgrove that led to the reversal of conclusions?"

"Yes."

"Did you think the new approach was appropriate?"

"It is not my job to tell the lead investigator he is wrong. He tells me what he wants, then I write the program and tell him the results."

"But you are more qualified to determine the statistical approach than Cosgrove. Do you think the new approach is better than the old one?"

Lee was starting to look angry. "It is not my job to argue with Dr. Cosgrove," he said.

I just sat there and waited for a better explanation. Lee came out with it after about half a minute.

"I do not have tenure. I am not a US citizen and I must have a job to stay in the United States."

This was what I expected him to say. It was an old story, and not one that universities should be proud of. Foreign nationals were exploited in academic jobs from the time they began their graduate studies until well after they should have been treated as equals to their American-born colleagues. This was especially true for PhDs working in medical schools. As graduate students, they were required to take classes for several years more than was really necessary because the 'classes' involved doing research for professors. After they had been awarded their doctorates, they were denied the usual job security of a university position. Of course, this kept people like Lee as compliant and cooperative as they could stomach; it was a matter of survival.

I sighed and changed the subject.

"Dr. Lee, do you happen to do know how Dr. Gupta died?"

"I believe he had a myocardial infarction, a heart attack."

"Did you know he had heart disease?"

Lee shrugged. "He was over sixty and overweight. Perhaps he did not eat enough fish."

"One more question. Did you know some Erecta pills turned up missing?"

"I know nothing about that."

"Thank you, Dr. Lee," I said. "I don't have any more questions for you."

The secretary appeared to very busy, so I asked for directions and set off on my own. Finding the administration building proved to be a challenge, but then I always got lost whenever I was going to someplace new, so it didn't bother me.

Betty tended to get frustrated with this aspect of my nature. Really, what difference did it make if you had to wander around a bit? The world was an interesting place and when you were lost you got to see more of it.

I was pretty sure that Betty had not gotten what she expected when she married me. She would have preferred a rich husband, for instance. I asked her about this issue one time.

"If your life had turned out differently, you might have married a wealthy guy and you could have been a rich wife. Do you think you would have liked that?"

"Maybe." She considered the possibility some more. "Being a rich man's wife is a pretty darn good job. You have plenty of money, so everybody treats you well. You can just do what you want to do all day long."

"If it's so great, why do some rich wives seem to be pretty unhappy?"

"With some of them, their husbands have dumped them and they are really angry because they're not rich wives anymore."

"Do you think they always were nasty and that is why their husbands dumped them?"

Betty considered that possibility for a moment. Any time the subject of divorce came up, her instinct was to side with the wife on the general principle best summed up with the phrase 'men are slime.' This time, though, she didn't do that. "Some of these women probably were nasty to start with. Their own kids don't want to have anything to do with them."

"The big question is still this: would you be happier if you had married a rich guy?"

She had to think about that one for awhile.

Chapter 7

Interview with James Jones

James Jones, Ph.D., inhabited a large office populated with a big desk covered with papers and a conference room table with half a dozen chairs around it. His secretary ushered me in, then closed the door behind her. Jones rose from his desk to shake my hand then directed me to take a chair at the table. He sat across from me.

Jones looked to be about sixty years of age. He wore his hair like Ronald Reagan: heavily greased, combed back, carefully parted on one side. He was a tubby fellow, heavy through the torso and enormous in the tail end. His rear was so large I wondered if he had some kind of disorder.

"Well, Dr. Schumacher," Jones said, "we are delighted to have you visiting with us. Dr. Cosgrove told me you would be talking to him this morning. I just wanted to take the opportunity to ask you how it was going and offer to facilitate in any way I can." He smiled insincerely, eyes bugging out like a bull frog.

"Thanks. I appreciate that." Having responded politely, I stopped talking. An awkward silence lay between us like last year's fruitcake: dry, tasteless, and difficult to eliminate.

Jones cleared his throat. "Hmmph. Do you have any questions for me?" He really wanted to ask me what conclusions I was likely to reach, but was not ready to pry. Not yet, anyway.

"Sure. Why is a vice president interested in a minor matter like this? After all, this is just one journal article. Your school produces hundreds every year." I already knew the answer to this question, but wanted to hear how he would respond.

"As you know, Dr. Schumacher, the study was funded by a major pharmaceutical company. If the paper is published with erroneous conclusions, it will reflect badly on our institution. Frankly, Pharmamax may not want to work with us again."

"You have been funded by them extensively in the recent past?"

"Very extensively. And when Erecta is successful, the company will come to us for a lot more work. I think you realize the enormous profit potential of a drug like this. The revenues will be staggering. Pharmamax will roll some of those revenues back into additional R&D so that they can find new applications for the medication. We expect to receive a lot of those R&D contracts."

I decided to play dumb. "Since the research funds you receive are all spent on research, there is no profit to speak of. In my experience, finding free data to do research with is pretty easy, and publishing that way is much faster than if you apply for grants, wait for them to come in, then take all the time it takes to collect your own data. Why do you care whether you get any money from a pharmaceutical company? As I said, there is no profit; the money is a pass-through."

Jones looked dumbfounded. Clearly, it had been a long time since anyone had questioned the value of getting more money in his presence. He had to gather his thoughts.

"I suspect you already know the answer to that question. First, grants and contracts include administrative overhead costs that are used to fund the Office of the Vice President for Research. We could not operate without them."

"Nor would you need to," I mumbled under my breath.

"Secondly, medical school rankings are determined by the amount of research funds they acquire."

"And not by the amount of new knowledge you produce," I mumbled again.

"And thirdly, our board of regents has mandated that we increase our research funding."

"The regents are academics who understand how new knowledge is produced?"

"Hummph. Actually, most of them are successful business people."

"Ah. So they understand making money, respect making money, but don't know much about academics."

Jones looked pained. "You may be overstating the case."

"Do they spend much of their time talking about the findings of research projects and what additional knowledge is needed to advance medical treatment?

"Of course not. Our basketball team has had coaching problems, so they concentrate on the athletic program. After all, they are managers; they don't have to know anything about research in order to manage a research University."

"That is an interesting point of view. And you, Dr. Jones, what is your field of research? I'll look you up on the internet and read some of your articles."

"You don't need to bother," he said hastily. "It's been a long time since I was on the production end of the process. These days I just function as a manager." He smiled proudly. Then he shifted uncertainly. "Would you mind, uh, giving me a sense, uh, a brief preview, uh, of what your conclusions on this matter might look like?" The sentence structure was awkward, but it was clear what he was asking.

"That would be inappropriate, I'm afraid. The publisher made it clear that I should be reticent."

"Oh. That's unfortunate."

The phone on his desk rang at that moment. Jones picked it up and said shortly, "I said to hold all calls (pause). Oh, it's him (pause). Go ahead and connect him (pause). Good morning, sir (pause). Yes, he's here now (pause). Not very well, I'm afraid (pause). Yes sir, I'll arrange it." Jones laid his hands in his lap and said formally, "Dr. Simpson would like to talk to you.

He happens to have an opening in his calendar right now. I will take you down the hall to his office."

"Who is Dr. Simpson?"

Jones finally showed a little irritation with me. "Dr. Hubert Simpson is president of the University."

"Let me ask you a couple of questions before we go." Jones looked nervous and impatient. "Don't worry; I'll be brief. First, I have to ask if you are aware of any financial conflicts of interest involved in the Erecta project."

"Physicians are an uncommonly ethical group. Dishonesty does not occur, or hardly ever."

"Yes, I agree that it's rare. But it does happen occasionally. The National Institutes of Health had to come down hard on some of its people for taking money on the sly. And the federal Securities and Exchange Commission found over twenty cases of physicians selling confidential research information to biotech companies. You know that if they found twenty, then they missed hundreds. And physicians have been prosecuted for trading on inside information about the results of drug research projects."

"If there were any conflicts of interest in this University, that information would be confidential. But be assured that if any conflicts of interest were reported to me, I would investigate thoroughly." Jones raised his wobbly chin and tried to look firm and steadfast. It was not very convincing.

"Next question. Are you aware of any serious procedural problems with the Erecta project?"

"Same answer as before. Confidential. We would investigate thoroughly if any problems came to our attention." Then he led the way to the Great Man's office.

Chapter 8.

Interview with the President

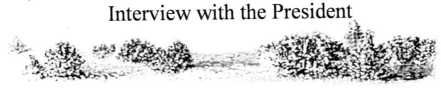

We checked in with the administrative assistant who guarded the president's door, and she led us into the inner sanctum. Simpson met us at the door with an outstretched hand. He dismissed Jones immediately, then led me into a large and luxurious office. Simpson was every inch the powerful executive. His suit probably cost as much as my car. He was slim, debonair, and every hair was in place. He also exuded good will. He sat behind his desk and waved me into a leather-upholstered armchair in front of it. He directed his full attention at me, smiling charmingly. This was the kind of man who could make you feel as if he cared about you personally the instant you met him. However, I knew it was a carefully cultivated act that he could turn off at will.

"How is your visit going with us, Dr. Schumacher?"

"Very well, thank you. I'm learning a lot."

"Excellent, excellent." He seemed to be genuinely delighted, even though I was sure he already had heard that I might be turning over more rocks than he would have preferred.

"Are you learning anything that I should know about? We take our responsibilities seriously as I'm sure you realize. If something needs to be corrected, I will make sure it happens."

"I'm afraid I can't say just yet. I'm still gathering information."

"Good, good. We all want you to do a thorough job, so we can put this matter to rest and get on with other things."

"Acmemedpub agrees with you. I hope to wrap up the fact-finding aspects of the inquiry today."

"That is great news!" He beamed a sparkling smile at me. "Is there any way I can help? Is our leadership team coming through for you? We have a strong leadership philosophy here, you know. Strong leadership has made the Medical University of Madison the strong institution it is today."

"Really?" I asked innocently.

That one-word question threw him off stride.

"Well, of course. That is why we are ranked as one of the best medical schools in the nation."

"Is it?"

He didn't answer, clearly at a loss for words.

"I would have thought that great doctors had something to do with it." I suggested.

'Yes, yes, of course. But having great physicians is not enough by itself. Leadership makes the difference."

"Does it really? Do you have any evidence to support that theory?"

"Theory? That's not a theory; it's a fact. You can't seriously question the value of strong leadership."

"You'll have to excuse me. I've made my career as a researcher. That makes me a professional skeptic. I need to see evidence before I accept an assertion as a proven fact. You clearly are operating with an hypothesis in mind. You believe that strong leadership results in better organizational performance. Have you tested that hypothesis? Has anyone?"

Simpson sputtered. "Of course, it's been tested. Everyone in management knows it to be true."

"I would be interested in seeing the research reports that support your claim. Frankly, I don't know how you would go about measuring leadership. And if you can't measure it, then you can't test an hypothesis about whether leadership affects performance. So tell me, Dr. Simpson, how do you measure leadership?"

He was starting to get a bit red in the face. "When an organization performs as well as we do, it proves we have strong leadership. That's because we stress accountability. Accountability is paramount."

"That's a circular argument, but still it's great to hear you say accountability is important. Not every executive is committed to accountability."

"But they should be, they certainly should be." He was trying to regain control over the conversation.

"Since good organizational performance is something the leadership can take credit for, is poor organizational performance their responsibility as well?"

"Eh?" He didn't know how to respond to that.

"In my experience, managers are like politicians: when things turn out well they tend to believe it is due to their own brilliance, but when things go badly, it's due to circumstances beyond their control."

"And that is usually the case."

"Surely you can see the inconsistency in that. If you are accountable for good results then you should be accountable for mistakes."

"Yes, yes, of course. We do that. We take responsibility for our mistakes."

"According to the local newspaper, a federal audit agency says your grant accounting was done poorly. Is someone accountable for that?"

"That is a complex issue. Too complex to go into now." Simpson was starting to get pretty upset with me. "Look, you can't seriously be questioning the vital role good management plays in our society."

"I'm sorry if I've upset you. It's only natural that managers tend to believe they are special. Every primitive tribe in human history has believed it was special, superior to all outsiders. But surely you can see how self-serving that kind of thinking really is." Simpson's mouth was hanging open in amazement. Did he just hear me describe managers as a primitive tribe with a self-serving philosophy?

"What amazes me," I continued, "is that every other type of chauvinism is regarded as unacceptable in our culture today. Racial superiority, gender superiority, superiority based on wealth—these are all seen as bigotry. But when managers create a leadership mystique and regard themselves as the chosen ones, no one questions it."

I held up my hand to stop an imminent outburst. "Now, I know I am goring a sacred cow and that sort of behavior always makes people angry. But in my own defense, let me say that I am motivated by a different sacred cow, and my cow is bigger than your cow."

"And what sacred cow might that be?" Simpson was gritting his teeth. He obviously wished he had never asked to talk to me. But now he was curious about what crazy argument I was going to make to defend my point of view.

"Why, the Judeo-Christian ethic, of course." His mouth fell open again. "Anybody who went to a church or synagogue learned that power and money are corrupting influences. Managers work with power and money every day. Radiologists wear little radiation safety badges that tell them how much exposure they have received. Managers should have to wear little corruption safety badges, so that everyone knows when one of you has built up too much of a dose. Then he can be pulled out of the game for a while. The problem is managers don't know when they have become corrupted. First, they are attracted to power and money. Then, they learn to love them. They idolize them. Then they feel entitled to do whatever is necessary to keep what they have, then to acquire more and more."

"Not all managers are corrupt!" He shouted. "That's nonsense!"

'No, not all of them. But think about the Bible. We all remember the good leaders in the Bible. Men like Abraham, Moses, and Solomon. But for every good leader the Bible tells about, many other nasty leaders are described. Someone should compute the ratio of morally good to morally bad leaders in the Bible and see if the same ratio applies today."

"The Bible described leaders from thousands of years ago" Simpson ranted. "Society was primitive, uncivilized. Corruption would be the norm under those circumstances. But things are different today. We're civilized."

"How different is it today, really? What about Enron, Worldcom and the rest? Chicanery is everywhere. And management attracts sociopaths like sugar attracts flies."

"I don't have time for this," said the president of the Medical University of Madison. He escorted me to the door, then slammed it shut behind me. I must say, it was a very enjoyable meeting.

I practically skipped down the steps in front of the administration building. Then I stopped suddenly. Wasn't I being hypocritical? I was being a holier-than-thou, hypocritical, pompous jerk! Of course universities were rife with greed, even driven by greed. But I was not innocent of that charge either. I was trying to sell electric bike motors out of my garage. That clearly was a case of pursuing profits to the utmost of my abilities. I had jumped at the opportunity to take this assignment. Once again, I was greedy. What a hypocrite! People who live in glass houses shouldn't throw stones. We should take the plank out of our own eye before we try to take the splinter out of someone else's.

Despite all my best efforts, I still was pretty pleased with myself. Maybe Betty was right; maybe I just liked to cause trouble.

That tendency caused her no end of embarrassment. Given how stressed out she was, I really should have tried harder to contain my own sociopathic tendencies. Unfortunately, they just tended to slip out.

But, I reminded myself, I needed this gig to succeed, if for no other reason than because Betty needed for it to succeed. If I had a regular income, she could relax. Until I did, she would be feeling extra pressure. The other night the conversation had gone like this.

"Tell me you are going to start making some money."

"I'm going to start making some money."

"You don't know that. You have to reassure me. Tell me you will get a job for sure! And be convincing!"

"I'm going to make millions."

"Now you are making fun of me. You're always minimizing my concerns!"

"But you want me to reassure you."

'You idiot! Yes, I want you to reassure me, but you don't need to minimize my fears.

"Just kidding. Look, we will get through this. Things will get easier."

For Betty's sake, I really needed to succeed at being a consulting ethicist. Still, I knew that, because of the kind of guy I was, I might mess it up. As Betty liked to say, we have to do the best we can with what we have to work with. I just hoped that what I had to work with was good enough to get the job done.

When I reached the bottom step in front of the administration building, a fresh-faced young woman approached me. "Excuse me, sir," she said, "are you a researcher?"

"Well, yes, I guess I am."

"I'm doing a report. May I ask you a few questions?"

A student wanted to pick my brain! I puffed with pride. It had been a long time since I had enjoyed the opportunity of pontificating to a student. When you were teaching, sometimes people actually listened to your ideas, which was very gratifying. Sometimes they even laughed at your jokes, which seldom happened to me otherwise.

"As it turns out, I need to grab a bite for lunch before going to my next meeting. There's a Wendy's over there. Let's talk while we eat.

She agreed. I bought a bowl of chili and a medium drink. The price for chili, crackers, hot sauce and a diet coke was only a couple of bucks. I offered to buy my new protege something to eat but she declined, thank goodness; young people have enormous appetites.

Chapter 9.

Interview with Madison Albright

We settled into a small table. The restaurant was filled with students, many of them lugging backpacks. The intense energy the crowd of young people exuded was exciting, but I knew I would not be able to tolerate it for very long. It would get on my nerves.

"Do you mind if I record this? It will help me get everything right." She pulled a small tape recorder out of her purse and activated it. I smiled indulgently; she was really taking this seriously.

"My name is Madison Albright," she announced. "What's yours?"

"Ed Schumacher."

"Are you a professor?"

"Yes, but retired from academics. I'm just visiting the University on business."

"Does it have to do with research?"

"Yes. I'm here to talk about medical research with some of the faculty. They needed help with a few ethical issues." I smiled modestly.

"What kind of ethical issues? I thought research was just science, you know, technical stuff."

"That is what most people think. But research involving human subjects always gets tangled up with ethical issues. We have to be very careful to respect everyone's rights and to not let our biases affect our conclusions."

"Is that what happened here? Is that why you came, because the research being done here is biased?"

"We're trying to make sure that doesn't happen."

"Are you working on that problem we saw in the paper? There was something in the paper about grant accounting being messed up. Are you here about that?"

"No, no. Finances are not my area. On the other hand, money influences everything. That is one of the reasons why we have to be so careful about not letting our biases influence our conclusions. Money can create a very strong bias, even if we don't realize it."

"Can you give me an example?" She looked at me with her eyes wide open and innocent, just like my cat.

"Well, take that new sexual performance medicine for women, Ambrosia. The drug company that makes it is making a lot of money from it. They just naturally will want the researchers who study it to find out positive things."

"Ambrosia? They come up with such strange names for medicines. I never can remember them. Or spell them."

"Maybe they should call it 'Superhot'," I suggested with a smile.

She smiled also. "Yes, that's much better. I think I will use that instead."

She was so naïve, I thought. You can't make up your own names for things. This will lower her grade. Or it would if I was grading her paper.

"Do they have something like that for men?" she asked.

"Yes. In fact, this University is studying a new one. It's called 'Erecta'."

"Oh, that's gross."

"Could have been worse. They could have called it something like 'Superstud.'"

"Oh, Professor Schumacher! You are so funny."

We chuckled together like old friends.

"You mentioned how drug companies pressure researchers to bias their research so that it makes their medicines look better than they are. Is that happening here, Professor Schumacher?" She was starting to sound more professional.

At that point I realized that a young man at the next table was pointing a video camera at us.

"Do you see that?" I asked.

"Oh, people do that all the time," she said.

"But you shouldn't take pictures of people without their permission."

"He's with me. And you said you would talk to me."

"You need a video for a term paper?" This was new one on me.

"Professor Schumacher, I said I was working on a report. I most definitely did not say I was writing a term paper. I am not a student; I'm a reporter for Channel 6 News. We are doing a story on possible research improprieties at the University. What can you tell us about that?"

"This is going to be on television news?" I was stunned.

"The editors will decide that, but I expect some of it will."

I feverishly reviewed the last few minutes in my mind, wondering how much trouble I had gotten myself into. "I'm afraid I can't talk to you anymore, Ms. Albright. I'm late for my next meeting. Bye, now." And I got out of there so fast I forgot my chili.

I ran for my car, which was difficult because I could not remember where it was parked. After about ten seconds, I slowed to a more sedate pace. As I wandered up and down State Street, dodging the drug addicts, students, parents, and tourists, I mentally kicked myself for being an idiot. Acmemedpub had specifically told me not to talk to the press. All I could do was hope the editors spiked the interview, or that it would be such a minor story that no one outside of Madison would hear about it.

That reporter had tricked me. But I had to forgive myself. After all, Betty always said I was easy to trick, so easy she had stopped bothering with it. Not enough of a challenge, she said.

Chapter 10.

Interview with Mrs. Gupta

The Gupta home was located in an up-scale residential neighborhood where the homes were well-maintained, the yards were neatly manicured, and the visible cars were all relatively new. Their house was a two-story place with bay windows and large trees on every side. The leaves had turned and the smell of autumn was in the air.

The woman who answered the door was in her fifties. She was more than a little plump and dusky. Her eyes were exuding sadness and had dark circles under them. She was wearing dark clothes, a blouse and a black skirt that reached nearly to the floor. When I told her my name she invited me in.

We seated ourselves in the living room, which happened to be the room with the bay window. Mrs. Gupta chose an overstuffed chair and I sat on the couch. The drawn drapes were heavy and made the room dark. She had turned on a couple of table lamps, but they did little to relieve the gloom. Mrs. Gupta was drinking white wine, which she offered me, but I declined.

"I'm sorry about your loss," I said. "Dr. Gupta and I never met, but what little I know about him is impressive. He must have been a man of conscience."

She teared up at that and sobbed quietly for a moment. Then she said, "Thank you. He was a good man. Many people will miss him."

"I don't want to intrude on your day any more than necessary, Mrs. Gupta. You invited me over, so you must have had something you wanted to talk about. What can I do for you?"

"Friends at the University told me about your visit," she said. "I thought it was important that you have some important facts about the project - facts you would not have heard from Dr. Cosgrove."

"Yes? And what facts do you mean?"

"First, you should know that Pharmamax is a horrid company. They are only interested in making money and they will go to any length to increase their profits. Of course, they produce some fine medicines, but the methods they use to sell them are, well, let's just say they are unsavory." She twisted her mouth in disgust.

"What do you mean?"

"Well, for example, they seduce their researchers to reach conclusions that will be good for sales."

"Seduce is a strong word."

Mrs. Gupta was starting to get upset. Her face darkened, she started breathing heavily, and she began to fan herself with a magazine. "Seduce is the word I meant to use, Dr. Schumacher. It is not too strong for what they do. They hold conferences in luxury hotels in the Caribbean. At these conferences they wine and dine the researchers and provide for their every whim."

"I imagine those meetings are well-attended."

"You can be sure they are. Everyone loves to go to those meetings. Pharmamax also gives most of their researchers consulting contracts that are little more than outright bribes. As you might expect, the researchers quickly become used to receiving a second paycheck." Her dark eyes flashed with outrage, but I sensed a hypocritical note; the nice home she was living in suggested to me that the Gupta family also had taken their share of side payments from Pharmamax.

"And they do more than that," she spat. "They send young women, whom they call sales representatives, to flatter and cajole the researchers so that they remain committed to company policy. Those women will do anything to keep the researchers compliant." She leaned forward and said in a whisper, "Dr. Cosgrove is completely wrapped around the little finger of that Smart woman. The way they carry on is shameful."

"That's interesting. I can't say I'm too surprised, Mrs. Gupta. Please be assured that all this will be taken into account when I write my report for Acmemedpub. But, please, could you tell me why you thought it was important that I know these things?"

"Because they are trying to undo my husband's work!" she cried. "They want you to believe that he was mistaken in his conclusions, but he wasn't! Erecta does increase the risk of heart attacks, or he would not have said so. They are maligning his good name and destroying his final contribution to scientific medicine!"

"And writing this final contribution the way he did required a great deal of courage on his part. You want him to receive the recognition he deserves."

She beamed. "You understand perfectly! I'm so grateful." She leaned back and fanned herself energetically. "It is so warm in here. I am going to get some ice water. Would you like some, Dr. Schumacher?"

"Thank you, but no, I will have to be leaving soon. May I use your restroom before I go?"

"Of course. It's just down the hall on your left."

We both left the room. While I was in the lavatory, I had an irresistible attack of curiosity. Was it possible that Gupta had taken the missing doses of Erecta for his own use? I opened the cabinet above the basin and began reading the labels of the pill bottles arrayed along the shelves. A bottle of Erecta was pushed to the back of the cabinet. I wondered if Mrs. Gupta knew it was there. In the process of finding it, I could not help noticing a bottle of Ambrosia was also present.

When I returned to the living room, there was something else I could not help noticing: Mrs. Gupta was different. Somehow her clothes were looser on her body and the top buttons of her blouse were unfastened. She urged me to stay for a moment longer, so I returned to my seat on the couch. She sat next to me, then put her hand on my arm.

"Dr. Schumacher," she purred, "I must tell you how glad I am that you came by to see me. I am so grateful to be able to tell someone the truth."

"You had a lot to get off your chest."

She giggled, causing her ample cleavage to shake in a disturbing fashion. "Oh, yes. There is nothing on my chest now." The woman had undergone an amazing personality change, from grieving widow to femme fatale. She scooted closer to me on the couch. "I feel strongly that I should express my appreciation to you as firmly as I can," she said.

"Ummm. That's not necessary, Mrs. Gupta."

"Oh, it's only what any good hostess would do, especially with such an intelligent and attractive guest." Her hand strayed from my knee upward. "Oh, Dr. Schumacher, I think you know what I mean!" she cooed.

I bolted off the couch. "That's my cue to go, Mrs. Gupta. Thanks for the hospitality, but, of course, there is work I should be doing." I started backing toward the door, but she immediately stood next to me and wrapped her arms around my waist.

"Oh no. I won't hear of it. You must stay a little while at least." She started undoing my tie.

I pulled free and ran for the front door, but she was too fast for me. She blocked the door with her body, then with a languid smile began taking off her blouse. The woman outweighed me by fifty pounds and I could see no way of getting past her without striking her. I ran toward the back of the house, searching for a rear exit. Her feet pounded on the floor behind me, so I dashed into the bathroom, slammed the door, and locked it. She was angry now, pounding on the door and screaming shrilly in frustration.

There is no other way to say it: I was scared. I admit it. Maybe a man should not admit he is afraid of a woman in heat but I was frightened right down to the bottom of my cowardly little heart. Pulling out my cell phone, I called 9-1-1.

When the operator answered, I said. "I'm being assaulted by a crazy woman!"

"Yes sir," said the operator. "Where are you right now?"

"I locked myself in the bathroom."

"Does she have a weapon of any sort?"

"No. Not that I know of."

"Are you in danger of physical harm?"

"Yes! She's twice as big as I am!"

The operator dispatched a police car to the Gupta address and they arrived just as the bathroom door began to splinter from Mrs. Gupta's assault. I could hear muffled sounds through the door, shouting and banging, but the noises were not right next to the door, so I opened it cautiously and peaked out. The action was taking place in the hallway. A young male police officer was down on his back with Mrs. Gupta astride him. She was shouting "yes, yes!" while a female police officer was trying to subdue her with a headlock. While they were shouting and wrestling, I slipped past them and headed out to my car. A small crowd of neighbors was beginning to gather, peering in the open front door to see what was happening. Perhaps I should have remained behind to make some kind of statement, but frankly the whole situation was too embarrassing. Besides, it was not clear to me who was going to win the battle, Mrs. Gupta or the two police officers. She might have ended up bedding them both. Discretion being the better part of valor, I drove away as quickly as possible.

Chapter 11

Interview with Allison Smart

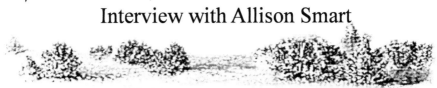

The experience with Mrs. Gupta had left me shaken, so I drove directly to the restaurant where Allison Smart and I were scheduled to meet, parked in a sunny spot, then lit my pipe while leaning against the car. The leaves were blowing a bit and the breeze made lighting the pipe difficult. Cigarette smokers never seemed to have this problem, but those folks were definitely a different breed of person. My grandfather used to sell cars. He said that when a cigarette smoker came in to look at cars, the salesmen were delighted because they anticipated a quick sale. Sometimes, though, when a customer had been shown a car he liked, he would pull out a pipe and start to set it up for a smoke. The salesman would have to stifle a groan, because pipe smokers could not be rushed into a sale. A pipe smoker would relax and think about the advantages and disadvantages of the car, its options, and its price. Eventually he would get around to saying the price should be lower. In the relaxed euphoria of nicotine absorbed through the lining of the mouth, he would not care very much whether he bought the car or not. This example, in a nutshell, captures the difference between pipe smokers and cigarette smokers: cigarette smokers seek the nervous energy the nicotine gives them whereas pipe smokers seek the relaxation they get from nicotine. Of course, both are bad for your health, but if you think both are equally bad for you then you are just being pig-headed.

By the time Allison Smart arrived, I was mellow again. The experience with Mrs. Gupta had been harrowing, but it was over. The entrapment by a TV news reporter had greater potential for causing me serious trouble, but what was done was done. The ten o'clock news that evening would tell me how much of a disaster it really was. I would just have to wait and see. With any luck, the news clip would end up on the cutting room floor.

Ms. Smart saw me in the parking lot when she disembarked from her jaguar. She had changed clothes and now was a bit overdressed for such an ordinary restaurant. She wore a short black sheath dress that molded itself to her curvaceous body and spiked heels. Her calves and the lower part of her legs were muscular, which some men may find attractive, but it didn't do a thing for me. In all honesty, beautiful as she was, my first impression was summed up in just one word: barracuda. This creature would eat me for dinner if I wasn't careful.

We had no trouble finding a table. Allison suggested drinks, but I declined since I was facing a thirty minute drive home. Besides, I wanted to keep my wits about me. So, we ordered our meals immediately and relaxed with glasses of iced tea.

"How has your day been going?" Allison asked me, after we had briefly discussed the nice weather and how quickly the seasons went by.

"Good enough," I replied. "Can't complain."

"You've learned how important this line of research is for men who have performance problems, I hope."

"It certainly could make a difference in a person's quality of life."

"I'm glad you realize that." She hesitated, wondering how to make her approach. "Professor Schumacher – may I call you Ed?"

"Sure thing."

"Ed, this new product will be very big. Many interesting research questions are coming up. We need skilled investigators who know something about the subject to help us get all of this sorted out as quickly as possible. You seem like the sort of person who could be invaluable to us. Would you have any interest in a consulting arrangement? I can promise you that we would pay the most competitive rates. Whatever you are getting from Acmemedpub and your other clients, I am sure we could offer enough to get your exclusive services."

"That's very flattering, but you know my doctorate is in public health, not laboratory science."

"We need epidemiological work just as much as we need bench science." Allison leaned back and crossed her legs, then began playing with her napkin. "We have conferences periodically where we bring in experts such as yourself to educate the bench scientists about the big issues. These are held in very nice locations and we treat everyone very nicely: luxurious suites, gourmet meals, all expenses paid. Many of our consultants appreciate the opportunity to blow off the stresses of their work in situations where they have complete privacy." She smiled. "I like to have a good time myself, as I'm sure you do. Admit it, you would enjoy a little dip in a secluded hot tub, wouldn't you? You can even wear a swimming suit if you wanted to, though no one else ever has." She flashed me a brilliant smile, with a knowing look in her eyes.

This made me swallow hard. But having escaped one predatory female that day, I was prepared to evade this one as well.

"You are tempting me, no doubt about it. But I would prefer just to stay close to home these days. Bad ticker, you know." I patted myself on my chest to make the point.

Allison's face showed irritation. She assumed a more business-like posture. "That's too bad," she said, immediately classifying me as a write-off in the bribery department.

"Now," she said, "I guess we should get back to business."

"All right. What did you want to discuss?"

"It's really very simple, Ed. As you know, Pharmamax has a great deal at stake in the Erecta research. We stand to make hundreds of millions. That means if anything delays it going to market, it will cost us hundreds of millions. Anyone who costs us that kind of money would have to expect a lawsuit for damages. You understand that, I'm sure."

"You can't be successfully sued for telling the truth."

Allison Smart threw back her head and guffawed like a longshoreman. "That's a funny one, Ed," she finally gasped. Then she laughed some more.

I didn't stay around for dessert.

Chapter 12.

The Report

The drive home was anything but uneventful, due to a major automobile accident on Highway 12 that pretty much put the icing on a bad day. I completely forgot about watching the ten o'clock news. A car accident can do that to you.

The next morning when I turned on the computer there was a message from Acmemedpub saying I should call at the earliest opportunity about an urgent matter. It was with the greatest reluctance that I dialed Afzal Arif in London. I was hoping that he was not near his phone, but my luck was not that good.

Arif began the conversation. "Jim, we have had some disturbing reactions from Madison."

"Oh? Who has contacted you?"

He sighed audibly. "Cosgrove called. He was disappointed in your interview with him. He thinks perhaps you have a bias."

"That's understandable."

"The Vice President called with the same message."

"That's unfortunate."

"Legal counsel for the University sent a fax, warning us of their intent to seek legal remedies if we don't agree either to change the article or reverse our agreement to publish it the way Dr. Gupta wrote it."

"Now that is really unfortunate."

"We also received a similar fax from Pharmamax."

"Your attorneys must be in a panic."

"Almost. They will be soon if this continues. I'm afraid I must tell you that we are very disappointed. We had hoped that you would proceed with discretion and the opposite has occurred. Instead of finding a way to calmly and judiciously soothe the situation, you seem to have created a firestorm."

I thought carefully for a moment before answering. "All I can say, Afzal, is that the situation was primed for disaster when I arrived. Pharmamax and the University have strong financial interests at stake. No doubt, they anticipated some resistance on our part and were prepared to bring out the big guns right away. The letters from counsel probably were written in advance of my visit and held in readiness. I assure you that I did not prejudge my conclusions. In fact, I am not finished with the report, and I am not quite sure about the exact nature of my recommendations even now."

"Even so, Ed, I must ask you to refrain from further communication with anyone at the University or with Pharmamax. I am sorry to do this, but our attorneys insist."

"I understand. Since I already have obtained sufficient information to allow me to finish the report, I will go ahead and do so. You do want my report, don't you?"

Arif was silent for a moment. "Yes, of course. Please send it to me when you are finished with it." He did not sound like he meant it.

I was desperate for a good word. "Didn't anyone say anything positive about my visit?"

"As a matter of fact, we received a call from Mrs. Gupta. She asked if I had mentioned your visit to her, which was a sympathy call, I gather. When I said you had not, she expressed her appreciation for your solicitousness. She also invited me to visit with her, next time I am in the United States. She seemed like a very nice person."

"She has many fine qualities."

"Please be assured that we appreciate your willingness to chat with the widow. It was no doubt difficult for you."

"You have no idea."

When the call was finished, I had the distinct impression that I had been fired, though in the nicest way possible. My dreams of a follow-up contract were evaporating before my eyes. It was still morning and too soon for a smoke, but I broke my own rule and went out on the deck to light up.

The most important question floating around in my mind at that point was this: was Gupta's death coincidental or did it have a more sinister aspect? Several possibilities came to mind beyond the obvious explanation of a natural heart attack. First and foremost was the very real chance that Gupta suffered a fatal heart attack as a side effect of taking the Erecta he had stolen from the research project. Researchers had been known to experiment on themselves, particularly if they thought the medicines they were studying might be dangerous. This may sound foolhardy to some, but others might consider it to be courageous. Direct experience in the form of chest pain, shortness of breath, or other symptoms of heart disease would have helped Gupta confirm in his own mind what his statistical analysis was leading him to believe.

Of course, a more selfish and less noble reason for taking Erecta could have been the real motivation. Gupta may have wanted to enhance his sexual performance, either because his energies were flagging or because he was striving for a gold medal in his personal sexual Olympics.

Having met Mrs. Gupta, I had to consider another possible reason for him to take the Erecta: perhaps he was just trying to keep up with her demands. Her libido obviously was out of control. Any good husband would want to meet his wife's needs and would feel badly if he could not keep up. He may have felt that he either had to take an enhancement drug or call 9-1-1 periodically, which would have been humiliating for all concerned.

If Gupta was taking the Erecta for the purpose of engaging in marathon sexual activity, then prolonged sexual athletics might have been the cause of the heart attack.

Finally, I had to consider the possibility that some over-zealous employee of Pharmamax had chosen to silence Gupta because of the revelations he was about to unveil about the dangers of the drug.

Which of the various possible causes of death constituted murder or some other crime? Obviously, if someone working for Pharmamax killed him, then it was outright murder. If Erecta caused Gupta's death, then the company might be liable for producing a dangerous drug and trying to cover up its side effects. True, the research and development phase was still underway, but if the company truly was trying to bias the findings, then perhaps they could be prosecuted for wrongful death.

If Mrs. Gupta humped her husband to death, could that be considered manslaughter? I had never heard of anyone being prosecuted for that one. On the other hand, maybe it was about time. After all, if they were taking sexual performance drugs for the benefit of one partner when the other partner was physically unable to keep up without the risk of a fatal cardiac event, should the authorities call it reckless disregard of another person's safety?

As I was mulling over these conundrums, Betty slid open the glass door and stepped out. "Where is your car?" she demanded.

Woops. I had forgotten about the wild auto escapade the previous evening. There was nothing to do now except confess all. "Well, there was this little car accident last night on the way back from Madison. The police towed my Ford away."

"How did you get home?"

"A County Mounty brought me."

"How did the accident happen?"

"My car just started accelerating and the brakes didn't work."

"Oh my God! How did you stop?"

"Emergency brake."

"Why didn't you tell me?"

"Because it would have made you anxious."

"Anxious! I need to know things like this! What do you mean, anxious?"

"I mean I was protecting you."

"Protecting me! Why would you need to do that?"

"Because you are a Nervous Nellie."

"Am not!"

"Are too!"

She gave up on that point and returned to the main issue: what went wrong with the car. "That's a weird mechanical failure. What caused it?"

This was the moment of truth. If I told Betty of my suspicions about sabotage by a drug company, she would either think I was crazy, become frightened, or both. But if it turned out that I was right but neglected to tell her, then she would be very unhappy. Despite a strong temptation to sweep it under the rug, I told her what I thought had happened.

Betty was understandably upset. "You're nuts! This is too farfetched." She mulled it over for minute. "What will they do next? We could be in serious danger. We better stay home."

"Well, I won't go too far without a car."

"Tell me it's going to be okay."

"It's going to be okay.

"You're just saying that!" Betty was not reassured. "This is too frightening. I'm going to call Andrew and ask him to come over and talk about it. Maybe he has some ideas." Andrew was Betty's cousin and he was some kind of investigator for the state of Wisconsin.

I sighed. Obviously, she trusted Andrew's judgment more than mine. On the other hand, maybe I did also. The guy was pretty cool. He had purchased his last car on ebay, which indicated an adventurous streak, combined with an instinct for penny-pinching. These were both traits that I respected.

Betty arranged for Andrew to come over for lunch. I used the next couple of hours to work on my report to Acmemedpub. Fritter the cat sat on the cable modem to watch me work. She must have liked it because it warmed her bottom. Also, it was directly under the desk lamp, which operated with pulls that turned the light on or off. Mostly, she just sat there, but sometimes she would put up a paw and bat the pull cords around, just for a bit of entertainment.

As I worked on the report, I became even more convinced that Gupta had gotten it right the first time: the medication had risks that were being underplayed by the manufacturer. Acmemedpub was ethically bound to print the original research. If Cosgrove wanted to remove himself as an author, he was free to do so. If the Medical University of Madison and Pharmamax chose to sue Acmemedpub, there was nothing I could do about it. Perhaps the publisher would fold under pressure. There was nothing I could do about that either. There, I had made my conclusions. Unfortunately, it appeared that no one would be very interested in reading my report.

After writing those eight or ten pages, I was ready for a break, so I sat down in front of the television to wait for Andrew to arrive for lunch. The Madison station announced that it was going to report on a research scandal involving the Medical University, so I quickly called Betty and we settled in to listen to the story.

It was a doozy as they used to say back home in Indiana when I was growing up. The station had pieced together shots of me to make it look like I realized I was being interviewed. They showed me saying that Pharmamax and the University were in cahoots to bias research findings because of the vast amounts of money at stake. I didn't remember saying it as strongly as they showed it, but there it was, right in front of my eyes. The camera cut to that cute little reporter, who told the world that Professor Schumacher had said that Erecta should be called

'Superstud' and Ambrosia should be called 'Superhot.' Then, she closed by saying legal action was pending.

After that, I had to turn off the television. I stared morosely at the empty screen, wondering if Arif would bother calling to officially terminate our relationship or would just send me a fax. There was no doubt about it; I had royally messed up this assignment.

When Andrew arrived, Betty was mixing up mayonnaise and tuna in a bowl for tuna sandwiches. "Hey, they had a news item about you on the radio," Andrew said. I groaned.

We sat down in the living room with plates and sodas. Betty made me tell my story from the beginning. There were many parts she had not heard before. She was especially interested in the conversations with Mrs. Gupta and Allison Smart.

"I shouldn't let you out of the house!" she spat after I was done.

"Wait a minute. What have I done wrong?"

She thought about it a minute. "I'm not sure yet. But nobody can get into this much trouble without doing something wrong."

Andrew had a more practical question. "Do you really think somebody sabotaged your car?"

"It sure seems like an odd coincidence for the brakes and the accelerator to malfunction at the same exact moment."

Betty broke in at this point. "You're paranoid. You always think someone is after you. Remember last year before you had your heart attack when you thought someone was chasing you around the back alleys?"

"Somebody was chasing me."

"Nobody else saw them. And remember the time you said somebody ran you off the road?"

"That really happened."

"Maybe and maybe not. And remember when we went to the state fair, you thought some guy was following us home. Remember that, Andrew?"

"Yes, I remember that," he said, then gave me an apologetic look.

"I never said he was following me, I said he might be following me. That's different."

"But why would you think some guy you didn't even know would bother to follow you?"

"Because when I backed my car out of its spot, I kind of dinged his Trans Am. He saw me and started waving his arms as I drove off."

"I didn't see that happen," Betty said.

"You were talking to Andrew. I didn't think I needed to mention it."

"You're incorrigible." Then she turned to Andrew. "Do you really think that somebody at Pharmamax would sabotage Ed's car?"

"I don't know," Andrew answered. "A lot of money is at stake. But I'm more interested in this business with the University. You say they are sweeping procedural violations under the rug in order to protect their contracts with Pharmamax?"

"I think we can be pretty sure that's true."

"The federal government might be very interested in that information after that business with the accounting violations."

"Well, I hope the feds look them over with a microscope. They strike me as a bunch of pompous sleazeballs pretending to be academics."

Then I asked Andrew the question that had been turning over in my mind that morning. "Do you think the coroner should consider Gupta's death to be suspicious and order an autopsy?" I went through the list of possible causes of the heart attack. When I was finished, Andrew agreed that the coroner's office in Madison probably should have this information, speculative as it might be. He said he would call them. It was possible that they already knew about all this, had performed complete toxicology tests, or otherwise had achieved definitive conclusions about the cause of death. But why would they bother doing a complete workup if they had no reason to see the death as suspicious? Andrew said he would call just to make sure the coroners knew Gupta was taking Erecta and Erecta could have caused the heart attack. He refused to mention the possibility that Superhot had induced Mrs. Gupta to ride her husband into the ground, so to speak.

We discussed the case a bit further, without resolving anything. None of us could be sure that the twin mechanical failures on my car were anything other than coincidence. We would have to wait until the police finished looking it over to learn the answer to that.

When Andrew left, we turned on a continuous news channel. The reporter was saying that a new scandal had struck the internet. Blogs were screaming about corruption in the pharmaceutical industry, specifically regarding the new sexual performance drugs popularly known as Superstud and Superhot. Pharmamax was being accused of skewing the research findings to hide the elevated risk of heart attacks associated with Superstud. Superhot was reported to be a recreational sex drug for women. The Medical University of Madison was mentioned specifically as having been willing to doctor research findings to suit the company. This story ran periodically throughout the afternoon, getting steadily more strident as the bloggers dug out more dirt on Pharmamax.

In time for the evening news, the FDA announced investigations into the safety of both Erecta and Ambrosia. In a related story, the FDA announced that a joint federal task force, including the Internal Revenue Service, was investigating use of research funds at the Medical University of Madison. Next, a blogger reported that Acmemedpub had valiantly fought legal pressure intended to force them to publish spurious research findings regarding the safety of Superstud. By 6 p.m., Acmemedpub was getting good press from Fox News for academic integrity. By morning, praise for Acmemedpub had appeared in editorials in *USA Today* and the *New York Times*. Miraculously, there was no mention of good old Ed Schumacher in any of the national news reports.

Chapter 13

Conclusion

The following week, I went to my scheduled doctor's appointment to refill my prescriptions for a cholesterol pill, an allergy pill, and a thyroid pill. In addition to those medications, I also took an aspirin and a multivitamin every day. As I dozed, half-awake, in the doctor's waiting room, I wondered if I was being a hypocrite in claiming Americans were overmedicated. Finally, I decided to declare myself innocent of that offense; my prescriptions were all for older, less expensive medications. However, that didn't make them cheap when you added up the entire bill. There was no doubt that access to basic medication was important to the well-being of every person who had the beginnings of a chronic disease. I would have to be careful as I made trouble for drug manufacturers that I didn't contribute to the false impression some people had that medications were not important at all. That would be throwing the baby out with the bathwater.

As the minutes continued to drift by, I mentally reviewed how the case had turned out. I had confronted Andrew with the news about the federal task force and its investigation of the University. He denied having called anyone to report my findings. Andrew said that the feds had probably just been waiting for an excuse to nail the University, and the bloggers had provided it.

The examination of my car by the police lab revealed no sabotage. The motor mounts had failed on one side of the engine, causing the motor to fall to one side. This ripped open the accelerator to its maximum and broke the brake lines at the same time. It was an unusual event, but not unprecedented.

This information had been reported to me by a delegation composed of Sergeants Broder and Schmidt and the county deputy whose car I had totaled. They had arrived at the condo without warning on Friday afternoon of the previous week. Schmidt gave me the news about the mechanical failure, then flashed a big grin, which I knew meant trouble.

"Mr. Schumacher, the forensic evidence is clear in this matter. Yes, your car experienced a serious mechanical failure. However, the way you stopped the car was outrageous. You endangered the lives of the deputy and any innocent bystanders who might have been in the area. It's a miracle no one was killed. You also caused a large amount of damage to an official vehicle." She smiled savagely. "I'm afraid we will be forced to bring charges against you."

The deputy, who had been silent up to this point, broke in to her diatribe with a firm voice. "Sergeant Smith!" We all looked at him; this was unexpected. "The accident did not occur inside the Fort Atkinson city limits nor did it occur in Cambridge. It is a county matter."

Schmidt was speechless, so Broder spoke up. "You mean you are not going to charge him?"

"No, we are not. Our review board has concluded that the heroic actions of the professor here, undertaken at my own request in a moment of dire need and at great personal risk of injury to himself, more than make up for the lapse of judgment that led to the accident. After all, how many citizens would have thought to turn their cars off and coast to a stop under those circumstances? No, we are not going to charge Professor Schumacher. However, we are going to ask that he accept two tickets to the annual policeman's ball." He turned toward me, holding out the tickets. "I sincerely hope that you will accept them." I took them without a word.

Broder had to lead Schmidt out by the arm. She appeared to be in shock. Schmidt had been wanting to nail me for something for nearly two years. Well, better luck next time, lady.

The deputy waited until Broder and Schmidt were gone, then reached into the pocket of his jacket and pulled out a brown paper bag. He handed it to me. Inside were my pipe, tobacco, and box of kitchen matches. His eyes twinkled. "I have been begging the county to buy me a new car for three years. Thanks for your help in moving that request along." We both laughed. He got up to leave, then turned back briefly. "By the way," he said. "The damage to your car was paid for by our insurance. All the repairs have been made and it's parked outside." He tossed me the keys, then left. He was a good guy. You just had to like a guy with that kind of style.

The final loose end remained unresolved. Andrew had informed me, after swearing me to secrecy, that the coroner's office in Madison had looked into Gupta's death. They found that he had indeed been taking Erecta. They could not say whether it had caused his death. Andrew did not tell me whether the body revealed evidence of intense and prolonged sexual activity, but there was no doubt in my mind about that being true.

The coroner found no evidence of foul play, so the dead man in the galley was not murdered. He died from taking Erecta or from intense physical activity that overtaxed his aging heart. If the Erecta killed him, then it was his own fault because he was not authorized to take it. After all, the drug had not yet been approved for use by anyone except experimental subjects. If the Erecta contributed to his death by allowing him to over-indulge in sexual activity, then it still could not be called murder. Instead, it was either a form of accidental suicide or a very special type of consensual manslaughter. I decided to call it an accident and forget it, since Mrs. Gupta had already suffered enough.

When I finally got in to see my doctor, he wrote out the prescriptions without any fuss, and I headed over to the pharmacy. A new Walgreens had recently opened on Main Street, so I went there. Getting my pills only took about twenty minutes. When I arrived home, my downstairs neighbor, Emily Eberhardt, was just returning home after walking her dog.

"Hey, Emily. How's it going'?"

"Just fine. Spot and I had a good walk."

"Emily, do you mind if I ask your opinion on something?"

"Sure, Ed. What do you want to know? I love to offer opinions."

"What do you think about all those television ads for new medicines? Do you think people should be getting the newest pills as soon as they come out?"

Emily hesitated for a moment. "I just saw another commercial for a weight loss pill this morning. People who spend their money on some of these new pills might as well be throwing it out the window. It's a rotten shame, taking advantage of people's fears in order to sell them useless pills."

"But some of those pills aren't useless; some of them really work."

Emily looked at me like I was daft. "Of course they do," she said, "but a lot of people don't know the difference between the useless pills and the good ones. I wish the useless ones weren't allowed to advertise. But what can you do, eh?"

"Good point, Emily. Thanks."

"Anytime, Ed. Now I have to feed Spot. He gets hungry after a walk."

I made it upstairs just in time to hear the phone ring. It was Afzal Arif.

"Ed? Afzal here. How are you?"

"Fine. Did you get my report?"

"Yes, and it was splendid. Succinct and right on target. The board is very pleased at how this difficulty was resolved. I must say we got a lot of good press from it."

"That is wonderful. I'm glad you are satisfied with how I handled it." I was fishing, of course. The last time we had spoken he had been very unsatisfied with my performance.

"Yes, we are very pleased. In fact, we are sending you a substantial bonus in addition to the fee we had agreed upon. I hope you will forgive us for that brief lapse in confidence. We were under a lot of pressure, as I'm sure you understand."

"Yes, of course. Quite understandable. No harm done. And the bonus is very much appreciated."

"Thank you for letting us off the hook on that one. Perhaps that means you will be willing to take on another assignment. In fact, we were hoping that you would accept a permanent retainer, so that we can call on you as needed. These problems with research ethics seem to crop up with no advance notice and require rapid action."

"What do you have in mind?"

"All expenses paid, of course. We estimate you might need to investigate at least one case each month, on average. Would five thousand dollars monthly be sufficient to keep you in reserve for us?"

Sixty thousand dollars per year, working two days a month? "Oh, I think that's fair. It leaves me time to work on other projects as well."

"Splendid! We will fax the contract to you post haste."

"I will be watching for it."

"I can't tell you how pleased I am. And the board will be delighted as well. I hope we can convince you and your wife to fly over here sometime soon to meet our principals. At our expense, of course."

"My wife will be pleased when I tell her of your invitation. I am sure we will be able to schedule a trip in the next few months."

"Your next assignment is a problem involving the Grand Poupon Institute. Have you heard of it?"

"I know the name. They are supposed to be even more elite than the Mayo Clinic, aren't they?"

"That's the place. The Institute is located in Poupon, Illinois, just south of the Wisconsin border. That is near where you live if I have read my map correctly."

'Yes, it's quite close. Just send me the background material and I will get to work."

We rang off and I sat back in my chair with a gasp of relief. You could never predict how things were going to turn out. In this case, the outcome was good, but I knew life would throw me a curve at some time in the future, some time when I least expected it.

When my conversation with Arif was over, Betty came in to ask me about it. After she had the scoop, she gave me a big hug. "You're so smart I bet your mother called you Sonny," she said. She said that a lot. I had tried to get her to change 'smart' to 'bright,' but she preferred it her own way, as usual.

"This is a good end to this story, but it's not perfect," Betty said. "You know, you are darn lucky you didn't get killed, sued, or arrested. Your family is right about you. They always say you could fall into an outhouse and come out smelling like a rose." Then she stopped criticizing me and took up my defense. "It's not fair that Acmemedpub got all the credit for being so ethical. If you hadn't stirred up a hornets nest, they might have quietly caved in to the threats from the lawyers." She was on my side all the way, that woman.

"Tell me this," I asked her. "Speaking as a physician: do you think it is possible that Gupta's death was due to too much sexual activity? I'm wondering if Mrs. Gupta's libido didn't do him more harm than the Erecta pills."

"She could have been a major contributing factor. By the way, I'm thinking about taking Superhot myself."

"You don't need that stuff."

"But I might like it. Maybe I don't know what I'm missing."

"If you want to, go ahead. It might kill me, but there are worse ways for a guy to go."

"No, dear, I am not really going to do that. I was just testing you."

"Testing me how?"

"Testing to see how much you loved me."

"Did I pass?"

"Yes, dear, you passed." She gave me a hug and a kiss on the cheek.

Later that evening we got into a discussion about a national medical program. I tried to convince Betty that our country could afford to give everyone all the medicine they needed if we would stop wasting money on unnecessary medicine that is extremely expensive. Betty wasn't buying my argument.

"You can come up with all the theories you want, but it's a waste of time. It doesn't really matter what is theoretically possible. The average taxpayer won't agree to switching from employer health benefits to government benefits, especially when you tell them they won't be able to get all the latest medicines."

"I'm afraid you're right. It's always the middle class that opposes true reform."

"What do you mean? That doesn't make any sense. Everybody knows it's the rich who are against government programs."

"No, the rich are against wasteful government programs. The middle class doesn't want any other kind. The middle class want a college education for every child instead of job training, which would be more useful and more affordable. The middle class wants big wasteful houses, big wasteful automobiles, and an educational system that offers music programs but allows kids to avoid learning how to read, write, and compute. Fact is, the middle class doesn't want government programs that eliminate poverty. They want government programs that will enable them to live like they're rich, instead of being middle class."

"You can't blame them for that," said Betty, who always appreciated as much luxury as she could get, preferably without having to pay for it.

"I just hope that someday the working class and enlightened conservatives will realize that they agree more with each other on government policy than they do with the middle class. If that ever happens, they could kick middle class butts all the way into next Tuesday. Then, maybe, some real improvements could be made in how society is organized."

Betty would not let me get away with that kind of rhetoric. "You talk like you aren't middle class, but you are. Deep down, you seem to be ashamed that you have a good education and you have accumulated a good retirement fund." She stood up to make her next point more forcefully. "Do you know what your problem is?" she demanded. "You are a sucker for lost causes."

She had a point there. "Okay, I admit it. I'm a sucker for lost causes. Don Quixote is my hero."

"No, dear," she said. *"You are Don Quixote."*

I brushed a sudden tear from my eye. "That's the nicest thing you have ever said to me."

Betty shook her head sadly. "You are a very strange man."

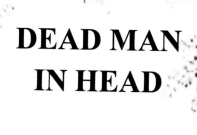

DEAD MAN IN HEAD

This book is dedicated to all the people in
the world who are afflicted with serious and
persistent mental illness.

Chapter 1.

When is a Turkey Not a Turkey?

The poor fellow was trying to push a freezer across Main Street. You might think I am making this up, but it is the absolute truth. The freezer was placed on some sort of dolly that had four small wheels. The man pushing it looked a bit wild, with his long, greasy hair and ragged clothes. No criticism was intended in describing him as greasy and ragged. If you were pushing a refrigerator up the middle of the street, you would be ragged and greasy in a short period of time. After all, it was sweaty work and hard on your clothes.

When I saw him, I was about to climb into my car after picking up a few groceries at the Sentry store. The freezer man had managed to back up a line of traffic, which was understandable, since people pushing freezers on dollies were bound to move at a slower rate of speed than the more common vehicles were able to achieve. He was scowling as he strained to push the freezer slowly forward. Or, perhaps, he was scowling because he knew the drivers of the cars behind him were staring and probably cursing him quietly.

The light changed and it was his turn to move across Main Street. The freezer moved forward at a snail's pace. I could easily imagine the impatience felt by the drivers in those cars; don't you just hate it when you know you won't make it through a perfectly good green light because someone in front of you is moving too slowly? On the other hand, the man pushing the freezer was doing the best he could, under the circumstances.

At any other time in my life, I would have just stood there and watched. This was not because I am lazy (though I am) or because I am insensitive (guilty again), but because I am not a fast thinker in crisis situations. On this particular day, my synapses were firing a little more quickly than usual, so I threw my groceries in the car then ran out in the street to give the man some help.

He glared at me when I started pushing, but said nothing. No doubt, he was saving his breath. He did move his pushing position slightly to the left, which gave me room to get a better angle on the right side. Together, we managed to pick up the pace a little, though not very much. I am an over-fifty, semi-retired college professor who has never lifted weights in his life, so the strength I brought to the task was far less than a working man might have expected. The man pushing the freezer had the look of a working man; his clothes were dungarees and a plaid shirt and he wore heavy boots. Though it was November in Wisconsin, he had on no jacket. He had worked up a good sweat performing his task, so a jacket would have been too warm. I, on the other hand, wore a black blazer, blue shirt with a button-down collar, and chinos. Fortunately, I was also wearing my usual foot-gear: Red Wing walking shoes. These shoes had good tread on them and were ideal for pushing freezers.

The air was brisk; it might have been about 40 degrees outside. The frost had melted off the road already, since it was about nine in the morning. Our first snow had not yet fallen, though with Thanksgiving only two days away, the possibility of a blizzard could not be ruled out. All in all, it was good weather for pushing a freezer up the road.

"Hey, this thing's heavy," I said, just making conversation. My co-worker ignored me. Who could blame him? That kind of comment, where one stated the obvious, was a form of low-key humor commonly heard in the Midwest. However, when you were engaged in an arduous task, dumb jokes were not funny.

"What you got in here, turkeys?" I tried again to make conversation.

"Just....one..," he replied.

"Must be a big one!"

"Yup...big.....turkey. For sure."

By this time we were in the middle of the intersection. Perhaps what happened next was due to the distraction I caused by making conversation with the freezer man. On the other hand, the fact that I was not physically very strong might be the only explanation necessary. Whatever the reason, my side of the freezer was not keeping up with the side being pushed by the wild-looking man. The bulky burden began to turn to the right. The street sloped downward there, which made the freezer difficult to control. Suddenly, it was rolling downhill.

Not wanting it to go rolling down Main Street on its own, I quickly shifted around to the front end of the freezer and dug in my heels. My shoes slid on the damp road as the freezer ignored my efforts and picked up speed. I lowered my center of gravity and pushed down harder on my feet and, at the same time, tried to push harder against the freezer. Unfortunately, the freezer just kept going.

Glancing over my shoulder, I saw a pickup truck close behind me. To avoid being pinned against it by the freezer, I scrambled on top, holding on to the strap that held it to its wheels. As soon as I leaped aboard, the freezer banged into the pickup. Its weight would not let it stop there, however. The other end of the freezer now swung around and we, the freezer and I, continued down Main Street.

My primary concern was to avoid allowing my hands or feet to be crushed as we banged off cars on either side of the street, picking up speed and caroming down the hill like a steel bearing in a pinball machine. The hill had just enough slope and the street was just slippery enough to allow the freezer-on-wheels to pick up a good rate of speed. We shattered glass, dented fenders, and tore off side mirrors on both sides of the street as our acceleration increased. I use the term 'we' because by this time my freezer and I had become quite close. We had bonded, so to speak. Jumping off would have been dangerous, so I hung on for dear life. The freezer was protecting me from the hard surface of the street, even as its increasing speed threatened me with consequences even more dire.

We broadsided a blue sedan in front of the city building, giving it a deep dent in the driver's side door. Just at that moment, a couple of police detectives I knew were walking out of the city building. Sergeant Schmidt was holding a cardboard cup of coffee, which she dropped when she saw what was happening. Whether it was the sight of someone she knew riding a freezer down Main Street or whether it was the damage done to her car that upset her the most, I couldn't say. But the scream she let loose may have provided a clue about what was upsetting her: "Schumacher!" That's my name. Since she did not shout "Mr. Schumacher" or "Professor Schumacher," I had to assume that she was upset with me again. The woman was biased against me for reasons I have never understood.

The freezer pinwheeled, so I lost sight of Schmidt and her partner, Sergeant Broder. We smashed some headlights and dented a few more fenders before reaching the bridge. For those of you who are not familiar with our little town, Fort Atkinson, let me describe the setting at this point in the story. Fort Atkinson has a nice little river running through the downtown area. The city's leadership has invested in creating a 'Riverwalk' that is quite attractive. The bridge connects one side of the downtown area with the other side. From the center of the bridge, you can look down to the see the Riverwalk and a few shops. It is really very picturesque.

The key point here is that the bridge rose a bit as it crossed the river. The hill down which I had been traveling reached its low point at the foot of the bridge. Despite the momentum we had achieved, we were not going over the bridge. Where, then, were we going?

The answer, as it turned out, was to the left side of the bridge. The freezer was moving quickly when it reached the foot of the bridge. It did not hesitate when the street began to rise, but shot to the left and off the road, taking out a chunk of cement railing and aiming for a concrete loading dock ten feet below.

I held on tightly while we were airborne. Some people say that your life passes before your eyes in the brief moment before imminent death, but those people probably were faster thinkers than I was. My mind just went blank until we struck the loading dock with a crash. The wheels of the dolly flew in all directions as we bounced and skidded off the edge of the loading dock into the river, then sank like a stone.

Fortunately, the river was not more than fifteen feet deep at that location. I say this was 'fortunate,' because I forgot to let loose of the strap until after the freezer came to a stop on the bottom of the river. Belatedly realizing my mistake, I gave a frenzied push with my legs and shot upward through the wet darkness.

Splashing around on the surface, with water obscuring my glasses, I was at first unsure which direction led toward the loading dock. Shouts got my attention and I began to stroke awkwardly toward the sound. My clothes were sodden and the water was very cold, so I tired quickly. Fortunately, the loading dock was nearby and, with the last of my remaining energy, I managed to reach out and grasp a helping hand that pulled me out of the water.

The hand belonged to Sergeant Broder. He led me back to the city building and took me inside. A blanket materialized from somewhere and I gratefully wrapped it around myself. Even so, I was shivering and felt light-headed.

Eventually, EMTs came and checked me over. Finding no cuts, abrasions, broken bones, or other injuries, they prescribed hot coffee and departed. My cell phone had disappeared, so I asked Broder if he would call my wife Betty and tell her where I was. I didn't really want to try to explain the situation to her; let Broder do that if he could.

After Broder made the call, he and Schmidt led me into one of their interrogation rooms. Broder was polite, as he always was. For the first time, it occurred to me that this might not mean he was a nice guy; maybe his job was to be the 'good cop' and Schmidt's job was to be the 'bad cop.' If so, Schmidt was type-cast because there was no doubt in my mind that she was downright nasty.

After we were seated at the table in the interrogation room with me wrapped in a blanket and drinking coffee, Broder began by asking me to explain what happened.

"Well, this guy was pushing a freezer across Main Street up by the Sentry store, so I gave him a hand."

"That was your idea of being helpful?" Schmidt asked with a sneer. "Wrecking a bunch of cars and throwing his freezer into the river?"

Broder interrupted. "Tell me about the man you helped. Who was he?"

"Never saw him before."

"What did he look like?"

"Wait a minute. You mean he's gone?"

"Mr. Schumacher," Broder said gently, "all the witnesses said you were alone on the freezer when it was rolling down Main Street."

"Of course I was! The other guy never got on the freezer!" Sometimes, these cops acted like I was nuts and it was very irritating. "I just got up there to avoid being crushed. I lost sight of him when we lost control of the darn thing."

"Can you describe this other man to us?"

"He was kind of grubby. Had on work clothes. Didn't look any too clean, frankly. I just figured he was pushing the freezer because he couldn't afford to have the thing moved on a truck."

"That brings me to my next question, Mr. Schumacher. Why was this man pushing a freezer through the center of town in the middle of the street?"

"He said he had his Thanksgiving turkey in there."

"Wouldn't it have been easier just to carry the turkey?"

"He said it was a really big turkey."

Schmidt slammed her fist down on the table. "This is the craziest story I ever heard," she growled. "And there aren't two people in this town crazy enough to push a freezer down the middle of the street. Admit it, Schumacher: there is no other guy. You pulled this stunt on your own."

"I never saw the guy before today or his freezer!" Was this my reward for trying to do a good deed? "I was just giving a guy a push. You know, like we do when somebody is stuck in a snowdrift."

Broder leaned back in his chair. "Yes, Mr. Schumacher, I see what you mean. However, when we push someone out of a snowdrift we try not to damage seven cars and end up in the river."

He had a point. Somehow, my good deed had gone wrong, though I was having trouble figuring out exactly where I had made my mistake.

At this point the door to the interrogation room opened and a uniformed officer beckoned to Schmidt. She stepped out for a couple of minutes, then returned with a grin on her face. This was not looking good.

"Mister Schumacher," she announced. "You will be happy to know that the guys from the service station managed to winch that freezer of yours out of the river. It's on the loading dock now."

"That's nice, but I would have left it down there until spring. That water is too cold to be working in if you don't have to."

"I just bet you would have preferred to leave it down there," Schmidt said, "considering what's inside it. Would you mind telling us again what you put in there?"

"I didn't put anything in there. The guy I was helping had a big turkey in there."

"The guy nobody saw put a turkey in there? More likely you put something in there. Only it wasn't a Thanksgiving turkey. It was a corpse, frozen solid."

Needless to say, it was a long time before they let me go home.

Chapter 2.

The Assignment

The phone rang while I was cussing at the cat. Our main cat was an orange tabby named Fritter who had been living with us for about a year after we rescued her from a rain-swept parking lot in Iowa. Fritter was a very nice cat. However, Betty and I had been concerned that Fritter might get lonely when we weren't around the house, so we decided to acquire a kitten. Besides, we didn't play with Fritter enough and we assumed that having a little buddy would let us off the hook. Another important concern was Betty's need for her own cat. Fritter had always been my cat, by Fritter's choice, and Betty felt left out. Betty wanted a cat that would sit in her lap and allow itself to be petted and hugged. Fritter rarely allowed Betty to do that.

As a consequence of these pressing concerns, we picked up another orange tabby cat, whom we named Bucky. For those of you who don't know the important facts of life, the mascot for the football team at of the University of Wisconsin is called Bucky. Since we were living in Wisconsin and since Betty had once attended UW, we named the new cat Bucky.

Bucky was lovable, but he was also a pain in the neck. He got into more trouble than Fritter had at the same age. Bucky would jump on my legs and dig in his claws. He scratched the furniture much more than Fritter ever had. He would throw things onto the floor. He would try to run out the door when he was supposed to stay inside. And worst of all, he would get up in the middle of the night and make noise when we were trying to sleep. Betty loved Bucky. So did I, but sometimes I cussed at him.

The phone rang while I was giving Bucky a lecture about not clawing my suit. I rarely bought a new suit, but at the rate Bucky was damaging this one I might be forced to replace it sooner than I wanted.

"Hello?" I asked the phone with some irritation at being interrupted in the middle of a lecture. "Professor Schumacher, please" a voice said.

"Speaking."

"This is Jim Jones, vice president at the Medical University of Madison. We met briefly when you were investigating a research problem we were having."

"I remember." That little situation had been a sticky wicket, as the British say. And Jones had not helped one bit. He was a bureaucrat who had developed highly refined skills in covering his pitootie. That may not sound impressive, but given the enormity of his pitootie, you can be sure that his skills in that regard had to be Olympic-class.

Jones cleared his throat noisily, then said, "We, eh, were wondering if we might be able to, er, ask your assistance on a little problem we are facing here in Madison."

My silence was motivated less by reluctance than by shock. The Medical University of Madison, MUM for short, and I had not parted on the best of terms. Yet, here they were asking for my help. This was very odd.

Jones broke the silence. "Of course, we want to assure you that we at MUM, hmm, have the utmost regard, er, for your abilities. That little difference of opinion we had, hmm, was not of your doing. Of course, you understand."

I almost felt sorry for the weasel. He clearly was squirming.

"What can I do for you, Jim?"

Jones clearly was relieved that the ice was broken. "Well, as you know, we do a lot of research here and always take great pains to comply with all federal requirements. In fact, we are eager to go the extra mile to meet the spirit of federal regulations regarding patient rights and safety."

Yeah, right, I thought, especially after that blowup when you got caught being a little too cozy with the pharmaceutical industry. My finest hour was when I turned up the dirt on that crowd.

"Jim, you can skip the PR," I said. "What's up?"

"Hmm. Well, you may remember an incident a few weeks ago in which a man was found dead inside a freezer. It happened right there where you live, in Fort Atkinson. "

"I remember." Darn right. The cops were far too rough on me. It would be a long time before I forgave them. "So? What about it?"

"Hmm. That dead man was enrolled in one of our research projects."

"Was he, now? That's interesting. And all deaths have to be reported, just in case they are caused by the research."

"That is correct."

"And the feds are being especially watchful over you guys, given the recent scandal."

"I wish you wouldn't use that word. It was hardly a scandal."

"Did the feds tell you that you had to find an independent investigator to look into this suspicious death?"

"You are very perceptive, Professor Schumacher."

"Why me?"

"Hmm. Well, the federal oversight agency regards you as being beyond any possible influence from the University, given that we were on opposing sides the last time we spoke."

"They are right about that; I am as independent as they come."

"Also, they knew from the newspaper accounts that you lived in Fort Atkinson, so hiring you would save on travel expenses."

That reason for choosing me was a little less flattering. Maybe I could get even for the insult by charging them a large fee.

"My usual fee is a thousand a day," I announced as if I had a 'usual fee.'

"That will be acceptable," Jones replied without hesitation. Perhaps I should have charged him more. "We will fax a contract to you immediately."

"Can you give me some more background on the situation? Of course, I will need to study the description of the research project, get the name and bio of the investigator, and have all of the information that was provided to the feds."

"We will run that information over to you by courier today. In brief, the situation is this: the research involved psychiatric patients..."

"Psych patients!" Vulnerable populations are supposed to be given special protection.

"The experiment involved a combination of medications and psychotherapy given to subjects sharing a similar delusion. The medications themselves were not experimental," he hastened to add. "The novel dimension to the research was that the subjects were all chosen because they believed in the same kind of paranoid delusion. They all believed that they could see deceased persons."

"They saw dead people?"

"That's right."

"Well, that's interesting, but not outrageous. Tell me, Jim, what is the real problem here? Psychotic patients live dangerous lives and accidents happen. Sometimes, unfortunately, they end up dead. The feds know that. So, why have they taken the unprecedented step of demanding an independent investigation?"

Jones hesitated, then laid it on the line. "Prior to the discovery of the deceased, one of the subjects complained that he was not fully informed about the purposes of the research before he agreed to participate. He said all of the subjects were misled, or they would not have participated. He made this complaint to the federal authorities. Then, a short time later, one of the other subjects was found dead. The oversight agency is concerned that serious irregularities might have been occurring in this project."

"It sounds to me like they have reason to wonder about that." I sighed. "Okay, Jim, I will need access to information that normally is kept confidential. I need to know the names of the subjects, so that I can interview them and find out what really happened."

Jones was silent for a moment. "We had hoped you would not pursue the investigation in this way, but even so we anticipated your request. We are forced to comply. The names and latest contact information for the experimental subjects will be in the packet we are sending you. We are also faxing you a confidentiality agreement that you must sign and return to us. It will be part of the contract between the University and yourself."

"Fair enough. If I have any more questions after studying the material, I'll give you a call."

"Please do. Despite our past differences, I hope you understand that we truly want to protect the interests of any persons who participate in our research projects." It sounded like a well-rehearsed statement, but it was no doubt sincere. After all, when the alternative to being good was a large financial penalty, even the sleaziest bureaucrat aspires to morality.

The packet of information sent over by Jim Jones was about two inches thick, containing a number of official reports to and from the federal agency responsible for monitoring research involving human beings (as opposed to animals or laboratory specimens). Using people as guinea pigs obviously has a lot of risks involved, especially since patients who suffer from serious diseases may be desperate enough to agree to almost any kind of experimental treatment.

The research project that I had been asked to investigate was a small one. Only a group of seven patients had been assembled. Signed documents were in the file showing that all seven had been informed about the purpose of the project and what would happen during the project. All seven had agreed to participate if you can believe that signing a long legal document proves that each person knew what he or she was agreeing to.

The theory behind the project was that psychotic patients who had similar delusions should receive group therapy together rather than being mixed with patients who had different kinds of delusions. This theory flew in the face of conventional wisdom in psychiatry. Many professionals who worked with the "seriously and persistently mentally ill," as they were called, believed that having two patients with the exact same delusion in the same hospital unit was a formula for conflict. What if a person who thought he was God happened to chat with another person who thought he was God? Would they get into a fight?

The psychiatrist who came up this theory, Dr. Zelicov, was a professor in the medical school. He seemed to have a strong interest in talk therapy, which was a little unusual for psychiatrists in the mid-west. The old fashioned idea of a psychiatrist meeting with his patients for hour-long weekly sessions was more often found in New York or Boston. Most modern psychiatrists concentrated on diagnosing the problem and prescribing medicines. Patients were referred to other professionals for counseling. The modern strategy was more cost-effective than the old-style approach. Besides, only very rich people could afford that much attention.

My first question was this: why had this project been approved in the first place? The number of patients was too small for serious research. There was no group of patients receiving standard care that could serve as a comparison group. And psych patients were very vulnerable to exploitation because they may not have understood what they were signing up for.

Now that I understood what the project was about I was ready to check into the complaint. The names presented in the rest of this report are entirely fictitious since it would be both illegal and unethical to reveal the identities of the people involved.

The seven people chosen to participate in the project were Miles Archer, Lew Archer, Archie Goodwin, Miss Marple, Sherlock Holmes, Archy McNally, and Dr. Watson. Miles Archer was the man who was found in the freezer. Dr. Watson was the patient who filed the complaint against Dr. Zelicov. Watson complained that none of the patients in the project understood what the research was about. Furthermore, he said that they were tricked because none would have participated if they had known. His argument was interesting. He said that all seven of the patients were recruited because they reported seeing deceased people. They were convinced that what they saw was real, and for each of them the ability to 'see dead people' was an important though frightening gift that made them feel special. Since the purpose of the project was to find a way to cure them of seeing dead people, these folks would have refused to participate in the project had they know the plan because they did not want to be 'cured.'

As I said, this was an interesting argument. Until I spoke to the other patients, I would not know whether any agreed with Watson's point of view. Maybe the rest understood what the project was about and desired to be relieved of the stress of seeing the dead. Maybe Watson was alone in his view. Maybe he was off his meds when he wrote the complaint and forgot that he had, in good faith, agreed to participate in the project at a time when he did, indeed, desire a cure for himself.

At the time the patients were recruited into the project, all were patients in a locked hospital ward in Madison. That means they were very sick at the time since hospitals discharge patients as quickly as possible, due to the cost. After discharge, they were dispersed throughout the Madison area, except for Lew Archer. Lew Archer had been discharged to his home west of Madison, but he was already back in the locked ward. Miles Archer had been homeless; I wondered how he ended up in a freezer in Fort Atkinson. Archie Goodwin was listed as living in Happy Acres, a large group home in Janesville, which was a few miles southeast of Madison. Miss Marple lived in a smaller group home in Watertown, which was a small city north-east of Madison. Archy McNally lived in an apartment building in Milton, a city located southwest of Fort Atkinson and southeast of Madison. Sherlock Holmes was living in a homeless shelter in downtown Madison. Dr. Watson apparently lived just outside of Fort Atkinson, not more than ten minutes from my own condo.

Making appointments with most of these folks would not be possible. I would just have to drop in and ask for them, one at a time. Dr. Watson was, of course, the exception. He had provided a cell phone number, so I could call him and invite myself over.

Chapter 3.

Interview with Doctor Watson

Dr. Watson's address was on the outskirts of town. Watson lived in a rusty mobile home nestled into the underbrush on an overgrown lot. I steered my car into his driveway at dusk, the headlights casting flickering shadows off evergreen bushes that waved in the steady breeze despite their overcoats of snow. Thanksgiving had come and gone and winter had settled in. A storm was coming. It was the third week in December, so the temperature had dropped sharply with the disappearance of sunlight.

A rickety step led up to his front door. I knocked on it, then heard movement on the other side. A moment later, the door swung open. The man behind the door was very tall and thin, with scraggly hair and beard. He looked to be in his middle forties, though he could have been quite a bit younger but worn out, given how difficult his life might have been. He was dressed in a worn black suit and narrow black tie. Incongruously, his feet were bare. Thick black hair curled around his toes and over the tops of his feet, which did not look particularly clean. In fact, his whole person emitted an odor of unwashed body and cigarettes.

"Yeah?" he asked.

"Are you Doctor Watson?"

"That's what they call me. What do you want?"

"I'd like to come in and talk to you for a minute."

He didn't move so I tried again. "You wrote a letter complaining about a research project. I need to ask you a few questions about it."

He grunted, then stepped back into the room, swinging the door wide behind him. I stepped directly into his living room, which was carpeted with a tattered rug and stuffed with shabby furniture. The windows were covered with sheets of black plastic. Watson had positioned an old metal desk in the center of the room so that it faced a futon couch. He waved me toward the couch and seated himself behind the desk. Picking up a well-gnawed pencil and positioning a smudged and torn scrap of paper in front of him, he glared at me from under shaggy brows and demanded, "So, what do you want to know?"

Watson leaned forward and glared at me. "There's one thing I need to know right off. Do you work for the university or the feds? Because if you work for the university, I'm not talking to you."

"The feds required the university to hire me because they see me as being an independent investigator."

"Oh yeah? What makes you trustworthy?"

"Did you hear about that business a few months ago when the university got in trouble because of its financial relationship with a big pharmaceutical company? It made a splash in the news for a couple of days. I was involved in that."

Doctor Watson leaned back in his chair. "Right. I remember that. So that was you? Good for you, man. They got what was coming to them that time." He grinned at me. "You're alright, man. You can call me Doc."

Still grinning, he leaned back in his chair even further and put his feet on his desk. "Well, let me tell you my story. Several of us were on the inpatient unit over in Madison. You ever been there?"

"Nope. Never had the pleasure."

"Hah!" He laughed loudly. "Never had the pleasure! That's a good one. Some pleasure. Shoot, man. It's rotten. I mean, what else can they do when a guy is out of control? But it's still rotten." He sighed. "I've been on that unit more times than I can count. Well, maybe I could count them if they didn't dope me up with Haldol so bad that I can't remember anything afterwards. Anyway, you need to understand the situation. Several of us were there that had been in and out a bunch of times. All of us were dopey from the drugs they gave us. And," he leaned forward, "this is the most important part: we all wanted out." He swung his feet to the floor and slapped the desk with the flat of his hand. "See what I mean, man? We were all desperate to get loose from that place."

I saw his point. "You were inclined to agree to the study because you hoped they would let you out sooner if you cooperated."

"Yeah, that's sort of right. See, we all know how the system works. We've all been around. We know you can't trust anybody. And some of these crazies, they think spies are after them or something. So none of us are inclined to believe anything the white coats tell us. On the other hand, when you want out you might take a chance. You think if you show some good behavior they will think you're ready. And besides, the drugs keep you from thinking straight. See, if they came to me with some forms to sign right now, I would know it was a trick. But in there, I couldn't see the trick because my brain was fuzzy."

Doc's eyes darkened with anger, then shifted to one side and he mumbled something under his breath.

"Why did they put you in there, Doc, if you don't mind my asking?"

"I don't remember this, but they said I was tearing up a bar over in Madison."

"If that was the whole story, they would have thrown you in jail, not the psych unit. So, why the psych unit?"

He considered the question for a moment, his eyes shifting back and forth, then replied. "You tell me."

"How would I know?"

"I bet you do."

"According to the project records, you see dead people."

"Maybe I do. You think that's impossible?"

"Heck if I know. The important question is this: did you want to stop seeing dead people when you signed the consent form?"

Doc twiddled his pencil around a little. "How would I know? I can't remember what I was thinking then. But I don't think so. Do you know why I think that?"

"Maybe because it's exciting and maybe it's the most important thing in your life. Very frightening, but important."

Doc grinned hugely. "You got it, man. Life's a drag when they put you on the meds."

"You mean the guy behind your shoulder stops talking to you?"

Doc froze, then jumped up out of his chair. "You see a guy behind my shoulder?"

"No, I don't see anybody."

"Then you seein' inside my head, man?"

"No, I can't see inside your head."

"You must be, you must be," he whispered, sitting back down in his chair. He stared down at the surface of his desk for a long moment, then spoke. "Okay, I got it. You know things, too. Things other people don't know. You're one of us." He gave me a sad smile. "Okay, I know you have never been locked up for it. But you're one of us." He chuckled at the look on my face. "Don't worry, man. I won't tell the white coats. And they wouldn't believe me anyway. So you're safe from me." He stood upright and leaned over the desk toward me. "Just watch out for the dead people. They'll get you into trouble."

At this point, Doc's mouth dropped open and his eyes opened wide. "Wait a minute! You're the guy who rode the freezer down Main Street into the river. Miles Archer was in the freezer. A dead guy already got you into trouble! See, was I right or was I right? You're one of us."

This conversation had gotten way out of hand.

"Hang on, Doc. You're way off base there, but I don't want to argue about it. I'm supposed to investigate this situation and find out whether you were tricked or coerced when you signed up for that research project. Besides talking to you, I need to talk to the other people who were in the project." I pointed my finger at him. "You feel that you were coerced with the implied offer of early release. Also, you were tricked because you did not know they wanted to find a way to stop you from seeing dead people. Is that right?"

"That's right, man. You got it. It isn't right that they should trick people that way."

He shook his head. "Life's hard enough. They take away my freedom too often and in too many ways. Tricking me into research projects is too much. It goes too far. They have no right to do that. I'm a person, aren't I? I'm not some kind of wild animal they can treat however they want."

"You're right, Doc. You're a person. You have rights. You should get to live your life the way you want as long as you don't hurt anyone else."

"You got it, man! If I want to see the dead people, I have a right to do that. If I want to live here in my house with my stuff, then I have a right to do that. Of course, sometimes I act wild. Then they have to lock me up for a bit, chill me out. Otherwise, they should leave me alone."

"I see your point." And I did. His trailer looked like a dump to me. The health department would have said it was unlivable. But Doc was clearly proud of his home. There was no telling what he saw when he looked at it. If he liked it, why should my standards take precedence over his? Heck, the caves lived in by early men probably smelled bad too, and we did not say early man was insane. The cabins lived in by frontiersmen a hundred years ago were worse than this mobile home, but we did not try to lock them up for being crazy.

Or maybe we did. Maybe the reason those guys lived out in the woods was because the city folk would have thrown them in an insane asylum for living in unsanitary houses or hearing voices or even for seeing dead people. Maybe the great adventurers were all crazy by conventional standards.

"Well, that about covers it, Doc. I will try to run down the other guys tomorrow and the next day. Then I'll write up my report and we will see what the feds decide to do."

"Cool, man."

"You understand that I have not made up my mind about what I'm going to say in the report, don't you? I might agree with you and I might not."

Doc smiled. "I get it, man. You have to say that. We're cool." He chuckled, then winked at me. "Hey, man. Why don't you come back and see me after you talk to those other guys? Maybe I can explain a few things to you. Answer a few questions."

That sounded like it might be helpful. "Thanks, I'll do that."

I headed for the door. "Thanks for your time. Catch you later."

He waved from his desk. "No problem at all."

As I closed the door behind me, I heard him call out, "Watch out for those dead people!" Then he roared with laughter.

Chapter 4.

Interview with Lew Archer

Scratch scratch scratch. Scratch scratch scratch.

It was dark in the room, but the scratching didn't worry me. It irritated me, but it didn't worry me. Bucky did this every night and being awakened at four in the morning day after day was leaving me exhausted. Usually, I would reach down beside the bed toward the floor, since Bucky always scratched the mattress on my side of the bed. Bucky would easily evade my grasp until I reached farther and farther, waking myself up even more, falling half off the bed. Then he would let me catch him and drag him by the collar up to the surface of the bed. Instead of choking and gasping, he would purr and snuggle into a warm spot.

After a week or so of this nonsense, I started taking my pillow out from under my head and swinging it down beside the bed. Bucky had no trouble evading the pillow. He would wait until I was tired of swinging at him, then start scratching again.

Betty pointed out to me that I was rewarding him with a game when what I really should have done was discourage him. She suggested I bring out the Big Gun in cat behavior modification: the spray bottle. The Big Gun was filled with plain tap water and the spray was gentle. We had purchased it from a pet store, so it was approved by all the appropriate pets' rights groups. And the darn thing was amazingly effective. The cats hated it. They would never repeat a behavior if they had been sprayed more than three times. At least, not while we were watching. I knew Bad Boy Bucky had met his match that night when I went to bed. The spray bottle was on the night stand, loaded and ready.

Four a.m. Scratch, scratch, scratch. I quickly reached up, grabbed the bottle, and sprayed myself in the face. Undeterred, I reversed the weapon and sprayed toward the sound. The scratching stopped. A shocked and offended silence arose from the direction of the floor that lasted a good thirty seconds. As I was nodding off again, I heard a tentative scratch-scratch. Having kept the bottle cradled in my arms I was able to fire off a fast volley.

Bucky was cured for the evening. However, he did not jump back onto the bed and go to sleep as he should have. Instead, he galloped around the house like a small buffalo. How a fifteen-week-old kitten running on carpet could make so much noise was a mystery to me, but Bad Boy Bucky could do it. Maybe it had to do with the size of his belly, since he ate more like a pig than a cat.

Fritter never acted out as badly as Bucky did; she was a lady cat. Betty said I was biased against Bucky in favor of Fritter, but who wouldn't be? Bucky could be a real pain in the neck. Yes, I loved him. But if he woke me again, I would spray him again, relishing the revenge.

Since my sleep had been interrupted night after night for weeks, I was a bit groggy when I set out on my quest the next day. My job would be to track down as many of the research subjects as I could find and interview them. I needed my wits about me, but would have to make do without them. Thank you very much, Bucky Boy.

That morning we went through our usual routine. I got up at dawn, showered, put on the coffee, then went over to the convenience store down the street to buy a newspaper. Actually, I usually bought two papers: the Milwaukee paper and the local paper. The local paper was a lot more fun to read. Sometimes the news was a regular riot. One time they reported on a program soon to be offered at the senior center in Cambridge about weird happenings in Wisconsin. One of the weird stores was about the local werewolf. Who would have guessed that you could find one of those living in rural Wisconsin? Or that folks at a senior center would enjoy hearing about it? Rural Midwesterners have more of a sense of humor than most city people realize. It's too subtle for them to notice, but it's definitely offbeat.

This particular morning the paper carried a story about a community foundation that was soliciting grant requests. They had $500,000 to give away for projects that would improve the quality of life in our little town of Fort Atkinson. This was not a trivial amount and it made me think about ways I would spend the money if it was mine to give away. Try that exercise sometime, and you may come to the same conclusion that I reached: almost any idea I could come up with would have only a short-lived benefit. How could you spend money so that it created a long-term improvement in the lives of people in the area? I had to set that problem aside for later study.

One of my favorite sections listed coming events. The paper that morning listed a duplicate bridge club, which I was glad to see, because sometimes it seemed that the game of bridge was disappearing from the world. Bridge required more mental effort than most people wanted to exert, especially if they grew up playing video games and watching action movies.

Another scheduled event was a meeting of the local chapter of the national alliance for the mentally ill. City people might think that all mentally ill folks lived in urban areas, but this was not accurate. One time the local paper carried a matter of fact story about a police call involving a man who complained that the voices in his head had gotten so loud that he could not hear anything else. The paper reported that the man's girlfriend had arrived on the scene and promised to take him to the emergency room for more meds. Rural emergency rooms saw their share of mentally ill people who had slipped off their trolleys a little bit.

Seventeen events were listed as occurring over the next two days. Interestingly, four were meetings of Alcoholics Anonymous groups and two were Weight Watchers groups. In fact, the state of Wisconsin was reporting a record number of arrests for drunk driving. It was obvious that local people were quietly struggling with their share of personal demons.

The thought of demons reminded me that I was due to get out of my chair and visit some people who had some serious demons to fight. My first stop was the hospital where Lew Archer was staying on a locked ward. The roads were icy and I didn't dare go faster than forty miles per hour. Everyone else was passing me. One turkey honked as he went by. I understood his irritation, but I was doing my best.

It was late in the morning when I checked in at the desk on the first floor of the building that housed the psychiatric patients. The locked ward was on the fourth floor and, naturally enough, visitors were not allowed in unless they had a reason to be there. Jim Jones, the vice president for research, had provided me with a letter signed by the chair of the psychiatry department that granted me access. Even so, the clerk at the front desk was cautious enough to confer by telephone with her counterparts on the unit before letting me pass by her. I gave her high marks for taking her job seriously.

The elevator took me to the fourth floor, then disgorged me into a hallway with no signs telling me which direction led to the locked wing. Wandering around brought me up against a door that blocked off the hallway into the unit. The windows were darkened so I could not see all the way in, but no one appeared to be directly on the other side. I pushed a button labeled 'talk' and called out 'hello?' After about twenty seconds, a voice responded, "Yes? May I help you?"

"I'm here to see Lew Archer."

"Visiting hours are this afternoon, sir."

"I have special permission for this visit."

Silence.

"This visit is not personal. It's official business."

There was a long silence. I assumed the person guarding this door had not yet been told about my impending arrival. Eventually a buzzer sounded, so I pushed on the door and it opened into a dimly lit hallway. The nurses' desk was about thirty feet down the corridor on the left. A few patient rooms were on the right side, but they were empty. Presumably the patients were in the day room.

I signed in at the nurses' desk, where a heavy-set, muscular man in white pants and a tee-shirt was busy filling out forms. The aide told me to wait while he went to get Lew Archer. He must have only gone a few feet, because the two of them were back in a few seconds. Lew was a big man, with skin as dark as it can get, who must have weighed close to three hundred pounds. He was wearing what looked like thrift store clothes and had a slow shuffling gait.

"You have a visitor, Lew," said the aide in a loud voice.

Lew looked at me blankly, but said nothing.

"You can go into the interview room," the aide told me, gesturing toward a room behind the nurses' station. He took Archer's arm and led us both into the room. As he left us, the aide said if I needed anything to 'just ask,' then closed the door.

Archer and I sat there quietly for a moment, then I introduced myself and told him why I was there. Archer said nothing in response, so I tried again.

"Lew, did you know you signed up for a research project a few months ago?"

After shifting in his seat, he replied in a deep, slow voice, "I did?"

"Yes, you did. A group of people who were staying on this floor all signed up to be in a special group. You were in the group."

Lew looked confused.

"Doc Watson was in the group, Miles Archer, and some others. Do you remember now?"

"Oh yeah. That group." He gave me a slow smile. I wasn't sure whether he remembered the group or not.

Lew smiled at me at this point. "Can I get out of here now?" he asked.

This question threw me off balance. "That isn't my decision, Lew." He just stared at me, waiting. I tried a different tack, which proved to be a mistake. "Lew, you must be in here because people were worried that you might get hurt out on the street, right?"

Lew's smile turned cynical. "You sayin' that safety is more important than freedom?" he asked.

"Sometimes."

His smile broadened. "Then let's you and me change clothes. You can be in here where it's safe and I'll go out and take my chances on the street."

I didn't answer; he knew I wasn't going to take him up on his offer.

He leaned back in his chair, eyelids drooping. "You a fool, man. Got no time for fools." He appeared to be dropping off to sleep. In the moment of silence that followed, we could hear shouting and laughing echoing from outside the room. The background noise was eerie. Then the door opened and a matronly black woman entered the room. She was carefully dressed, her hair was nicely done, and she was not wearing white. She did not look at all like the staff members I had seen up to this point.

"Lew," she said. "I need to get your signature on some forms."

"Hey, Mama," he responded, "you gonna get me outta here?"

"Yes, dear," she said soothingly. "Soon. When it's time."

"I'll get my bag," he said, starting to rise.

"No, no, not yet," she responded, putting her hand on his shoulder and pushing him back down into his chair. "Just sign these forms for the nurses." She pushed the forms in front of him and held out a pen.

Lew pushed them away and ignored the pen. "I don't wanna sign no forms."

"Why not, Lew honey?"

"Don't know what they for. Could be anything."

She sighed. Obviously this conversation was going about as she had expected. She pulled the forms over to her side of the table, sat down, and started to sign them herself. She had beautiful handwriting, very clear and firm.

I leaned over to look at what she was doing. She was writing "Lewis Archer" on each form. She shot me a suspicious but defiant glare. "You must be a school teacher," I said. "Your cursive looks like you've been practicing it for a long time."

"Thank you," she said. "And yes, I have been teaching K through 12 for thirty years." She finished the stack of forms and turned toward me. "Now, what business do you have with my son?"

"I'm auditing a research project Lew was enrolled in. I needed to ask him a few questions about it."

"Did he give you the information you needed?"

"Not really. He does not seem to remember much about it."

"That's no surprise."

"Maybe you could tell me about it. I'll buy you a coffee or a soda. Are you available any time soon?"

"Yes, as soon as I turn these forms in at the desk." She stood up to go.

Lew looked up. "Can I go now, Mama?"

"No, dear, not just yet. You just rest while everybody does their paperwork. You know the paper comes first."

"Yeah, I know," he said resignedly. We left him sitting in his chair. After we went through the locked door in the corridor, she led me back to the elevators, then turned to me with an outstretched hand. "Margaret Archer," she said. "Ed Schumacher," I responded, bowing slightly as I shook her hand. Her eyes crinkled a bit at the corners as she suppressed a smile. We rode down to the ground floor in silence. A few chairs formed a waiting room outside the reception area. It was empty at that moment. Margaret showed me the coffee vending machine, located behind the elevators. We punched in our selections then seated ourselves in a couple of vinyl-clad aluminum-framed chairs.

After we were comfortable, Margaret fixed me with a direct stare and waited for me to explain myself.

"Well, it's like this," I began. "I can't give you all of the particulars, but the main issue you might be interested in is simply this: Lew was enrolled in a research project that involved a small group of people who all happened to be upstairs on the locked unit at the same time. They also all had similar delusions."

"Yes," Margaret said. "I remember that. What about it?"

"The federal agency that monitors research directed the university to contract with an independent investigator to audit the project. That's me. My job is to find out if all the important procedures were followed."

"There has to be more to the story than that," Margaret said. "Random checks I can understand, but bringing in an outside investigator can't be routine." She was a smart woman.

"You might have a point there, but if you don't mind, let's just skip ahead to the essential facts as they relate to Lew. First, you have already confirmed that Lew was in the project. Do you think he knew what he was signing up for?" I gave her the most wide-eyed and guileless facial expression I could muster up. She was not fooled one bit.

"You mean, did I sign the consent form for him."

"Did you?"

"Why would I want to admit to such a thing?"

"Maybe I should just pull out the form and see if the handwriting is as beautiful as yours."

Margaret laughed. "Yes, I imagine that could prove something. Lew writes like a ten year old. But what difference does it make anyway?"

"Nobody is supposed to be enrolled in a research project unless he knows what it's about and has agreed to be in it."

"Lew gave me his power of attorney years ago. I am his guardian and the payee on his disability checks. Besides that, I'm his mother, and since his judgment is impaired, I have to make choices for him."

"Even children have to agree to be in a research project. Their parents can't just sign them up without talking them into it."

"That's ridiculous. Look, you don't understand how it is with mentally ill people. The medical care system is a mess when it comes to people with chronic mental illness. Unless parents get deeply involved and push hard, the patients won't get what they need."

"So I've heard." She looked at me with some suspicion in her gaze. "There's a lot of truth in what you say."

"It's completely true. Anyone who has had a family member in the system knows how quickly they get dumped on the street with no services. And dumping them is easy since the sick person often does not want any services. They just want to be let out the door."

"Like Lew."

"Yes, like Lew. He just wants out now. He's not thinking about where he will sleep or where he will get his next meal. He definitely is not thinking about where he will get his meds. Without those meds he will be back in the emergency room in less than a month, if he hasn't been killed in a fight before then." She was breathing hard from her passionate outburst. At the same time, it sounded well-rehearsed.

"I understand the problem."

"I don't think you do. The system gives an insane person rights that he can't handle, then makes me break the rules if I want him to get services. Yes, I sign his name. Yes, I make sure the doctor gets all the information he should have about Lew, even if the doctor doesn't want to take the time to talk to me. I have to fight and fight and fight to get anything out of this system. People like Lew need to be placed in supervised apartments. They can't be just dumped out on the street. Families that give up the fight against the system get nothing that they need." She was really steamed.

"Believe me, I understand what you are trying to do. Still, the law says Lew has rights. If the law needs to be changed, then our society should change it. "

"While we wait for that to happen, Lew and thousands of other people like him could die of exposure or violence." She stopped talking and the silence between us began to stretch uncomfortably.

"Margaret," I said finally, "upstairs when Lew asked me to let him out I mentioned safety and he asked me if I preferred safety to freedom. That made me think about what I would prefer if I was the one locked up. Would I want to be able to make my own choices, even if my judgment was impaired?" I took a swig of my cold coffee. "Sure I would. I do it all the time. We live in a complicated world. Most of my important decisions are based on guesses about what might work out best. When you go to the polls, do you really know that you are voting for a candidate who will do a good job? When you park your retirement money somewhere, are you sure it's a going to be a good investment? We make choices and sometimes we guess wrong."

"It doesn't usually make us homeless or hungry when we make a bad choice," Margaret said through clenched teeth. "We aren't likely to choose to take a ten mile walk in the snow, barefoot and hatless."

"That's true. But I have to tell you, the older I get the more I realize that life is tragic. Everybody gets sick and dies, some sooner than others. It's part of the Grand Plan, whether we like it or not."

Margaret was done with me by this point. She got up and went out the door without another word, throwing her full cup of coffee into the trash as she went. She was angry, and who could blame her; life had dealt her a nasty hand of cards. She was left holding two's and three's when she needed aces to protect her son. Unfortunately, even if she had all the aces, there was no way to protect her son from all the dangers he faced. Lew was a very vulnerable guy, despite his enormous size and obvious physical strength.

As I left the hospital, I was mulling over the problem faced by the families of mentally ill people. If you advocate strongly on behalf of your loved one and you succeed in forcing the system to provide services, will the patient be happier than he would have been if you had left him alone? And what kind of ethical boundaries do you have to cross to be a 'strong advocate?' When you fraudulently sign the patient's name to a form, you have crossed a line. When you exaggerate the patient's symptoms to the doctor so that he will crank up the meds, what kind of harm might you be doing? When you tell the patient where to live and how to live, you have imposed your values and preferences on someone who sees the world through an entirely different lens. Is all this to make the patient happier? Or is it really intended to make the parent feel better about the tragedy of mental illness?

To the uninitiated, the guilt felt by the parent of a mentally ill person is hard to imagine. Modern science knows that unless you tortured your child, you probably did not cause his psychosis. Even so, parents feel that the way the child 'turned out' reflects on their parenting. And when living in the same home with an adult psychotic turns out to be an unacceptable and unsustainable option, the parent gets a double dose of guilt because many other parents simply do not understand why the sick person cannot just live at home.

Of course, many parents make that sacrifice. But, unless one person stays at home all day on guard, drug dealers or a crowd of other undesirables are likely to end up in their living room, eating their food, and stealing their television. A shadowy crowd of low-lifes make their living by exploiting the mentally disabled. When the monthly disability check arrives, the creeps come out of their dark corners and buddy up to – or beat up - the people who should be benefiting from those checks. Unless we intend to lock up all the mentally disabled people in the world for their own protection, someone will find a way to periodically exploit them.

The tragedy of mental illness does not just affect the sick person. It affects the mental health of their families as well. A person with a serious and persistent mental illness is often fated to live a dangerous life. Parents are forced to observe, to help a little when they can, but mostly they just watch. Parents of mentally ill persons face a double-whammy when it comes to emotions: guilt and powerlessness, both of which are very hard to bear.

The interviews with Lew and Margaret Archer gave me a lot to think about. I drove home at a sedate pace, then parked myself in the garage to smoke my pipe. Smoking in the house was a bad idea, but smoking outside in December was not a pleasant experience. Consequently, I had placed a chair, a space heater, and a side table in a corner of the garage. With a warm coat and hat, I could relax and consider the complexities of modern life for as much as an hour at a time before becoming chilled.

After returning from the psych hospital, I zeroed in on my smoking spot like a homing pigeon. The ethical dilemmas facing parents had no simple answer, so I gave up on that issue. Instead, my mind turned to the mysterious circumstances of the dead man in the freezer. Each of the patients in the research project had at least one dead man in the head. How did imaginary dead people produce an actual dead person? Not being an expert on the occult, I was pretty sure that dead people did not directly cause the death of real people. Maybe this would sound like an unenlightened attitude to some. After all, Hamlet said there are more things in heaven and earth than were dreamed of in Horatio's philosophy. He said that because he was in dialogue with a ghost.

Despite the possibility that ghosts might exist, I was going to attack this mystery scientifically. I was going to assume that the dead cannot reach through the veil of tears and crush the life out of us. Perhaps that sort of thing could actually happen, but it had to be so rare that it should be ignored as a possible explanation for the death of a particular person, i.e., Miles Archer.

Shaking off the chill, I returned to the basic challenge of any person who plays detective: asking the right questions. In this case, the key question on the table appeared to be the following: was Miles Archer's death connected to the research project? If so, who killed him and why?

The news reports after the body was found in the freezer had said little about the circumstances of the death. Apparently, the outrageous way the body had been discovered was more newsworthy. They reported the victim's name, that he was homeless, and that he had apparently ingested a large quantity of alcohol prior to death. Very little else was known. My investigation of the research project had turned up more background on the victim than the reporter had found.

Assuming for the moment that Archer's death was connected to the project, my list of suspects was limited. It included the other patients who had been in the group and the researcher, Dr. Zelicov. I was willing to rule out Lew Archer, despite his history of violence, because he had been locked up too much of the time and because the placement of the body in a freezer seemed to require far more subtlety than Lew could display.

The most obvious suspect for the murder was the man who had been pushing the freezer. Nevertheless, to assume that someone had killed a man, placed the body in a freezer, then pushed the freezer down the middle of Main Street was jumping to conclusions. That would lack discretion, if you know what I mean. You would have to be nuts to do that. For now, I was willing to accept the working hypothesis that the man pushing the freezer was not the killer.

Sometimes the most obvious answer is the correct one, but I intended to keep an open mind on the subject.

After finishing my pipe, I went upstairs where I found Betty reading a book.

"How is your day going?" she asked.

"Just fine. Interesting. This investigation of the psych research project has some fascinating ethical twists and turns."

"That's nice. I'm glad you are working on a project." Betty did not have much interest in the projects that I got involved in, but she generally liked to see me busy. She knew I was the sort of person who had to work to avoid getting depressed. And she also knew that, once drawn into a puzzle, I would give it my full attention until it was solved. Obsessive and compulsive were two of my more prominent traits.

Walking into the spare bedroom where we kept the computer, I turned it on and waited for a connection. It was time to check for messages and pay a few bills. Fritter came in, jumped on my lap for a little petting, then moved to her favorite spot: the modem. The modem was warm and also was under the desk lamp. By sitting there, Fritter was warmed from above and below, which she really seemed to enjoy. She would sit there for hours if I was working on the computer. Bucky came in next, attempted to jump on my lap, fell off, and had to be picked up. He immediately rolled onto his side and began purring. When I tired of petting him and began working on the computer, he sat on the table and watched me. When I lifted my hand to move the mouse, his head would turn to follow the action. Fritter's did as well. The two cat heads moved in synchrony: forward, back, left, right. This went on until I stopped noticing them. The fascination with my computer work was unfathomable, who could know what a cat was thinking? Their mysterious nature was part of the reason humans loved having them around.

Betty came in after half an hour or so. She was wearing an unfortunate black dress.

"How do you like my new dress?" she asked. "I just bought it."

"Mmhmph" I said to buy time. Every husband knew when he was in a dangerous situation. He knew it because he had erred on the side of honesty early in the marriage and still bore the scars.

"What does that mean?"

"Very nice." Okay, so it was an outright lie. But when dealing with women's fashion, the normal rules of ethical behavior simply do not apply.

"Do you think it's too tight?"

Darn, a direct question. "Your butt never looked smaller." This was the stock answer. Trial and error had revealed that it was always acceptable.

Betty turned to look at her behind. She considered it's magnitude for a moment, then asked, "should I wear it to the holiday dinner with the clinic staff?"

At this point, some courage on my part was required. If she wore that thing to the dinner, she would decide halfway through the meal that it was too tight.

"That other one you have is better."

"Which other one?"

"You know, the one I like."

"Which one do you like?"

"The one with a belt. It shows you have a waist. And makes your bodice more prominent."

"Bodice? What have you been reading?"

"Bodice is a real word."

"Maybe it was a hundred years ago. You should get out more." Then she whirled around and left the room. In five minutes she was back, wearing a looser dress that was longer, had more color, had a belt, and displayed her charms admirably, both of them.

"I decided this would be better," she announced.

"It's great. It makes you look like Barbara Streisand."

"Why do you think Barbara Streisand looks good?"

"Because she looks like you. By the way, Andrew and I are going out for a beer tomorrow night." Andrew was Betty's cousin. He lived in Fort Atkinson, also.

"You're impossible" she declared, then left. Sometimes a stupid remark combined with a change of subject is the best strategy for ending a conversation. Try it sometime. See if it doesn't work.

Chapter 5.

Interview with Archie Goodwin

The next day I was eager to get back to work on my investigation. My first task of the day was a visit to Archie Goodwin who lived in a group home called Happy View in Janesville, near Madison. Janesville was only about half an hour away, down Highway 26. When I drove up to the building, I was surprised to see that it was very large. It obviously had begun its life as an apartment building or hotel. It must have contained several hundred rooms.

The sidewalk out front and up the street in both directions was dotted with people who looked like they might be residents of Happy View. Many had an air of unkemptness, with shabby clothes and hair in disarray. Buildings in nearby strip malls were boarded up. It appeared that being near Happy View was not an attractive location for businesses.

A crowd of people were standing around the reception desk joking among themselves. At first I could not distinguish the residents from the staff. However, it gradually became apparent who was more alert, so I guessed they must be the people in charge. On the other hand, I may have guessed wrong.

Archie Goodwin's name was called repeatedly. His room was called via telephone and the day room received the benefit of several loud shouts. Eventually, somebody found Archie out on the patio. He approached me with some caution, but when I suggested driving over to the Dairy Queen he quickly signed himself out and away we went.

Archie did not ask why I was visiting him. He just waited quietly until he got his Blizzard, then dug into it with enthusiasm. That fellow really knew how to enjoy his ice cream. He seemed to forget everything going on around him as he consumed it. Finally, he set aside the empty cup with a sigh and leaned back in the seat.

Archie was a young man, probably in his twenties. He was skinny, boney even, with hollow cheeks. He looked as if he had been seriously malnourished at some time in his life.

I decided to try an indirect opening. "Say, Archie, what's it like living in that place?"

Archie looked at me with amazement. "How do you think? How would you like to live with a bunch of crazies? Those people are nuts. Ain't a soul there I would hang out with if I had a choice. Wish I could get outa there. But they ain't never letting me out. It's like a prison."

"Why can't you get out? They let you sign out with no problem."

"Yeah, I could walk away. Lots of people do that. But I don't have no job. Nobody is going to hire me. With no job I can't get a place to live. Can't get no car so can't drive to a job, anyway. I'm trapped, man."

At this point he turned to me and asked, "who are you? And why did you buy me an ice cream?"

"My name is Ed. I need to ask you some questions about a research project you were in back when you were on the inpatient unit at the psych hospital. And I'm sure glad I bought you that ice cream because it's been years since I saw anybody enjoy one as much as you did."

Archie snorted. He obviously thought I was scamming him. "What research project are you talking about? I wasn't in no research project."

"It was like a therapy group. Doc Watson, Sherlock Holmes, Lew Archer, and some others were in the group with you."

"I remember some of those guys. That was research? I thought it was just another damn boring group thing. They made us do groups every day."

"Would you have said 'no' if they asked you to be in a group for research?"

"Damn right. Groups are a drag." He hesitated for a moment, then asked, "What did we talk about in the group? Sometimes groups can be fun. Were there any women in the group?"

"Yes, there was a woman in the group--Miss Marple."

"Marple! She was hot. But way off in the 'zone, if you know what I mean. What did we talk about in the group?"

"You talked about seeing dead people."

Archie froze. "No way," he said.

"Yes, that was what the research was about."

"They was researching our dead people?"

"Uh, no, they were trying to figure out how to help you stop seeing them."

Archie was silent for a moment. Finally he said, "no way."

"Would you have signed up if you knew that was what they were trying to do?"

Silence. Then, "I'm ready to go back now."

We drove back to the group home without talking. I pulled up in front of the place and, as he started to get out of the car, I stopped him with a question. "Archie, did it work?"

Archie stared at me with his big starvation eyes dominating his skinny face. "What do you think, man? How in the hell would talking in a group keep dead people away? That's just stupid." He slammed the door and slouched away.

Goodwin certainly had a point. The whole premise of the research project seemed ridiculous. Had the investigator really believed this treatment was going to work? Who could be that dumb?

As I drove back to Fort Atkinson, I remembered that I was supposed to meet Andrew for a beer. We generally met at Sal's, since that was convenient for both of us. Come to think of it, no place in Fort was more than ten minutes away from where either of us lived.

Going directly to Sal's parking lot, rather than stopping off at home first, I found that Andrew was already at a table, nursing a beer.

"Hey, how's it going?" he asked.

"Just fine. Been here long?"

"About five minutes."

After ordering a Miller for myself, we talked about the weather a bit, then Andrew asked me, "so, Betty tells me you've got yourself a new case."

"Yep. Sure do."

"How did that happen?"

"The med school in Madison called me and asked me to look into something for them."

"I thought you and them weren't on the best of terms."

"Well, you can sure say that again. But it turns out the feds told them they should call me in. An independent perspective was needed."

"Why independent?"

"Because the feds knew those guys at the med school would cook their investigation till it came out right if they had a chance."

We both chuckled at that for a bit.

"Well, are you turning up anything interesting?" Andrew was an investigator for the state of Wisconsin. He found my little amateur investigations amusing.

"For sure. Somehow it's tied up with the dead guy in the freezer."

"The one you rode into the river?"

"Yup. The dead guy was one of the patients in the research project. The feds suspect that the death may have somehow been due to the project. That tells me that if I can figure out how the two are connected, I might solve the murder case."

"You can't investigate a murder. You're not qualified and you have no legal standing."

"True. But I'm not investigating the murder. I'm investigating the research project. It's not my fault that the two are connected."

"How could they be connected?"

"I don't know. I was hoping you could give me some ideas. The facts are pretty skimpy at this point. All the people in the research project are mentally ill, including the dead guy."

'Mentally ill? What's wrong with them?"

"Psychosis. They have some serious delusions. They see dead people."

"You're trying to get at the truth by interviewing these people?"

"Yup."

"Well, good luck. And you better stay away from the murder issue. You'll get into big trouble." Andrew sighed, then relented a bit. "I don't have any ideas for you. When you get more information, let's talk about it again. Maybe something will come out later. What else are you learning?"

"The way our society deals with people who have serious mental problems is really shameful. I say it's shameful because of the way it turns out, but I don't really have a clear idea of how to do it better."

"What do you mean?"

"Well, these folks have trouble coping. It's not their fault; they just don't understand the world the same way everyone else does. In some ways they just don't get it. In other ways, they understand their situation very well, but still can't manage to cope very well. We seem to be telling them just to go out and get a job and work hard and everything will be fine. But not everyone can do that. As a last resort, we give them a disability check, but that doesn't solve all the problems. It's a mess."

"What's wrong with just giving them a check?"

"Well, for one thing, the cost of living is quite a bit more than a disability check will cover. Until we find ways to keep the cost of living down, lot's of people, not just psych patients, will continue to be deep in poverty, not able to afford basic food and medicine and housing."

"Oh, this is where you say everyone should drive electric bikes." Andrew liked to tease me about the time I got into selling electric bicycle motors.

"An electric bike sure would be a form of cheap transportation. It's environmentally safe and it's affordable."

"Well, I see your point," Andrew said. "But the price of gas has gone up and now renewable energy sources are going to be used a lot more. That should make you happy."

"Happy? You must be kidding. These days it seems that everyone is on the renewable energy bandwagon. Rising oil prices have created the impetus, and a variety of businesses and governments have experienced suspiciously sudden conversions to the Green camp. It looks to me like the political support for energy conservation is rapidly being diverted into profits for business interests rather than lower energy costs and a lower cost of living for consumers."

"Do you really believe that? Give me a for instance."

"Okay, think about this. In Northern Ireland the government plans to develop a Renewable Energy Strategy. The Ulster Farmers' Union praised the decision, pointing out that their members are happy to grow the crops. A boom in the local agriculture industry appears imminent, at taxpayers' expense."

"Farm subsidies are pretty popular around here. You better be careful what you say against them."

By this time I was on a roll. "Even the garbage business is getting in on the gravy train. In Malaysia, the Jana landfill, located 40km outside of Kuala Lumpur, is one of the city's main municipal storage waste sites. Landfills are a potential source of 'free fuel' that would otherwise be flared or vented. This sounds like a good opportunity for tax payer savings, but we shouldn't jump to conclusions about who will benefit. GE built the plant and opened it in 2004 before the current oil price hike, presumably because they anticipated a profit. The government of Malaysia has been giving a 70 percent tax break for five years to companies that develop renewable energy sources. They now are proposing to increase the tax break to 100 percent and extend it for ten years. How can the cost of living be reduced for the average consumer when business is getting deals like that?"

"Okay, maybe our utility bills won't go down. But hybrid cars are available now and they reduce how much the average consumer pays for gas."

"Yeah, right, hybrid cars. What a crock. Hybrid vehicles are not affordable for working class families."

"Not affordable?"

"Right. The last car you bought was a Dodge Neon. A hybrid would have cost you more than twice as much. The savings at the pump will never be enough to make up for the higher price of the car. Besides, low income people can't come up with the monthly payments for an expensive car, no matter how good their mileage is."

"Are you trying to say that the renewable energy policies are all cooked up by corporations so they can increase their profits?"

"Many of these policies will benefit businesses more than consumers. Here is another example for you. The state of Connecticut is 'incentivizing' businesses to use renewable energy sources such as fuel cells or solar panels. Millions in grants are available for businesses to set up such renewable energy generating facilities at their sites. Taxpayers are paying the bill for these changes. A tax on businesses that refused to switch to renewable energy sources would have had the same effect, at less cost to the taxpayer."

"Where do you get these stories? They sound pretty outlandish to me."

"Off the internet, of course. I just do a Google news search and it pulls up the newspaper stories." I took a sip from my beer, then went on. "Try this one. In Washington State, Puget Sound Energy has acquired 100 percent ownership of a big wind energy project. The CEO of the company had the gall to praise the hard work of local and state officials who made this monopoly possible for his company. He didn't explain why local ownership of smaller wind energy generating sites wouldn't have been better for the people of the state of Washington."

"Okay, that one sounds a little out there. I'll give you one."

"Let me try for another. The governor of Georgia said the devastation caused by recent hurricanes had motivated him to push his state toward greater 'energy security.' This was smart. He managed to bring up the words 'security' and 'disaster' in the same sentence. Anyway, he wants to give tax credits and incentives for people who drive fuel-efficient cars, homeowners who convert to solar power, and businesses that create new forms of energy. Unfortunately, the governor did not say how the people who lost their jobs and homes due to hurricanes would benefit from the tax credits. With no jobs they won't be paying taxes."

"Okay, one more point for you. Betcha can't get another."

"Bet I can. Try this. The governor of Vermont said big industrial wind energy factories with tall turbines 'don't belong' on Vermont's mountaintops. But, at the same time, he is supporting a commercial wind project to be placed on top of a mountain that will include four 330-foot tall strobe-lighted turbines located on government land. He says he is not being inconsistent because the project is just a demonstration project. It sounds to me like government land is being provided so that big business can get the kinks out of industrial wind technology. Once again, the taxpayers foot the bill so commercial interests can cash in on the energy crisis. What will the little guy get out of it?"

"You sound more like a socialist every day." Andrew said.

"When you are retired and trying to live on a social security check, you will wish the cost of living was lower. And if you or one of your kids develops a serious mental illness and can't figure out how to keep a check book, I might just tell you to go out and buy a hybrid car. You remember what Marie Antoinette said when she was told the peasants were starving?"

"Yup. She said 'let them eat cake.'"

"Here's to cake," I said, raising my glass. Andrew raised his in response, we clinked them together, and drank them down.

Chapter 6

Interview with Miss Marple

Bucky was being his usual self that morning, bounding around like mad, clawing my wool slacks, clawing my office chair, and pulling my ties off the hanger onto the floor. I didn't mind because this was the day Bucky went in to be neutered. How often do we get to behave in a socially responsible manner and also get revenge at the same time? Don't get me wrong; I loved Bucky, but I was still gleeful about having his goods snipped off.

I picked him up to pet him, then popped him into his carrying bag. Betty was worried, of course. She thought he might die under the knife.

"Poor guy. Don't you feel bad for him?"

"Not really."

"He might die during the operation."

"He won't die during the operation."

"He might. It happens."

"He's young and very healthy. He'll be fine." After that exchange I hustled him out the door. When we were ushered into the vets examination room, Bucky was his usual, lovable self. He purred so much that the vet had trouble listening to his heart and lungs. The vet and her assistant loved him.

"He is very friendly, isn't he?"

"Yes indeed. He loves everybody. Say, do you think he will be a little less rambunctious after the operation?"

The vet shook her head, "No, I'm afraid not. Would you like more information about the procedure?"

"I'd rather not know the details, frankly." The vet and her assistant found my squeamishness amusing. They said I could pick him up anytime after noon. "Oh, one more thing."

The vet had been on her way through the door. She stopped with a quizzical expression. "Yes?" she asked.

"This is kind of a big event. My wife is nervous about the operation." I hesitated, unsure about how to go on. "Yes, Mr. Schumacher?" the vet asked.

"Could you save the parts for us?" I blurted out.

"Excuse me?"

"Well, you know, old people like to show their scars after a big surgery and when you pay a lot of money to have your car fixed they offer to give you the old parts, so I put those two ideas together and thought I would just ask for Bucky's parts."

The vet thought for a moment. "I can't think of any reason why not," she said, then left the room shaking her head at the strangeness of customers.

The next stop after the vet clinic was a small group home in Watertown, which was located about 45 minutes north of Fort Atkinson on Highway 26. This was where I had been told I could find Miss Marple. The drive over took less than an hour, but then I got turned around, as I usually do, and wasted nearly an hour trying to find the address. It turned out to be an ordinary looking house in a residential neighborhood. The streets were lined with trees, leaves were mixed in with snow on the ground, and toys were laying abandoned on the drifts.

I parked on the street in front of the house, then climbed the steps to the front door. Ringing the bell brought a heavyset man to the door. When I explained my errand, he acted as if he had not been told that I had a legitimate reason for talking to Miss Marple. On the other hand, he did not appear to care one way or the other. He led me into the living room, where an attractive young black woman sat in an easy chair with an afgan covering her lap and legs. My escort did not introduce us. He just waved me toward her, then left the room.

"Hi. My name is Ed," I said. "Do you mind if I ask you a few questions?"

Miss Marple did not answer, but she favored me with an angelic smile. I took that as permission to charge ahead.

"A few weeks ago when you were in the hospital you were part of a research project. Do you remember that?"

"Maybe," she said still smiling.

"Some of the other people in the group were Doc Watson, Lew Archer, and Miles Archer. Do you remember those guys?"

"Maybe."

"Can you tell me anything about the group you were in?"

Miss Marple hesitated, then said, "I've been sick."

That was when the realization finally struck me: she had no idea what I was talking about. The smile was angelic, but the mind was vacant. As we used to say back home, the lights were on but nobody was home. There was no point in asking any more questions. I found the heavy set man in the kitchen and told him I was leaving. He didn't seem surprised at the brevity of my visit. He also didn't seem to care.

Chapter 7.

Interview with Sherlock Holmes

I went directly from Miss Marple's place to see the last person on my list, Sherlock Holmes, who was reputed to be living in a homeless shelter in downtown Madison. The place was not hard to find, being a large and relatively new building on one of the main streets. Inside the front door, visitors were confronted with a receptionist who sat in a glassed-in enclosure. I wondered if the glass was bullet-proof. Down the corridor behind her, I could see a large room walled off into sections with what looked like floor-to-ceiling chain link fencing. Living there would be like living in a dog kennel, I thought.

When I asked for Holmes, I was told that he did not reside there anymore. The receptionist suggested I try another shelter, just down the street. The other shelter was called "Saint Martha's Mission."

When I found the place I realized that not all homeless shelters are equal. Holmes definitely had taken a step down when he moved to this place. It was a large building that was in poor repair. Scruffy men were hanging out around it, leaning against the building smoking cigarettes. It reminded me of the large group home where I had found Archie Goodwin. Perhaps the only difference between the two was that Archie was given medicine in Pleasant View while Saint Martha's had no health services. Yet, when I stepped in the front door I quickly reached the conclusion that a lot of the residents could have benefited from some pysch meds. One man was dressed in a bed sheet and had a trash can on his head. Much of the conversation that could be overheard seemed to make no sense at all.

They found Holmes for me. That was when I received the biggest surprise of the day. Sherlock Holmes was the man with the freezer. He was the man whom I had helped, much to my detriment. He had abandoned me to the police when the freezer ended up in the river. And he definitely had some explaining to do, starting with the biggest question now on my mind: how did Miles Archer's body get into the freezer?

When he got in the car, Holmes asked me for a cigarette. When told I had none, he became even more withdrawn, so I pulled over behind a convenience store and gave him some money go in and buy a pack. He scooted out in a hurry. While he was gone, I called Betty on my cell phone to tell her where I was and how long it would be before I came home.

During the call, I got out of the car and leaned against the driver's side door. Holmes returned, with a lighted cigarette in his hand. I told him "just a minute" and turned away to finish the call. He needed time to finish his cigarette, anyway. I did not want him to smoke in the car.

Five minutes later we were driving away. We quickly became entangled in traffic, however. All the cars on the street froze in place as a fire truck and a couple of police cars rushed past us with sirens blaring. After they were gone, traffic resumed its flow. Holmes and I ended up at a Wendy's, with me having a bowl of chili and him having a large value meal. He was vacuuming up his food like a ravenous Hoover when we first seated ourselves, so I said nothing until he finished. Then, I went through my spiel about what I was trying to learn and why I was talking to him.

"Do you remember the group sessions, Holmes?" I asked him.

"Yeah. Sorta."

"Did you know you had signed up for a research project?"

"Yeah. I guess so. It didn't matter. Something to do."

"Did you know what the project was trying to do?"

"Maybe I did at the time. Don't remember. It wouldn't have made any difference to me. I still would have signed up."

"Why wouldn't the purpose of the project make any difference to you?"

"You say they were trying to stop us from seeing dead people by having a group? That's dumber'n dirt, man. Waste of time. But what the hell; wasting time is all you got to do when you're in the psych unit."

"Well, that's great. You gave me the information I needed." Now it was time to change to a more interesting subject.

"Holmes, we've seen each other before, you know."

'Yeah?" His eyes became hooded and cautious.

"Yep. When you were pushing that freezer across Main Street in Fort Atkinson, I stopped to help. Remember that?"

"What about it?"

"What about it? You left me in the lurch there, fellah. The freezer ended up in the river, with me going along with it."

Holmes chuckled at that image.

"Yeah, you might think that sounds funny. But after they dragged me out of the water, the cops found a body in that freezer. They had a lot of questions I couldn't answer, like who put the body in the freezer? I wish you had been there to explain things a bit."

"Don't like cops. So I split."

"Well, at least you can tell me what was going on. The dead guy was Miles Archer. He was in your research group. Somebody killed him by sticking him in a freezer when he was loaded and letting him suffocate or freeze to death or maybe both. Who did that and why?"

"He asked for it," Holmes blurted out.

I was stunned into silence for a moment. My mouth hung open. Had Holmes just said what I thought he said? It came close to an admission of guilt.

"Are you telling me..." I started to ask him, but it was too late. He was out of his seat and through the door before I could finish the question. He was moving fast, so I didn't bother to try to catch up with him. He did not appear to want to discuss the subject any further.

With my interview terminated so abruptly, there was nothing to do except go home. I picked Bucky up at the vet and took him back to the condo. He didn't seem to be particularly uncomfortable. Then I smoked my pipe until Betty returned home. The garage door went up to let in her car around two in the afternoon. Betty was working half days in a medical clinic. She was a physician who had been a university professor, as I had, before we moved to Fort Atkinson. Betty had rushed home because she was planning to do a little shopping, which was definitely more interesting to her than work.

We were headed to Cambridge to visit the pottery store. Cambridge was about ten miles down the road from Fort Atkinson. Before we started out, however, I had to buy Betty a Happy Meal at McDonald's. She never seemed to have time for lunch when she was working, so she was starving. We needed to get something for her quickly, so McDonald's was the best bet. Besides, sometimes she just got hungry for a Happy Meal. Actually, she really developed a periodic hankering for one of the toys that comes in a Happy Meal. When that happened, it was best not to be slow about providing one.

We drove up to the drive-through because Betty was convinced that she was committing a felony by ordering a child's meal when she was an adult. At the drive-through window, she could feign innocence. The conversation at the speaker box went something like this.

"May I help you, sir?"

"We would like one Happy Meal with a coke and one burger with a diet coke."

"What kind of hamburger, sir?"

"What kind is on the dollar menu?"

"Excuse me, sir?"

"The dollar menu! What kind of burger is on the dollar menu?"

"A regular hamburger, sir."

"Then that's what I want."

"Excuse me, sir?"

"I. Want. A. Regular. Hamburger."

"What did you want to drink with that, sir?"

"A. Diet. Coke."

"Yes, sir. That will be five forty-nine."

"Wait!"

"Yes, sir?"

"We want a girl toy!"

"Excuse me, sir?"

"WE WANT A GIRL TOY IN THE HAPPY MEAL!" In the rear view mirror, I could see the people in the car behind me were laughing.

"Yes, sir. Please pull up to the next window."

When I pulled up to the next window, the cashier handed me the food and accepted my money. Betty was trying to make herself invisible by looking out the passenger window and pretending she was not in the car. When the Happy Meal was handed over I said, "It's not for me. I would have asked for a boy toy."

"Really, sir?" asked the cashier with a smile.

"That didn't sound quite right, but you know what I mean."

"Yes, sir. I think I do. Have a nice day."

When we drove away, there were several moments of silence. Finally, I announced, "I hate drive through-windows."

Betty did not answer at first. Then she said, "I am so humiliated."

"It's better to get out of the car and go in for your food. That way, they can at least understand what you want."

"Most people in the world can manage to use a drive-through window. You are the only one who has problems."

"Really?" Was it possible that she was correct on that point?

We rode in silence to the pottery store in Cambridge. Betty was determined to enjoy herself despite the fiasco at McDonald's, so she went in. I opted to stay outside and smoke my pipe.

Before lighting up, I cleaned the trash out of the car, stuffing it into a can by the door of the pottery store. Then I loaded my pipe, lit up, and leaned against the car to puff. After ten minutes or so, some other customers arrived. A young couple tossed their half-empty soda cups in the trash can. A family came by and threw in their fast food trash. This prompted a certain level of uneasiness in my mind, but I could not quite put my finger on what was bothering me.

I puffed a few more minutes when suddenly I realized my mistake: I had thrown away the McDonald's bag. Quickly, I searched the car for the girl toy. It was nowhere to be seen. This was an emergency. If, after all that embarrassment, Betty did not have her girl toy to show for the trip to McDonald's, my life would not be worth a plugged nickel.

There was no alternative. I went over to the trash can and plunged my arm in up to the shoulder, feeling around for the bag I had thrown in and the treasure within it. The side of my face was pushed against the cold metal of the trash can as I rooted around in its bowels like a gastroenterologist with a scope.

While I was so engaged, I heard a car drive up. Footsteps approached me. A voice spoke out somewhere beyond my left ear.

"So, Mr. Schumacher, you taking up dumpster diving?"

"First of all, this is not a dumpster. Dumpsters are bigger. Second, I'm not diving into it. I'm just feeling around. So this is not dumpster diving because it involves neither a dumpster nor diving. Any dodo should be able to tell that." Ordinarily, I was not that grumpy, but under the circumstances, anyone would have been testy.

Turning my head, I could finally identify the speaker. It was my old arch-enemy Sergeant Schmidt of the Fort Atkinson police department. She appeared to be very angry about the lack of respect I had shown her exalted position. Standing next to her was Sergeant Broder. He was trying to suppress a grin. Whether he was laughing at me for my awkward position, at Schmidt for having been on the losing end of a zinger, or me for the trouble I had caused myself by zinging Schmidt, was hard to determine. Most likely, it was all three.

Schmidt ground her teeth. "Listen, Schumacher. We don't have time for your guff. We're taking you back to Fort. We need to talk."

"Now?"

"Yes, right now. Get out of the trash can and get in your car. You can follow us back."

"Can't right now."

"Can't? What do you mean, can't? When we say 'go,' you 'go'." She was yelling now.

I couldn't go off and leave Betty in the store. And I couldn't give up on finding the girl toy. So I told a little white lie.

"Stuck."

Broder started to laugh.

"You want me to bring the trash can with me?" I asked. "I can't drive this way, but I can drag it into the back seat of your car."

Broder was guffawing while Schmidt sputtered with rage.

Fortunately, my hand closed on the girl toy at that moment and I was helped to pull my arm out of the can. "Ah, that was a close one," I said. Then Betty came out of the pottery store.

Broder explained the situation to her. "Mrs. Schumacher, we need to talk over a few matters with your husband. You can drive yourself home, can't you?"

Betty was fine with it. "No, I don't mind driving myself home. And, Sergeant," she said as he started to turn away. "Keep him as long as you like."

I had stuck my arm into a trash can for that woman and that was all the thanks I got. The world can be very unjust at times.

When we arrived at the city building in Fort Atkinson, Broder and Schmidt led me into the interview room. We sat down on opposite sides of a small wooden table. A television was in one corner of the room.

Broder began with some small talk. "You and the missus go over to Cambridge often?"

"Now and then. That's a nice spot down there, you know."

"Yes, it is. Oh, in case you were wondering, we knew you were there because there's an all-points out on your car and one of the locals called it in. Since the plates turned up your name, we said we would come get you. After all, we have gotten to know you pretty well over the last couple of years." He was referring to some contretemps that had arisen due to circumstances entirely beyond my control.

'Why is there an APB out on my car?" I knew I had run a stop sign, but that did not seem like reason enough for an APB.

Schmidt suddenly slammed her fist onto the little table, making it shake and rattle. "Don't pretend to be innocent with us, you creep! Give us one good reason we shouldn't charge you right now with public endangerment?"

"Public endangerment? For running a stop sign?"

"No, you moron. For arson. You not only contributed to arson, you also cost the city of Madison a lot of money. They had to send two fire trucks and two patrol cars to the scene. The fire damage will run into the thousands. You are in big trouble and you better come clean with us."

"I have no idea what you're talking about."

She snorted. "I figured you would say that." She turned on the TV and fiddled with it a bit. "This was recorded this morning," she said. As we watched the screen brighten up, we could see a silver hatchback drive up next to a dumpster in an alley. Two seedy looking characters got out. One was talking on a cell phone, while the other went out of sight. When he returned, he lit a cigarette, then set about starting a fire in the dumpster. He pulled the most flammable bits up where they could get some air and lit the pile in several places. The two seedy characters, one a pyromaniac and the other an idiot, got back in the car and drove away.

We sat in silence for a moment. Frankly, I was at a loss for words. The other two were just watching me think about the mess I was in. Finally, I rallied a bit.

"Okay, that was me alright. On the phone. But I didn't see the other guy lighting the fire. This is a complete surprise to me."

Schmidt sneered at me. "You expect us to believe that? A guy lights a bonfire right next to you and you don't even notice?"

At this point, Broder intervened. "Now, now, let's not get ahead of ourselves here. I think it is safe to say that Professor Schumacher here may be the only person in the state of Wisconsin who can provide a long series of documented instances where he did not notice what was going on around him. Anybody else who claimed not to notice the fire would get laughed at. Not the professor here."

"Thanks," I said to him. He was not offering me a compliment, but I would settle for mercy.

Broder turned to me. "We can let you get on with your day if you just tell us who that man was who set the fire and where he is now."

"Well, I can do one of those things. His name is Sherlock Holmes and he lives in the shelter in downtown Madison. But he ran off so I have no idea where he is now."

"Ran off?"

"Yes. We were eating lunch at Wendy's and he ran off." Broder looked doubtful. "Holmes has a history of mental illness," I added. That seemed to cause Broder to accept the story.

"All right then," he said. "I guess you can go now. Do you need a ride home or can you walk from here?"

"I can walk. No problem." If there had been three feet of snow outside, the answer would have been the same. I just wanted to get away from those guys.

Broder opened the door so I could leave. As I was walking out, his face grew puzzled and he asked, "what did you say to Holmes that made him run off?"

"It wasn't so much what I said as what he said. He practically admitted killing the fellow we found in the freezer last month."

The door slammed shut. Broder took me by the arm and led me back to my chair. The interview wasn't over after all. In fact, I didn't get to go home for a long time.

Betty was reading a book when I staggered into our living room after the long interrogation the police had imposed upon me. She did not look up when I entered the room. "Still mad at me?" I asked.

Betty gave me a cold stare. "Do I have a reason to be mad at you?"

"I embarrassed you at McDonald's. I'm sorry. I have trouble with drive-through windows."

She sighed, relenting a bit. "I know you do."

"Am I forgiven?"

"I'll think about it." She changed the subject. "What was that about with the police? Are you in trouble again?"

Again? That seemed hardly fair. "The guy I interviewed in Madison today set fire to a dumpster. The police wanted to know his name and whereabouts."

"That seems pretty simple. Why did it take so long?"

"Well, at first they thought maybe I knew he was setting the fire."

Betty decided not to probe into the reasons behind that misunderstanding. "What else? You were there a very long time."

"Well, you remember the body in the freezer? The fellow I had lunch with today said something that sounded like he might have killed that guy."

"What?" she shouted. "You had lunch with a murderer? You might have been killed!"

"I was in no danger. We were at Wendy's, for Pete's sake."

"You know this kind of thing makes me crazy! You can't take risks like that! It's not fair to me!"

"I know. But don't you see: there was no way I could have known he was a murderer before we started having lunch."

Betty gave me a glare. "You're always scaring me."

"I'm sorry. I didn't mean to." We hugged and I think she forgave me. I hope so, anyway.

"Hey," I said. "This has been a rough day for both of us. How about if I make us a martini?"

"I'm way ahead of you, mister. I had a martini an hour ago."

Betty laughed at the disappointed expression on my face. "You can go ahead and make one for yourself, though."

While I mixed it up, she chatted with me. "You better believe I enjoyed that martini. It was just what I needed. Those pickled mushrooms were a little old though." Betty liked to put pickled mushrooms in her martini instead of olives. I never understood the attraction, but different strokes for different folks.

"I thought the pickled mushrooms were all gone."

"So did I, but you forgot to throw the jar away. I found it in the fridge with a couple of little bits of mushroom floating in the brine. With a couple of teaspoons of brine to make it a 'dirty' martini and those bits of mushroom, I think I may have invented a new drink. What should we call it?"

There was a long moment of silence while I considered my options. Finally, I said, "how about a Bucky Banger?"

"Oh, that sounds good." Betty liked the idea. I felt kind of sick, myself.

Chapter 8.

The Voice in the Night

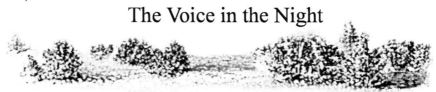

The next morning I went through my usual routine. Start the coffee, shower, dress, pick up a newspaper at the convenience store, bring Betty her coffee and part of the paper. After Betty and I had finished the papers and she went off to work, I poured the last of the coffee into my cup and sat down in my living room chair. From my Morris chair, I could see through the sliding glass door across the deck. The sky was a light blue with a few clouds. It looked to be a fine December day. Most likely, our downstairs neighbor, Emily Eberhardt, would take her dog out for a walk within the next hour. Emily was a reliable character who could be counted on for a sensible perspective on this complicated case. Immediately, I resolved to hold a council of war before finalizing my report. Emily, Andrew, and Betty could help me make some sense out of the available information.

Help was desperately needed because I was confused. While it seemed likely that Holmes had killed Miles Archer, a few loose ends remained. Like, why did he do it? Why was the body in a freezer and why was Holmes pushing the freezer across Main Street? And did this death have anything to do with the research project? Another fact occurred to me: Archer and Holmes were reputed to be bosom buddies. Why, then, would Holmes kill Archer?

Emily, Betty, and Andrew would be invaluable in helping me clarify the issues. However, one personal issue of my own was definitely not coming up for discussion because it was a secret that I had kept to myself for several years.

Betty had gone out of town on a business trip. Before she left we argued about something trivial. The first day of being a bachelor was quite pleasant. The second day was boring. The third day I started to get very uncomfortable. Edgy and restless, I took walks, tried watching television, ran errands, but nothing helped. Finally, about nine p.m. I gave it up and went to bed, even though I was not sleepy. Shortly after I lay down, I heard a voice say my name.

Quite frankly, it spooked me. The voice had sounded like it was in my bedroom. It could have been either a man or a woman. It was clear and loud. Somehow it contained a note of mocking humor, as if there was something very amusing about the situation.

I got up and searched the house. I looked over the deck, thinking that perhaps someone was down below on the sidewalk, calling up to me. There was no one around anywhere.

A dream, you say? This was extremely real. No dream in my experience had ever had this quality of reality.

Of course, I had to consider the possibility that I was out of my mind. Hearing voices was the classic symptom, after all. One thing was very clear to me, unfortunately: that voice was so real that if I heard it very often I would not be able to convince myself that it was imaginary. It might all be in my head. Even so, it would be as real as anything else that I could perceive.

Getting back to sleep took a long time since I was scared out of my wits. Eventually, I dropped off. The voice never came back. But I never forgot the experience. It was one of my most indelible memories.

The investigation I was currently pursuing made me think about that voice. How different was I, really, than Doc Watson and the others? How much of a push would it take to tip me over into their circumstances? And could it happen to the average person? Could it happen to you?

Honestly, I did not know how close I was to serious mental illness. Nor could I say how much stress was required before the average person would lose his tenuous grip on reality. Maybe we all had demons in the back of our minds that we actively sought to repress at a subconscious level. Given a weak moment, the demons might escape. Then we would be the ones locked in the hospital, trapped in a group home, or evicted from a homeless center.

Our natural tendency is to avoid thinking about people with serious mental illness. This is shortsighted. There but for the grace of God go you, me, or our loved ones. If and when it happens, we will wish we had done more to create a safety net that allows even the most confused person to live comfortably and safely in a world that is filled with terrors.

Chapter 9.

Interview with Archy McNally

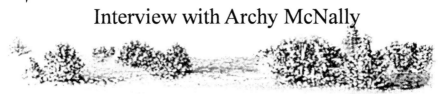

That day I went in search of the last research subject, Archy McNally. McNally was recorded as living in Milton, which was about twenty minutes south of Fort Atkinson on Highway 26. No one answered the door at his apartment. His work address was listed as the local Goodwill store, so that was where I went next.

McNally was working the checkout counter. He was a thin, nervous young man in his late twenties. When I said I needed a few minutes of his time, he called in a substitute to watch the register and we went outside, where he immediately lighted a cigarette.

"What can I do for you?" he asked.

I ran through my spiel about the research project.

"Yeah," he said. "I remember the project. I signed up for it on purpose."

"Why did you agree to be in the project?"

"Because they asked me to. I was being helpful."

"You had no concerns about the purpose of the project?"

"You mean about maybe being cured of seeing dead people? That was what I wanted to happen. I wanted to get my life back on track. By doing everything the doctors and nurses and social workers want, you get to move on with your life. And because I did that, I have this job and I have an apartment."

"That's great. It sounds like you are doing really well."

McNally waved his arms around excitedly. "I'm doing great!" he said, shifting his feet around excitedly. "And after this I'm going to law school, then I'll run for Congress. Who knows, maybe I'll be the first guy to run for president who was ever in psych treatment."

"Actually, there was one guy I remember. A vice presidential candidate. The news stories said he had been treated for serious problems with depression."

"Really? I never heard of that."

"Well, it was before your time. You're a young guy. You have plenty of time to accomplish your goals."

This got McNally back on his theme. He started waving his arms again. "That's right. On track. First law school, then Congress, then the Oval Office."

"I wish you luck."

McNally stared at me hard for a moment. Perhaps he suspected that I did not rate his chances of being president too highly.

"Oh, by the way, Archy," I said. "Did you know Miles Archer was dead? Somebody put him in a freezer. Did you hear about that?"

McNally was withdrawing, looking over his shoulder to see if anyone could overhear our conversation. "No, I didn't hear that," he said.

"Do you have ideas on who might have done it?"

He actually jumped, as if he had been stabbed with a pin. "No. No idea."

"Do you think Sherlock Holmes might have done it?"

McNally's reaction surprised me. Instead of getting more anxious, he actually relaxed when he heard the question.

"Did Holmes kill Archer? No way, man."

"Why are you so sure?"

"Well, they were good buddies. Holmes would have done anything for Archer. And besides, Holmes wouldn't hurt a fly. He looks scary, but that's just an act. He runs like a rabbit whenever he gets a little nervous. And everything makes him nervous."

I laughed. "Yeah, I know what you mean about him running like a rabbit. But if he didn't do it, who did?"

"That's obvious. It was the dead people, of course."

My jaw dropped open. McNally immediately recognized his error. "Ah, just kidding. There aren't any dead people. Just testing you! Ha, ha! Hey, I gotta go now. Catchya later, man." And he ran back into the Goodwill store.

Chapter 10

Interview with Dr. Zelicov

My final interview was with Milo Zelicov, MD, who was the genius who dreamed up the research project I was investigating. Even before meeting with him, I assumed the man was an incompetent researcher. His project was ill-conceived and, based on the interviews completed up to now, most of the 'subjects' had not met the standards of 'informed consent': they either did not know they had signed up, did not know what they had signed up for, or denied that they had ever signed up.

Since I was a few minutes early, I stopped at a McDonald's for a coffee on my way into Madison from Fort Atkinson. In my mind, I imagined what response I would receive if I discussed Zelicov with the crowd of elderly folks who were holding down chairs and coffee cups in one corner of the restaurant. The conversation would have gone something like this.

Geezer 1: "Are you tellin' me....."

Ed: "Yessireebob."

Geezer 2: "Oh m'gosh, you can't mean it."

Ed: "It's the God's honest truth."

Geezer 3: "Well geewhilikers. Don't that just beat all."

Ed: "Don't it, now?"

Geezer 1: "It's a free country. You can do what you want. But if people'd grow a brain they would plan ahead better, if you know what I mean. That's my opinion. It's just my opinion but that's what I think. No point in beatin' 'bout the bush on these matters."

Geezers 2 and 3: "You can say that again. Yup."

Feeling reinforced by my imaginary conversation with the geezers, who were sure to agree with me if we actually had discussed it, I was ready for my meeting with Zelicov. I was 'loaded for bear,' as the geezers would have put it.

Zelicov's office was in the Department of Psychiatry and Psychology of the Medical University of Madison. This told me he probably was expected to see patients in addition to doing his research. If he had been in a liberal arts college, I would have classified him as a teacher, rather than a clinician.

A secretary directed me toward Zelicov's office, which turned out to be an examination room. A vinyl-clad chair was placed in front of a small metal desk on which a computer terminal sat. Another chair was placed next to the desk. You could almost visualize a patient and his wife, or a patient and her husband, or a patient and her mother sitting in those chairs, anxious and perhaps defensive. This, clearly, was a room in which patients were seen and the information taken from them was entered directly into the computer. If any research went on in that room, it clearly was not regarded as the most important activity. An office where research was a priority would have had a bigger desk and it would not have needed two chairs for visitors, especially not chairs upholstered in vinyl. Vinyl was used when the occupants of the chairs were likely to be wet or dirty or destructive.

The chair that was placed behind the desk and in front of the computer was occupied by a small man with a goatee who was wearing a long white coat. He welcomed me with a gesture toward one of the chairs and a warm smile.

"Professor Schumacher! How good of you to come," he said cheerfully. For a moment I forgot that I was the one who had requested the meeting.

"Doctor Zelicov," I said as I offered my hand to him. "Thank you for being available on such short notice."

"Delighted, delighted, I'm sure. This is a very serious matter. One which will be easy to clear up, but when the federal government is demanding answers, one doesn't dilly-dally, no?"

"Not if one is smart," was my reply.

Zelicov slapped his knee and laughed. "Yes, yes. Quite right you are. But first, the amenities. Amenities are very important to good working relationships, I find. So, would you like some coffee? There is one coffee pot in the area that has excellent coffee. It is the personal machine of a colleague of mine. He will let us share some, if you like. Come, I will send for it, yes?"

"That would be nice."

Zelicov made a brief call, then put the phone down and leaned back in his chair. "You live near here, I understand, in the town of Fort Atkinson?"

"That's correct. We moved there recently from the panhandle of Texas."

"Yes, I detected an accent there. But you are not originally from Texas, I think. Somewhere in the Midwest, perhaps?"

"Very good. Yes, I am from Indiana originally."

"And you are some kind of government investigator?"

We were interrupted by the arrival of our coffee. It came in porcelain mugs, not Styrofoam cups. The aroma was rich, but the coffee turned out to be flavored. I tried not to grimace when swallowing it.

"Government investigator? Not really. I describe myself as a consulting research ethicist, which is a niche I fell into by accident. This is my first case in which the federal government asked for my services."

"A consulting research ethicist?" Zelicov was nonplussed. "Forgive me, but that sounds a bit pretentious."

"It sounds pretentious if you focus on the ethicist part because the title suggests that the consultant pretends to be more ethical than anyone else. In practice, however, many people are experts in research ethics. Every conscientious researcher thinks about ethics. Every member of a research review board, and there are many, thinks about ethics. All of us who have served on those boards have been trained to look for certain rules to be followed. Was the patient shown respect? Was he lied to? Was he fully informed about the project before he agreed to participate? Did the risks exceed the benefits? Was confidentiality protected? These rules are so clear that any researcher can learn them. That is not the hard part about being a consulting research ethicist."

Zelicov pondered for a moment. "You make an interesting case. But do go on: what is the important skill required by a research ethicist?"

"You have to be an experienced researcher. Experience matters because it helps you judge the most important issue: do the likely benefits of the research exceed the risks to the human guinea pigs? And I don't mean the benefits expected by the researcher because that person has trouble being objective about the benefits of his own project. Besides, he might be an inexperienced researcher and not realize that his research plan is flawed. If the research design is flawed, then no benefits are likely to result, which means even a low risk project should not be undertaken."

"I see. You are here to judge the quality of my research." Zelicov had gone pale.

"I don't pretend to be an expert in your field of research. On the other hand, the general principles of good research design are well-accepted. I would not be able to tell if your theory is wrong."

He relaxed a little at that. "Now I understand. This begins to make some sense to me." He spread his hands wide. "So, ask your questions."

"First, let me address the issue of informed consent."

"Yes, yes, of course. All of the subjects were explained about the project. They all signed the forms in front of a witness."

"These were psych patients. Some were heavily medicated. Did you take any special steps to ensure that they understood what they were signing?"

"We explained the project to them until we were sure they understood. We are experienced clinicians; we can judge when a person understands what he is being told."

"Let's take a few of the subjects and deal with them specifically. Do you remember them?"

"I reviewed the files in preparation for this meeting."

"Okay, Lew Archer."

"Yes, Mr. Archer. He happens to be an inpatient again right now. I know him well."

"You consented him yourself?"

"Yes, I did. He understood perfectly."

"Were you present when he signed the form?"

"Yes, of course."

I said nothing at that point. Instead, I just sat there and looked at him. Zelicov looked back calmly at first, then the cogs in his brain began turning over. The moment when he remembered what actually happened when Lew Archer was consented was obvious: he turned pale again. Then he had to decide whether to lie to me or confess. He chose to do neither.

"Dr. Zelicov, did you actually see Lew Archer sign the form?"

"Well, that was a long time ago. I don't actually remember. Why do you question it?"

"Because he does not remember, he is generally uncooperative, and the handwriting looks exactly like his mother's and not like his own."

Zelicov was sweating. "I see your point," he said.

"It turns out that the other patients don't remember consenting, deny that they would have consented, or say that their consent was predicated on anticipated rewards. You know, I'm sure, that offering rewards for consenting can be coercive. I'm forced to conclude that your consenting process did not follow approved procedures."

"I'm sorry you have reached that conclusion. However, I am sure you realize that this is a tempest in a teapot, so to speak. The project was risk-free. No one was hurt."

"Someone died."

"That could not have been caused by the research!"

"Couldn't it? These were mentally impaired patients, highly vulnerable. You were undermining delusions that might have been important to them." I held up my hand to stop his protests. "No, stop there. I understand that the therapeutic process is intended to address those delusions. But this was a research project. It must be held to a higher standard. To say that there was no risk at all is simply not true. What we have to address is this: was the risk greater than the likely benefits?"

Zelicov was still trying to put up a brave front, but it was obvious he could tell he was doomed. "The potential benefits were enormous," he whispered.

"You mean curing delusions? The chances of that resulting from this project appear to be nil."

"Nil?" He was aghast.

"You had no control group. Your sample size was too small to lead to any conclusions."

"This was a pilot study! Those issues don't apply to a pilot study!"

"Even a pilot project should offer more benefits than risks. If you weren't going to learn anything from doing the project, then you shouldn't have done the project. The university should not have permitted you to do the project."

He held his head in his hands.

"Dr. Zelicov," I said. "How much research experience do you have?"

"I worked as a laboratory assistant back in Moscow before coming to the United States. Here, I have been a busy clinician. Too busy with patients to do research."

"Why did you change direction and try to do this project?"

"The university has been pressuring everyone to get research grants. And if we get grants, our patient load will be reduced."

"You're a little burned out on seeing psych patients?"

"You have no idea," he said.

I had to sympathize with the guy. But I also had to bar him from research if I could manage it. As a researcher, the man was a menace. I hoped he was better as a clinician, but somehow it seemed unlikely.

Chapter 11.

The Report

Andrew, Emily Eberhardt, Betty, and I convened our meeting in the evening after my meeting with Zelicov. None of them had heard all of the details of the case and Emily had heard none of the story before that night. First drinks were handed out to everybody, beer for the men and wine for the women. Then I started talking. After I had summed it all up for them, Andrew voiced an opinion.

"Ed," he said. "It sounds like you have already made up your mind about what you are going to say in your report. You are going to come down hard on Zelicov. So, what do you want from us?"

Betty chimed in at that point. "Do you just want us to say you are right? There must be more to this meeting than that." Emily was looking a bit disgruntled as well. To avoid a rebellion, I rushed ahead.

"Hey, you guys, calm down. I really do need your help. For one thing, I might be biased and if I am you will be able to talk me out of my position. For another thing, there might be some issues involved that I have not considered. And the most interesting problem is one that I have no solution to: who killed Miles Archer and why? As long as we don't know the answer to that question I will have to wonder if we aren't missing something important to the investigation. A research subject is dead and we don't know why. How can we be sure that the research project did not lead to his death? If so, then my report would be seriously flawed for failing to say so." With that, I leaned back in my chair and waited for a reaction. I didn't have to wait very long.

Betty spoke up immediately. "Basically, you feel like you can safely say that the research project should not have been approved by the university in the first place, and also that Zelicov broke all the rules when he recruited his patients into it. So, let's just agree that your report will be very critical on those points. But the more important issue has to do with the relationships between families and patients and how they might have been affected."

Emily agreed. "That's right," she said. "Those relationships must have been strained or even destroyed by the stresses affecting them. If the project hurt the relationships, that is the most important issue. But if it helped, then we can forgive the professor for breaking a few rules."

Betty added more at that point. "The fears the parents had for their family members might have been reduced if the project offered some hope. Who cares if the hope was a pipedream? All that matters is that something was being attempted that might offer a slim chance of a cure. Eventually those families have to move on with their lives. They have to forgive themselves and everyone else so that they can rebuild what's left of their lives."

Andrew was looking at his shoes. "Do you understand what the heck they are talking about?" I asked him.

"Sort of," he answered.

"No kidding? Then maybe you can explain it to me."

"It sounds sort of like something I heard on Oprah."

"You watch Oprah?"

"No, but once when I was channel hopping her show came up. They were talking about that stuff."

"Which stuff?"

"You know. Relationships."

Betty was outraged. "Men! You don't understand anything. How do they get through life?" she asked Emily.

"Women have to do it for them," was the answer she got back.

"Hey, if you wise women want to write down something for me that I can put in the report on this relationship stuff, I will be glad to put it in. Right now I'm clueless, though."

"You got that right, Buddy," Betty said.

I couldn't let her have the last word. "Look, from my point of view, what matters is whether the patients get to live their lives the way they want. Forget about some dream of a cure. If they want to have jobs, then they should be able to work. If they want to control their delusions, they should have meds. If they want a place of their own to live in, they should have it."

"Where can people work if they have a serious mental illness?" Andrew asked.

Betty had an answer for that. "Wal-Mart hires them sometimes."

This brought up the debate that seemed to be going on forever in Fort Atkinson about whether to let Wal-Mart open a store in the county. The critics were still winning the fight, but some of their arguments were starting to sound a little off-base.

Emily chimed in at this point. "We don't want a lot of low-wage jobs coming in here. Besides it will put the local businesses out of business."

"You don't see them hiring the mentally ill," I replied. "The local businesses claim that Wal-Mart is bad because it doesn't offer health insurance, but neither do they. In fact, it doesn't matter about the health insurance. All the big corporations will start backing away from their health insurance plans eventually. Wal-Mart just got there first."

"I suppose you think we should have a national health insurance program anyway," Andrew said.

"Sure, that's what I think, but I know we won't get one." It would be cheaper for everybody and everybody would have coverage, but it's just not the American way."

"Then what is going to happen when all the corporations stop offering health insurance benefits?" Andrew asked.

"Then most medical care becomes a cash business," I answered. "We will buy services on ebay for very low prices. When we get sick, we will send an email message to our health care company, they will try to deal with us by sending us prescriptions without ever actually seeing us or even talking to us. If we insist on talking to someone, it will mean a long distance call to India or somewhere like that."

Betty was not too concerned. "So what? Doctors like me can't cure most of the problems people see us for. Genetics and unhealthy habits shorten our lives and medical care can't make much of a difference."

That remark, coming from a doctor, left the rest of us speechless for a moment.

"Well," I said, "at least we can agree that psychotic people are helped by getting their meds." That point brought no arguments from anyone. But nobody had much confidence that the government would always be willing to pay for those meds.

Emily had the last word to say before we broke up the group. "Ed," she said. "You say that the research project was so weak it had no hope of doing any good. That means it could not have done much harm either. So maybe the whole thing is a tempest in a teapot."

After Andrew and Emily left, I set to work writing up the report. Basically, it just said that the project should not have been approved and the rights of the research subjects were not protected. It also said that while the cause of death for one of the subjects was unknown, it probably was not caused by the research. I recommended that Zelicov be barred from research and that the university undergo an exhaustive audit by the feds to see if they were failing to protect the rights of research subjects involved in other projects. I sent the report to the university as an email attachment, then washed my hands of it. All in all, it was very unsatisfying.

Chapter 12.

Christmas Party at Doc's

When Betty and I pulled into Doc Watson's driveway on Christmas Eve, there was another car already there. I wondered who it could be. As far as I knew, none of the other people who were expected to attend our little party owned cars. When I called Doc and offered to buy take-out chicken for an informal get-together, he said he would round up Sherlock, Lew Archer, Archie Goodwin and Archy McNally. Miss Marple was assumed to be too ill to attend. This was a two-bucket party. I chose one bucket of crispy and one of regular.

Everyone else was present when Doc let us in. Doc introduced everyone to Betty. One person was present whom I had not met. He was introduced as Mycroft Holmes, Sherlock's brother. Mycroft had a short haircut and was wearing a sport coat and slacks, with an open-collared dress shirt. He appeared to be a quiet man, somber but with obvious intelligence. He was a bit on the portly side and bore no resemblance to his brother Sherlock at all.

Distributing paper plates, napkins, and chicken did not take long. Soon everyone was munching happily. A cooler of beer was under the table, so within twenty minutes, the sound of smacking lips was supplemented with occasional belches.

Eventually, Betty and I could eat no more. Mycroft had stopped after one piece. I gathered that take-out chicken was not part of his usual diet.

When he saw that we were finished, Mycroft stood up and cleared his throat. "Gentlemen," he said, "and Mrs. Schumacher" he added with a nod to Betty. "We have a little business to take care of." He pulled a fold of papers out of his jacket pocket. "As you know, I am the executor of Miles Archer's will. Now that the police have closed the investigation of Mr. Archer's death, we can settle the estate."

I raised my hand. "Hold on a minute, Mycroft. First, I didn't know the police investigation was over. Second, if you are going to read a will, then Betty and I should leave because we didn't even know Miles Archer." I started to stand, but Mycroft held up his hand to stop me.

"Professor Schumacher," he said, "please wait. All will be made clear to you. And I assure you that your presence here is appropriate."

As I settled back down in my chair, I sensed that, aside from Betty, everyone else in the room was aware of what Mycroft was going to say.

"First, of all, I should provide a little background. My brother Sherlock and Miles Archer were friends, so two years ago when Sherlock brought Mr. Archer to me for the purpose of making up a will, I agreed to do so, even though the case was assumed to be pro bono and there might be some who would question whether Mr. Archer was of sound mind. However, since Mr. Archer had no heirs, I thought it would be safe and appropriate to accede to his wishes, despite their somewhat unusual nature." Mycroft consulted his papers with a frown, then proceeded with his oration.

"Mr. Archer wanted his assets to be placed in trust in the event of his death. The purpose of the trust was very clear: Mr. Archer wanted the trust to provide support to persons who were in a special minority group. Mr. Archer called that minority group "persons with radically alternative perceptions of reality who have financial difficulties due to those perceptions." He wanted the trust to provide housing and cash assistance to eligible persons in such a manner when two requirements were met. First, the assets would not be transferred to payees in amounts that were sufficiently large so as to jeopardize disability payments. Second, the assistance provided to payees would in no way restrict their freedom. Mr. Archer understood that sometimes difficult judgments would be required to carry out the intent of the will, so he specified that a director of the trust be chosen who was acceptable to a board of persons he regarded as trustworthy. To wit, these gentlemen." Mycroft looked up, then waved his hand in the direction of Lew Archer, Doc Watson, Sherlock, Archie Goodwin and Archy McNally, all of whom applauded.

Turning to me, Mycroft asked, "Professor Schumacher, do you have any questions so far?"

"I'm too fascinated to have questions. Maybe later."

"Then we will continue. Each member of the board of the trust has interviewed a candidate for the director position. All have found this candidate to be acceptable to them. If the candidate accepts the position, then we have some forms to sign. Professor Schumacher, the board would like to offer the position to you. Do you have any questions now?"

Betty gasped. "Wait a minute," I said. "When did these interviews take place?"

"You spoke to each of the board members."

"But I was interviewing them!"

"If you like. They choose to view it as the other way around."

"But the police were still investigating Archer's death, so the will had not been read yet when I spoke to them."

"True, but not relevant to the board. They know now that they needed to conduct interviews so they choose to consider the meetings with you as meeting the requirement." Mycroft hesitated, then added with a twinkle in his eye, "the members of the board are not as committed to conventional views of space and time as are most governing boards." That was certainly an understatement. He went on. "Do you think you might be willing to accept the position?"

I turned to look at the board members. "Doc, do you think this is a good idea?"

Doc smiled. "You're one of us, man."

"Lew?"

"You a fool, but you not stupid."

"You mean, I'm ignorant but teachable?"

Lew smiled at me as I used to smile at a grad student who provided the correct answer in class. "That's what I mean."

"Archie Goodwin?"

"You get my vote. And I'm first in line for some help. Get me out that group home. It's nasty."

"Archy McNally?"

"Sure. But I don't need any help for myself."

"Of course. Sherlock?"

"The legs are all gone," he replied. Sherlock was feeling around in the chicken bucket.

Next I turned back to Mycroft. "I'm touched and honored at the trust these folks have in me. But I must ask a question. Is there any money in this trust? Would I be taking on a responsibility without the means of accomplishing anything?"

He obviously had been waiting for me to ask this question, "Mr. Archer had been a successful stockbroker for several years before he was first hospitalized. After that, he became homeless, but most of his assets remained intact, at least at first. At the time he came to me to make out his will, he had just converted all of his funds into a cash purchase of a single stock. This was a new stock offering. Mr. Archer spent all of his money on that stock in the belief that it would increase in value and thus provide the resources for the trust he envisioned."

Mycroft stopped at this point. All the eyes in the room were on me. I took a breath, then hazarded a guess. "Was it Google?"

Everyone in the room applauded me except Betty, who asked "what's so special about Google stock?"

"It went up. A lot." Turning to Mycroft, I said, "that answers the question. The trust has enough funds to do some good."

"Please understand that the director is limited to a salary of ten thousand dollars per year."

"That seems fair." I looked at Betty and she nodded. "I accept the position."

After that, Doc handed out presents to us all. He even had one for Betty. She got a chipped flower vase, about two inches tall. She said it was beautiful. Sherlock got a carton of cigarettes. The two Archies and Lew each got a small brown paper sack, which they accepted with enthusiasm. Mycroft got a tie clip. And Doc handed me a cap made out of aluminum foil. "Keeps out the radio waves," he said, deadpan. Everybody laughed.

After we had admired our gifts, I remembered the big, unanswered question. "Hey, wait a minute you guys. Nobody explained to me what happened to Miles Archer"?

Mycroft looked at Sherlock and waited, but Sherlock was ignoring him. Mycroft sighed, then said, "The police picked up Sherlock shortly after the dumpster fire. I was called to represent him, as usual. Eventually, we were able to put together the facts that enabled the authorities to close the file on Miles Archer." Mycroft took a breath, then began the story that I had been waiting to hear since I was pulled out of the river.

"Mr. Archer felt that his alternative perception of reality was becoming too much of a burden for him. He believed that the only hope of escaping the visitations he experienced was to place himself behind some heavy shielding, such as by getting into a freezer. He found a freezer on a vacant lot that seemed to belong to no one, so he took advantage of the opportunity. The temperature was below zero that night."

"Didn't he understand that climbing into the freezer would be fatal?"

Mycroft looked at me with pity. "Of course he understood. He asked Sherlock to push the freezer into the river to provide additional shielding. Sherlock was irritated with him and tried to talk him out of it. They parted ways. When Sherlock returned to the freezer in the morning, he found Miles inside, dead. Sherlock decided to carry out his friend's last wishes. And that is how he met you. You were helping carry out Miles Archer's last wishes. This is where the board's flexible attitude toward time comes into play again. You see, from the point of view of the board members, you accepted the position of trust director at that time. What happened today was merely an administrative detail from their point of view."

And maybe they were right. Shortly after that, the board members opened their brown paper sacks and took out baggies packed with something that they started rolling into cigarettes. Betty, Mycroft, and I decided it was time for us to leave. Mycroft announced that he would come around the next morning to pick up anyone who needed a ride home. He was told to make it after noon.

Chapter 13.

Conclusion

The next few weeks were a lot of fun since I was spending someone else's money. Archy McNally and Archie Goodwin each got a trailer to live in, at the expense of the trust, and start-up funds for their own ebay businesses. We also bought a trailer for Sherlock to live in, but his was consumed in a fire within a week. After that, I learned that the reason he had been evicted from the first homeless shelter was an unfortunate disagreement about a trash can fire. My next step was to buy a surplus storage canister from the Army. It was left over from Desert Storm. It was about the size of a mobile home and had been outfitted with a toilet and a metal door. The whole thing was metal. There was no way Sherlock could burn it down.

I also bought an old taxi for Lew Archer. His job was to be a driver for the other guys. He really enjoyed the role. He was never in a hurry to get anywhere and so was a safe driver. How often he actually took people where they wanted to go was unclear to me, but nobody complained. Maybe they all just enjoyed driving around.

We were starting to find new customers for the trust to help. Our board members recruited them in mysterious ways. Usually, Mycroft would just call and say that Doc had found another one. We would meet at McDonald's and discuss the person's needs and limitations, then Mycroft would write out a check for whatever goods or services we thought might be useful and appreciated.

The university received a public wrist-slap from the feds, but that news story was quickly forgotten. Presumably they went back to their old ways.

Betty complained that she was never able to reproduce the taste of the original Bucky Banger Martini, so she retired the name. She was happy that I was enjoying my new job as a director of a charitable trust.

"You seem to get along awfully well with those guys," she noticed.

"They are a lot of fun."

"Birds of a feather."

"That's why you like me."

"What do you mean?"

"If I was entirely normal, I wouldn't be as interesting."

"Interesting is an understatement," she said. But she was smiling when she said it.

Bucky proceeded to get fatter and fatter. Fritter got thinner and thinner. Betty said that Bucky was not letting her eat her share of the food. I put her dish up on the kitchen counter, but she preferred to eat down on the floor with him, even when he bullied her out of the way. He wasn't being deliberately cruel to her, just insensitive. He pursued his appetite in a clueless way, not noticing how much harm he was causing his house mate. Betty said that was just like the behavior of males of any species.

Of course that made me wonder if I was causing her harm in an unthinking way. If being unthinking was the problem, then I would cure it by thinking. So, I thought about it and could not see anyway to improve right away, so I quit worrying about it. But I resolved to try harder to be alert to the possible adverse consequences of my actions. Betty was a Nervous Nelly, so anytime I went on an adventurous investigation it made her anxious. Next time, I would try harder not to worry her. But, heck, the only way to keep her from worrying would be to stay in the condo and not come out. A guy can't live that way all the time. At least, I couldn't.

We discussed all this. She decided, as usual, to forgive me for being, as she said, 'a galoot.' What more could a guy ask, after all, than a woman who would forgive him for being a galoot?